THE HOUSESITTER

TARA MARLOW

Wildlight
PUBLISHING

For Rich, my partner in 'crime'.

PROLOGUE

Neeminah River, Tasmania
Farmhouse in the Huon Valley

Name: John Young
Nearest major city: Hobart, 45 mins drive
Sitter required for: June 6 – July 5 (30 days)
Dates are flexible: Take over from previous housesitter. Crossover dates okay.
Own bathroom and bedroom.
Pet sitting required: 3 dogs, 10 goats, 15 chickens (free-range)
Housesitter pets allowed: No

About this housesitting position in NEEMINAH RIVER

Large farmhouse with a wrap-around verandah on five and a half acres, nestled in the Huon Valley. The Neeminah River is on the boundary of the property. The property is positioned in a quiet community nestled between river and mountains. Wood heater with plenty of wood, heat pump, and electric blankets will keep you warm, while unlimited high-speed internet, wi-fi, smart TV, and multiple streaming services will keep you entertained.

There are three dogs that need walking/running every morning and afternoon: Ruby, my cocker spaniel with velvety ears; Billy, a lazy but sweet rescue greyhound who defines the term 'puppy dog eyes'; and Charlie, the most lovable, soppy German shepherd you'll ever meet.

The chickens are free-range but will need to be locked up away from wildlife each night. There are devils, quolls and feral cats around.

The goats are free to roam in the two paddocks, which can be opened between. They are low maintenance but love the occasional Weet-Bix.

There is a local farmers' market every Saturday, and a supermarket 15 minutes away. The chickens will give you all the eggs you can eat.

Amenities:

- High-speed, unlimited internet and wi-fi
- Washing machine and dryer
- Heat – various sources
- Dishwasher
- Oven

Close to:

- River
- Park
- Supermarket
- Farmers' market
- Walking trails

1

S he could not let him win.

Em McKinney had put up with the drugs and partying, even the prostitutes, but when Callum had taken her ATM card and almost stripped her account, she had finally had enough. She'd walked out of the house and their marriage, taking very little but his secrets with her. Callum had done some stupid things in their fifteen years of marriage, but his latest stunt had shocked her more than anything else: accusing her of embezzling from her own business.

Now, housesitting in southern Tasmania on the other side of the world from her dumpster-fire of a life in California, and letting the lawyers handle the clean-up, she was as far from her normal life as she could get.

Returning to Australia had brought her a sense of peace. This was comfort. Home. It was where people told it like it was, rather than saying or doing anything to get ahead – like her husband did. Here, even if you were famous, people generally left you alone to get on with things, they didn't trail you with mile-long lenses.

But there were weirdos everywhere. She knew that.

Wearing faded black jeans, a thick black cable-knit jumper and worn R.M. Williams boots, Em had dressed to reflect her relaxed state of mind. Her auburn hair was stuffed under a thick black wool beanie, and she was makeup-free for the first time in years. She loved it here. Who knew that in the middle of southern Tasmania she would find herself content?

From the middle of the dirt track, she could hear the river gurgling down the hill on her right, while eucalyptus trees danced in the afternoon breeze. In the distance, ominous clouds were slowly making their way up the valley. Smoke puffed in single streams from nearby farmhouses, while birdsong from the wrens and willy wagtails sang out from the bushes along the fence lines. Something sweet in the air, like the scent of blossom she couldn't quite pinpoint, wafted by as she continued more quickly down the track. Around her, the three dogs were having a field day scouting out whatever scents had caught their attention.

The moment she had arrived at the housesit the day before, she had instantly fallen in love with all three of the dogs. Charlie, the German shepherd, had quickly taken on the role of her protector, but he was also a huge softy, constantly looking back for her approval. Billy, the storm-grey greyhound, was happy to plod along, sniffing at whatever the other two dogs were into, so long as it meant there was a long nap at the end. And Ruby, the red cocker spaniel, possessed velvety ears capable of inducing a state of relaxation no matter how stressed one was. Em imagined the feel of those ears would challenge any of the expensive meditation sessions sought after by her LA friends. But right now, Ruby was plastered beside her, her ears flapping in the wind as she trotted along the gravel road.

It wasn't just the dogs that had captured her heart. The goats loved Weet-Bix, just as the homeowner had claimed in the advertisement (although she'd initially believed he was teasing until she saw it for herself). The chickens made up a whole quirky community of their own. She'd already named the rooster Leo DiCockrio because of his flock of young things, but he had his sidekick, Kate Wingslet, to keep him on the straight and narrow.

Life was calm here. Serene. It was the perfect place to work on her long-neglected passion project – writing a cookbook. She had everything to keep her safe, cosy and focused. She could imagine living in a place like this. She just needed to take her bakery in California and transplant it somewhere nearby. Em imagined it would make her mum happier to have her closer, especially if it meant she was far away from Callum. But Em and her mother were better if they weren't too close. Her mother valued her independence, and Em had lost that close connection with her years ago, when words were spoken and her mother had disappeared to the other side of the country, right before Em and Callum relocated to America.

Shaking the negative thoughts away, she emerged from a copse of birch trees. The wind whipped strands of her hair into her mouth. She quickened her pace. She needed to get the dogs home before the rain came, and to get the chickens safely tucked into their coop.

As she walked past a neighbour's house, a man in his forties, dressed in saggy, light grey track pants and an old woollen jumper, stopped dead in his driveway and watched her with steely eyes. Staring. Judging. Assessing. She knew that look. It was the same one Callum threw out when she didn't do something to his liking. Reluctantly, Em waved hello, but the hard stare continued. *Shit.* Had the neighbours worked out who she was? She closed her eyes, trying to stay calm. It wouldn't be hard to work it out. Her face had been splashed over every celebrity gossip website, the media portraying her as an uncaring bitch who'd left their favourite Australian A-list actor heartbroken while she employed one of LA's top divorce attorneys. The truth was, Callum was most likely partying hard with his friends in Malibu. Ah, but the media didn't know about any of that. Callum made sure his PR team kept it under wraps. Meanwhile, she was hiding out in Tasmania, away from the harsh ridicule of the paparazzi and tabloid magazines. But with the false accusation that she was embezzling money from her Venice Beach bakery, the media had become even more vicious.

Fucking Callum. She wanted to kill him for this latest bullshit. They had an agreement. He would leave her bakery alone if she didn't reveal any of his secrets. Callum was particularly concerned about one that had advanced his career, although his lawyers were more worried about the other gems they were constantly covering up in his wake.

Callum's latest texts came to mind. The one that really stuck with her made her nervous: *What's your next move?*

He was taunting her. She almost expected the next text to say *See what I can do to you? If you fuck with my reputation, I will fuck with yours.* To him, it was a game, but Em had no interest in playing. She was simply trying to get on with her life. Move forward. Write her cookbook. But most of all, she was trying to get away from Callum and his antics. She needed to ignore his texts. They weren't doing her any good. If anything, they just took her back to feeling like a puppet on strings, dancing to his manipulation.

She took a deep breath, trying to calm herself, but after the creepy guy's stare, she felt wobbly. Callum always made her feel unsure of her emotions. But she'd be okay. *I'll be okay. I'll be okay.* The mantra repeated like a broken record, but she needed to say it. The problem was that the message wasn't quite getting through.

When she made it to the dirt driveway, Charlie bolted under the fence on their left and behind the woodshed, his snout never leaving the ground. Ruby went on alert, then zoomed back and forth across the driveway, her nose quickly discovering whatever trail Charlie had found. Billy followed, more curious than urgent. Before long, all three dogs had disappeared behind the shed.

"What are you guys—" She stopped in her tracks. Blood.

An icy chill ran through her. Em yelled to the dogs to return to her as she opened the gate to the paddock where the woodshed sat alongside the chicken coop. Em called the dogs again to put them into the house yard and was shocked when they complied. Charlie was first, his head down and his tail between his legs. Ruby trotted behind, her ears flapping against her head, the blood around her muzzle staining her red fur. When Billy came last, he looked up at Em, his eyes reflecting the same confusion she was feeling. She patted him as he slunk by.

With the dogs secure, she followed the trail of blood. At first, she noticed a few drops, but as she approached the end of the shed, the grass was stained red with blood. Taking a deep breath, she pushed the bushes aside.

She screamed, the sound echoing off the surrounding mountains.

She turned around quickly, caught her breath, then turned back slowly to assess the massacre. Chicken feathers were everywhere. She pushed the bile down in her throat when the smell hit her. There was so much blood. Slowly, Em counted three chickens in all. One of them was Kate Wingslet. Her gorgeous, multi-faceted feathers hung from a nearby bush, while a few others stuck to the blood seeping into the ground. What was more shocking was the fact that the chickens were headless.

What the hell had happened? Had something got into the chicken coop? Surely this hadn't occurred in the last hour while she was out walking the dogs. She took some calming breaths, and, with her hand over her nose, scanned the vicinity. The smell was overwhelming.

She stepped back and took another deep, cleansing breath, but panic quickly overtook her. The other chickens! She raced back around the shed, searching to see if any other chickens were about, but the place was empty. When she made it to the chicken coop, she was relieved to find the rest of the chickens already roosting inside, including the rooster, Leo DiCockrio. They seemed completely oblivious to what was outside. There were no signs of the gate being broken or tampered with, but a shoe print was in the mud, one that was too big to be hers. It could have belonged to Lukas, the previous housesitter. At least, she hoped that was the case.

When the dogs began barking, her guard went up. She wasn't tuned in to their different barks yet, but the sound wasn't coming in her direction. It was directed at the front of the house.

"Hello?" a woman's voice called, urgently, from a distance.

Em poked her head around the side of the shed and saw a woman gazing up towards the verandah. An old black Labrador stood beside her, looking nonplussed. The young woman stood back from the fence, just out of reach of the dogs. What was she waiting for? Why didn't she just go through the gate to the door? The dogs didn't seem to be barking angrily. It was more to alert her that someone else was there.

Em recognised the woman. She'd seen her walking the Labrador while Em and the dogs trailed behind on the road. Up close now, she looked to be in her mid-twenties, slim, but not the Hollywood-thin Em was used to seeing. God, this woman wasn't Hollywood at all. Not with her ponytail of dirty blonde dreadlocks, multiple piercings, and an army jacket with bold, multicoloured leggings covering her long legs underneath. Chunky combat boots finished off her edgy look. Beside her, the old black Labrador sat down, tired from standing.

Em didn't know who the woman was. For all she knew, she could be a reporter, here to scout out some dirt about her life. Great, that's all she needed. Bloody paparazzi.

Em's emotional walls locked into place – her fortress, a resilient shield protecting her. Her goal with the housesit was to find the strength to dismantle these walls and reclaim her freedom. Eventually. But for now, she knew she wouldn't get rid of the woman by skulking behind the shed.

"Be water," she whispered, trying to convince herself that she would be okay. "Be flowing yet flexible. Powerful yet open." The words felt flimsy, but her therapist insisted she repeat them whenever she felt threatened. It felt strange trying the words on, but she stood upright and put her shoulders back, and stepped out into the open. As soon as she did, the woman zeroed in on her like a raven on roadkill.

"Hey! Are you okay? I heard screaming from the road," the woman said.

Her face looked etched with concern, but Em didn't trust it. There was always a reporter or photographer lurking in her life.

"Yes. Great. Just great," Em said, sarcasm dripping.

"Oh, you're ..." the woman began, clearly recognising Em instantly. Yeah, the woman knew exactly who she was.

"Yep. I'm Mathilda Walsh, although I'm known to most as Em. And yes, I'm Callum Walsh's wife. Or soon-to-be ex-wife," Em said. She added a mumbled "Thank God" under her breath.

"Is, um, everything okay?" the woman asked again, looking behind Em to see what she was screaming about.

But Em had had enough of people digging, probing into shit that was none of their business. So, fuck it. She'd give this woman a story if that's what she'd come to get.

"Is everything okay? You tell me. Here I was thinking I had finally found the perfect place to retreat from my bullshit life. Dogs with velvety ears and puppy dog eyes. Rocking chairs on a wrap-around verandah, where I can sit and relax while drinking my beverage of choice. So, yes, it's all lovely. All beautiful. All those things listed on a housesitting ad, making the place sound absolutely idyllic," Em ranted.

The woman stood ramrod straight, her green eyes blinking rapidly.

Em went on, "But now I have my mother doing a little jig, as she sings 'I told you so', reminding me how she advised me to leave my dickhead husband years ago. Doesn't help that the dickhead is sending me texts every five seconds about what a bitch I'm being, all the while threatening to ruin me and my bakery and my life. Oh, but I may not have a bakery or a life, because my business partner, Asher, has just dropped a bombshell that he's thinking of pulling out. Probably because he's sick of the paparazzi running off our clientele. Or maybe he's questioning whether the embezzlement rumours swirling around social media are true. Even though," she said, her voice going up multiple octaves to a pitch that would normally scare a raven from its feast, "he knows the rumours are bullshit because Asher and I do the fucking books together. Every. Single. Month! But I'm here, in the middle of fucking nowhere Tasmania, wondering how to fix it and wondering if there's someone lurking behind every fucking tree, or driving by in every fucking car I see, because that's been my life for the last five years. I mean, how fucked up is all *that*? I just want my bloody life back! I want to find some peace and fucking quiet because I'm so sick of selfish people running my fucking life. I just want to bake and finish writing my cookbook! But right now? Now I find three massacred chickens. I don't even know what caused it. And I can't find their heads! The heads have fucking vanished!" And with that, she flailed her arms and stomped her feet in the middle of the paddock like a five-year-old having a hissy fit in the middle of a supermarket when their mother has refused to buy them sweets.

Em finally stood still in the paddock, spent from her rage. But she looked up when she heard laughter ring out and felt a wet nose nuzzle her hand. The dreadlocked woman was doubled over, heaving in a fit of laughter. The black Labrador, who had been beside the laughing woman only moments before, was nudging Em's hand, his nose sticky and wet. Em bent slightly and stroked the dog's head, calming him, even though he had come to calm her.

Billy looked down from the verandah with his forlorn eyes. Ruby stood wiggling beside him, staring at Em, desperately wanting to comfort her. And Charlie was now at the gate, clawing at it, trying to get through to her. But the laughter continued to reverberate off 'The Chick Inn', behind which three dead chickens lay headless, the surrounding grass a dark, vicious red.

"What the fuck are you laughing at?" Em screamed at the hippy-dippy chick.

"Because I never thought this would be how I'd meet some celebrity's wife. Throwing a tantrum in the middle of – what did you call it – fucking nowhere Tasmania!" The woman wiped away tears.

"Oh, fuck off!" Em threw back at her, wiping away her own tears and smearing chicken blood across her cheek, the smell piercing and metallic. She looked at her hands and became nauseous at the sight. She wiped them across her jeans, regretting it immediately. "And now I'm going to have to throw out my favourite fucking jeans because I'll never get this blood out of them!" Em screamed.

The laughter grew louder. "I'm sorry," the woman said, desperately trying to stop laughing and failing miserably. "It's just that … Lukas told me that the housesitter taking over from him was demure and nervous. From what I'm seeing, either you're not the new housesitter, or he was seriously mistaken!" She called the Labrador back, as he'd clearly caught a whiff of the dead chickens.

"Well, did Lukas have to deal with dead chickens on day two of *his* housesit?" Em yelled, remembering how easily she'd been wooed by the beauty of everything when the Dutch backpacker had shown her the ropes.

"No, he didn't," the woman said, and the laughter eased. "I'm sorry. But you've got to admit. You aren't the typical housesitter. How in hell did you end up in Neeminah River? Shouldn't you be in LA battling the dickhead in some nasty divorce hearing?"

"That's what my lawyer is for," Em said, her tone deadpan.

"Yeah, okay. Well, I won't say anything about you being here. Promise." She stuck up her fingers in a botched Girl Guide sign. "I'm

Anna. I'm a housesitter too, looking after a property a little further up the road."

Em didn't know if the woman was being sincere or just spinning a story. Could she trust this hippy? Just because Anna had mentioned Lukas didn't mean she wasn't a reporter. And, Em knew, if word got out that she'd thrown a tantrum in "nowhere Tasmania", it would be one more thing the media would crucify her for.

But Anna hadn't reacted like Em would have expected a reporter to, and when Ruby trotted down and stuck her head through the gate, her tail twirling like a spinning top, she reached down and said hello to Ruby by name. Em watched Anna closely. She really needed help with the chickens. Considering the risk, Em decided to give her the benefit of the doubt. But she'd stay on her guard. Keep the walls up. She may be water, but she had ice in her veins when it came to the media.

2

———————————

Once she'd calmed down a bit, Em was embarrassed about how she had behaved. She never lost her shit like that. Asher had once called her the most level-headed person he knew. Which was why she was pissed off that he seemed to be doubting her about the embezzlement fiasco. But she couldn't deal with what was going on in LA right now, nor could she worry about what people thought of her. She was on a farm in Tasmania, and she needed help with three dead chickens. This reality was way out of her league.

"Look, I'm sorry. I really didn't mean to unleash like that," Em said. "I'm Em. I've just been on edge lately. A lot has been going on."

But Anna probably already knew most of that. The media had slain her. No one was happy she was breaking poor Callum's heart. And Callum, as was his usual way, was lapping up the attention, not correcting them with the truth, all the while sending her scathing texts.

"Don't worry about it. I'm not sure how you deal with any of that, to be honest. You know, being in the spotlight all the time. It's got to be exhausting."

"You have no idea," Em said, feeling the tiredness down to her bones.

"Do you need some help? With the mess, I mean," Anna offered, surprising Em. "I had a fox get into a chicken coop when I was doing a Queensland housesit earlier in the year, so I know what it's like. The clean-up is no fun."

Em hesitated. She really had no choice but to trust the woman. The dogs would be into the mess if she didn't deal with it.

"No, it's fine. But thanks. I just don't know what may have happened. Would you mind having a look and seeing if you can work it out?"

As soon as the words left Em's mouth, she wanted to gobble them back up. What was she doing? If this woman called the media, she would be exposed completely.

"Of course," Anna said with a reassuring smile. "Let me just put Sachin up with the other dogs. They're old friends."

The old Lab was restless, sniffing the air. Anna opened the gate to the house yard. They watched him amble up the stairs to where the others lay waiting on the verandah. But the three other dogs weren't interested in their friend. They stared in the direction of the shed and the chicken coop.

"So what do you think happened?" Anna asked. "About the chickens, I mean."

"I really have no clue. The dogs were barking last night, but I went out with them to check, and again this morning. Nothing seemed amiss, and they didn't go behind the shed either time."

They turned the corner of the shed, and Em pulled aside the bushes to reveal the bloody mess.

"Oh shit! I was going to make some joke about needing clean-up in aisle three, but this is nasty," Anna said, covering her nose. The smell of blood was overpowering. "Do you have a shovel and some gloves? A wheelbarrow would be a bonus. Then we wouldn't have to carry them. But we'll need to bury the carcasses and wash away the blood, otherwise you'll have the devils here tonight."

"Oh, no, you don't need to help. I just needed to know what to do," Em said, shocked. But then what Anna had said stopped her. "Wait. What? Devils?"

"Yeah. Tasmanian devils are scavengers. When I was housesitting up north, one of the older locals told me that if you break the pelvis, head and shoulders on a human body, the devils can consume the entire body. Like, all of it. And, if there are a few around, they'll devour it in one night. Except for leather boots. They like to gnaw on those like a chew toy."

"Holy shit," Em whispered.

"Yeah, I thought the guy was just having me on, just joking with me, you know? But I've heard it a few times now," Anna said. "The devils have incredibly powerful jaws. When I asked a wildlife expert, they told me it's possible for them to do that even without breaking the larger bones first."

"Wow, I had no idea," Em said, stunned at what lay just outside her door every night. "Do you think this could have been caused by a Tasmanian devil?"

"It's possible. I read they are known to go after poultry if they're really hungry. But dead chickens are an easy dinner, and it doesn't look like anything's tried to eat them. Look, it's no problem to help. Besides, it'll go faster with two people. And I wouldn't worry too much about it. This happens on farms all the time," Anna said.

Em wasn't so sure. She went to get what she needed from the shed nonetheless, and when she returned, Anna was on her haunches, assessing the mess like she was a detective on *CSI*.

"It looks fresh. Like it only happened in the last hour or so," she said, while Em set everything down.

"Well, the dogs were with me on a walk, so I know it wasn't them," Em said, shovelling the carcasses into the wheelbarrow and trying her best not to vomit.

"Look, I don't mean to freak you out, but I don't think this was caused by an animal," said Anna. "I mean, it could have been an eagle, but where are the heads? And look," she said, bending down and pointing at the neck of one of the poor creatures, "it's a clean cut. I reckon a human did this."

"A … a human?" Em froze, gazing at the blood and gore around them.

Anna nodded.

Would Callum send someone to scare her like this? She considered it. It certainly wasn't beneath him.

"Whoever it is, they are a sick motherfucker," Anna said. "I mean, Bryan across the road is a bit of a weirdo. Could be him? We should call the police."

Em hesitated. Once she got the police involved, people would find out she was here. The media was her main concern, although the Australian paparazzi weren't as vicious as the Americans. And if it was Callum who was connected to it, she'd find out on her own.

Anna stared at her, waiting for her answer.

"No, I don't think so. I mean, it could be a prank, or it could be some wedge-tailed eagles going out for lunch," Em said, trying to blow it off.

"Hmm. Yeah, maybe," Anna said, but her look said otherwise. "But …"

"No," Em said definitively. "The last thing I need is photographers and journalists camping out, disturbing the place. And I don't want to be offside with the neighbours either, for something that could be dismissed as a prank. Even if someone is pissed off that I'm here, this is a way for me to stand up. I don't scare easily. I think it's best to just clean it up, so the dogs can't get into it again."

"Are you sure? I mean, I'd be calling the cops if this happened on my housesit. Especially given …" Anna said, pointing at the severed neck and running a finger across her throat.

"I'm sure. Look. Don't get me wrong, I feel bad this has happened on my watch. Really bad. I was just getting to know the chickens and their personalities. I named that one," Em said, pointing to the older, now headless, bird with her multicoloured coat. "I called her Kate Wingslet. The rooster is a bit of a rogue, always after the young things. That one was a bit of a mother to the rest."

Anna said, "I've got one chicken that follows Sachin around. She thinks she's a dog too."

They were both quiet for a moment, staring down at the dead chickens, giving the moment its due.

"Where do you want to bury these poor things?" Anna said, just as sprinkles of rain began to fall.

"Lukas, the previous housesitter, mentioned a pit," Em said, and pointed towards the back of the house. "He said if anything happened with the animals, the homeowner said to just toss them in there. I doubt he thought this would happen, though."

Anna nodded, solemnly.

Em scanned the trees at the perimeter of the property, looking for someone watching them. Despite what she told Anna, she knew someone was behind it and that someone had to be watching for her reaction.

MINUTES LATER, Em stared down at the dark metal sheeting covering the pit but resigned herself that the task had to be done. She was surprised by how heavy the lid was and, when she grunted at the effort, Anna moved in to help. With the lid to the side, they tossed the headless chickens into the deep, dark hole. Em was sorry that this was the end for these souls. As she and Anna walked back to the crime scene, Em's heart felt heavy. The poor chickens. It wasn't their fault this happened. It was hers. As they filled buckets with rainwater from the tank, Anna told her the story about the fox during her Queensland housesit.

"It was a mess. Much like this. Feathers everywhere. And the chickens stopped laying for two weeks. I didn't know what to do."

Em was relieved that Anna was keeping the conversation going. An internal battle had begun within her in earnest, and there was one nagging question she needed to ask Anna before she left. When she invited Anna in out of the light rain for coffee, Anna declined, saying she needed to get Sachin home before the skies really opened up.

"Can I ask you a question?" Em asked, her tone so sharp that Anna froze. Even in the poor light, Em could see Anna's face pale.

"Sure," Anna said, nervously.

Em leaned forward, her eyes sharp as she fixed them on Anna. "Are you a reporter?" Her words were icy and accusing, and her fingers twitched with frustration as she waited for Anna's response.

Anna straightened, her cheeks flushing pink and her eyes widening in shock. Em wasn't sure if she was startled by being caught red-handed or merely by the accusation itself.

"Christ, no!" Anna exclaimed, but Em's right eyebrow shot up.

"I'm a scientist. I've just finished my degree in Marine Biogeochem-istry in Canberra," she continued, "and now I'm waiting until the new year before I start a Graduate Diploma of Marine and Antarctic Science in Hobart. My goal is to work in Antarctica."

Em's mouth dropped open.

"Look, I'm sorry if I gave you a different impression," Anna said, her cheeks quickly returning to their normal colour. "I don't mean to make you nervous or not trust me. Believe me, I'm on your side. What-ever is going on with you and your ex, I know what it's like. Okay, maybe not exactly what it's like, since my ex wasn't famous, but it can be hard breaking away. And yeah, sometimes you do need to scream and yell at a total stranger, even when she's coming to make sure you weren't being killed by an axe murderer. I mean, that scream of yours is Oscar-worthy. Maybe *you* should have been in the pictures, and not your ex?"

Em smiled, instantly relieved to know who Anna was, but even more relieved to know someone was on her side for once.

As Anna and Sachin ambled down the driveway towards home, Em wondered how Anna would go as a scientist in Antarctica. Would they allow a scientist into Antarctica with body piercings? Wouldn't they freeze to her skin in such cold temperatures?

3

Your brand-new 4WD looks like it's been bathed in crystals.

It looks pampered… just like you.

I hope the seatbelts work because strap in, princess, you're in for a ride.

The road ahead is about to get … bumpy.

4

As the fire crackled and the scent of coffee wafted through the room, Em sat down to write an email to her mum and Asher. She had talked to both of them the day before, to let them know she'd arrived. Now she was stumped as to what to say.

Her relationship with her mother was strained, and she couldn't rely on her for anything. Meanwhile, her business partner had threatened to leave her in the lurch. As she tried to process Asher's comment about leaving their partnership, a whirlwind of emotions consumed her. She wondered what could have pushed him to consider such a drastic move, and what she would do if it actually happened. Even though he hadn't made a firm decision yet, just the thought of losing him sent her spiralling. She was willing to negotiate with him if it came down to it, but she wasn't sure what bargaining chips she had. Right now, she missed his friendship and guidance. He was like an old soul who brought balance to her chaotic life.

Em nervously rubbed the back of her neck, wondering if Asher would be willing to talk her off the metaphorical ledge. He was always her rock when things got overwhelming. Though he wasn't related by blood, he was the closest thing she had to a caring and supportive brother. And in some ways, he understood her better than anyone else in her family. When she had confided in him about Callum's latest antics with the embezzlement, Asher's hands balled into fists, and when they'd talked about how the rumour would inevitably affect the bakery, the vein in Asher's neck had started pulsing almost instantly. It wasn't long after that that he'd dropped his bombshell about wanting to dissolve their partnership.

She desperately hoped it was just anger towards Callum that made him say those words. Should she talk to him? Or could she continue burying her head in the sand over the whole scenario? That seemed a better option for now.

She wasn't sure if she wanted to share the headless chicken incident, but she had no one else to tell. No matter how long she spent in the shower or vigorously scrubbing her skin, the stench of blood lingered. Was Anna correct in her theory that a human was responsible for the chicken massacre? It seemed unlikely that she would say something like that just to scare her, but it was still a possibility. With a deep breath, she started writing her email.

Hey guys,

I'm happy to report everything about the Huon Valley is just as advertised. Rolling hills, apple trees, curvy roads, sailboats docked along the river ... and quiet. So quiet. The handover from the other housesitter was smooth. No dramas there. The guy was incredibly nice.

The three dogs – Charlie, Ruby and Billy – are snoring by the fire now. It's cold and raining here this afternoon. While I thought the homeowner was only kidding, apparently goats DO like Weet-Bix, although you've got to be careful feeding them. I almost had my hand bitten off! I guess there's a technique to learn there. (Asher – I'll leave you to google Weet-Bix to understand what I'm talking about.)

The chickens are kinda funny. The rooster is a total cock (pun intended). I've nicknamed him Leo DiCockrio. He had a sidekick who kept him in line, and she was gorgeous with her russet and gold feathers. Except, well, poor Kate Wingslet is no longer. I came back from a walk with the dogs today to discover three headless chickens. Seriously! (What the hell did I sign up for, Mum?) I am a bit freaked out about it, to be honest.

After she heard me screaming my lungs out, a neighbour came to my rescue. Although, truth be told, I thought Anna was a reporter lurking about, and as such, completely unloaded on her. That was before I discovered she was a scientist, and another housesitter, looking after a property up the road. She's housesitting while she waits for her academic stuff to recommence in Hobart. I'm fairly confident the news of the murder scene (and my tantrum) won't be leaked to the media anytime soon. At least I hope so. Anna seems trustworthy.

Not sure what to do about the chickens, though. Anna wanted me to call the police. She thinks someone did it intentionally, but I decided to hold off on calling them. It's bad enough that people know I'm in southern Tasmania thanks to the embezzlement rumour Callum started. I don't need them to know exactly where I am.

Anyway, the house is gorgeous. Total farmhouse from the outside, but inside is something else. The kitchen! It's a dream. There's even a marble section in the countertop for pastry work. Seriously! I don't know much about this homeowner, but it seems he knows his stuff. I'm attaching some photos so you can see.

Em took a long drink of her coffee, sat the cup back on the side table, and continued with the email. Ruby was splayed across her feet and, even with Em's movements, the dog didn't move.

There's a clawfoot tub in the GUEST bathroom (I'll take pics of that tomorrow), and a garden I could spend hours in. Obvs when it's warmer. The garden is bare now. Oh, and SNOW is forecast. That should be interesting. I may need to buy more winter clothes. Thank God for the wood heater. The previous housesitter chopped enough wood for at least the next few days, so I don't have to deal with that yet. But I'm here for a month, so I'm going to have to tackle that at some point.

Not sure how you knew about this place, Mum, but thanks. It seems like the perfect place to get my book finished. And I'm determined to do just that.

I won't be posting anything on my socials (you know why, but I have to admit I'm itching to, especially with the amazing kitchen), but know I'm okay.

In fact, better than okay. I'm feeling peaceful (even with the chicken incident) and for that, I'm grateful. It's a far stretch from life with Callum and California.

I'll write more soon.

Love,
M
Xoxoxox

Em leaned back, taking a moment to contemplate again how different her current situation was from her usual life. The contrast was stark between this tranquil location and her busy home in California. She had spent the last five years constantly on the move – rushing to work, attending events, running errands for her business. But here, she could finally slow down and focus on what she truly wanted in life. She gazed out the window and, with Ruby still across her feet, Em let her mind drift to thoughts of her future.

What did she want to do? Where did she see herself going? All she knew was that she wanted to live without being surrounded by scandalous rumours. The view outside, from the farmhouse perched on top of a gentle hill overlooking the Neeminah River, reminded her of the romance novels she used to devour as a teenager. She couldn't help but imagine a rugged man in flannel sitting beside her, gently brushing away strands of hair from her face. She let out an exasperated sigh, realising that the last thing she needed – or wanted – was some knight in shining armour coming to rescue her.

Em closed her eyes, fighting off emotions that threatened to overwhelm her. Callum's cruel words echoed in her mind. She knew deep down that they were not true, but ... Useless. Stupid. A fat cow.

Ruby sat up and came over to her. Em bent down and stroked the dog's soft ears, finding comfort in the simplicity of this small gesture. Should she leave Los Angeles for good? The thought was too daunting to consider at the moment. All she knew was that she wanted to be far from the toxicity of Hollywood and Callum's manipulation. But what did that mean? There were endless possibilities before her, but none seemed easy to pursue.

For now, the only thing she had control over was the cookbook. She would make use of this kitchen and push forward with her work. Too much time had already been wasted, and giving up was not an option. With this kitchen setup, she could focus on baking and taking photos for the cookbook. Then she'd figure out her next steps.

5

The sky had yet to brighten beyond the mountain range when Em's phone chimed beside the bed. When her mother's face smiled up from the screen, she picked it up quickly, raking out a hoarse hello. She peered out the nearby windows. Leaves drooped with dew while birds, looking plumper than Hollywood stars over-filled with collagen, clustered together, shivering. Through the foggy glass, Em heard the frigid breeze blowing through the valley – a chill that would accompany her walk later. But right now, her mother's voice had more bite than the wind.

"Headless chickens?" Kat shrieked over the phone. "And what's this crap about embezzlement? What is Callum up to, Mathilda?"

Em swallowed. When her mum used her full name, she knew she was more than angry, and judging by her questions, she'd most likely been online doing some digging.

"I don't know about the chickens yet. As for the embezzlement thing, it's not true," Em replied, throwing off the covers.

She pulled on her ragged old cardigan and slippers, then made her way down the darkened hallway to where light was filling the lounge room. The dogs jumped up from their beds and raced to the door, ready to relieve their bladders.

"Well, of course it's not true!" squeaked Kat. "You wouldn't be that stupid. This bullshit is more of his lies. Although I must admit, it seems to be a new low, even for him. Which is why I asked what he's up to."

With a firm tug, Em opened the door slightly, holding it against the wind. The dogs took off into the chilly morning, happy not to wait any longer. But before she could close the door again, someone on the road caught her attention. A lone figure in a long dark coat, hunched against the wind, wearing a backpack. Who was that? Why were they walking on the road so early in the morning? Was it the person who'd killed the chickens?

"Em?" Her mother's voice prompted her back to reality, away from her paranoia. When she saw the dogs race to the fence, happy to greet the walker, Em put her worries aside and turned back into the house. Whoever it was, the dogs clearly knew them.

"The lawyers aren't certain if it was Callum who released the embezzlement piece," Em said calmly after she closed the door again.

She walked to the wood heater and, noticing the coals were no longer viable, grabbed some kindling and a firestarter from the basket beside her. She needed to ward off the chill.

"Well, that's bullshit!" Kat exclaimed.

Em wanted to toss the phone or hang up on her mother. She didn't need this today. She mumbled her agreement and carried on stacking the wood fire. She lit the firestarter, relieved when the kindling caught quickly.

"They disclosed where you are, for Pete's sake," continued Kat. "That little prick knows where you've gone, judging by the article mentioning 'southern Tasmania'. And, since only a few of us know your exact location, let's narrow down who could have shared your whereabouts, shall we?"

Em knew better than to interrupt her mum when she was on a tirade. Especially about Callum.

"It could be your lawyer," Kat went on, "but it's not in their best interests to reveal any information about you or the case. There is Asher, but he knows he'd have to contend with both you and me, if he let it slip. And we both know he's loyal to you, so that leaves ... ta-da! The little prick."

"I'm aware, Mum, and it's most likely him. Given we haven't finalised our divorce yet, I think this is just one last mind-game on his part."

At least, she hoped that's all it was. And she didn't want to think about Asher's loyalty at the moment, either.

"What about The Bakehouse? How will Asher handle it all?" asked Kat.

Em's mum had been so excited when Em finally realised her dream and opened the bakery, and even more pleased when she made Asher her business partner. Her mother's only issue was that Em opened The Bakehouse in California. She'd hoped it would be somewhere in Australia, away from Callum. For years, her mother had wanted her to cut ties with him. He'd charmed Kat initially, just as he'd charmed Em, but once her mother saw the real Callum, she was hell-bent on helping her daughter out of the marriage.

"I talked to Asher yesterday morning, and he said he'll take care of it. We don't know what kind of reaction it's going to get. It could bring out the freaks and the stalkers. Or it could get a positive reaction from our loyalists. I'll know more today, once I find out how things went yesterday. But Mum, Asher is thinking of leaving the partnership. He said so before I left."

Em stared into the fire that had just taken hold. Flames danced against the roof of the wood heater.

"Why would he do that?" Kat asked.

But when Em had asked the same question, Asher had only said, "It's time." She didn't believe him. He loved the place as much as she did.

"I don't know," Em finally answered. Now she regretted bringing it up. Her mum would offer some advice to her now, then take a completely different approach the following day. She was as indecisive about Em's life as she was her own, except when it came to Callum. There, she remained resolute.

"Well, at least The Bakehouse is taken care of for now. Are you okay there in Tassie? Do you feel safe? You need to make sure you stay under the radar."

Em turned towards the glass door when she heard scratching noises. There, three faces peered back at her. Billy was shaking violently from the cold. The other two dogs didn't look too pleased with the cold weather, either.

"Yeah, I'm fine. I have three dogs keeping me company," Em declared as she stood and walked to the door to let them in. She stood and the three dogs rushed to the wood heater, desperately hoping for warmth. Following them, Em stacked more wood onto the burgeoning flames.

"Are they sappy dogs who'd let any stranger in, or are they going to protect you?" Kat asked. Billy flopped down on his bed next to the fire, but the poor dog was still shivering. Em walked to the mudroom in search of an old towel or blanket to cover him. Poor love.

"Billy and Ruby are pushovers, but Charlie will protect me. He's the German shepherd. When I arrived, he waited for the previous housesitter to give him direction. He's pretty good at obeying orders. And since I've allowed them all into the house where it's warm, I think I've earned their loyalty. I'll be fine here. But I will keep an eye out, don't worry."

She looked through two cupboards in the mudroom and made her way to a third. Surely there was an old blanket or towel in here somewhere.

"Hmm," Kat said. "Just be vigilant, okay? Promise me."

"Don't worry, Mum. I'll be okay," Em said. "Now, tell me. Why the hell are you up at seven o'clock in the morning? Your campervan must be freezing! Where are you, anyway?"

She finally found an old red blanket to cover Billy. She walked back to the lounge room, covered the shivering dog, and was rewarded with a look that melted her heart.

"I bought a little heater for the van last week. Works a charm. And I'm in Hawks Nest, just north of Newcastle. But I'm setting off early to get through the city traffic before it really builds. I'm probably already too late."

"Why are you heading south? I thought you were heading to Queensland!" Em was confused, but not surprised.

"Oh, change of plans. You know me. I'm heading down to Victoria to see someone I knew a long time ago. We're meeting down along the Surf Coast."

"That's quite the change of plan," Em said, sitting on a floral uphol-stered chair.

Ruby came over for a pat, and the softness of the dog's ears soothed her nerves. She knew her mum was a careful driver, albeit with a terrible sense of direction, but Em still couldn't help being anxious. When it came to blood relations, her mum was it. Even if she couldn't rely on her.

"Oh, it's fine, love," Kat said, chuckling, and Em could hear her packing things away. "I just need to get to the other side of Sydney today. I know it's a long drive to Victoria, but don't worry. I won't push myself too hard."

"Are you driving down via the south coast or going inland?" Em asked, knowing the drive from their years of travelling when she was younger. From where her mother was in Hawks Nest, it was over a thousand kilometres to where her mother was headed. It would take a few days, at the very least, in her mother's battered old VW campervan.

"I haven't decided yet. Wherever I stop, I'll let you know where I land."

"Okay. Just be careful, okay?" Em implored, although she knew her words fell on deaf ears.

"I will," Kat said, placating her. "I'm more worried about the situa-tion with Callum. He's a bastard. We know that much. But this seems ... I don't know. It's always behind the scenes with him. This shows he's spiteful. Vindictive. I worry about how this could impact your reputation and everything you and Asher have built. You can overcome it, like you always do, but ..." Although she didn't finish the thought, Em felt its weight. Tears filled her eyes, and she struggled to swallow the lump in her throat.

"Em? You've gone quiet."

"I'm still here," she whispered, trying to steady her voice. "I'm okay."

"Shit. I'm sorry. I didn't mean to pile it on. I know this is tough," Kat said softly.

But did she really comprehend what Em was going through? To have someone manipulate you emotionally and verbally, while keeping it all hidden from the public? Her mother had some knowledge about the situation between Em and Callum, but not all of it. There was a fragility to Kat. Em had been young when they lost her father, but she still remembered the days of her mother's breakdown afterwards, especially the day she was dragged to the psychiatric facility. Now her mother travelled, not to see Australia, but to run away from the dark thoughts tormenting her.

"You didn't pile it on, Mum. It's okay. It's just been a few crazy days. I'll be all right. The embezzlement thing is in the lawyers' hands at this point. I just hate that this has exposed where I am. I was hoping to enjoy this place a little longer, but now I'll be spending the time looking over my shoulder." She put more wood on the fire, then stood and headed to the kitchen, desperate for coffee. "On the upside, I made some delicious chocolate ginger cookies around two o'clock this morning."

Em rummaged in the pantry for her coffee beans. She could have sworn she'd left them beside her coffee grinder on the counter.

"Baking has always been your way of calming the world around you," said Kat.

Em scanned the freshly baked cookies on the counter and realised how true that statement was. She switched on the coffee maker and topped up the water canister at the back.

"I hear the coffee maker going, so that means you're staying up. So, while I start ol' Lorelei's engine to warm her for the drive, tell me more about this housesit. The pictures looked divine." Em heard the van's engine purring softly against the sounds of bird calls and kookaburras laughing in the background.

As she ground the coffee beans, Em peered out through the bi-fold doors to the valley beyond and allowed herself to relax into its beauty. The sunrise had lit the hills with a warm glow, and the ground sparkled like it was covered in tiny diamonds from the overnight frost. Rows of bare apple trees lined the far distance, and the Neeminah River meandered through the gum trees below.

"The photos don't do the place justice," she said with a smile, then described the scene before her.

"They don't call Tasmania the Apple Isle for nothing," her mum said, while Em began to scoop coffee.

"Oh, that's right. I forgot about that," Em said, then sighed. "I wish you were here. There's a wrap-around verandah with wicker chairs. I can imagine us sitting there, catching up over a cup of coffee or a glass of wine. But it's probably too cold to do either of those things now. I'm still not used to the weather here."

"Yeah, I remember," her mum chuckled, but before Em could inquire further as to her mother's recollections of Tasmania, Kat said quickly, "Go on. What else?"

"Um, there are raised garden beds inside a professionally built enclosure. It looks new. I didn't notice it in the photos, but it's got to be at least thirty feet wide … um … ten metres? It's a gardener's dream."

"What about the inside?" her mother asked. Em heard her move around the van, securing things before she left. "You didn't send many photos of the inside."

"The living room is large yet has a cosy vibe. It's an eclectic mix of old and new. At one end, there's a wood heater with a brown leather couch nearby. It's that delicious soft leather that's been lived in for a while. Opposite that are two vibrant red, floral upholstered chairs, each large enough to curl up in. At the other end of the room are these huge, floor-to-ceiling glass bi-fold doors. The side that overlooks the valley is the main door inside. There is a front door, off the lounge room, but when I got here, the other housesitter brought me through the side door."

"That's how it is in the country. No one uses the front door," Kat said.

"Exactly. I forgot about that. Anyway, the other glass bifold doors overlook the river at the bottom of the hill. Next to those doors are floor-to-ceiling bookcases, filled with all kinds of old books. I haven't seen a new release in there, but I'm still looking. There's a long wooden farm table, in between the two spaces, that looks like it's had its fair share of wear and tear, but it's been refinished, and it fits the vibe of the room perfectly. The best part, though, is an old record player on the sideboard behind the couch. I haven't tried it yet, but there's a great mix of records next to it, so hopefully it works! It reminds me of my record collection back in my bungalow in LA."

"You'd better get those out of your house before Callum dumps them all," Kat said.

Em's heart caught, hoping that wouldn't be the case. Surely Callum wouldn't do that. Would he?

"Before I go," said Kat, "let me ask you one last question. The important one: how's the kitchen?"

Her words snapped Em out of her thoughts. She heard the slide of the campervan door and the crunch of gravel beneath her mother's feet. Time was ticking to get on the road.

"A dream," Em answered, gliding her palms over the wooden countertop, feeling the linseed oil on her skin.

"Your email said it was gorgeous. With that kind of kitchen, they'll have to drag your dead body out of there!"

Her mother was joking, but Em's mind returned to the poor dead chickens, now lying lifeless in the bottom of the pit.

6

I see you've settled in. Made yourself at home.

Do you feel comfortable there?

Take. Take. Take. That's all you do.

Your time will come.

Just when you think your world is as it should be ...

7

After saying goodbye to her mum, Em took a deep breath and opened the article that had been posted online. She'd already read it a million times but felt compelled to read it again. It was short. To the point.

DIVORCE TURNS NASTY: CALLUM WALSH ACCUSES WIFE OF EMBEZZLEMENT

The Australian actor Callum Walsh has now created a notably darker portrayal of his soon-to-be former wife, Mathilda Walsh. In the wake of their highly publicized separation, Mathilda, now known as Em McKinney, has been accused by Walsh of embezzling funds from her celebrated bakery The Bakehouse in Venice Beach, CA. A source close to the couple confirms the veracity of these claims, revealing that McKinney is currently seeking sanctuary in southern Tasmania, in her home country of Australia.

"Fuck!" Em screamed. She stood up from the couch quickly, narrowly avoiding spilling her coffee. As she paced around the room, her mind was consumed with thoughts of her recent conversation with

Asher. She was at a loss as to how to deal with the fallout, and she knew The Bakehouse was at serious risk.

"That's absolute bullshit and we both know it," Asher's voice had boomed through the phone when she called him, his usual calm demeanour replaced by anger. "And Christ, it's going to bring out the freaks and the vultures," he'd added with a heavy sigh.

He was right: Em had already received numerous interview requests the day the news article had come out.

"I really don't have time for this!"

She knew he was right. Asher had been managing The Bakehouse without her since she returned to Australia. He'd insisted she take a break from the drama of her divorce and reflect on what she wanted in life. But it wasn't until she'd arrived in Australia that Asher had stated he wanted to end their partnership. Had it become too overwhelming for him?

But that wasn't the immediate concern. Callum was. She'd anticipated her soon-to-be ex-husband would stoop low with the divorce. She just hadn't anticipated how big a bastard he could be. How could he be so heartless? Was it some sort of challenge or way to humiliate her? Trying to show that he still held power over her? She was done being manipulated. But would standing up to him really benefit her?

The bakery on Abbott Kinney in Venice Beach was her baby, and Callum knew that. She had worked tirelessly to become a skilled pastry chef in Sydney while he pursued his acting dreams. After moving to the US and obtaining residency status, she'd opened the bakery with Callum's support. As soon as she could afford to bring on more staff, she'd hired Asher for his exceptional baking talents and quickly made him a partner. Their teamwork was unparalleled; they'd been told repeatedly by customers and staff alike that it was like watching Fred Astaire and Ginger Rogers perform a perfect dance routine.

While she focused on pastries, Asher perfected his bread recipes, earning them a loyal following in the bustling city of LA. People lined up around the block every weekend just to get a taste of Asher's croissants and bagels. She knew that without him, their bakery would not be as successful as it was now – an award-winning establishment with a solid reputation among both locals and tourists. And, despite the drama surrounding her personal life, she needed to keep the business running with Asher; it was her main source of income until her divorce was finalised.

And Callum knew that. Fucker.

"Listen, Asher, I understand. I'm angry too," she had said, the frustration clear in her voice. "We both know this is just Callum being his usual self. He knows how much the bakery means to me, to us!"

Asher had abruptly ended the call, leaving her wondering if he questioned the validity of the story. But they both knew the truth. They always did the books together, and they were meticulous about it because she knew she would have a target on her back as long as she was married to Callum. So why was Asher suddenly considering ending their partnership?

Em had to figure out a way to mend the rift between them. He was rightfully angry, but it wasn't her fault. And his suggestion – "Call the bastard and tell him what you really think" – wasn't going to fly either. Em knew she wouldn't do that. This was Callum playing his usual games of control and manipulation.

Staring at the article, Em considered the fallout. It had the potential to be catastrophic. Their professional reputations ruined. Callum knew exactly how to go for the jugular. He was seeing how far he could push her, knowing she'd never reveal his biggest secret. Suddenly she began to wonder what was stopping her from fighting back.

She turned away from the computer and was about to make herself another cup of coffee when Charlie started barking outside. Not aggressively, but enough to alert her to someone's presence in the yard. Em opened the door and stepped out on to the verandah.

"Now, Charlie, you know me. Why are you barking?" Em heard an older woman say as she stepped up to the gate.

The woman was dressed in a vibrant caftan over black pants and a long-sleeved black top, her curly dark hair damp and showing off a striking silver streak at her forehead in the morning light. It was early, before nine, yet here was a stranger with a border collie by her side, holding a Tupperware container. Clearly a neighbour.

"Hello," Em said, reaching the edge of the verandah. Charlie looked back at her from the gate. Ruby trotted over to say hello to the other dog, their tails wagging in unison.

"Good morning. I'm sorry, I know it's early. I was just heading into Huonville, but wanted to stop by before I left," she said.

Em leaned down to pat the border collie, who had nudged her leg.

"I'm Margo. I live next door with my wife Shirley," she explained. "And that's Gracie. She's usually shy, but it seems like she likes you." Margo's face softened as the dog lapped up the attention Em gave her.

"She seems a very sweet girl. Are you sweet, Gracie? I'm sorry … I'm Em," she said, straightening up.

"Lovely to meet you," the older woman said, smiling. "I bumped into Anna this morning. She told me about your encounter with the chickens last night. I know that can be a traumatic experience, so I thought I'd check up on you."

"Oh?" Em wondered how much information Anna had disclosed, but the only way to find out was to invite her up to the verandah. "Please, come through. I was just about to make a coffee if you're interested. I take it Gracie knows the other dogs. Anna's dog, Sachin, seemed to be old friends with these three."

"Oh no, that's okay. I know there are rules for the housesitters, inviting people in and all that, but I also know John, the homeowner. He wouldn't care, but I don't want to make it awkward for you. I just wanted to drop off some peppermint slice to you, and introduce myself, since we live just next door." Margo held out the container.

Em smiled. She hadn't had peppermint slice since she was a kid, when the woman across the road used to make it every week. Em always thought she'd get sick of peppermint slice, but she never did.

"Thank you. That's very kind," Em said, taking the container.

"Sounds like Anna was able to help you, which is good. And you found John's very strange pit. The thing is a bit creepy, but we've used it ourselves from time to time. To dispose of carcasses and the like. Kind of handy to have around, to be honest," Margo said.

"It would be a good prompt for writing a horror movie," Em joked.

Margo laughed. "Indeed it would. Especially during this dreary season. Anyway, I just wanted to stop by and say hello. If there's anything you need, just yell. One of us is usually around; Shirley

35

mostly, but don't be put off by her gruffness. She's a diamond in the rough. You just have to chip away at her."

Em thought that a very interesting way of describing one's partner. She'd seen Shirley out in the yard but hadn't met her yet. She'd seemed friendly enough, offering a wave when she walked by with the dogs, clearly aware that Em was the housesitter.

"Anyway, Anna said you did okay with everything, but if you do need help, we're around. Oh! Speak of the devil!" Margo said, as Anna made her way up the driveway with Sachin in tow. "Hello, Anna darling, how are you?" Margo bent down to pat the old Labrador. "Morning Sach, your old legs creaking like mine this morning, love?"

Sachin looked up at Margo, wagging his tail.

"Morning Margo. Looking fabulous as always. We're doing fine today although Sachin had a hard time getting going. I thought a slow wander might help get the legs moving. Morning Gracie," Anna said, and watched Gracie wander over to see Sachin.

Sachin just sat and let Gracie nuzzle him. It seemed everyone knew everyone, canines included.

"Well, I must get going," said Margo. "I have my literacy group meeting this morning at the library and have to stop in at the shop for Shirley before I head there. Lovely to meet you, Em. I'm sure we'll see more of you. You're here for a month, is that right?"

Em nodded. "Yes, that's right. Nice to meet you too. And Gracie."

Charlie trotted down to say goodbye to his friend through the fence. He sat patiently at the gate, waiting for Gracie to make her way over. Eventually she did, and they had a quick sniff, but Gracie moved on when Ruby butted her way in. Em laughed at the smaller red dog. It was as if Ruby was making it clear to Gracie that Charlie was hers, and she wasn't up for sharing him. Especially with a dog as beautiful as Gracie.

The interaction with Margo, and seeing her greet Anna, had Em yearning for something she hadn't had for a long time. Community. Support. She wondered if she'd ever had that. Apart from Asher, there had only been Callum, and when she thought back on it, she'd had little of it from him at all. He was too obsessed with his own career. Even in high school and culinary school, she'd had limited friends, but

Callum was there, too. Maybe he was the reason she'd missed out on those connections?

With a wave, Margo was off, calling Gracie to join her. Sachin looked back longingly at his friend leaving.

"Hey Em. Thought I'd stop in on our way past to see how you were this morning," Anna said.

"I'm okay. Bit of a rough night. Had a really weird dream, then woke to about fifty texts from Callum," Em said, and Anna scrunched her nose in disgust. "Other than that, life is golden."

"Up for a walk? We're just meandering down to the park and back. Sachin is feeling his arthritis this morning, poor love. And I want to get a walk in before the weather turns."

Em gazed up at the gloomy sky. "Sure."

"Do you mind if I use your toilet before we go?" Anna said, but Em hesitated, thinking of Margo's words about housesitters and rules. Before she could say anything, Anna added, "I won't snoop, promise."

"Yeah, sorry. Habits. Come on through."

Anna opened the gate and Sachin ambled through, waiting at the base of the stairs. When they walked inside, Em pointed to the hallway and said, "Down the hall, first room on the left. It's the guest room but there's an ensuite." She headed to the mudroom for the dog leads.

"This place is impressive!" Anna said when she quickly returned. "But I noticed you have a locked room down the hallway," Anna added sarcastically, with a grin. "Wouldn't want the sitters getting into the silver. I've had loads of homeowners locking cupboards and rooms before. Not unusual. But wow, you lucked out with this one. It's nothing like the place I'm looking after!"

They walked back outside and, seeing their leads, all three dogs in Em's care swished their tails to and fro. Sachin stood now at the base of the stairs, his backside swerving so excitedly that he almost fell off balance.

"You didn't come inside while Lukas was here?" Em asked, as she locked the door.

"Nah, he was a stickler for the housesitting rules. No guests," Anna said, and walked down the stairs. That was twice now someone had mentioned the rules. Em had no idea there even were rules. She probably should have asked her mum before she took the housesit. But it made sense. If you were asking someone, trusting someone, to look after your house, you didn't want any old person walking through. She felt bad now, letting Anna in, but if Anna knew the rules, why had she come inside? Em suddenly wondered again if Anna had an agenda. Surely a reporter wouldn't go to these lengths to get a story on some celebrity's estranged wife. It was possible, she mused, but she couldn't imagine any reporter cleaning up chicken carcasses as Anna had.

"As a baker, you must be in heaven with that kitchen," Anna said.

"I am. It may be the inspiration to actually finish my cookbook!" Em said as they turned left past the rosebushes lining the front of Margo and Shirley's house. Though they were pruned now, Em imagined them in full bloom, their scent sending wafts of sweetness into the air.

"You're writing a cookbook?" Anna asked over the crunch of gravel under their feet.

"Yes. I'm incorporating recipes with the stories behind where I found them. A lot of them were discovered while I travelled on location with Callum, before I started The Bakehouse."

She'd said as much to the press before, so she wasn't really giving anything away. Further down the road, a massive gum tree danced in the breeze, the wet leaves glinting in the sunlight.

"Oh, look at that tree. Do you see it?" Em stopped suddenly and Ruby, who'd been trailing behind with Sachin, ran into the back of her leg. "Oh, sorry, Ruby." She bent down and gave the dog a pat, then looked back up at the tree again.

"Wow, that's magic," Anna said.

"It's better than watching the Eiffel Tower twinkling its lights at night," Em said as they both stood there, watching the tree sparkle like it was full of diamonds. Em had goosebumps.

"It's nature on display," Anna said before pointing at the sky. Heavy clouds were moving towards them.

They continued on, navigating around a deep puddle along the side of the road.

"With the peace and quiet around here, you're bound to have lots of time to work on your book," Anna said. "Nothing happens around here. Well, except for your chicken thing. Margo even said that's the first thing that's happened since Gerald went walkabout, naked, about two years ago."

"Gerald?" Em asked.

She noticed curtains flutter in a window to her right. She looked over. It was the creepy guy's house. The one who'd been staring at her last time she walked past.

"He's the old guy who lives in that house," Anna said, pointing to where the curtain was moving. "His son Bryan moved home to help him out, apparently. Gerald is a lovely old man when he's lucid. He has Alzheimer's. He has a llama out the back he named Lucy. Lucy the llama. Bryan hates it. Spits at him all the time."

"How old is he?" Em asked, thinking Bryan must be the creeper who stared at her from the driveway.

"Gerald or Bryan?"

"Bryan," Em said, looking back at the house again.

"Don't know," Anna said, shrugging her shoulders as they turned at the fence post on the other side of Margo's house. Now they were on the dirt track and off the road, heading towards the river. "My guess is about forty?" The four dogs put noses to the path in search of the best smells they could find.

"Hmm. I think I saw him yesterday," Em said.

"Yeah, Bryan is a bit of a weirdo. I've actually only seen him a few times the entire time I've been here, which is about six weeks. The neighbours mostly don't talk to me much. They see the dreadlocks and assume they know what I'm like. You know, like just another back-packer. Margo's the only one who's really asked me anything of substance about myself. Oh, and Aubrey and Tom who live next door to me. They've been lovely too. But with Bryan, I make shit up about myself, just to screw with him."

Em had to wonder why Anna would do that – make stuff up about herself. She wanted to ask, but Anna ploughed on.

"Now I think of it, Bryan has been a lot more active in the last few days than he has in three weeks. Maybe he's curious about you? I don't know. He told me he came home to look after his dad, leaving his high-end mining job in Western Australia. Bit of a misogynistic dickhead, if you ask me."

Em was pensive, taking this information in. She'd have to keep an eye out for him. What if Callum had hired the guy to mess with her? But that was stupid. Even Callum didn't know exactly where she was. She hadn't told him. So it would be strange if Callum knew this guy, especially a miner from Western Australia.

"So, how'd you hear about the housesit?" Anna asked, changing the subject. "I didn't see this sit listed on the three sites I'm on. I would have jumped on it if I had."

"My mum told me about it. She's been housesitting on and off for a long time now and she was told about it by someone she knows. But she hates Tasmania, so she didn't want to do it. She'll be relieved she didn't after the chicken incident. Anyway, she suggested it to me when I told her I was looking to come home for a while. Away from …"

Em didn't finish the sentence. She saw Anna understood and was relieved not to have to explain. Then Anna asked a question that shot Em's walls back up.

"How are you feeling about it all, if you don't mind me asking?" Anna must have sensed her defensiveness. She hastily added, "I meant about the chickens yesterday! Not about … you know."

"Oh, right. Sorry," Em said, blushing, relieved when they had to go single file down the narrow path.

Sachin walked behind Em, Ruby behind him. The other two were up ahead in front of Anna, but Em could still see them from where she was.

"I'm okay. I'm still freaked by the missing chicken heads and, to be honest, wondering what I've got myself into. I've never housesat before. Not like this, anyway. I looked after my best friend's place when he went to Europe for a month, picking up his mail and all that. But never on a farm, and never with animals. I mean, I love dogs and cats, but I don't have any of my own. I'm never home. I have a hard time keeping a plant alive. I don't know what I'll do if something else goes wrong. I mean, this happened in the first week! I've still got another three-and-a-half to go!"

"Don't worry about it. Lukas, the housesitter before you, said he looked after a place where the woman didn't disclose her rabbit breeding business before his arrival. He had four baby bunnies die on him in the first week. He told the homeowner's best friend, who was his point of contact, and she had no clue how to handle it either. When they contacted the homeowner, she blew it off completely. Said something flippant, like "It happens all the time". All the time! How can someone run a business like that?"

"Is that usual with housesits? Do you sometimes have to look after their businesses, too?" Em asked. She couldn't think of anything worse. Looking after someone's private property was bad enough. "Like, what if they have an Airbnb? Do you have to play host? I'd suck at that."

Anna laughed at Em's admission.

"No, seriously! I have a housekeeper for a reason!"

Anna turned around and stopped midtrack. "Don't worry. It's not something you have to do. What that woman did was most definitely not in the rule book. She should have disclosed it. Lukas should also have reported it, but said it wigged him out so much he stopped housesitting for three months." She turned around again and kept walking.

"How long was Lukas here for?" Em asked. She'd hardly spoken to him when they'd done the handover. He'd had a ferry booking on the north side of the state he had to catch.

"About a month. He said he would have extended his stay except the homeowner had already found someone."

"Yeah, Mum only told me about it a week ago. It was good timing for me, to be fair."

"Well, Lukas had the ferry booked anyway. He was meeting up with friends from the Netherlands while he was in Melbourne, so he wasn't too put out."

Em was relieved to hear that.

The dogs sniffed the ground as they walked along, though none of them veered off into the native grasses lining the path. The track itself was well worn under the large gum trees and a smattering of native wattle trees.

When they reached the park, the place was empty but for a white campervan. A rental, from one of the larger rental companies. Em glanced at the numberplate on the back end and saw it was Victorian. She looked around but saw no one nearby. Probably a tourist happy to have found a free camping spot for the night. At least, she hoped it was, and not some photographer staking her out.

Beyond the campervan was an elaborate playscape, and Em imagined it filled with children in the summertime, with its canvas awning keeping them protected from the high UV rays. Now, it sat lonely. There was a community centre too, perched high above the river, dark and vacant now too. Battered old recliners, a picnic table and a collection of white plastic chairs, some half broken, sat under an awning. A toilet block was off to the side of the community centre, large enough to support a cricket game crowd at the nearby oval and various other events during warmer weather.

"I'm surprised the toilet block isn't locked," Em said. "Tasmania seems to be a pretty trusting place. You'd never see that in LA. Maybe on the interstates at the rest areas, but not in a public park. It'd be paid access only."

"Probably why the campervan is parked here. Free toilets and showers, no doubt," Anna said, just as Em heard a twig break. She noticed Anna's sidewards glance.

Em looked around, not able to shake the feeling that someone was watching her. A raindrop hit her eyelashes as she scoured the area.

"Time to head back," Anna declared.

Five minutes later, they found themselves at the intersection where Anna would head right to get back to her housesit while Em would go left.

"I really appreciate the walk, it was great to get some fresh air and have good company," Em said to Anna. She waved goodbye, calling out for Billy and Charlie who were investigating something on the side of the road.

"Snow is forecast, so stay warm, okay?" Anna said as she walked away.

With the dogs back on their leads, she noticed Billy starting to shiver. Poor love. She'd get the fire going as soon as they got back. Looking up, she saw the dark clouds coming down the valley. It was approaching faster than predicted. Even with her woollen beanie pulled low on her head, the icy breeze prickled the back of her neck, the scarf doing little against the wind. She took a deep breath in and felt the crisp air hit the back of her throat, giving her an almost burning sensation. The dogs huffed and puffed around her, expelling the cold air from their nostrils like they were releasing steam from their inquisitive minds.

Despite the biting cold, Em saw that the scenery surrounding her was picturesque. Houses puffed smoke from their chimneys, while their interior lights spilled into the empty paddocks surrounding them, making shadows dance. The gum trees' branches swayed in the wind, reflecting the soft lights' glow and casting eerie shadows. The storm made things darker, but it was a canvas of dark blues and greys, creating a moody backdrop. And Em loved that. She preferred the winter weather, and storms were perfect for snuggling up in a cosy chair by the fire with a good book – which she planned on doing tonight.

It was so peaceful here; all she could hear was the rustling of leaves in the chilly breeze, the sound of rapids down at the river and, in the distance, the faint buzzing of a chainsaw. When the breeze nipped at her neck, she pulled her coat more tightly around her and thought, again, how different this all was from the last few years of her life.

Living in LA had been one continuous stretch of crazy. She was always rushing to be somewhere. If she wasn't at The Bakehouse, she was being dragged along to one of Callum's Hollywood events. She hated those things. They were always full of judgemental people, dissecting what she wore or whether she was the right person to be married to a handsome movie star.

The match that had lit the fire, the one that left their marriage a smouldering mess, was a tall woman wearing nothing but a faded pair of Lululemon pants. When Em discovered her with Callum on a Tuesday afternoon, the woman turned to Em with a sneer, a trace of white powder dusting her left nostril. It wasn't the first time Em had caught Callum sleeping around, but this woman was a definite cut below his usual type. With her cold eyes and crooked yellow teeth, the woman looked like a cheap hooker. Her hair, a greasy, vomitus-orange mop, looked like a drunken home cut, although it may have been deliberately styled by a high-priced LA salon for all Em knew. She wanted to suggest to the woman that she ask for her money back. But it was the air, smelling like cheap, sweaty sex, that made the situation feel like a living inferno, and Em knew then that the fire was about to consume everything in Em's life. Between this woman, and Callum's other recent actions, Em knew then that she was done with the marriage.

Now, standing in the middle of a road in Tasmania only weeks later, Em was relieved to have walked away. The woman was welcome to her ex-husband.

LATE THAT AFTERNOON, stroking Ruby's soft ears put her into a meditative lull as she watched the soft rain falling outside the large bi-fold doors. Charlie and Billy lay nearby on thick dog beds by the fire, sated from their dinner, while Ruby's head rested in her lap. Em sipped tea, her plate on the coffee table empty now after tasting one of the recipes she'd add to her cookbook, a lemon drizzle cake. Em was proud of this recipe. It was one of the best sellers at The Bakehouse.

Life was good, she thought. Finally. She felt, for the first time in a while, at peace. Maybe this housesit was just what she needed. At least the media didn't know where she was. She jumped when the wood fire spat an ember. Okay, maybe not as relaxed as she could be, she chided herself.

Seeing the fire was low, she nudged Ruby off her lap and walked to the door to get more logs from the wood box. She'd have to haul more up from the woodshed in a few days. Lukas had been nice enough to fill the wood box, but after two days, she was depleting it faster than she'd expected.

The dogs followed her out and began racing down the verandah stairs to relieve themselves. But Charlie stopped midway, returned to the verandah, and sniffed his way around the corner to where the front door was. Crap. Not this again. Em dropped the logs she'd gathered and followed him around the corner.

Her hand flew to her mouth. Sitting on the doormat was a lone chicken head, propped up and posed like an offering.

Em called Charlie back and looked around. Who would do this? *When* did they do this? But as she looked beyond the fence and around to the shed, she could see no one. The neighbourhood was quiet but for the soft rain falling around them. In fact, everything was *eerily* quiet.

Em began to shake uncontrollably. Although she didn't want to believe it, she had to agree with Anna's conclusion that the beheaded chickens were not the work of an animal but of a human. Now she was sure of it. Especially since there was a note attached to the head left on the doorstep, with a clear message written on it:

Welcome to the neighbourhood.

8

Em was forced to call the police. She didn't want to, but the note completely freaked her out. In hindsight, had she known who'd end up standing in front of her, she wouldn't have called them at all. Now, an hour since making that call, Detective Joshua Ryatt stood before her, dripping wet after dashing from his unmarked vehicle to the side verandah where she stood. The dogs barked from inside the house. Em turned to quiet them before turning back to the man she'd thought she would never see again.

"Hello, Mats," he said, his cheeks flushed.

Mats. He was the only one who'd ever called her that. Everyone else called her Mathilda or Em, but Ryatt's name for her took her way back, and she found she didn't mind.

"Josh," she said, simply.

His presence was so unexpected that she felt like her heart had stopped. She hadn't seen him since the week before they were due to start Year Eleven at Pennant Hills High School in Sydney. Although it had been years since she last laid eyes on him, his face still looked as familiar as ever.

"I go by just 'Ryatt' nowadays. Only Mum and Dad call me Josh anymore. It's, ah, been a long time," he said.

"Ryatt," she confirmed, although the name felt strange on her tongue. But using it distinguished between the boy she once knew and the man standing in front of her now.

He'd been a gangly kid back then, tall and skinny, but he'd grown into his body over the years. He was at least six foot she guessed, and muscular. But maybe that was a bullet-proof vest, hidden beneath his clothing? Still, with him standing there in the dark, with only the harshness of the verandah light to illuminate his face, he looked at least ten years older than her. His brown hair was peppered with grey. Most likely from the job, she assumed. His eyes held an inquisitiveness, but there was something else there as well. Embarrassment? Pain?

She hoped he felt both. The way he'd left her had been sudden. But when he smiled at her, it was like a light switch was turned on, brightening his blue eyes.

"It's good to see you. It has been a while," she said, feeling the pain of their breakup as if it had happened only yesterday.

She tried to put it aside. She didn't know why he'd left so suddenly.

"Look at you now. A police officer in Tasmania?" she said, growing angry as history invaded her thoughts. He'd left so suddenly at the beginning of Year Eleven. No goodbye. No letter. He'd just vanished.

"Detective, actually. I saw your name on the emergency list and figured it was probably someone else, but the dispatcher said she'd read somewhere that you were in Tasmania, so I took the call-out. What are the odds I'd run into you here, hey? I thought you'd moved to America."

His hands were in his pockets, she assumed to keep warm, and his embarrassment had turned now to amusement.

"The dispatcher? Will she tell people I'm here?"

Ryatt shook his head. "Nope. She can't say anything. Against policy. But I know Terrie. She wouldn't even if she could. She's as discreet as they come. But let's get to why I'm here, shall we?" he said, pulling himself up to his full height. "Chicken head, I was told."

"Isn't this call below your pay grade?" Em asked. "If you're a detective, I mean."

"Well, technically it is. But if it was actually you that called, then I wanted to be the one to help. Is …" Ryatt looked behind her, as if looking for someone else.

She saw a flicker of anger pass through his eyes, but he quickly shut it down. "Is anyone here with you?"

"No, just me," she said before realising that if she were in Los Angeles, this question would have her on edge. But she trusted Ryatt with her safety. She always had.

"Right. Okay," he said.

Em sensed his relief. Callum, his high school tormenter, wasn't here.

"Let me show you why I called the police. It's at the front door." She led him around the corner to where the chicken head remained propped up on the welcome mat.

Ryatt crouched down and inspected it closely.

"Did, ah, Callum remain as vindictive as he was in high school? Or did he finally grow up?" he asked as he gloved up.

Em considered the question. How much was she willing to tell Ryatt? She considered lying, but she was done lying for Callum. "No change. If anything, he got worse," she said.

The flicker of anger returned.

"Sorry to hear that. Truly. Do you think he may have had something to do with this?" Ryatt asked, stepping to the other side of Kate Wingslet's head and reading the note lying at its base.

"Callum?" she asked, as Ryatt pulled out his phone and took several photos.

"Yeah. Do you think he may be behind this? Is he still in America?" He pulled a plastic evidence bag from his jacket.

"I don't know. As far as I know, he's still in LA, but honestly, I can't be sure. We haven't spoken in weeks, except for the texts he keeps sending me."

Em wondered whether she should have mentioned the texts at all. She hadn't responded to them, so they were one-sided at this point, on the direction of her lawyer.

"Texts? Do you mind if I take a look at those?" he asked, and she made a note to contact her lawyer in the morning, in case Callum was behind it.

"No, I'll show them to you. But given the note, wouldn't it make more sense that a neighbour is sending a message?"

Ryatt straightened, after securing the note in the evidence bag.

"Most likely. But I just need to be sure I don't rule anything out. And, since I know what your ..." Ryatt hesitated, briefly grimaced, then continued, "... husband is like, I want to be sure I'm thorough."

Em nodded. "Soon-to-be ex-husband," she added. "We're in the middle of getting divorced."

Ryatt looked at her, pain replacing the anger.

"I heard," Ryatt said. "But I can't say I'm sorry."

What did that mean? Because it was Callum? If he wanted to know why she'd married Callum, he'd ask. The Josh Ryatt she knew was never one to hold back his opinions. Not with her. At least that's how they were when they were teenagers. But he probably wasn't that person anymore. She certainly wasn't the same person she was back then. She let it go.

"Well, if you have what you need there, come inside. My phone is in the kitchen, and it's a lot warmer inside than it is out here." Em was shivering, her socked feet wet from the rain-drenched verandah.

"Is there somewhere I can put this chicken head for you?" offered Ryatt. "I have the evidence I need, and it's best now to dispose of it." He poked it with a pen and watched it fall over on the mat.

"There's a pit behind the house. But leave it there. I'll drop it in there when we're done."

"No. I can do it for you," Ryatt said.

But Em just wanted him gone. Between the hurt from eighteen years before and her humiliation that she'd married Ryatt's bully, she just wanted to run and hide. She was silent.

"Mats. Just direct me to this, ah, pit and I'll dispose of it. Then you can show me the texts and I'll get on with my job. Okay?" His eyes were intense.

"Behind those bushes. Close to the fence," she said.

He nodded, then left her on the verandah, opened the boot of his car and grabbed his raincoat. He returned, gloved up once more, and picked up the chicken head with both hands. Em shuddered at the sight of the hacked neck, then left Ryatt to it and headed inside to the warmth and the dogs.

She moved the dogs into the mudroom to keep them out of the way for now, but as soon as she closed the door, all three began to whine. Shit. She felt guilty for locking them in when they were used to the warm fire, but she resigned herself to it. They'd be okay. It wouldn't be for long. She left her wet socks at the door and hurried to her own room to find her slippers.

A few minutes later, Ryatt knocked on the door, stomping the water from his feet. Em opened the door just as he was unlacing his boots.

"Thanks," he said and stepped into the warm room. "Oh, much better. Snow's forecast. There'll be some on Vinces Saddle for sure later."

Em had no idea what he was talking about but nodded just the same.

"So, you're housesitting this place?" He looked around with cop eyes, taking in every detail of the room.

"Yes. Mum told me about it. She was asked to do it, but she refuses to come down to Tasmania. Too dark, she says. So she suggested me for it."

Ryatt nodded. "Your mum still travelling the country?" he asked, as they stood awkwardly at the door.

"Yes," she said. She wasn't sure whether to offer him a drink or just answer his questions, so he'd leave sooner.

"Ah, do you have your phone? I'll take a look at those texts," he said.

She nodded and walked to the kitchen counter, wondering briefly if he needed a warrant to see them. It really didn't matter. She was happy to volunteer her phone, although she probably wouldn't have been if it was another detective. With the phone unlocked, she handed it to Ryatt.

"Thanks," he said, and she watched his eyes skim text after text as he scrolled through. "Still a dick, I see." He looked up quickly, blushing. "Sorry, that wasn't very professional of me."

"It's okay. I'd be surprised if you said any different," she said. "Sadly, yes. He's still a dick. But he wasn't always that way with me."

He looked at her with confusion. She thought he was probably trying to work out how she could have dated Callum in the first place. Blinking, he looked back down.

"You said he's still in the US. I'll do some checking to confirm that. You never know. Do you know if he has any connections here?" He handed the phone back to her.

"None in Tasmania. He keeps in touch with Robbo and Kitchy from high school, but they're in Sydney, I think. Oh, Robbo might be on the Gold Coast. I'm not sure. But no one else. He had some colleagues from his early acting days, but most of them are out of the picture now. I don't think he's talked to anyone since we moved to LA." She didn't want to say it was because Callum thought he was better than his past colleagues, calling them all two-bit acting wannabes.

"Okay. Well, it could be a neighbour, of course. Does anyone else know you're here?"

"Mum knows where I am. My business partner in America. A neighbour, Anna, who figured out who I was pretty quickly. She lives further down the road. And she's another housesitter, so I'm pretty confident she didn't do it."

"Why?" Ryatt asked. He got to the point; that was for sure.

"Um, because she helped me clean up the mess when I came across the chickens yesterday."

Em filled him in on what had happened the day before and saw him trying to bury his smirk when she told him exactly how she'd met Anna.

"What? I've been under a lot of stress lately, and I was just over it. The chicken massacre was the last straw. So I threw a tantrum. It's not like it's a common occurrence," she said, exasperated.

"No judgement here," he said, hands in the air. "Just imagining it, that's all. But, since you described it as a chicken massacre," he said, the smile disappearing and the cop face returning, "I'm going to check with the neighbours. See if anyone saw anything or knows anything. If I get lucky, someone will admit to it and say it's a prank. I'm thinking that's all it is at the moment. Having said that, I know what your ex can be like, so that's why I was curious about what his connections may be. But you need to keep a watch out, Mats, just in case. And call me if anything else happens, okay?" He pulled out a business card from his jacket pocket and handed it to her.

"Do you think something will?" she asked, feeling the blood drain from her cheeks as she took the card.

"I doubt it. But just be careful. Whoever did it, it's harassment. Plain and simple." And with that, he opened the door to the rain.

EM SIFTED through her emotions after Ryatt left. He had changed. But then, so had she. When Callum's name had been spoken, she'd felt an underlying resentment emanating from Ryatt. She didn't blame him. Em had married the guy who'd taunted him in high school. The guy who'd flushed his head down the toilet more than once – and that was one of the kinder things he'd inflicted on Ryatt.

There was every chance Ryatt would come back and ask what had happened with Callum. She could turn the question around on him – he had disappeared first, after all. And she hadn't started dating Callum until nine months later. But she didn't just date him; she married him. That was the key difference. What could she tell Ryatt when he asked why? That it was because he left her? Em knew it was more complicated than that.

Life with Kat had been challenging. It had felt like her mother couldn't stand to be in the same room as her. Callum had been her life-line, offering an escape from that isolating environment. He made grand promises and showered her with love and attention, but it came at a cost. While he treated her like royalty, he was cruel to those around them. At first, she was enamoured of his kindness and support, but once they moved to the United States, another side of Callum emerged – the same side that Josh Ryatt remembered from before.

During her time dating Josh, Em had witnessed the simplicity of a normal family and longed for that kind of love, support and stability. She'd cherished the warmth and acceptance she received from his parents whenever she visited. They were vegetarians and grew their own produce in a lush garden, a stark contrast to the unkempt weeds covering her family's yard. While her mother relied on gallons of instant coffee, Ryatt's family brewed peppermint tea. They gathered around the dining table every evening for meals, while at her house it was more common to eat microwaved dinners in front of the television. On Friday nights, Ryatt's family played board games, while Em spent her time packing up for her mother's early morning Saturday markets. The idyllic family life that Ryatt had grown up with was something Em held on to dearly, knowing she had experienced nothing like it since her father had passed away.

Almost twenty years on, that lifestyle seemed like a fairy tale. Marrying Callum had certainly been as far from that kind of life as she could ever imagine, and she would have been kidding herself if she'd thought otherwise when she'd married him.

Em thought about texting her mum, eager to tell her about Ryatt showing up. But she had serious doubts her mother would even remember him. It was a time her mum was always in a stoned fog, while she made bunting for her market stalls. Besides, telling Kat about Ryatt meant Em would have to explain why he'd shown up, and she wasn't ready to burden her mum with that news yet.

Not until they knew more about who was behind it.

9

You seem perplexed by the note, Mathilda.

That's good.

You need to stay on your toes.

But pay attention.

Because I'm only just getting started.

10

With a steaming coffee between her gloved hands, Em sat on the verandah the next morning while the dogs did their usual sniffing around the yard. She was expecting Ryatt at any moment. His call hadn't surprised her. Not really. She was just shocked that he'd called her this quickly. Didn't he have other cases to solve? Hers was hardly a murder investigation.

She hated the thought that she was the visitor to the neighbourhood and now the police were snooping around. Not to mention that it was Josh-bloody-Ryatt! And God knew, she had enough dramas in her life without dead chickens and Ryatt showing up.

As the sound of crunching gravel echoed along the driveway, all three dogs bolted towards the gate, barking ferociously at the unfamiliar car approaching. Em, caught off guard, jerked her arm and accidentally spilled her coffee all over herself.

"Fuck!" she screamed, as she felt the scalding liquid soak through her gloves. She jumped out of the chair, shaking her hands and ripping off the gloves. She called to the dogs, hoping to put them into the outer paddock before Ryatt reached the gate, but all three ignored her. When the car door slammed, she called them again, this time clearly agitated.

Ruby obeyed, prancing back to her as if Em was offering her a treat. Billy followed. Charlie stayed at the fence, not barking, but definitely on alert.

"Charlie, *come!*" Em yelled again, and this time he turned, looked at her, and finally followed her orders as she kept wiping at the coffee on her jeans.

"Morning, Ryatt. Hang on. Let me just put the dogs out into the outer yard."

Em rushed down the stairs. Believing they were going for a walk, all three dogs raced to the other gate, tails wagging with anticipation. Em felt guilty putting them out, but she'd only seen how they behaved around the neighbours. Granted, she'd been a stranger when she'd first arrived, but the last thing she needed was for one of them to have a go at a police officer.

"Morning. You could have left them in," he said, unhelpfully, when she returned.

She looked over at the dogs who were looking back at her with what she was sure was disappointment on each of their faces.

"It's fine. I'll walk them when we're done. Want a coffee?" She immediately wanted to bite her tongue. This wasn't a social visit!

"Wouldn't say no. It's bloody cold this morning," he said, stating the obvious.

Maybe he was nervous too, she thought, sending him an awkward smile. "I thought it was just me being a wimp and feeling the cold," she said, walking inside in her coffee-soaked stockinged feet.

She ripped the socks off at the kitchen island and threw them down the hallway towards the mudroom, hitting the other wet pair from yesterday. She'd deal with them later. Ryatt stood at the door and took his boots off.

"Cappuccino, flat white or ..." she offered, turning the coffee machine on. "Wait. Do you drink coffee?"

"Yeah, I do. A flat white would be great. Thanks." He followed her inside.

"I remember your family only drinking peppermint tea," Em said as she pulled the milk from the fridge.

"Yeah, they still do. I went to the dark side and started on the hard stuff when I began in the police force," he said. "Still like the tea at night, though. Totally relaxes me."

"How are your mum and dad? Still around?" Em asked, instantly berating herself. What was she doing? She really didn't need to be walking down memory lane here.

"Yeah, Mum finally retired from nursing last year, and Dad's still working as a carpenter. Although it's part time now. He's getting too old for it." Ryatt took a seat at the long wooden table. "What about you? Kat still roaming the country?"

Em smiled. "Yeah. Right now, she's heading to Victoria to see a friend. Probably some old fling. She's had a few of those. No one ever sticks. Probably never will, to be fair. Not after Dad."

"Still mourning him then?" Ryatt asked, and Em nodded. "I remember the one time I brought him up. Wanted to cut my tongue out when she went quiet and pale."

"Yeah, it's a forbidden subject. She can't even be around me much anymore. Apparently I'm just like him, which has never made sense to me, but I guess being with me just makes her grief worse."

She turned to make Ryatt's coffee and, while the frother did its magic, she watched him in the window's reflection. He'd turned and was now looking around the living room. His hair still curled at the back like it did when he needed a cut.

Ryatt seemed lost in his own thoughts. When she placed the cup in front of him on the table, he started.

"Oh! Thanks. Was just thinking back," he said.

Em walked back to the kitchen. Thinking it would only go to waste otherwise, she grabbed a couple of slices of lemon drizzle cake, along with her own coffee.

"All that was so long ago. I've changed a lot since then," Em said, indicating her voluptuous curves before taking her seat opposite him.

When Ryatt blushed, she wanted to laugh. She'd been a size eight, maybe a ten, when she'd known him. Now she was sitting between a sixteen and an eighteen. She'd blossomed, as her mother liked to say. Callum just told her she'd got fat.

"Can I ask you a question before we get into the official stuff? I assume you're here with an update. Or is this purely a social visit?" She passed him a slice of cake.

Ryatt sat up straighter, as he'd done the night before when she'd tried to steer the conversation to police matters. "Official visit, and I'll get to that. But go ahead. What did you want to ask?"

"Where did you go? When you left?"

Em was surprised when he looked confused.

"What do you mean?" he asked. "I left you a letter with my new address on it. I gave it to Kat when you were away with what's-her-name." He flicked his fingers, trying to remember the friend's name, as if that was the important piece of information. "Your friend with the frizzy blonde hair," he added.

"Gretchen," she said plainly, annoyed at the deflection. A letter? He hadn't left anything for her. He'd just disappeared. "I didn't get any letter," she said, calling him out on his lie.

"Really?" he said, his face full of regret. "I handed the letter directly to your mum while my parents sat in the car. After that, I wrote you tonnes of letters. At least twenty. Maybe more. When I didn't hear from you, I assumed you were pissed off that I left, and that you didn't want to write to me. Did you not get any of the letters?"

Em shook her head.

"God, Em, I'm so sorry."

Em flashed back to the afternoon she returned from that trip with Gretchen. "When I got home from that trip, Mum was really distracted. She'd just broken up with someone. Mike? Peter? Bob? I can't remember his name. Someone clearly forgettable."

Her mother had been upset, smoking cigarette after cigarette in the back doorway, her hands shaking every time she inhaled.

"When I went back to school the next day, you were gone," Em continued. "No one seemed to know where you went." She clenched her hands around her coffee mug.

Looking at the hurt on Ryatt's face – the same hurt she was feeling – she wanted to rage at her mother. How could she have done that? Why would she not have given her the letter? Had she thrown out the rest he'd written? Letters were the only way they had to communicate in those days, before cell phones and email became the norm – not that they'd have been able to afford such luxuries in those days. And a breakup wouldn't be enough of a reason for her mother to withhold the letters from Ryatt.

She knew how upset Em was at his sudden departure. She'd cried for a week after the office told her he hadn't re-enrolled at the school. When she went to his house, there was a For Sale sign in the front yard and no trace of the family at all. She had felt lost and betrayed. Abandoned, just as Kat had when Em's dad had died. Ryatt had been important to her. He was her first love. The one she confided in. The one she trusted.

"So, where did you go?" she asked again, trying to keep the pain from her voice, but she could feel that her face was flushed from her inner rage.

She got up quickly from the table and went to poke the fire. She needed to calm herself. Being angry at her mum wouldn't solve anything. And it wouldn't solve what was going on here, either.

"Here. Tasmania," he said as he watched her close the wood heater door. "Mum got a new job at the Royal Hobart Hospital as a theatre nurse. Apparently, she had some specific skills they desperately needed, and they wanted her to fill the position as soon as possible. They offered housing along with a package she couldn't refuse and, since Dad wasn't working then, it made sense to go before school started. I wanted to tell you as soon as I knew, but you were away on the boat with Gretchen and her family, and I had no way of reaching you. Hence, the letter I left with your mum. I'm sorry, Em. I thought you knew."

"Nope. One day you were there, and the next you were gone. When I came back to tell you all about the trip, you weren't there." She returned to the table and took a seat.

"I'm really sorry," he repeated, and she could see he meant it.

Nothing could be done about it now, other than some harsh words to Kat when she spoke to her next. Ryatt wasn't at fault.

"I guess now we know," she said. "So, what have you found out about the note?" She wanted to bring his attention back to why he was here, instinctively putting up a protective barrier to shield herself from any further hurt.

"Well, other than your neighbours being either concerned for your wellbeing, or pissed off that their privacy has been invaded, I haven't got any solid leads. But I would keep my distance from Bryan if I were you. He was purely reactionary, and my visit did not go down well."

Ryatt took a bite of his cake and groaned, his eyes rolling back in his head. Em smiled a little. She'd seen this reaction to her pastries before.

"Holy shit, Mats. Did you make this?" he asked, his mouth still half full. He held up a finger, chewed, swallowed and apologised for his rudeness. "Sorry, but this cake is unbelievable. Seriously, did you make it? You run a bakery in LA now, right?"

Em nodded, her cheeks heating.

"You always said you'd be a baker one day," he said, going in for a second bite.

"I did?" she asked, surprised at the comment. She didn't remember ever saying that at all when she was younger. She remembered deciding to be a baker towards the end of Year Twelve.

"Yeah, you used to tell me about this old lady who lived across the street when your dad was alive. You said she inspired you to bake. I remember these scones you used to make. Pumpkin ones. It was like you were obsessed with trying to replicate the woman's recipe. Tell me you finally cracked it."

She'd forgotten about that, and she couldn't remember the woman's name. Wow, she'd forgotten all about her.

"Yes, I finally got there," Em said. "Took me years, but I think I finally worked it out."

At least she'd figured out the professional part of her life. But she was questioning the direction the rest of her life had taken after hearing Ryatt's story about the letter.

WHEN RYATT LEFT fifteen minutes later, after receiving a call, Em let the dogs back into the house yard. As she disappeared into the house to go to the mudroom, all three dogs stood looking at the door, bitterly disappointed.

"Don't worry, I'm just getting your leads. We're still walking, don't worry!" she called.

When she returned, the dogs noticed their leads and dashed back to the gate where they sat patiently, ready to go.

"Good doggies," she said, unlatching the gate. Charlie was first, followed by Ruby, then Billy ambled through like he had all day. But as soon as he was in the open space, Billy sprinted off, zooming around the paddocks like he was a dog on a mission to show her all she'd missed while she was inside talking to Ryatt. Watching him, she thought how nice it was to see a rescued greyhound now living his best life. The smile on his face as he raced around the paddock brought a lightness to her heart. Charlie began chasing Billy, trying to keep up, but there was no chance the German shepherd would keep pace with the greyhound. Em looked down and saw Ruby plastered to her side. The dog looked up, looked across to the boys running around the paddock, then looked back at Em again, as if to say, "Boys! Am I right?"

Em reached down and patted the sweet girl, as if to agree. "Come on Rubes. Let's join them."

By the time Em and Ruby made it to the bottom gate, the one near the track, Charlie waited patiently with Billy. Seeing the track empty, save for a million footprints, she decided against leashing them. She'd keep them close to her, though, just in case. When she unlatched the gate, all three dogs went left automatically, towards the park.

Further along, black cockatoos munched on some dead branches, making one hell of a mess below. Charlie watched the birds from the base of the tree trunk, only to have rotten bark fall on his head.

"Guess the birds want you to walk away, Charlie. Come on, let's keep going." Charlie shook off the remnants and galloped over towards her. She patted him and called Billy back from the river. After the rain, the river was a powerful force, with the water jumping over itself in rapids before splashing into the depths below. The waterline was even reaching the base of the enormous gumtrees. Maybe she should have leashed the dogs, she thought. But it seemed such a peaceful time to be untethered, and all three seemed happy to stay nearby.

She tried to enjoy the walk, but Ryatt's comments weighed heavily. What direction would her life had taken had she received that letter? What if she'd responded to it, and she and Ryatt had continued their relationship, long distance? She was almost seventeen when Ryatt had left. No doubt her life would have been different. She'd loved Ryatt. He was her first boyfriend. The first boy she'd ever felt a connection with. He was the first person she had revealed her pain to. She'd shared how hard it was to move around so much while her mother fled the pain of her father's death. She'd shared her worries about her mother's mental health and the struggles her mother had carried, as well as what it was like for her to lose her father so young, and all the things she'd missed out on because of that loss.

And then she'd lost Ryatt.

In hindsight, she was certain that Callum had sensed her vulnerability and swooped in like a predator to take advantage of her. He'd played the part of her rescuer, nursing her through her pain, only to trap her in his web once she was dependent on him.

Shaking her head, she brushed off the feeling of entrapment and thought back to the conversation with *Detective* Ryatt, not ex-boyfriend Ryatt. He had warned her about Bryan, but even he wasn't convinced that Bryan was truly responsible for what had happened. Just before he'd left, Ryatt had said Bryan had been alibied by his father.

Em had laughed. "The man has Alzheimer's!"

Bryan clearly hadn't mentioned this; and Ryatt clearly shared her uneasy feeling about him.

When she reached the park, the place was empty. She let the dogs run around for a little while, calling them back when they raced down the path towards the river. There was no way she wanted to be rescuing a drowning dog today! And God knew that was the last thing she needed to tell the homeowner. Dead chickens, then a dead dog. Nope. Not on her watch. The chickens were bad enough.

Walking back towards the house, the dogs now leashed, Em looked at the houses set back from the road. Some were quite elaborate and clearly lived in. Others looked vacant. She admired the variety of letterboxes at the front of people's driveways, large enough for the odd grocery drop-off by a thoughtful neighbour or a parcel delivery. They weren't boring old letterboxes here. Some were made of old milk churns; another was made of wood painted to look like a cow. Her favourite was the one that had a bright, detailed painting of three chickens on the side; when she approached the driveway, she saw it housed eggs for sale as well as being a repository for mail.

The letterbox for her housesit was an old black plastic drum, cut out to hold mail, but devoid of anything but the number of the house. Em felt disappointed to find John's letterbox boring in comparison with the beauty of the house.

As she rounded the corner to head towards the housesit, she saw Anna standing at the end of the driveway chatting with Margo and her wife Shirley. The diamond in the rough, as Margo had called her. Em hadn't spoken to Shirley yet, and given Shirley's stance and gestures as she stood talking on the driveway, she wasn't sure she would if it were just the two of them. Oh, Shirley had waved to her when she was out walking the dogs, but now the expression on her face made Em want to keep a wide berth.

Em wondered whether it was because she'd called the police. Shirley's face screamed resentment, while Anna's and Margo's faces reflected concern. Shirley said something under her breath, and Em thought she could make out "There she is".

Margo scowled at Shirley, then smiled as Em came closer. "Hello, Em darling, how are you?"

Margo was the epitome of style in this country setting. Today, she was dressed in black trousers with matching black square-toed boots, a black cashmere top, a chunky silver necklace and a long maroon coat that complemented her black outfit perfectly. Beside her sat Gracie, and when Ruby approached, Gracie turned her cheek and looked over at Sachin, who was getting loving pats from Anna. Charlie and Billy were too busy sniffing the ground around them to notice anyone.

"Are you okay?" Anna asked. She was in her usual colourful leggings, combat coat and boots, with her blonde dreadlocks pulled back with a red scarf.

Gracie sashayed her way over towards Em, looking for a pat. Em bent down and gave her a pat until Ruby pushed her way in, reclaiming her human.

"You don't need to leash those dogs. Not here. There's no big bad boogie man that's out to get you here," Shirley said, grumpily.

Her frizzy grey hair was held back on the sides with long bobby pins, and she wore a large cream-coloured Irish fisherman's jumper that looked to be three sizes too big and was so ratty it had to be at least thirty years old. She'd even paired with it with stirrup pants, clearly of the same era. Topping off her look were a pair of faded grey Skechers which had seen better days.

"Shirley," Margo said, harshly, but Shirley ignored the reprimand. "Now you've met my very delightful, full-of-sunshine wife, Shirley. Darling, this is Em."

"I know who she is," Shirley said.

"Nice to meet you," Em said, reluctantly, although she wasn't sure "nice" was indeed the right word to describe meeting this curmudgeon.

"So, what happened yesterday? Are you okay?" Anna asked. "Margo said some detective visited them."

Em hesitated. Shirley already had her mind made up. But Ryatt hadn't said anything about not saying what she'd found. All three women looked at her expectantly. Should she tell them?

"Just tell us what happened. We know something did," said Shirley, impatiently.

"Shirley. Maybe she doesn't want to. Or maybe she's been told not to," Margo said, giving Em an empathetic smile.

"No, it's not that," Em said, and looked to Anna.

If it was just Anna who'd asked, she would tell her what happened. But she didn't know Margo and Shirley, and who knew: maybe it was one of them? Shirley was definitely giving off the vibe.

Before Em could say anything, the creepy guy from across the road sauntered towards them, his hands deep in his tracksuit-pant pockets, posturing like he was God's gift. Was this Bryan?

"If it's not Miss High-and-Almighty. The celebrity's wife. The one who's swept into Neeminah River and accused us of something none of us done," he scoffed, his brown eyes holding Em's green ones, zoning in on her and not letting go.

When he reached their huddle, he stood just outside the circle of women, spreading his feet just slightly wider than shoulder width, and crossing his arms across his chest. He looked menacing, and with his stained grey tracksuit pants and rugby hoodie, he would qualify easily as a thug. Gracie gave a low snarl from behind Margo's leg. That got Charlie's attention, and he pulled on his lead towards Bryan. Em pulled him back and patted him, appreciating his loyalty.

"Oh, shut your mug, you stupid bitch," Bryan said, looking down at Gracie now cowering on the ground behind her owner.

"Leave Gracie alone, Bryan. You know she's a traumatised rescue," Margo said, turning around to calm her dog.

"And she hates men. Or those who *think* they're men. So why don't you do us all a favour and take a short walk off a long jetty," Shirley added. "We were having a pleasant conversation until you came along with your belligerent bullshit."

While Em wouldn't say it was a pleasant conversation, she appreciated Shirley's defence. Charlie sat in front of Em, providing a barrier between her and Bryan.

"Well, it wasn't too *pleasant* having a fuckin' copper knock on my door yesterday. Did they come around to your place, or just mine? Because I can see that," he said. "Coppers always give preference to the women."

"Go home, Bryan. You're embarrassing yourself," Margo said. Anna looked like she wanted to hit the guy, but Em's feet were rooted to the ground, and she was mute. Bryan's eyes were cold as they glared at her.

"I'll go. But know this, *Mathilda Walsh*, I'm *not* your fuckin' problem. So keep your fuckin' Hollywood drama away from me. Okay?" he spat, venom in his voice and his finger pointing straight at her. And with that, Bryan stepped towards her, flipped her his middle finger centimetres from her nose, then turned and walked back to his house. Em was trembling uncontrollably as he stalked away, and when Anna reached out to her, Em jumped.

"Hey Em, are you okay?" Anna asked, her eyebrows drawing together, her face tilting towards her.

While Em heard her words, she couldn't speak. He'd sounded just like Callum. The words. The inflection. The hatred. Maybe he was the one behind the chickens, despite what Ryatt thought?

"Come on, let's get you back to the house," Margo said, and Em felt a soft touch at her elbow, steering her up the driveway.

"Give me the dogs," Shirley demanded. "I'll deal with them. You two take care of her."

11

Sitting at the kitchen table with a hot cup of tea in front of her, Em watched as Margo flitted around the kitchen searching for something. Em lifted the cup to her lips, but her hands shook so much that she placed the cup back on the table. Bryan's demeanour reminded her of a nastier time in her marriage. A time when Callum was high and full of hatred towards anyone who got in his way. His wife included.

"Do you have any sugar, love?" Margo asked. "I've looked, but I can't seem to find it."

Em nodded. "In the pantry on the right. A container with a green lid." Her words, the first she'd spoken since they'd come inside, were wobbly and faint.

Anna got up from building a fire to help Margo find the sugar, poking her head into the pantry behind Margo and pointing to the container.

"I swear I looked there," Margo said, smiling at Anna. "Thank you, sweetness."

Anna returned to the fire.

"Shirley has more sugar in her tea than actual tea," said Margo. "And Em, I know this is against the rules for us to be here, but I think we can make an exception. I honestly don't think John would mind us being here. Besides, you were clearly shaken by that little bloody upstart. If we have any good-for-nothing bogans in Neeminah River, then Bryan Owens is it!" Margo shook her head, exasperated, as she refilled the kettle.

"Dogs are dealt with," Shirley said, coming in from the mudroom and looking around. "Took off the harnesses and gave them all some dog treats. Sachin too. Hope that's okay?"

Anna nodded and said thanks, but Shirley looked at Anna's fire-building efforts and tutted.

"Let me show you how to build a fire properly," she said, nudging Anna out of the way.

Em watched Shirley lay a firestarter in the centre of two sticks of kindling, then stack two more sticks in the opposite direction. She continued with three more layers of kindling in a hash pattern, then finished with two large logs on top. When she stepped back, Em saw the wood heater was full.

Anna said, "That'll never light," her hands on her hips, and received a glare in return from Shirley.

Margo stood in the kitchen, cradling her own tea, smiling. "I thought that too, Anna, but just you watch. It's crazy how it works," she said.

"Got any matches?" Shirley asked, after riffling through the wicker basket next to the fire.

"Yes, they should be in there with the firestarters," Em said, shakily.

Shirley shook her head.

"Really? They were there last night. Maybe they're on the mantle?"

Anna looked up and searched the mantle, then shook her head too.

"Weird. Okay," Em said, completely confused. "I'll get some from the mudroom. I think there's a few boxes in there."

"You stay put. I'll find them," Shirley said, then groaned as she got vertical. "Bloody knees."

She went back to the mudroom and returned victorious. After checking the flue was open, she lit the firestarter in the centre of her stacked wood creation and closed the door. "Watch and learn, girls. Watch and learn." She stood back as the fire flared.

"Here's some tea for you, darling," Margo said, handing Shirley a steaming cup and pushing the container of sugar towards her. "And there's the rest to make it drinkable for you." Margo smiled, then leaned over to kiss Shirley's cheek, making the older woman blush.

"There are some blueberry muffins in that large container beside the stove. I made them this morning," Em said.

She got up from the table and walked to the kitchen, all three pairs of eyes following her, full of concern.

"I'm fine. Really. He just rattled me," she said, finding four small plates and a larger one for the muffins in the cupboard.

Searching the pantry for some paper serviettes, she was surprised to find cloth ones. When Em brought everything to the table, Margo picked up one of the floral blue serviettes and chuckled.

"Ha! I bet these have never been used," she said. "I made these for John last year when he finally finished renovating the house. There are some placemats to match these too, although I have to admit, it was more of a hint than a genuine gift. I didn't want this gorgeous table ruined." Margo ran her hands along the rustic table, which had been refinished and sealed beautifully.

"Ooh, but don't these look scrumptious," said Shirley, taking a muffin and placing it on the plate in front of her.

Em picked up the large plate and offered it to Margo and Anna, taking the last muffin for herself. "Have you lived in Neeminah River for long?" she asked Margo, who nodded to Shirley to answer the question as she took a long sip of her tea.

Behind them, the fire crackled. Shirley turned to check on it and smiled smugly when she turned back around.

"I moved here forty years ago," she began. "My house is the original house out here. Mine and John's are the oldest in the area, although his house didn't look like this for quite a few years. John bought it about five years ago and renovated it slowly over that time. He's done a remarkable job. I thought the house needed to be demolished, but he's brought it back to life."

Shirley laced her tea with two full teaspoons of sugar and stirred it aggressively in the delicate teacup before going back for two more.

"He's done a beautiful job," Em said, looking around. "The kitchen is a dream. Between the large commercial stove, the marble countertop and the gorgeous farmhouse sink, it's easy to bake in!"

"He did a lot of research on it, which is funny since he's not a cook, nor is he a baker," Shirley said, her mouth now full of muffin.

Bits of muffin flew this way and that as she spoke. Em had to look away, suddenly wishing she had made the bite size versions of muffins her bakery was famous for. Em looked at Anna who had her head down, focused on her own muffin.

"He asked a lot of questions," Margo interjected. "About the kitchen renovations. What people liked. That kind of thing."

"Everything in the kitchen looks to be brand new. Lukas mentioned nothing looked used when he first arrived. I felt guilty using the Mixmaster yesterday," Em said, realising Shirley had already almost devoured her muffin in only a couple of bites.

"Is he thinking of selling?" Anna asked.

Margo shrugged, but Shirley held up a finger, seemingly knowing the answer. It took her a moment to answer, given how much was in her mouth. Once she'd swallowed, she took a long slurp of her tea, but Margo gave up and answered instead.

"All I know is he told me he was renovating the house with someone in mind, but we've never seen him with anyone. Maybe that's who he's with on his trip around Australia," Margo said, with a glint in her eye. "He's very private. Lovely man, though, and very helpful when we've needed an extra hand. Quiet otherwise."

Em had only communicated with John through the housesitting service, then briefly via email. She'd never spoken with him or met him, and she wondered now what he looked like. She imagined a tall skinny man in his mid-sixties.

"Everyone tends to keep to themselves around here," Shirley said, throwing a barb in Em's direction.

Em realised that she still hadn't told her neighbours what had happened the previous afternoon with the chicken head.

"There are the Smiths," Margo said. "Deb and Bill. Their house is the one Anna is looking after. They're a lovely couple. Retired. They spend part of their winters in Queensland, where it's warmer. I'm surprised they are coming back to Tasmania so early this year."

"New grandbaby coming, I think. Anyway, there's the new couple who just bought next to them. Shit. What's her name? Audrey?" Shirley asked.

"Aubrey, darling," Margo said to Shirley, then turned to Em. "She's gorgeous. A creative, like you. Her partner, Tom, is building her a studio at the moment, with the help of a family friend. The things you do for love. Oh, that reminds me. Was your electricity off for very long, Anna?"

"No, only a few hours," Anna answered, then turned to Em. "The sparky came out to put electricity in for Aubrey's new studio, so they had to turn the electricity off for the day last week. Good thing I had the wood fire going!"

"Indeed. But you could have come by our place if you'd got stuck. You know that," Margo said.

Em wondered if Anna would have taken her up on it. She didn't know Anna well enough to say, but the way Anna was wriggling in her seat had Em thinking no.

"Well, as you saw, Bryan is not a happy chap," Margo said.

"I reckon there's more to the story there, with that one," Shirley said.

Em had wondered about that, too.

"Bryan's dad, Gerald, has lived here for about twenty years, I'd say," Shirley went on. "He hasn't been well. He was diagnosed with the Alzheimer's a while back. Then he had a fall, which he didn't recover well from, so now that little son of a bitch lives with him. Bryan's got issues of his own. Seemed pretty convenient that his dad had the fall, then he came home to live full-time, if you know what I mean. A little too convenient."

"Well, we don't know the full story, and it's best not to speculate. Then there's Pete and his son Tyler, across the road," Margo said, smiling warmly. Clearly, she had a soft spot for them.

"Right," said Shirley. "They moved in about a year ago, maybe longer. Moved down from Melbourne, originally with Tyler's mum. It was for, what do you call it, Margo? A tree change?"

"Yes," Margo said. "They wanted out of Melbourne and into a slower pace of life. Pete works as a chef at the Mad Dog Blue restaurant in Franklin, and juggles trying to be a single dad. Pete's a good parent. He's trying to do what's best for Tyler."

"Hmph," muttered Shirley, but the others ignored her response.

"What happened with Tyler's mum?" Anna asked. "I wanted to ask Tyler, but I didn't want to pry."

"Ginny didn't like Neeminah River, so she lives up in Hobart," replied Shirley. "She's some kind of house decorator in Hobart, but I wouldn't be surprised if she went back to Melbourne. She seems pretty self-absorbed to me. All about her career. When she is around, she's not very engaged, if you know what I mean. Comes down every couple of months to see Tyler. He goes up there once a month, I think. She's one of those city people who's always thinking about work – or talking about it constantly at least. Total name-dropper." She rolled her eyes. "She's a bit too much of a hoity-toity for Neeminah River, I reckon."

"Tyler's a lovely kid, though," Anna said to Em, as Shirley picked at the crumbs on her plate.

Shirley looked up sharply. "Oh, that's phooey! That boy is so full of rage, he looks like one of those boys who commit those mass shootings in America, with his long coat and combat boots. I once caught him playing one of those violent video games with Suzanna's grandson." She sucked the muffin crumbs off her fingers.

"Shirley, you know that's not a fair assessment. He mows our yard, for goodness sake," Margo said, taking a very small bite of her muffin.

"Well, I avoid him. Pete seems nice enough, but that kid of his, I just don't know."

Shirley certainly had her opinions, but Em noticed Anna shaking her head ever so slightly.

Shirley looked pointedly into her empty teacup then up at Em.

"Would anyone like more tea?" Em asked.

"That would be lovely," replied Shirley. "And do you have more of those muffins? They were delicious. Although Suzanna's buttermilk scones would give them a run for their money. Suzanna is a member of my knitting group, and an award-winning baker in the Huon Valley." Em ignored the barb from Shirley, suspecting Shirley had probably done her research, and therefore knew exactly what Em did for a living.

"Shirley," Margo warned, confirming Em's suspicions.

Em looked over and saw Margo shoot a look of exasperation towards her wife. Poor Margo. She really was trying to rein Shirley in. Em smiled and rose to make the tea, taking the empty muffin plate with her.

As she waited for the kettle to boil, Em looked over at Anna. The muffin on her plate was mostly uneaten; she'd probably been put off by the eating display Shirley had given them. While Em hadn't asked for the neighbourhood gossip, somehow these women had decided Em needed to know who was who and what she was dealing with. It may have been just gossip, but seeing them sitting around the table, Em felt a sense of community.

"It sounds as if Neeminah River is pretty tight," Em said, setting the plate with a few more muffins back on the table.

"Oh, yes, I suppose you could say that, but we do keep an eye out for the odd stray," Shirley said, popping more sugar into her teacup. "Not that I would call you a stray. We just don't tend to get a lot of traffic through here, as you may have noticed. Just the odd campervan."

"Have you noticed the campervan down at the park these last few days? Looks to be the same one," Anna said, directing her question to Margo and Shirley.

"I doubt it's the same one," Margo said, brushing off Anna's comment. "There's a campervan down there every week or so. Sometimes they stay for two days and do day trips around the area."

"It is very quiet, that's for sure. Peaceful. A lot different from my life in California," Em said, just as Shirley broke her second muffin into four pieces.

Em glanced at Anna, then cautiously in Shirley's direction. Surely she wasn't going to eat the oversized muffin in four bites. But yep. Yep, she was. Em looked away but saw Margo shaking her head in her peripheral vision.

It took another hour before Margo and Shirley left, with more muffins in hand, and as Em watched them turn the corner towards their house, Anna burst into laughter beside her.

"Geezus. That woman has drained me," Em said.

"Yep, that's Shirley," said Anna.

"But I've got to hand it to her. That wood fire is raging, with no further intervention, so I tip my cap to her for that."

"Right?" Anna said. "I'm going to have to try that trick with the fire myself tonight. Anyway, I'm going to go, too. But I wanted to make sure you're okay first. You seemed reluctant to get the police involved when you found the chickens, so I figured something else more serious had happened for you to ring them. I didn't tell Margo or Shirley that I thought that, by the way."

"One of the chicken heads turned up," Em said, relenting. "On the front doormat last night when I went out to get some firewood. It was accompanied with a note that said 'Welcome to the neighbourhood'."

Em watched Anna's face closely and was relieved when Anna's eyebrows shot up and her jaw dropped. Em knew then for sure that Anna was not the culprit.

"Holy shit! Well, clearly Bryan isn't liked around here, so maybe he is the one who left it? But your reaction to him earlier had me worried …"

"Yeah, I'm okay. He just reminded me of someone," Em said cautiously.

As much as she was bonding with Anna and learning so much more about the neighbours than she'd ever thought she would, she wasn't quite ready to tell any of them the complete truth about her estranged husband.

12

E m felt more unnerved after what Margo and Shirley had said the day before about the neighbours. Especially after finding the 'welcome' note on the mat. Clearly, someone wanted her gone from the neighbourhood. It may have been Bryan. Hell, it may have been Shirley. She certainly had her opinions about everyone. But whoever it was, Em knew why they wanted her out: she wasn't like them.

It was the story of her life. She'd always been the outsider. She thought of all the times people gave her sideways glances, or gossiped behind her back, especially in LA. She was the overweight wife of the movie star. She was a business owner, not a housewife. She was a redhead, not a blonde; and when she was a blonde, she was not blonde enough. Even with her childhood, she was always the new kid, not the one they'd grown up with. It was always the same. She was not like them. They never fully accepted her because she was too different.

And Em knew it wouldn't be any different here either. Someone was making it very clear she was unwelcome. But she'd dealt with this kind of thing before.

"Suck it up, Buttercup," she imagined Asher telling her, as tears formed. Asher had been her rock for the last two years, always her voice of reason. The fact that he seemed to be stepping back from their friendship was harder than anything else she was dealing with, if she was honest. Even the threatening note. She missed him, but she held back from reaching out to him. He'd said what he wanted to say.

Taking a deep breath, Em straightened and wiped away her tears. She looked through the window, out past the verandah, and took in the sheer beauty of the landscape before her. Fog had enveloped the rolling hills earlier that morning as if a kindly old woman had covered them with a comforting blanket, but the morning sun had burned it away. It was past noon now, and dark clouds were beginning to crawl across the sky towards her, the wind picking up ever so slightly. Even the gum trees shivered in the chilly breeze. The weather here changed more quickly than the hottest starlet in LA.

Em's phone dinged behind her on the kitchen counter. She reached for it, hoping it was her mum. She'd sent her a text two days before but hadn't heard from her since she'd started heading south. It wasn't unusual. She'd probably lost her phone. It wouldn't be the first time. But when she opened her phone, she saw it was an email from the homeowner, John.

Hello Em,
I hope you are settling in, and everything is to your liking. I wanted to let you know that my neighbour Shirley will most likely be popping over to say hello. She's a bit opinionated, but a good person. Oh, and she tends to have a sweet tooth. Just a word of warning. I hope you're enjoying the property. I will be out of touch for a while as I drive north. If there's anything you need, please let me know ASAP.
Sincerely,
John

Em gave a short laugh. She'd certainly met Shirley and her sweet tooth and did not want to repeat that experience anytime soon. She started a reply to John's email, thanking him for the opportunity and letting him know she was enjoying it. She paused, thinking. Ryatt had recommended she inform the homeowner about the chickens. She kept typing, explaining about the dead chickens, apologising and offering to replace them before she left. She left out the detail about it being caused by a human, and she held back from telling him about the chicken head. She figured the threat itself wasn't relevant to John.

His response was swift.

Not a worry. It happens. Just throw them in the pit.
Take care,
John

Well, he was a lot more understanding than she would have been! She was relieved. Maybe, as Anna had said, this happened all the time on farms. Except the way this one had happened was not usual. But with Ryatt looking into it, she was pretty sure it was best to keep the part about the threat from John.

She put her phone aside, then picked it up again to check if there was anything from her mum. Nothing. But then she saw a message from Asher telling her to call him as soon as she got the message. He had sent it an hour before. Checking the time difference, she saw it was close to eight in the evening in LA. She hoped she would catch him before bed, given his baker's hours. She dialled his number.

"What's cookin', good lookin'?" Asher answered merrily, his use of one of his usual quips throwing her off.

"Hey Asher," she said, cautiously.

"How's it going there on the island state?" Asher asked.

He seemed very perky for … she checked her watch again. Yes. It was just after eight in the evening. He would have been up since three-thirty that morning. He was usually asleep by nine, and that was a late night for him.

"You're rather chipper for this time of night. Usually you're in chill mode," Em said. She heard soft music, James Taylor, in the background. Which was most definitely not his usual taste in music. "Um … do you have company? I can call you later."

"Well, I do. But I really needed to talk with you," he said and slightly muffled the phone as he gave some direction about where his potato peeler was in the kitchen. "Sorry. I, ah, have news. And I wanted you to know before it became public knowledge."

"Public knowledge?" This wasn't good. She lowered herself into the nearby kitchen chair.

"Yeah. I'm, um, dating someone. Well, I have been for a while now. But with everything going on at the bakery, with your divorce and everything, I wanted to be completely transparent with you. Because it may come out."

"Okay," Em said. "Who is it?"

She actually couldn't remember the last person Asher dated. He'd only been seriously involved with someone once in his life. Usually, he was pretty casual about it, given his schedule. Most people weren't understanding about baker's hours.

"It's …" He paused, and she could hear him take a long drink of something. Well, shit. Her leg began shaking with anxiety. "Okay, it's someone you will not be happy about. But I want to tell you that there's more to the story, and she's on your side. Completely. One hundred percent."

"Just tell me, Asher," Em said, her tone coming across as way more abrasive than she meant it to be.

"It's Kennedy Wright," Asher said, and Em's leg stopped shaking immediately.

She got up from her chair, indignant. "Kennedy fucking Wright? You're sleeping with the enemy? The blood-sucking celebrity reporter from C News?" she screeched, and she heard Asher whisper, "Not happy".

"Em, it's not what you think. We've been seeing each other quietly for about six months now. She's a good person and she has worked with guys like Callum. She's heard things about him too. Look, I'm going to put you on speaker—"

"Don't you fucking dare!"

"Hello Em. I hope it's alright that I call you Em. Asher calls you that all the time. But I can call you Mathilda, if you'd prefer," said the woman in a sweet Californian accent that Em found annoying.

Em stayed silent.

"Em, don't be mad," Asher said. "Kennedy caught wind of something that we thought you may need to know."

"Look, I know you'd want to keep your distance from me," said

Kennedy, "and I get that – I do – but as Asher said, I am on your side. Your ex is an asshole. And I can help you."

Em snorted. She doubted that. She'd seen Kennedy's work before. How she'd decimated people, their careers, their reputations.

Kennedy continued, "I've kept my boss at bay on this one, because I knew there was another side. He's not happy. Hell, they may fire me for turning the story down so many times on this, but I want to help you. Your ex is a sexual predator."

Em inhaled quickly. No one referred to Callum as either an asshole or a sexual predator. He was both, but usually behind closed doors. That's what he paid his agent and public relations team to keep from being public knowledge. And away from people like Kennedy fucking Wright.

"Em, you can trust her, okay? I do. And you trust me. Can that be enough for now?" Asher asked.

"Let me think about it," Em said, and promptly hung up.

She trusted Asher – or had. But he'd thrown sand in her face by telling her he was considering walking away from the partnership. How much could she trust him now? And Kennedy Wright? She was a whole other story.

Her phone pinged, making her jump. Asher had sent a message.

Call me later. But Kennedy wanted to let you know Callum is in Melbourne, quietly shooting a movie. It's not public knowledge. Yet.

At least now she knew Callum was in the country. So maybe he was behind the chicken massacre after all?

Hearing a scratching at the back door, Em looked up to find Billy peering in. She looked out to the gate and saw Ruby and Charlie waiting expectantly, ready for a walk. She looked down at her Apple Watch, then back at the clouds. She had five minutes left until her cheesecake squares would come out of the oven, then she'd take the dogs for an early walk and hopefully beat the storm. Maybe she could walk off the storm within. This news was just the cherry on top of everything else.

Twenty minutes later, they were trailing the river path. It was bitterly cold, colder than she expected when they'd set out, and snow began falling around them. The walk had been good for her to clear her head a little. She was angry about Kennedy and Asher dating. If they'd kept it quiet for six months, it meant they'd been dating while she was still there, and she'd had no indication that it was going on. She remembered that Asher had taken up yoga a few months ago, which had been odd. He was more of a runner. She'd teased him about it, given his build was more like that of an all-star quarterback than of a limber yoga instructor. But he insisted he was enjoying it, that it was keeping him centred, which only made her laugh more. Obviously, that had been Kennedy's influence. She wasn't surprised she had missed any other signs. She'd been so focused on getting out of LA and away from Callum that there could have been a major earthquake, and she would have missed it.

But the timing was odd. Was Kennedy dating Asher just to get closer to her? Closer to the story, or to her and Callum? It was possible. Celebrity journalists could be cunning in their approach. But Kennedy's words "sexual predator" had become an ear worm in Em's head.

As she turned down the road leading to the house, Ruby looked up at Em and a snowflake hit her in the left eye. Shaking her head, she beat her floppy ears against the sides of her head as she tried to remove the foreign substance. The quick movement made her stumble slightly. Em stopped so Ruby would, and while she waited for the dog to recover, she held out her bare hand and felt the flakes touch her fingertips then melt away quickly. Ahead, white smoke rose into the sky from chimneys along the road. The scene reminded her of a Christmas tale, despite it being June. It was magical, especially in the afternoon light.

Just as they approached the driveway, Em saw a dark figure in a long overcoat duck behind the shed.

"What the fuck?" she whispered.

Who would be here, lurking? Was it Bryan, as Ryatt had warned? Anna had mentioned she'd seen Bryan more than usual. Maybe it was Callum screwing with her. Would he have worked out where she was? Somehow, she doubted it. He'd most likely be up to his usual antics, which meant nightclubs, drugs and prostitutes back in LA. Or Melbourne, if Kennedy was to be believed. So who was skulking near the shed?

"Hello? Who's there?"

There was no reply.

Em walked cautiously towards the house, feeling a chill in her spine. The dogs headed straight for the mudroom door, showing no fear of whoever lurked outside, while Em peered out into the paddocks. Where had the person even gone? The surroundings fell eerily silent as soon as she stopped.

She eased her way over to the shed and opened the door, switching on the light, hoping to give the surrounding area more visibility. Everything was silent. Empty. Looking into the shed, she started to scour it for any stolen items, but then she realised she didn't know what belonged there to begin with.

Charlie stared bewilderedly at Em's anxious motions, whereas Ruby and Billy began sniffing around the ground. Ruby came to her and nudged her calf gently, as if telling her that everything was alright. Em felt oddly calmed by the gesture. She grabbed some Weet-Bix and grain for the goats from the shed and nervously threw them over the barbed wire fence. The cluster of goats gathered around. Em stopped again. She could see nothing and hear nothing but goats bullying their way in for grain. She hurried to make sure all the chickens were secure. Seeing them roosting, away from the chilly night air, Em said good-night and locked them into the coop.

As she made her way back to the house, she could sense, now more than ever, something strange looming in the air. Approaching the verandah, Em saw something lying on the front doormat. It was a brown paper bag, sitting just where the chicken head had been before. Before she could investigate what was inside, Charlie barked from the bushes nearby. Em jumped, but his leg was still raised in mid-stream as if nothing was wrong. He was just letting the world know he was there. Ruby came to her side immediately, while Billy continued sniffing his way around the native garden at the bottom of the verandah.

Em crouched down, dread filling her chest. Coldness seeped into her bones. She wasn't sure what was in the bag, but she knew something was wrong. Her gaze lingered on the bag for a moment before she plucked up her courage and slowly unfolded it. Charlie barked again, startling her. As she peered in, the contents filled her with both surprise and confusion. Billy joined them on the verandah, shivering in this greyhound skin.

"Onions?" she said, incredulously. Ruby nuzzled in to look into the bag. "Why would someone leave a bag of onions here?"

She surveyed the surroundings one last time, but nothing seemed to move or answer her question. Still seeing nothing, Em picked up the bag and hurried inside as Charlie barked wildly at something in the shadows.

"*Now* you're going off, Charlie? Really?"

Shaking her head, she let the dogs in and watched as they zoomed to the warmth of the fire. In the kitchen, Em peered into the bag again under the down light. There was something white towards the bottom of the bag. She reached in and pulled out a piece of paper.

Time to peel away the layers, Mathilda.

Hands shaking, she read the typed line again. The letters blurred before her eyes, but she forced her gaze to stay focused on the paper. With her heart pounding furiously in her chest, Em read the words repeatedly until a wave of dread swept through her body. Even though a part of her was desperate to know what it meant, another part of her was too afraid to find out.

13

E m baked to find control. It had been her coping mechanism for years. It was just after ten o'clock at night and she'd already made brownies and another batch of muffins.

She wasn't sure why she'd made more muffins, other than that Shirley had been on her mind. She'd been thinking through who would leave her the 'welcome' note and the note buried in the bag with the onions. What did it even mean?

She'd called Ryatt almost immediately, as if on instinct. He'd advised her to set the bag aside and not touch it again, telling her he'd be out as soon as he could. He was stuck in Hobart, as Vinces Saddle, the pass between Hobart and Neeminah River, was closed due to snow and ice. But he promised to be down to see her as soon as it reopened. Hopefully that would be in the morning.

That left her on her own for the evening, mulling over who could be so cruel.

Cruel. At first she'd been convinced it was Callum behind it. But the longer she thought about it, she just couldn't see him going to such effort. His level of cruelty from afar had been harassing texts. Or calling her to berate her. This seemed different. Then again, Kennedy's news about Callum's whereabouts was whirling in her mind as well. Melbourne was only an hour's flight away.

Em's bare feet were numb against the kitchen floor, and her legs were aching. She had been baking non-stop for hours. She needed her slippers. She walked back to the bedroom and turned on the light. Her slippers weren't where she'd left them beside the bed. She poked her head into the bathroom, finding the floor empty but for a thick grey bathmat. That was odd. They weren't in the living room, either. Maybe one of the dogs had taken them.

That made her think of the Tasmanian devils Anna had mentioned and how, when she'd researched it further, she'd discovered that devils used boots as chew toys. Maybe the dogs had done the same with her slippers? But none of the three seemed the type to do that, and she'd not seen a single chew toy around.

Resigning herself to finding her slippers later, she pulled out the thick, striped socks she'd bought at the Salamanca Markets in Hobart and wiggled them on to her feet. They'd do for now.

A few minutes later, with a steaming coffee beside her, she worked the sourdough. Asher had spoiled her with his sourdough creations, so store-bought bread just wasn't the same. As she kneaded the dough she thought over, once again, what she knew about the neighbours. And what she knew wasn't much. Mostly just the gossip from Anna, Margo and Shirley.

She started with Shirley. While Em didn't think the older woman was up to the task of beheading chickens, she did seem to have an opinion about everyone. She clearly didn't like Bryan, but she did seem to have a soft spot for John. And when Em had her panic attack, Shirley was quick to come to Em's side and help her, along with Margo and Anna. Shirley was a busybody, but Em couldn't see her as the culprit.

Sensing her anxiety, Ruby got up from her dog bed and trotted over to the kitchen. She nudged Em's leg with her head.

"Sorry sweetness, but my hands are full of dough at the moment. Go lie down with Charlie and Billy. I'm okay," Em said softly.

The other two dogs were sleeping soundly on their beds in front of the fire. Billy was snoring. Suddenly, Charlie's head popped up. He didn't bark or growl, but simply looked towards the door. Em felt her heart race. Whoever had meant to scare her had accomplished their goal.

She walked to the front window and saw a car driving slowly past. A dark four-wheel drive by the looks of it, but it was hard to see without moonlight. It pulled into the driveway across the road. Margo and Shirley had mentioned the neighbour's name. The single dad, Pete. And his son, Tyler. He was someone else Shirley didn't like. Pete was a chef at a local restaurant, the Mad Dog Blue, further south. Em remembered the restaurant name, only because it sounded cool.

She walked back to the kitchen, telling herself that it was just Pete, probably getting home after the restaurant had closed for the night.

Shirley had called Tyler trouble, and almost seemed scared of him. But hadn't Margo and Anna quashed that idea? They'd said he was a good kid, although when Em had seen him lope past the house that morning, his head down and headphones firmly in, he did look rather menacing in his long black coat and combat boots. When Ruby had barked at him, startling Em, he'd looked over at the house. Which meant his headphones weren't blasting Metallica or whatever band angsty teenage boys listened to nowadays. Em had raised her hand to say hello, and he seemed to hesitate, but then surprised her by raising his hand in return, coupled with a partial smile. Maybe Anna was right about him. The smile didn't look menacing. It was more like disbelief. Surprise that someone would say hello.

Her mind returned to Bryan. His father had Alzheimer's, and everyone agreed Bryan was not a happy guy. Yesterday proved that. Maybe he was bored enough, or pissed off enough, that he thought it would be fun to screw with her. Especially if he was stuck here after a bad divorce, or whatever it was that brought him here. Em agreed with Shirley. There had to be more to it. He didn't seem to be the type to move home to look after his dad.

Ryatt had warned her about Bryan. So had Anna, but she'd also said he was lazy. Would he go out in the cold to do such a vicious thing? Em had heard about rapists doing more in far worse conditions, so yes, it was possible. Especially since he knew exactly who Em was. Which meant it was likely he'd been spying out the windows when she took the dogs for a walk, a thought that creeped her out too. The more she thought about Bryan, the more convinced she was that he was most likely the one pranking her.

But was it just a simple prank? A cold, heartless one. Killing innocent animals just to spook her. Could it be possible that Callum had reached out to Bryan? To pay him to mess with her? It was possible, but how would Callum know where she was? She hadn't told him. She'd been very secretive about where she was. Only her mother and Asher knew. Except now the neighbours knew who she was, and it was very possible that one of them had leaked her whereabouts. Maybe even Bryan.

She hadn't looked at the media outlets or the celebrity pages since she'd arrived back in Australia, so she didn't know what information was out there. Instead, she'd buried her head in the sand, trying to ignore the media frenzy. Her lawyers had emailed the day before, updating her and asking her if she wanted to sue Callum for defamation over the embezzlement accusation. It was tempting, but she needed to talk to Asher about it and see what the fallout was at The Bakehouse first.

Maybe it wasn't a bad idea to find out what was being said online. It had been a few weeks since she'd looked. But she didn't want to get sucked into the negative vortex either. The whole thing was mentally damaging, and she was here to escape that.

Her call with Asher came to mind: Kennedy would know.

Having formed the dough into a log, she greased the bread pan and placed the dough in it to rise. The room was warm enough, now the fire had been going for hours, so she was confident she'd get a good rise going on the dough. Leaving the pan on the counter with a wet towel over it, she washed her hands then picked up her phone. Calling Asher at work would mean she could talk to him alone, given it was after five in the morning already. Sometimes baker's hours came in handy.

She sent him a text to let him know she was about to call him. If he had his hands in dough and music blasting, which were both likely scenarios, he wouldn't be answering his phone. When she hit the call button two minutes later, he picked up.

"Morning, cherub," Asher said, his voice gravelly, indicating she was the first person he'd spoken to all morning.

"Hey Asher," she said, plopping down on the couch and feeling deflated and tired from the emotional day.

"How's things?" he asked, casually.

"Not as quiet as I'd hoped," she said.

Ruby came over and collapsed on Em's feet, her fur warmer than Em's own socks.

"Why? What's going on?" She could hear ovens purring in the background and Asher's assistant moving trays around, the clanging ringing out in the large room.

"I can't remember what I've told you. Things have been a blur," she said, realising that the last time she'd told him anything about the housesit was in the email she'd sent him on her second night. It had been three days since then, but it seemed more like three weeks. "Apparently the chicken massacre behind the shed was just the prelude."

"What do you mean?" Asher asked.

"Well, the following day, I came back from walking the dogs to find a chicken head propped up on the front mat with a note welcoming me to the neighbourhood."

"Oh shit," he said.

Em continued, "Then today, I saw someone lurking behind the shed, and later in the afternoon, a bag of onions was left on the same front mat, with another note. This time saying it was time to peel back the layers."

"Onions? What the actual fuck?" Asher exclaimed. "What does that even mean?"

"No clue. I think it's a neighbour screwing with me. There's a weird guy living across the road. He knows who I am and seems pretty pissed off."

"Have you called the cops?" Asher asked, which, for him, was a stretch. He hated dealing with the police. He may be a successful business owner in Venice Beach, but he was still a black man living in Southern California. He'd been pulled over more times than she could count.

"I have. After the chicken head, I called them and, you won't believe this, but the detective who came out was my old boyfriend from high school. Before Callum," she added, still not believing it herself.

"I thought Callum was your first and only?" Asher asked, which made Em wonder what had given him that impression. But Callum was her first in many ways and, when you were thirty-four and had been married for fifteen years, it was a safe assumption to make.

"No. I dated Josh for a year, before he left town. Turns out he wrote me a letter, explaining why he was leaving. I just didn't get it. Either Kat forgot to give it to me, or she deliberately tossed it and didn't tell me." Em wished her mother would get back to her so she could ask her what happened.

"Would she do that?" Asher asked.

Em laughed. "Yes. If it meant I was serious about someone who would whisk me away from her, of course she would. She was a wreck back then."

"She's still a wreck," Asher said plainly, and it was true in many ways. "But what about Callum? Didn't he do just that? Whisk you away?"

"Yeah, but he also wooed my mother. Charmed her off her feet. Speaking of Callum, I wanted to ask you a question."

Em paused. She was risking a lot by taking this route, but she had always trusted Asher. And seeing as the discussion about the business seemed to be on hold, she would cling to whatever friendship she had left with him.

"What's the dealio, Emilio?" he quipped. "How can I be of service?"

Em smiled. His words were enough to settle her. "Kennedy. An interesting choice of bed partners, I have to admit—"

Asher cut her off. "It's more than that. But go on."

Em was surprised. More? Seriously? What did they even have in common? He was a baker. She was a celebrity journalist who preyed on the innocent. She took a deep breath.

He spoke again. "What's your question?" His tone had changed. He was ... cautious. Defensive. And not of her.

"Kennedy mentioned that Callum was in Melbourne," Em said. "I haven't really looked at the gossip pages or anything online since I left. Just the press release about the embezzlement."

"And isn't that a joy," he said, reminding her again that she needed to ask how much fallout there was.

But that wasn't what she needed to ask him right now. "Does anyone else know where I'm staying? The press release mentioned 'southern Tasmania', but not where. I'm curious, with all this other stuff going on, if there's been any leaks. I'm wondering if ..." She paused. "If Kennedy has heard anything about it. Whether she knows if anyone from here may have leaked where I am. I wouldn't be surprised if this creepy guy said something."

"So you're pissed off that I'm dating Kennedy, but it's convenient for you that I am? I'm confused," Asher said. When he said it like that, she felt awful. "We tried to tell you last night that there's stuff going on, Em, but you wouldn't listen."

Shit. Well, what was she supposed to say? He'd blindsided her with the news. She stayed silent.

"Look, I know she's not who you'd like for me to date, but it is what it is. Kennedy is a good person and I think you'll realise that, if you get to know her. She fell into the celebrity reporting gig by accident. And if you look at what she reports on, it's mostly domestic abuse and misogynist power plays. Look it up. You'll find I'm right about that."

Em remained silent but took in every word.

"I'll ask her later about what she's heard. She's had her ear to the ground. As I told you last night, she's on your side. She's heard a lot of stuff about Callum, word of mouth stuff, and she's also been on the receiving end of his bullshit, before he knew who she was," Asher said.

"What do you mean?" Em gasped.

"You'll need to ask her. It's her story to tell, not mine," Asher said. "She'll be around later this afternoon, so I'll have her ... wait. Time difference. I'll have her reach out to you via text, if you're okay with that?"

Did she want to give a celebrity reporter her phone number? Hell no. But if what Asher said was true, then she'd risk it. She could always get another phone number.

"Sure," she replied.

"Look. Just remember why you're there, okay? And you're working on your book, right?" Asher asked.

"Yes. I baked up a storm tonight after the bag of onions showed up," Em said, looking at the plethora of baked goods cooling on the wooden table. What was she going to do with it all?

"Okay, that's good. You've been talking about that book forever, so just stay focused on that. Don't let some guy get in your head. And I'm talking about the neighbour, not Callum. You're already in a better place being away from Callum."

"But why am I here? Why not in a hotel with room service and security? Why didn't I stay in the cottage in California? I could have just holed up and been in my own kitchen," she said, her voice rising to a whiny pitch.

"You know why. The media would be still hounding you. Besides, hotels don't have ovens. Not the hotels you've grown accustomed to staying in. Look, Callum is playing the clubs, right out in the open now. Or he was. At the moment, everyone is wondering where he is. No one knows he's in Australia. But that will change soon enough, I'm sure."

Em groaned. Of course – and the public probably loved it. He was probably playing up that he was newly single. Which he was, but Em wondered just how openly he'd play.

"You need to remember that you are a kick-ass businesswoman. You're instinctive and confident when Callum isn't around. You are an award-winning pastry chef. You need to tap into that confidence. Listen to your instincts like you do with the business. From what I'm hearing right now, you're being led by someone else's intention. And that's not who you are. Don't let the neighbours get in the way of finding some solace, yeah? People are still wondering where you are, I think, and that's good. Kennedy can confirm that, but the regulars here are asking about you. The ones who are used to seeing you here."

"You don't think Kennedy is with you because of me, do you?" Em asked, but Asher laughed.

"No. I promise you, she's not," he said.

"Sorry. It's just … I don't know. I feel anxious all the time. Like someone is watching me. And I hate that. I hate feeling paranoid."

"Then don't be. Just be aware of what's going on around you and focus on what's important. You. Your book. Let the rest go. I'm still here for you Em. I'm not going anywhere."

"But you said you wanted out?" Em said, finally bringing up what was weighing her down.

"No, I said I was considering it. I wonder if it's not time. Nothing is holding you in the States anymore, so why be here? Why still be linked to Callum when you could start fresh somewhere else?"

"Because I don't want to do that. The Bakehouse is our baby. It's what I've always dreamed of doing. And you're the best partner I could have."

"Well, I appreciate that," said Asher. "But you have to think about what's right for you now. Take the men in your life out of the equation, including me, and think about what you really want."

Em was quiet. That was a tall order.

Asher changed the subject. "Okay. So this cop-slash-ex-boyfriend. Is he on the up and up? Is he going to help? Or is he just starry-eyed about helping you out?"

Em took a deep breath. Asher was cynical about anyone getting close to Em, which is why she was confused about his dating Kennedy. She'd definitely be doing some research on Kennedy's pieces before she responded to her later.

"Callum used to bully Ryatt in high school, so I think I'm in good hands," Em responded.

"Seriously? So Callum was an asshole, even then? Why hasn't that come out in the media?"

"Probably because he charmed everyone, just like he does now. And let's remember, he is Australia's Favourite Son," she said, syrup lacing the sarcasm. "Back then, he targeted the weak."

"Hasn't changed, then. Not that you're weak. But you do have a weakness for him. If I were in your shoes, I'd been screaming from the rooftops about what a fucking shit he's been to you. Kennedy thinks so too. She's ready whenever you are to pull that lever."

But Em knew she'd never pull that lever. Callum's secrets would destroy not only Callum's career, but possibly hers too.

14

The following morning, Em picked up her phone from the side table and brought it under the covers. The room was glacial. Colder than it had been over the previous few days. Clicking her phone on, she gasped when she saw it was almost nine o'clock. Geezus, how did that happen?

She quickly scanned her messages and saw there was still nothing from her mother. But there was a text from Kennedy.

Morning Em.
Nothing about where you are. Just what Callum's release said:
Southern Tasmania. I'd love to share with you what I know. I'm here
when you're ready, but as a friend. Not as the media.
Kennedy x

Em stared at the text message. Did she dare trust her?

She'd done extensive research on Kennedy the night before. She'd been reluctant at first, but her conversation with Asher had compelled her to open Google and type in Kennedy Wright's name. Kennedy had published puff pieces, as Em had expected, but her in-depth articles were exactly as Asher had said: she focused primarily on domestic abuse and misogynist power plays. It made Em wonder what Kennedy's story was. Why, as a celebrity reporter, would she choose to go down that route? It was like pulling the pin out of a hand grenade in Hollywood.

Em wasn't sure if she was ready to chat with Kennedy yet, so for now, she put it into the too-hard basket. Asher was right. She needed to focus on herself and her book. But there were other things nagging at her. Her mum's silence was one of them.

Racking her brain, Em thought back to the last time she'd spoken to her mum. She'd said she was travelling in her campervan down the east coast of Australia and, considering how many days it had been since that conversation, her mother would be somewhere on the south coast of New South Wales, maybe even on the Surf Coast in Victoria if she'd driven longer days. She was meeting someone down there. Maybe that was it? Maybe she was just distracted with her friend. Or maybe it was a new lover. It wouldn't be the first time.

Her mum was flighty about charging her phone, not to mention connecting to email, but she was pretty good about returning Em's phone calls. She had gone without speaking with her mum for days on end before, but that was years ago, and long before this blow-up with Callum. For the last few months, she and her mum had either spoken or texted every other day. It was unusual now to have her messages ignored.

Keeping the covers over her arms, Em dialled Kat's number. It went straight to voicemail. She texted her mother instead. She was more likely to respond to that anyway.

Hey Mum. Starting to get seriously worried now. Are you ghosting me? Call me back, okay? Love you! xx

Em stared at her phone, willing a response, but there was nothing. No dots blinking. She scrolled back through and saw that two previous messages had been read, so her mum was seeing her messages. Why wasn't she responding?

When she heard whining from the bedroom door, she looked up and saw Charlie staring back at her.

"Oh God. Sorry Charlie. Are you desperate for a wee, sweetness?"

She threw back the covers, making the dog leap back and dash to the outside door. She grabbed her cardigan, still missing her slippers, and looked outside. Snow covered the ground outside.

She snorted. "That's going to make for an interesting day."

In the living room, she opened the bi-fold door and felt the cold coming off the snow, the frigid wind sweeping its way into the house. Once all three dogs were out, she closed the door quickly. She didn't know how people dealt with this kind of cold for months on end. She had been spoiled living in LA. But the room seemed a lot colder than it should be, given she'd stoked the fire the night before. She'd been able to keep the fire going all night before, but now she noticed the fire was completely out. Weird, she thought. Had she put wet wood on it? She didn't think so.

Approaching the wood heater, she saw the flue was wide open. Crap. That would explain why the fire had gone out. God, she was losing it.

Once she had the fire going again, she rose and walked to the kitchen, switched the coffee maker on, then slathered a thick slice of homemade sourdough with some jam she'd picked up at the Salamanca Markets. With the machine warming, she grabbed a mug from the drying rack, a white one with delicate blue flowers wrapped around, which was quickly becoming her favourite of all of John's mugs. She wondered if he'd miss it if it happened to make its way into a suitcase at the end of her stay.

Laughing to herself, knowing she'd never do such a thing, she stepped into the pantry and grabbed her coffee container. Popping the lid off, she saw that the coffee scoop was missing. Huh. It was always there. Had she washed it the day before? She looked at the drying rack, then in the utility strainer, but the scoop was in neither place.

Strange. First the matches, then the slippers, then the fire ... and now the coffee scoop. She really was losing it. She grabbed a tablespoon from the drawer and heaped coffee into the portafilter, then twisted it onto the machine, making a mental note to search the kitchen. First she needed coffee, especially if she was going to face another day seeing Ryatt. She just didn't know where things stood with him anymore, especially when it came to her being Callum's wife.

She wasn't sure what time Ryatt was coming to see her. Once Vinces Saddle was open, he'd said. But now the idea of him coming all the way to Neeminah River over a bag of onions and a note seemed stupid. She'd sent him photos. Wasn't that enough?

Her thoughts returned to the onions. Who'd put a bag of onions on someone's doorstep anyway? And that note? It didn't make any sense.

She thought to call Ryatt and tell him not to come, but Asher's words about trusting her instincts nagged at her. Fine. Just as she started frothing the milk, the dogs began barking outside and she heard the crunch of tyres on gravel. Surely Ryatt wasn't here already? She wasn't even dressed yet.

She left the milk jug on the counter and ran back to the bedroom to throw on her clothes from yesterday. When she glanced quickly in the bathroom mirror, she laughed. She had the worst bedhead she'd had in years. Looking through her toiletry bag, she found an elastic and quickly piled her hair into a topknot, hoping it looked a little better. Stepping back into the living room, she saw Ryatt through the glass door, bent over and patting Charlie behind the ear, who looked at him like he was God's gift to dogs. Suddenly she began to doubt Charlie's ability to guard anything.

She opened the door, noticing that the cold wind had picked up even more. All three dogs dashed inside before Em realised their feet were soaking wet. Muddy footprints marked their path to the fire.

"Shit, sorry. I should have held them back," Ryatt said, standing at the door.

"Doesn't matter. Come in, come in," Em said, then laughed at Ryatt taking off his boots. "Seriously? After these three? Just come in and leave them inside the door. It's too cold to stand out there."

"Right, sorry," Ryatt said, stepping inside and closing the door behind him.

"I just need to get an old towel from the mudroom to wipe their feet. I'll be right back." She raced down the hall.

"Bring two towels and I'll help," he called.

When she returned, Ryatt was seated at the farm table with Ruby's head on his knee, the dog taking in all the love Ryatt was willing to give her. Em handed him an old brown towel and he began wiping Ruby's paws. Em went to the other two who were already on their beds, curled up. Poor Billy was shivering. She pulled the old red blanket over him while she worked on his paws.

"I have news for you about who was skulking behind the shed," Ryatt announced as they worked on the dogs.

Em's head shot up.

"It was Tyler," Ryatt said. "And not for the sinister reason Shirley would have you believe."

Em raised one eyebrow.

"Yeah, Shirley was clear she wasn't a fan of Tyler's when I talked to her. But it turns out that the kid was looking for a coat for the greyhound there. Billy?" Ryatt indicated the dog licking her hands as if appreciating her soft touch while she cleaned his paws.

Em nodded.

"He saw Billy wearing a coat when he was first adopted, a few months back," Ryatt explained. "Said there had to be one around somewhere, and he thought John may have put it in the shed. He said he knocked on the door, but you weren't home, so he went looking in the shed. Apparently he helps John out here and there for some extra money, so he knew the shed was unlocked. He didn't see you coming home. Poor kid. He feels really bad about scaring you like that."

"Of course. His long coat. Now that makes sense," Em said as she moved to Charlie. Seeing the others getting their feet wiped, the dog was hesitant at first, but Em whispered sweet nothings to him until he reluctantly complied.

"Yeah. Shirley isn't a fan of his. Seems to think he's got a dark streak," Ryatt said and went on patting Ruby once he was done.

Em nodded, then said, "But Anna, the other housesitter, seems to have a good impression of him. She said Tyler is a good kid. She's had a few conversations with him." Em worked on Charlie's front paws now that she was done with the back.

"I think he's lonely, to be honest," Ryatt said. "When I talked to his dad, he said one of the reasons they left Melbourne was because Tyler was being bullied. Thought Tasmania would give them all a fresh start.

When I eventually talked to Tyler, I told him that I knew what it was like. To be bullied, I mean."

Em's face paled.

"I didn't tell him who it was that bullied me," added Ryatt, hastily. "No one would believe it anyway. Besides, it's in the past. But I also told Tyler that I knew what it's like to move somewhere new at his age, where you don't know anyone. I just wanted to make sure the kid knew he wasn't alone."

"Okay," Em said, her heart returning to a normal pace. She stood to return to the table. "Did you discover anything about the bag of onions?"

She walked to the kitchen counter and grabbed the bag. The note was still inside. Ryatt pulled out gloves and put them on.

"Oh crap. Sorry. I forgot," Em said, dropping the bag in front of Ryatt and stepping back.

"Well, I knew you'd already handled them. Has anyone else touched them? Other than the person who placed them on the mat, I mean."

Em shook her head. "Not that I know of."

Ryatt pulled out the piece of paper from inside the bag. "Good. I showed the pictures of the bag to Shirley and Margo earlier," he said as he read the note.

"You've already talked to the neighbours this morning?" she shrieked. "It's barely nine!"

"Yeah, of course. When did you think I talked to Tyler and his dad? This is Tasmania in the winter, Em. People are up with the sunrise. We only have eight hours of sunlight."

She took a breath. Right.

"Shirley thinks the bag looks to be from the local farmers' market," continued Ryatt, "so it's likely someone local; and, look, Bryan isn't too happy with me knocking on his door again this morning. I think he may be behind it. He made a comment about my questioning him about a bag of onions and a few stupid notes being a bit over the top. Right now, I have nothing to connect him, but my advice is to steer clear of him."

"Bryan. You're sure?" Em asked.

"As sure as my gut says. I'm still in the process of doing a background on him, as there's something about him that I don't like. Better to know who we're dealing with. I think you're relatively safe, but just take precautions, okay?"

"Anna did say she's seen Bryan out and about more lately," Em said. "But you don't think …" She wanted to ask if it was possible that he could be connected to Callum but saying it out loud seemed far-fetched.

"Do I think Callum is involved?" Ryatt asked.

Em nodded.

"No, not at this point."

"Okay. Well, thanks for looking into it. I'm kind of relieved, actually. I've felt like someone has been watching me, but that could just be my paranoia. You know, from living in LA and dealing with the paparazzi with the divorce."

"Right. Sure. Well, if anything else pops up, call me. Okay?"

"I will, thanks. Do you want some coffee for your efforts? I have muffins, bread and brownies too," Em said, blushing. "I bake when I'm anxious."

Ryatt chuckled. "Yeah, I remember. And I'd love some, but I've got to get over to Kingston."

"Want some for the road? Seriously, I can't eat everything I've baked myself, and even if I deliver apology baskets to all the neighbours, I'll still have plenty left over."

"Well, if you're offering free baked goods, I'll take them," Ryatt said.

She blushed again.

WHEN RYATT HAD GONE, Em sat down at the table, relieved. Now that she knew who the prankster was, she could get back to her cookbook and just give Bryan a wide berth.

She picked up her phone to check if there was a message from her mum yet (still nothing), and read the message from Kennedy again. Maybe it was time to talk to her. It may not hurt to befriend Kennedy if she was in Asher's life. And if Kennedy had her ear to the ground, Em could be prepared as the divorce case continued. She checked the time and saw it was just after five in the afternoon in LA.

She texted Kennedy.

Hey Kennedy. Thanks for letting me know that my whereabouts are still under wraps. Spoke to A. I'm open to chat when you have time. Em.

The response was immediate. Not a surprise. The word 'vulture' sprang to mind.

Hello Em. Now's good? I'm at A's now.

Biting her lip, Em dialled Kennedy's number. It rang once before Kennedy picked up.

"Hello?" Kennedy said, which made Em laugh to herself. It's not like she wasn't expecting Em to call her.

"Hey Kennedy. It's Em," she said. She waited, leaving it to Kennedy to open the conversation.

"Hi Em. I'm glad you called. I thought I'd come over and make Asher dinner. How is it that he's a genius with baking, but he hates cooking? Has the man ever used the cooktop since you've known him?"

Em laughed. She'd teased Asher relentlessly for years about his lack of cooking skills. He was the king of sandwiches. If he ate anything hot, it was either take-out or microwaved.

"He doesn't even know how to boil an egg," Em said.

Kennedy gasped. "*Seriously?* Asher. Do you not know how to boil an egg?"

Em waited while Kennedy waited for Asher's answer in the background, knowing what his response would be.

Kennedy spoke again. "He tells me it's a—"

"—skill he doesn't need to know," Em finished. "He knows pastry and bread. That's it."

"Shocking. Anyway. That's not why you're calling me. I know I'm probably not someone you would trust easily, given how abhorrently you've been treated by my—" Kennedy fake-coughed— "colleagues.

But let me tell you two things. Then you can decide whether you want to continue with our conversation. Is that fair?"

"Yes," Em said. The woman was good; she could admit that.

"Alright. First of all. I have met you in person before. At the G'Day USA event. It was about two years ago. The year you left with gastro, I believe."

Em remembered it well. She'd been so ill she'd ended up in the ER at Cedars-Sinai hospital and had been admitted for two days. But that information was public knowledge. And Asher could have told her about that.

"Callum stayed at the event after you left. Do you remember that?" Kennedy asked.

"Yes."

"Well, later that evening, Callum accosted me as I came out of the bathroom. As in, he had me against the wall and wasted no time before he was groping me under my dress. I didn't report him. I didn't say anything, as it happens a lot in Hollywood. Too much, to be honest. But I stomped on his foot and told him he needed to remember where he was. He didn't know that I was a celebrity reporter, but after the groping, I let him know. He stormed right off to talk to someone. His PR rep, Graeme someone. He was attending with you, I believe. Graeme came to speak with me immediately. He was trying to keep what happened quiet and offered me quite a hefty sum to do so."

Em remembered Callum telling her the next day about some bitch who'd almost broken his foot at the event. His version was a lot more innocent than Kennedy's – he was just trying to buy the woman a drink – but Em knew Callum and was inclined to believe Kennedy's version.

"The second thing I wanted to tell you is that I know what men like Callum are like, and he shows all the typical signs," Kennedy said.

Em's hand began to shake. This was the part she was worried about with Kennedy. Callum had threatened her with retribution if any of his secrets came out.

"It's not what you think," Em began.

"Please don't," Kennedy said with a sigh. "I've been watching you both for two years, since that incident. I've seen how he speaks to you, how he treats you. The embezzlement release is a power play, to see how far he can push you. Am I right?"

Em stayed silent.

"Let me help you. Not as a reporter, but as a friend. I've been in a relationship like yours myself. Look, I know it's hard for you to trust me, given I'm in the media, but *use* me. Use me to your advantage. I can tell you when stuff is happening, so you're prepared. I know you went to Australia to lay low, and that's a great idea. You're away from the bullshit. Stay there. Stay away. And if Callum decides to pull anything else, I can help you prepare. He's in Australia now too. In Melbourne. The rumours are swirling. No one knows if he's there talking to some producers about an upcoming film, or if he's already working on one. My network is trying to nail it down. They want me to fly out and dig. But if I dig, I'm doing it for you. I have your back. I just don't want you to be accused of anything you haven't done."

Em was silent. Surely Kennedy didn't know about ...

"All I know is, everyone has secrets," Kennedy added, before Em could finish the thought. "And I am telling you, whatever it is you're hiding for him, I want to protect *you*."

15

Are you feeling … forgetful?

Like you've lost something?

Something you felt you could rely on?

16

Em agreed with Ryatt about Tyler. While the long, dark coat and combat boots were a little off-putting, especially on a teen who kept to himself and rarely made eye contact, they were practical for the weather. When Em walked past Tyler's house with the dogs later that morning, Tyler was hauling out the rubbish bins, battling the gusts of wind that were sweeping their way up the valley. When Em said good morning, his blush expressed his embarrassment over the shed incident. He waved to her in response.

When she was on her way back from her walk a little while later, Tyler followed her. This time, she stopped until he caught up. As cold as it was, and despite the wind howling around them, she needed to talk to him.

"Morning Tyler. Cold one this morning," Em said.

He nodded in response.

Em wondered what she could ask the kid that could open up the conversation. She thought about the shed incident, and remembered he'd gone there to try to help Billy.

"I'm sorry to have misunderstood about the shed thing. Poor Billy, he really does feel the cold. I have been looking for a coat around the place myself but haven't found one yet. Do you remember what it looked like? The one you were looking for?"

Tyler looked up, his cheeks so red that Em wasn't sure if it was from embarrassment or the cold. "I'm so sorry about that. I really didn't mean to scare you." His voice was deep but soft. She had to really tune in to hear him over the wind.

"Oh! No, no. It's okay. Really. It's just I had some chickens that had been …" She shook her head. "Doesn't matter. Your heart was in the right place."

"I'm just really sorry. I won't do it again. I did come up and knock, but I know Mr Young leaves his shed unlocked, so thought I'd have a quick look, in case it was there. It wasn't likely, though. To find the coat there, I mean. It's probably in the house somewhere, but I wanted to make sure."

Em wanted him to just take a deep breath. He was so apologetic, it broke her heart. He may be sixteen and look like a serial killer, but there was no sense of evil about him.

"Do you remember what the coat looks like? I'll take another look today."

"Um, it was a dark green colour. Checked? No, that's not the word," he said.

"Tartan?" Em asked, and Tyler nodded. "Okay, that helps. I'll take another look around today and let you know if I find it. If not, I'll search online and see if I can find something like it for him."

Tyler looked sideways at her, surprised.

"I'm with you Tyler. It's not fair that he's suffering in the cold."

THAT AFTERNOON, Em saw Shirley's aged four-wheel drive in their driveway. Given how she and Margo had helped her with Bryan two days ago, and then suffered Ryatt's continued questions, Em decided to deliver some caramel slice she'd made that morning. She'd drop some to Tyler, too.

By the time Em reached the front door, Shirley was standing in the doorway. Her dishevelled grey hair was barely constrained by her bobby pins, and she wore what must have been pyjamas: baggy, blue-checked flannel pants and a green pullover, one sleeve pushed up to her elbow.

"Em! How's it going?" the older woman said, her eyes zeroing in on the old round biscuit container in Em's hand. "Now, what do you have there?"

"I made some extra caramel slice. Thought you might like some?" Em held out the tin.

"Well, if it's like your muffins, I'd be happy to have some. Come in, come in. I'll pop the kettle on. Margo's out at the moment but should be home shortly." Shirley held the door open a little wider.

Em considered her options. Should she decline and say she needed to continue walking the dogs, or should she go in, drink the tea and be neighbourly? She liked Margo, but she was still on the fence about Shirley. Still, Shirley did remind her of her old neighbour, from when they lived in Queensland when she was around twelve or thirteen. The phrase 'salt of the earth' popped into her head. How could it hurt?

"Thanks, Shirley. I'd love a cup of tea. Are you okay if I leave the dogs here in the yard? I was just out on a walk with them."

"Oh, yeah. They're used to it. John has popped in before and left them out there. And Gracie will be back with Margo soon, so they can have play time together."

Em looked at the dogs. While Ruby was sitting politely beside her, the other two were sniffing the yard like they'd never been there before.

"Come on. They'll be fine," Shirley insisted.

Em stepped into the house and was hit with the smell of urine. In the corner was a playpen for children, but this one had a mesh top. Weird, Em thought.

"Do you have grandkids?" she asked. Margo and Shirley hadn't mentioned any when they'd been over the other day.

"God no," Shirley said.

Em chuckled and pointed at the playpen, confused.

"Oh. That's for Kumquat," Shirley said, tilting her head towards an overweight tabby perched at the top of a cream-coloured cat tower.

The contraption was almost two metres in height, and right now,

Kumquat was staring her down like a jaguar after its kill, his tail snapping back and forth.

"Please ignore the smell. I've been cleaning up after the damn cat. He wasn't happy to be in his pen this morning, so as soon I let him out, he walked over and pissed all over the curtains in retaliation."

Em wasn't sure how to react. On one hand, she wanted to high five the cat. Who'd want to be locked in a cage while he could have the whole house to himself? Then again, peeing on the curtains was pretty defiant and it was not an easy smell to get rid of. So she did as Shirley requested and ignored it, instead changing the subject.

"I saw Tyler this morning," Em said, following Shirley as she disappeared into the kitchen to make the tea. "I thought I'd drop off some slice to them as well later. Seemed like Pete might have been busy when I went past earlier. There was another car in the driveway."

"Probably romping around with Blaze. That's his sous chef. Pete thinks he's being discreet, but it's pretty obvious when Blaze's car is parked there all day until they leave for work." As she gossiped, Shirley dangled tea bags in two mugs. No teapot in sight here. "And Blaze is a good egg. So is Pete. He's much better off with Blaze. Pete's wife, Ginny, is a bit of a glamourpuss. Maybe she's his ex-wife by now? No idea. Anyway, yeah, he's better off. Ginny is a piece of work. All about appearances, that one." Shirley wrinkled her nose. "Don't get me wrong. They seemed like the perfect couple when they first came down. But they're a cricket pitch apart, like two wickets staring each other down from either end. Better off apart, I reckon."

Em held her tongue. No response seemed necessary, anyway.

"And take it from me," Shirley continued, throwing the used tea bags into the sink. "I know all about what it's like to be in a loveless marriage."

She yanked open the fridge, pulled the milk out and held it up, looking at Em. When Em nodded, Shirley splashed a little in each cup, returned the milk to the fridge, and led the way to the dining table, where she'd left the caramel slice.

"Oh, now don't they look good," Shirley said, her fingers reaching in for the largest piece. "We should wait for Margo, but ..." She shrugged. "I'll save a piece for her. I bet this'll be in the running to beat

Sue's caramel slice. She's in Cygnet. She sells her slices to the local cafés. But this looks scrumptious, too."

Em smiled at the back-handed compliment. It was just like the comment about Suzanna's scones. But Em knew this slice was damn good. She'd been tweaking the recipe for years now and was finally ready to include it in her book. Shirley took a bite, letting crumbs scatter. She'd not provided a plate for either of them, or any napkins, and since Em had already experienced eating once with Shirley, she looked away.

Around the cosy room were bookcases, floor to ceiling, filled with knitting books and an assortment of craft books. Mixed in were what her mother liked to call 'penny dreadfuls', Mills and Boon novels. Nearby, on the side table, was a collection of photos. Most were of Margo and Shirley, arm in arm, smiling. Some were older photos. There was another woman with Shirley in two of the photos – a woman of about the same age as Shirley was, with brunette hair in a pixie cut. In one photo, the woman was looking at Shirley as if she'd hung the moon.

"That's Linda," Shirley said, noticing where Em's gaze had landed. "She was my partner before Margo. She died, oh, going on about thirty years ago now. Died in a car accident. Drunk driver." Shirley took another large bite of caramel slice.

"Oh," Em said. Another layer of Shirley peeled away. "I'm so sorry."

Shirley waved her away. "I was married to a miserable son of a bitch for about twenty years while I was with Linda. My husband found out about her. You couldn't be open about your sexuality in those days. So I'd married Ronald to cover up my secret, and when Ronald figured it out, he threatened to tell my family. Held it over my head for years. Bastard, he was. But he had his reasons, I guess. I doubt anyone would be happy if they'd married someone who refused to have sex with them." Shirley took a deep breath in, exhaled, then took a large slurp of her tea.

She continued with her story. "Ronald leaned towards the violent side when he got drunk. Linda was always the one to patch me up, kiss my wounds. She had a little cottage in Cygnet. I'd duck over and see her at lunchtime, and after work most days. But that was the extent of our relationship for a long time – a series of trysts, you'd probably call it. At least until Ronald died. He had a heart attack. Suddenly, I was free. Anyway, Linda and I lived here after that. We rented out Linda's cottage and had a good life here for about ten years. Then she went out for a reading at the local library and got t-boned by a drunk driver coming home. She was a poet. A beautiful one. Quite renowned in this area. Well, all of Tasmania, really." Tears welled in Shirley's eyes.

"I'm so sorry, Shirley," Em said, reaching over to take Shirley's hand.

Shirley nodded, then stood and walked to the bookcase. She pulled a book from the shelf. "One of Linda's books. Take it with you. I only ask that you return it when you're done. I think you'd enjoy it."

Em looked at the cover and saw a gorgeous hand-spun blanket, a mix of bold primary colours, tossed over a muted upholstered chair. She turned her head and saw the blanket from the book cover slung over the same chair in the corner of the room. Em ran her hand over the cover and knew there'd be love written in these pages. She'd cherish the reading.

"Thank you. I will no doubt devour every word," Em said, and meant it.

When Charlie let out a friendly bark outside the front door, Shirley turned and looked up at the clock on the nearby wall. "That may be Margo, but my guess is it's Tyler, coming home," she said, turning back around and reaching for another piece of slice. Maybe she was serious about leaving Margo only one piece. "He works in Huonville on the weekends. Charlie and Tyler are friends, although I'm not sure why. The kid is a menace."

"Why do you say that?" Em asked, standing to take her empty cup to the sink.

"Look at him. He's a loner who wears a trench coat," Shirley said, staying seated at the table. She'd already inhaled two slices of the caramel slice, and Em suspected another would be gone before she got to the end of the driveway.

"My guess is he's lonely," Em said, thinking back to what Ryatt had said. "And he wears the coat to stay warm. With his parents living their own lives, and him living in a remote place where there's no one his age around, I don't see a menace. I see a lovely young man who's wanting company. And after my conversation with him this morning, I think he's a kid with a big heart. Maybe you should invite *him* in for tea sometime. I daresay you'd both enjoy the company." Going by Shirley's surprised expression, Em knew she'd hit a nerve. "Anyway, enjoy the slice. I'm off to finish walking the dogs. Please say hello to Margo for me. And thanks for the tea. And the book."

When she walked outside, she saw Margo's Subaru pulled up beside Tyler, Gracie's head sticking out, her nose sniffing the air. Seeing Tyler laugh at something Margo said, Em knew she was right about him. With the dogs already dashing ahead, Em walked down the driveway and joined Tyler at Margo's car.

Margo's face lit up. "Hi darling! How are you doing?" Margo could make Em feel included immediately. "I was just telling Tyler here that I'm needing some wood chopped. How's your supply?" She turned back to Tyler before Em could reply. "Think you could manage two households, Tyler?"

He looked at Em and blushed.

"I'd love some help with it," said Em. "I was wondering how I'd manage it, to be honest. I'd be a total klutz with an axe. Would probably slip and chop off my leg."

While Margo laughed, Tyler shook his head.

"I'm serious!" protested Em.

"Nah. But I'm happy to do it. Just let me know when. Anyway, gotta get home. Ton of homework," Tyler said, and after Em promised to drop him off a snack of caramel slice later, he blushed again with his thanks, patted Gracie through the window, then turned to go.

Charlie trotted up after him. Tyler bent, patted him, then pointed for Charlie to return to Em. Yeah, he was a good kid, Em decided.

"I really don't know what Shirl has against that boy," Margo said, watching him go. "I think he's the sweetest kid I've ever met."

"I agree," said Em, and they watched him disappear around the back of his house.

"How are you holding up? Is there anything I can do to help?"

Gracie wriggled in the back seat, strapped in by her harness. "Oh Gracie, love, we're nearly home. Just hang on a bit longer."

"I'll leave you to go. You may need to fight Shirley for the last piece of slice I just left with her. I wanted to thank you for the other day. And now, for today." Margo looked confused. "For thinking of me with the wood pile."

"Oh, that. That's just neighbours helping neighbours," Margo said, and put the car in gear. "Well, you know where we are. Yell if you need anything, and I'll be sure to remind Tyler that you need help. He's a bit shy, that one. Sometimes you have to nudge him." Margo smiled.

With a wave, Em called for Billy and Ruby. Charlie was sitting beside her, staring up at Gracie with love twinkling in his eyes. "Come on, Charlie. Let's finish our walk," Em said, getting the shepherd's attention again.

A few hours later, Charlie, Ruby and Billy were settled down next to the hearth, the fire was at a low burn, and Em was feeling this was definitely the best place she could be right now. Especially considering the temperature was due to drop below freezing overnight. They'd forecast snow again.

At five o'clock, she made an early dinner of scrambled eggs to go with her sourdough. Breaking the eggshells, she remembered a time when she was little, when her mother would crack open their eggs when they were still warm from the nest. Em had hated eggs as a kid for that reason. Here, the chickens were champion layers, and she found that if she put the eggs from the coop in the fridge for a day after she'd washed them off, she could pretend they were from the fridge section at the supermarket.

Thinking of her mum made her check her phone again as she waited for the eggs to cook. God, she was really freaking out now about not hearing from Kat. Six texts and numerous phone calls had gone unanswered. She had even checked her location tracker, but it hadn't moved in days. Knowing her mum and her feelings about being tracked, she'd probably turned it off. Kat was adamant about her privacy, and Em had to respect that, but she considered calling Ryatt to see if he could find out anything. She wasn't sure, though, if their relationship was one where she could ask that kind of favour.

Kennedy's words returned to her. "Everyone has secrets."

Em thought the only logical explanation was that her mum had found a lover and was spending a few uninhibited days somewhere. In the past, she'd told Em what was going on. This time, she'd just dropped off the face of the earth. But she had said she was meeting someone she knew before.

"Everyone has secrets."

Putting her phone down on the counter, ignoring it all for now, Em stirred the eggs, and thought of the secrets she held herself. Callum's secrets, mostly. They were doozies. What if the news outlets found out about them? The thought tempted her to offer up something to Kennedy, just so she'd post something online, to reveal a little of the truth. God, it was so tempting. But no. She'd take the higher road. She knew she was better off without Callum, and she didn't need to dredge up the past just to feel better. Besides, she already felt better being away from him.

The toaster popped behind her.

As she slathered butter on her sourdough toast, she laughed to herself. She wasn't forced to wear Spanx four sizes too small to contain her curves, to fit in with Callum's starlets. She didn't have to cancel her own plans so she could attend his events. She no longer had to miss her own award ceremonies because of her husband's less important movie premieres. The rumour she'd heard, right before she left Callum, was probably what Callum believed: he'd married her because he could mould her into whatever he wanted.

And maybe he was right, then. It had been her and her mum against the world, always on the move, always chasing the best market scene for her mum's business. Then, after Ryatt left, she was wrecked that their relationship was over so suddenly. Em had felt lost. She hadn't known what she wanted to do with her life at that point. In truth, Em had been adrift when she first dated Callum, and he knew it. She'd been heartbroken, and Callum had swooped in and 'saved' her. If only she'd saved herself. Callum was worse than a lech. He was a con artist.

Yes, she was far better off. She just needed to work out what was next for her.

Deciding to make that decision for herself – and soon – she took her eggs off the stove and placed them on the toast, steam rising into her face. Her stomach rumbled.

When her phone rang fifteen minutes later, Em saw "Unknown caller" on the screen. She ignored it and placed it back on the side table next to her glass of wine. Then her phone pinged. This time, a voicemail.

She picked up her phone, unlocked it and opened her voicemail.

"Hi love. It's Mum. Sorry. I lost my phone again. You know how I am. It's hard to keep track of the bloody thing. Plus, I had to wait until I was in a town big enough to buy another one. Don't know why I even have one. You're the only one I call on the stupid thing. Anyway, they couldn't transfer my number. Some tech mumbo-jumbo, and you know how I am with that. I zone out. So here's my new number." Kat rattled off her new number so quickly Em thought she might need to replay the message ten times to make sure she got it right. "I'll call you again tomorrow. Hope you're still alive in Tassie. Love you. Mwah."

Em breathed a sigh of relief. She didn't know where her mother was or what she'd been up to, but at least she knew she was still alive. And that was something.

She looked down at the notepad where she had written down her mum's number and hoped it was right. She dialled the number, expecting voicemail, and was surprised her mum picked up so quickly.

"Hi love!" Kat said, her voice perky and louder than necessary.

Em wasn't sure where she was, but she heard crashing waves in the background.

"Hi Mum. I've been so worried," Em said. "Where are you?"

"Surf Coast. I picked up a new phone in Geelong, then came back down here. It's so peaceful here in winter." Her mum was talking like nothing had happened. "But yeah, sorry to worry you."

"I sent emails to you as well. Did you not see those?" Em asked, exasperated. Her mum was unbelievable sometimes.

"Nope. I don't know where my laptop is. It's probably under a cushion or in the back of a cupboard somewhere. Probably stashed it when I parked somewhere, then forgot where I put it," Kat said casually. "I haven't needed it, so …"

Em could imagine her mum shrugging nonchalantly. It wasn't like her campervan was all that big, either. It was an old Volkswagen. Not too many nooks and crannies. She probably didn't even look for the damn thing.

"Well, I'm glad you're okay," Em said, resigned.

"Yeah, I'm fine. I'm probably going to hang here for a couple of weeks. There's a good festival on here that I'm going to try to get into. So I'll be sitting here by the ocean, sewing bunting for a while, I think. My stock is a bit depleted."

Her mum was always around markets, her source of some quick money.

Em's phone pinged in her hand. "Hang on, I just got a text," she said.

She saw a text from Kennedy, then gasped. There were five missed calls from Kennedy, too. How had she missed five calls? Scrolling, she saw there were also two missed calls from Asher.

What the hell was going on?

She returned to Kennedy's text and read it once more.

Em. Call me. It's urgent.

"Mum, I've got to go. I'll call you later, okay? Glad you're okay," then she promptly hung up.

17

You weren't paying attention.

You don't get to decide what people know about you. I do.

Time to let the world know how you destroy people's lives, Mathilda.

18

Em debated whether to call Asher first, but Kennedy's text compelled her to dial her number instead.

"Kennedy. Hi. What's going on?" Her pulse raced, and she placed a hand on her chest in an effort to regain her composure.

"Hi Em. Asher is here with me. Are you sitting down?"

Em straightened in her chair. A chill ran through her body and the three dogs shifted their gaze to her. Charlie sat up, ears pricked. Ruby trotted over and nudged her leg, while Billy stared.

"Yes, I'm sitting. What's happened?"

"A video has surfaced. Posted at midnight, our time. It's a video of you and another woman, with Callum's voice in the background."

Em clenched the phone. "What?" she whispered. It was all she could get out.

No. No. *No, no, no.* This wasn't happening. That video was supposed to have been destroyed. Like, years ago.

"Yeah. I'm trying my best to quash it, but it's out there, making its way around the internet," Kennedy said, her tone soft and empathetic.

"Can you tell—" Em began.

"That it's you? Yeah," Kennedy said. "Yeah, it's pretty obvious. And people have connected that it's Callum, too."

"Fuck."

Asher's deep voice boomed from the background. "Don't look at the news, whatever you do. It'll just spin you out."

The thought of Asher seeing the video made her want to cry. The shame was overwhelming. She wanted the earth to open and devour her. She stood up, stalked to the kitchen, paced back and forth a few times, then turned and walked down the hallway to the bedroom. Ruby stayed on her heels. Em stood in the bathroom, staring into the mirror. As she contemplated the fallout, her chest tightened, and suddenly, she couldn't catch her breath. She knew there was more at stake than just the sexual content.

She heard Kennedy's voice, then Asher's, but couldn't hear the words. She had to focus. She blinked. Once. Twice. She needed to know what she was up against.

In her hand, her phone vibrated, then vibrated again. Shit. Shit. Shit. She looked down and saw message after message reel through, from numbers she didn't recognise.

"Oh my God. I'm getting messages on my phone. How the hell did people get my number?" She raced to her laptop. "And my email, too. Damn, that was quick. I have thirty emails ... no, make that forty emails in my inbox."

She scrolled down and found an email from Callum's PR rep near the bottom of the unread emails. One of the first she'd received, she noted.

"Okay, this is interesting," she said. "There's one from Callum's PR rep, Graeme."

"What does it say?" Kennedy asked.

Em read it aloud.

Mathilda,
Sorry to be the bearer of bad news, but we've just had a story mailed to us. I'm afraid there is no stopping the freight train now, but we can try to do some damage control. The video seems to have been distributed to all news networks and Associated Press. Without viewing the complete video – I'd like to respect your privacy – it looks like someone may be out to blackmail you and Callum. I've spoken to Callum already. We

are keeping an eye out, but they have made no threats or demands. We
may have a legal problem as well. Please call me ASAP.
Regards,
Graeme

"Fuck," Em exclaimed. "Well, at least we know it didn't come from Callum."

"Not necessarily." Kennedy's response was chillingly clear. "It could be a way to get some attention. I mean, this is way more acceptable than, say, being arrested for lewd conduct with a sex worker in a public restroom."

Em gasped. How did Kennedy know about Callum's arrest? Graeme and the lawyers had buried that. The police had released Callum without a blip on his record. The prostitute, however, was another matter.

Kennedy continued, "But if you were all consenting adults, then who cares? My question is ..." She paused.

Em heard Kennedy whisper the words "I *have* to" at the other end of the line.

"*Were* you all consenting adults?" Kennedy asked.

Em was silent, still reeling from what Kennedy knew.

"Okay," Kennedy said simply, as if a non-answer confirmed her suspicions. "Graeme said legal issues. We don't know what that means. So let's say Callum, or someone in Callum's camp, posted it. I'd be wondering why."

"Maybe they're just trying to pin it on Em, to make her look vindictive?" Asher suggested, now speaking closer to the phone.

"Maybe. But my guess is they believe Em posted it, and they're fishing to find out why."

"I didn't post it! I didn't think the video existed anymore!" Em scrolled through her email then her texts, looking for something from Callum. Nothing. "Callum told me ..."

"Hang on, hang on," Kennedy said. "I didn't say you posted it. I'm saying maybe they *think* you did and they're fishing."

"But why post it for all to see?" Asher asked. "And that goes for Callum as well!"

"I don't think he'd take the risk, to be honest," Kennedy said. "Callum is cunning, as we would all agree, but I don't think he'd do something that would tarnish the superhero reputation he likes to spread around."

"Well. The only way we'll know is to call Graeme. Find out what he means by his email," Asher said.

"No," Kennedy said sharply. "Em, have your lawyers do it. Is there any communication from them?"

"No. Nothing." Em scrolled through page after page of emails, now flooding her inbox. "No calls, either, which is strange too."

"Contact them first," said Kennedy. "See if you can get a cease and desist, for whatever platform it originated from. There's no stopping it, I'm afraid, but at least putting something out there will slow it down. Then we can work out who posted it. I'll work on it from my end."

"Okay, I'll call them as soon as they're in the office," Em said, frantically.

"Email them so they get it first thing," Kennedy added.

Em looked at the clock on her laptop to calculate the time difference. "God, it's close to one in the morning there!"

"Kennedy is a pit bull," Asher said. "Luckily, she's a pit bull on your side of the fence. I'm heading into The Bakehouse now to get the mixes going, then I'll come home and sleep. I've got two guys coming in to help me this morning. Don't worry. The show goes on."

"Meanwhile, I'll ask some questions about who posted it," said Kennedy. Em gasped but Kennedy caught it. "Using a pseudonym, of course."

Kennedy's words from their first conversation came to mind again: "Everyone has a secret." This wasn't something she wanted the world to see, but what the tape masked was another secret they didn't need the world to know. A secret she was trying to keep buried for Callum.

Kennedy spoke again. "But Em, you also need to know, I'm heading to Melbourne for this."

"You are?" Em croaked out.

"Yeah, the network has pushed me to the edge. But I'm on it, with your interests at heart, okay? Please trust me." Something in her tone convinced Em her intentions were pure.

"Okay," Em said, not altogether convincingly. But right now, she was more worried about whether Callum would think she had released it.

"Call me back later, okay?" Asher said. "And Em? We're here for you."

Em ended the call. She walked to the kitchen, poured a large glass of red wine and downed it in four large gulps. Then she poured another and sat down with her laptop to email Sue Jackson, her lawyer. She stared at the blank screen, wondering for a few minutes how she could even begin. She took another gulp of her wine and began typing.

Dear Sue,

By the time you open this email in the morning, you will most likely be aware that a sex video is circulating, involving both myself and Callum, and another woman. I became aware of the video being online through friends and, although I haven't seen it online, I am aware of the video they are referring to.

To my knowledge, there was only one copy, taken on my phone and transferred to a laptop, but Callum informed me it was destroyed years ago. Clearly that's not the case.

I am not aware if Callum, or his team, released the video, but I assure you, I did not. I have scoured my emails and messages, and I've received no threats or blackmail demands. I have, however, received an email from Graeme Parsons, the head of Callum's public relations team, which I'm forwarding to you here. He mentions a legal issue. About what, I have no clue.

To be completely transparent, the other woman signed an NDA.

Please advise.
Sincerely
Mathilda McKinney

Em drank the rest of her wine and breathed deeply, trying to take some time out before her life was held up for the world to dissect, ridicule and judge.

When her phone pinged again, she looked down and saw Callum's name on the home screen. Here we go, she thought.

Steeling herself, she opened the message.

WTF?! What game are you playing?

The phone pinged again. Another message from Callum.

Don't fuck with me, bitch. Srsly. Don't fuck with my life!

Ping. Ping. Ping. Shaking, Em threw her phone across the room.

19

The news was... *e v e r y w h e r e.*

Em watched the local station and, although it wasn't at the top of the news (thank God), it was in the top ten stories. There was no containing the story.

But who had done this? She'd heard from Kennedy three times that night, letting her know she'd combed every outlet she could think of, asked every secure source she could ask, but no one knew where it came from.

Someone did. Who?

Just after nine o'clock, her phone buzzed again. Another text. She glanced at her phone and saw it was Anna. Should she answer? She opened the text.

Hey. Guess you're having a fun night – not. Need some company? I have tequila.

As tempting as it was to get blasted and lose herself in alcohol – she'd already had four glasses of wine – she needed to keep her wits about her. Two thoughts were on repeat in her head: Could they contain this secret? And was any of what had happened lately connected to this?

Suddenly tequila sounded like the answer. At least for tonight. She picked up her phone.

Come on over. Shit just got real.

Fifteen minutes later, Anna was knocking on the door. In the time between Anna's text and her arrival, Em had pulled out the sketchpad she was using to plan the outline for her recipe book, flipped to a new page, and written down every name of every person she'd pissed off in the last ten years.

Anna's knock brought her back to the present.

"Hey there," she said, when she opened the front door. "Welcome to hell."

She was joking, of course. At least, she hoped she was.

"Is this where Mathilda Walsh, harlot wife of Australia's Favourite Son, is staying?" Anna said, grinning cheekily.

"Ha!" Em said as Anna stepped into the warm room. She quickly closed the door on the cold outside.

But Anna was right. That's how everyone was talking about her – like she was plastic or didn't have feelings. She'd scoured the tabloids, of course. One reporter had been bold enough to liken her to a whale in comparison with the other, much skinnier, woman.

"Geezus. What a shitshow. And over something stupid like a three-some? I mean, come on. What planet do people live on? Threesomes now are like what a dinner party was in the fifties."

Em laughed. It was nice to have someone seeing the funnier side of things. Em wasn't quite there yet. "Yeah," she said, her smile fading.

What else could she say? Something that was fairly commonplace in Hollywood was being blown way out of proportion. It wasn't the video itself that had Em freaked out, though. But she couldn't tell Anna that.

"Sorry. I can't imagine what it's like when the sharks are circling," Anna said, handing over the tequila then taking her jacket off. "Are you okay?"

"Yeah. Or I'm getting there, anyway. Do you want wine, or do you want to go straight for the tequila? I have a bottle of wine open already if you drink red?"

"Actually, I haven't really been drinking a lot lately. I, um, went stupid on Southern Comfort over the holidays last year, and declared myself sober ever since."

"Then why do you have tequila?" Em asked, placing it unopened on the counter.

"I had it in my car, just in case there was an occasion. Just didn't imagine this to be the occasion. Fuck, Em, I'm really sorry this has happened. Do you know who released it?"

Em shook her head. "Not yet. But we will find out eventually." She refilled her wine glass. "Okay, so…. I have fresh juice. Or I can pop the kettle on for some tea, or make you a coffee?"

Anna pulled out a reusable Ziplock bag with some herbal tea bags inside. "I came prepared, so kettle for the win," she said. "I really just wanted to make sure you were okay. I mean, I know you probably have friends to talk to, but I just figured this would be a really shitty thing to go through alone."

Em stepped forward suddenly and hugged her. When Em pulled back, Anna began laughing.

"Now, just to be clear, this doesn't mean I want to jump into bed with you," Anna said. "I mean, we are short one person. Maybe Shirley or Margo would like to join us?" Anna laughed.

Em smiled, grateful for the joke.

They settled into the lounge room with drinks. Em took the couch, while Anna took the red upholstered chair. They started talking about some of the crazy things they'd done. Hearing some of Anna's antics, Em felt herself blush more than once, and she was not a prude by any stretch.

Two more glasses of wine later, Em said, "I thought I could escape the madness, you know? I figured Tasmania would be the last place this could all touch me. Turns out, it doesn't matter where you are. Your past always follows you." Her voice trembled.

Anna looked at her with concern. "It'll blow over, just like this stuff always does," she said.

But Anna didn't know what the media was like. They were vultures.

"Maybe. I'm getting more wine. Do you want more tea, or something else?" Em asked, walking to the kitchen.

She poured another glass of wine, having lost count of how many she'd had by now, and grabbed some caramel slice from the pantry to share with Anna.

"I'll take another tea. Thanks." Anna stood and brought her empty cup to Em.

"Oh! I finally heard from my mum," Em said, placing some slice on plates and pulling one of Anna's tea bags out of the reusable bag while the water boiled. Em smiled. Peppermint tea. Just like Ryatt's family used to have all the time.

"Oh? Had it been a while?" Anna asked, bringing Em back to the present.

"Wait. Did I not tell you my mum has been missing for a week?"

Anna shook her head, shocked. "God, no!" she gasped. "With everything else, too?"

"Yes, and it's been freaking me out." She poured boiling water into Anna's mug.

"Yeah. I'd be freaking out too. I'm close with my mum, so not hearing from her for a week … I mean, she texts me like twenty times a day, so that would have me going bonkers. Is your mum okay?"

"Yes, she's fine. Seems everything has been coming hard and fast this week. The last time I heard from her, she was just north of Newcastle, in Hawks Nest. She was heading south to meet up with a friend. But she said she lost her phone, and finally bought a new one in Geelong."

"Well, that's a relief!" Anna said.

Em handed her the tea and they returned to the lounge room. Em placed the slice on the coffee table between them. Anna nibbled on hers. Not like Shirley's devouring.

"I mean, it's not the first time Mum's lost her phone. She hates the thing. She's left it on picnic benches before, or in restaurants, without realising it for days. My mum is a bit flighty. Always has been."

"Geez, my mum is the opposite," said Anna. "She's a major control freak. I think she invented the idea of lists. There's a list for everything. And she won't go to bed until she's accomplished her daily list. It used to drive me insane growing up, but I appreciate it now I'm an adult. The habit got me through university, but don't tell Mum that. I'll hear 'I told you so' in every conversation thereafter."

Em laughed. She did sound the total opposite of her mother.

"I can't imagine that. Mine is very woo-woo. Every major decision she makes has to first be thrown to the universe, or she confers with her tarot cards. We've moved from one town to the next based on what the cards have said, or because of some sign she received from the universe or the gods. She's left people hanging more times than I can count. At first I thought she was on the run from something. You know, looking over her shoulder, waiting for the boogie man. Growing up, we were always moving. Moving schools. Moving houses. Moving towns. She was pretty unhinged for a while. When I suggested she try therapy, when I was in my second or third year of culinary academy, she took off the next day. To Western Australia!"

Em remembered the parting words her mother had spat at her before she left: "You're just like *him*." Em assumed her mum had been referring to her dad and some major fight they'd had.

Em continued, "Now I've lived away from her, I worry about her. A lot."

"And your dad? Is he in the picture?" Anna asked.

The question was not an easy one to answer. Em looked down and swallowed. She took a deep breath.

"No. He died years ago. Car accident. I was barely five at the time. It was a horrible night. I only remember flashes of it. It was his birthday, so Mum and I were bouncing off the walls with excitement because he was coming home early for it, after being away for a while, droving. She and I had baked his favourite cake." Em chuckled. "A pretty rudimentary effort when I think of it now. It was a rich chocolate cake, probably a cheap supermarket cake mix. It was slightly burned, and lopsided too, but we slathered it with chocolate frosting and sprinkles." Em said. She smiled at the memory but then her face dropped thinking of what happened next.

"What I remember really clearly was the cake sitting on our white

Formica table with thirty-nine candles randomly plunged into it. Mum's way of covering up the lopsided part, I think. Since then, I've always associated birthday candles with my dad's death. Random, I know."

She paused.

"Anyway, we knew he was coming home later in the day, but as the hours went on, Mum started to get manic. She began washing dishes. She vacuumed the house for the second time that day. She did a load of laundry at ten o'clock at night and hung it on the line. But most of all, she was pacing back and forth behind the couch, while I watched television. When I finally asked, probably for the millionth time, when Dad would be home, Mum sent me to bed. Mobile phones were still a luxury in those days and not something either of my parents owned. I remember asking why Dad didn't just stop and ring us from a phone box, but Mum just started chewing her nails after that question."

Anna sat patiently, listening to Em while sipping her tea. She'd pulled her legs up under her and settled in.

"The police arrived in the middle of the night. I was in bed, dead asleep, but I will remember my mother's scream for as long as I live. It was guttural, like someone had reached into Mum and ripped out her soul. There was a song playing on the radio when I stumbled out to find out what was going on: 'Imagine'. I turn it off every time I hear it now. It brings it all right back. Mum was inconsolable for what felt like weeks, although it could have just been days. She didn't shower after she learned about his death. And the smell! It was feral! I still remember that smell. But I couldn't do anything. She was in her own world. She didn't care about anything. Even me. We'd run out of cereal and milk, the only food I was allowed to get for myself. So I ate my dad's birthday cake after a while. I didn't want to. I guess I was still waiting for my dad to come home. But I was so hungry, and I remember making myself sick."

Em repositioned herself, pulling up the throw blanket and tossing it over her socked feet.

"Wow, Em. That's terrible. I can't imagine going through something like that at such a young age. Did you have anyone to turn to for support?" Anna asked sympathetically, scratching her leg as if she could erase the painful memory for Em.

"Eventually the neighbour across the street came over. After that, a man arrived and took Mum away. He took her to some hospital, so I stayed with the neighbour. I will always remember that woman's kindness. I think that's where my love of baking came from. Ryatt even mentioned her to me the other day. God, what was her name? Mrs Baily? No, that's not right. Mrs Banes? No ... Boyle. That was it! Mrs Boyle!"

"I wonder if she's still alive," Anna said, but Em shook her head.

"Probably not. She was pretty old, even back then. But she was so lovely. She taught me lots of things. Like how to iron. I remember ironing handkerchiefs and tea towels for hours. At least it seemed that way. But it's the baking I mostly remember. Her pumpkin scones were out of this world. I tried to replicate them for years when I was going through culinary school. That was what Ryatt mentioned, when he was here a few days ago. He said that when I mentioned this woman to him, years ago, I said that I wanted to be a baker like her."

"So you know the detective pretty well?" Anna asked.

"I used to. I know him from way back. Totally random that he's here." Em definitely didn't want to go into that tonight.

"What happened when your mum got out of hospital?" Anna asked, sensing her unwillingness to discuss Ryatt.

Anna reached forward to set her cup down on the coffee table between them, and Em got up and added more wood to the fire. When she was done, she turned and faced Anna, warming her back by the fire.

"We packed up and left. I remember looking out the back window of Mum's car with Mrs Boyle waving sadly from her front steps. It all seemed so sudden, especially after Dad died. I remember being on a boat after that, sleeping in a top bunk. Wow, I'd forgotten that. Mum was super clingy with me then. I do remember that."

She stopped talking and tried to remember more, but the memories from around that time had faded.

"Anyway, that's the long version. He died in a car accident. Brakes failed when he hit a kangaroo. Mum said he never wore a seatbelt, when she told me about it much later."

"Do you remember your dad?" Anna asked.

"Snippets. I remember him being a great dad. I was totally a daddy's girl. When he was home, he was fully present, you know? He was always playing with me. He'd sit and have tea parties with me. He was a big guy. Or he seemed that way to me as a little girl, so he looked really weird sitting at my little table. I'd always make him wear this pink feather boa and a sparkly crown, which probably looked as ridiculous as it sounds, but he was always up for it. He was just … there. Like I was the most important person in the world."

"You were lucky, even if you only had that for a little while," Anna said, and Em nodded solemnly.

"I was. What about you? You said it was just you and your mum?" Em settled back down on the couch.

"Yeah, just the two of us. I've been on my own since I was about sixteen. I have no clue who my dad was. Mum said I was the result of a one-night stand when she was drunk and stupid. Mum worked three jobs back then, and later on, too. We were always struggling financially. She has always told me to go out and conquer the world. Make it a better place. She kept pushing me to become a therapist at first, but she's proud of me. She likes that I want to save the planet."

Eventually the conversation returned to the sex tape. Anna had stuck with her tea, but Em had continued with red wine. She just wanted to dull the reality.

"So, you and Callum. Now that I know you a bit better, I just don't get it."

"What do you mean?" Em asked.

"Your relationship. I mean, you're smart, creative, kind. And from what you've told me, he's none of those things."

Em laughed.

"I mean, publicly, he's charming," admitted Anna. "Gives off a bit of a Hemsworth vibe. That Australian beach vibe, you know? All-Australian. Everyone's 'Favourite Son', as the media likes to call him."

Em gave a short laugh. "When Callum read that he was being compared to the Hemsworth boys, he took up surfing, just to keep the comparison going. He thought that comparison was his greatest compliment."

"But his acting has never been as good. I mean, come on! Thor?"

"Callum has bought into his own hype. He believed, still believes, he's as good as the Hemsworths, or the Matt Damon types."

"Far from it. Which is why I'm confused. Why do you think you and Callum got together in the first place?"

"Actually, I've been thinking about that myself, lately." Em paused. "I think it's probably because I could be moulded into what he wanted me to be."

"Really? So, who is the real Mathilda Walsh?"

"McKinney. I'm Mathilda McKinney now. I went back to my maiden name. I've always used McKinney for the business, too," Em said, but she was really just avoiding the question.

"Okay, so who is Mathilda McKinney?" Anna pushed.

Em took another sip of her wine and pondered the question. It was the part she couldn't figure out. Not really. She was so overshadowed by Callum.

"I don't know," she said eventually. She was sad to admit it out loud.

"You will eventually. I think it starts with knowing what you want. Then you figure out who you are. It took me a while to figure out who I was."

"And what is it you want?" Em said, happy to turn the spotlight on Anna.

"Right now? Space. Independence. Freedom. Being able to go where I want to, when I want to. But next year, I'll buckle down and learn everything I can, so that I can make a difference in the world. A positive difference. Leave a legacy of a good kind."

That all sounded good. Em wished she had that kind of insight into herself ten years ago. But Anna's words made Em think about what she wanted. Space sounded good. Not being overshadowed by the Great Callum Walsh. Not being put down by the Great Callum Walsh. Freedom to be who she wanted to be. To make decisions about her future, about her wants and needs, not just because something looked good in the public forum. She wanted space and freedom to be creative with her business, too. Maybe expand. Maybe create more books or start a cooking school.

But she also liked the friendships she'd begun here in Neeminah River, the community that was here. It was something she'd never experienced before.

"Penny for your thoughts, or whatever that saying is," Anna said, smiling softly.

"Oh, I was just thinking about how much I like it here. I like the space too, the time to think, to ponder, to get to know people a little more. I missed that growing up and it's made me realise, too, that there's been an absence of friends over the years."

"I guess that happens when you live in the spotlight?" Anna said.

"Yeah, there's that. But then … well, now there's all this other stuff going on. I can't quite relax and enjoy being here and I really, really want to. I mean, why is this all happening to me? Why me in particular? And why now? I just can't work out how it's all connected. I mean, there was the note with the chicken head, then …"

Em knew she was rambling. The wine was taking effect. She had to be careful. She tended to be introspective when she was drunk, and a Chatty Cathy.

"I can't see how the tape could be connected," Anna said. "I mean, the rest just seems like someone's pranking you. You know?"

"I know, right? That's the bit I can't work out either!"

Em's phone pinged for what seemed to be the hundredth time that night. She figured it was Callum still harassing her, but when her phone then actually rang at eleven-thirty, she was surprised to see Kennedy's name on the screen.

"Hang on," Em said to Anna, as she answered the call. "Kennedy!"

"Hi. Are you okay?" Kennedy asked.

"Sure! I've had a few glasses of wine and now I'm here with Anna. My housesitter friend, from down the road. We, well I, am having drinks. Anna is being a good girl and drinking tea."

"Well, you're rambling, and you sound way too happy to hear from me, so I'm going assume you're drunk. I'll call you in the morning," Kennedy said.

"Noooo," Em shouted into the phone. "No, it's okay. We're just sitting here, talking. Having a chat. But it's late, right?" She looked over to the kitchen clock, closed one eye and tried to focus on the clock hands, but she couldn't quite make out the time. "It's eleven … something at night. You've got to be calling me for some reason. Right? I mean, whaz up? What other shiz has hit the fan?"

Kennedy hesitated. "Can you put Anna on the phone, please?"

"Um, yes, I can. But why?" She tried to sound serious, but Kennedy's tone made her want to giggle.

"Because I need to speak with her. Can you hand the phone over to her, please?"

Em was confused. Why was Kennedy wanting to talk to Anna? She looked over at Anna, who looked calm and all kinds of innocent, but she had to admit that Kennedy was right. She *was* drunk. She handed the phone to Anna.

"Kennedy wishez to speak wif you," she said, hearing the slurring in her own voice. "I'm going to go to the toilet while you two gab."

She stood up, unsteady on her feet and wobbled her way towards the hallway.

When she returned, Anna was quiet and watching Em closely. She was also no longer on the phone with Kennedy.

"What happened?" Em said.

"She'll call you tomorrow. She asked if I'd stay. If I could. Until she talks to you. She said that Asher – is that his name? He says you're not good when you get drunk. So I'm going to go back to the house to get Sachin and a change of clothes." Her tone was serious. "I'm really sorry. I thought this was a good idea."

"What? It's fine! But wait, why is Kennedy calling again tomorrow? What's going on?" Em said. "But yeah. Stay. That's okay."

Suddenly, the room started to spin. She turned, too quickly for her head to keep up, and found herself nauseous. Anna was beside her quickly.

"I'll help you to bed, and maybe give you a bucket. Then I'll be back. Okay?" She guided Em back to the hallway.

"Okey-dokey!" Em said.

"Lead the way," Anna said. Em pointed to the spare room. "You can stay in John's room, or on the couch. Whatever you want."

"I'm happy on the couch. I'll keep the dogs company," Anna said, and eased Em onto the bed.

Em felt like she was on a merry-go-round, so she put her hand down to steady herself.

"The dogs. I didn't let them out for the night," Em slurred, but swivelled to lie down as she was speaking.

"I'll let the dogs out when I go," Anna said. "I'll be back with a bucket and a towel."

She left the room and Em heard her opening doors and fumbling around. She soon returned, saying, "Here you go. Okay, I'll be back and don't worry. I've got you covered."

"Ha! If only I'd kept myself covered years ago!" Em said. "Then I wouldn't be in this mess!"

Within a few seconds, Em was sound asleep, and Anna was heading out the door.

20

Her head pounded. And the sun was way too bright, blinding her when she rolled towards the window.

Wait. Was that someone in the house? Someone opening the door?

Em sat up quickly and wanted to hurl every last particle in her stomach. Not that she hadn't already tried to do that at three in the morning.

Yes. There was someone in the house! And it wasn't even her house.

She threw the covers off and noticed she was still dressed in the clothes from the night before. Geezus. How drunk had she been? Not that drunk, surely, but she couldn't remember anything past sitting on the couch, talking with Anna. Wait. Anna. Anna had stayed last night, hadn't she?

Em pulled herself up and walked tentatively to the lounge room. The fire was going already. So maybe Anna had stayed. Or John, the homeowner, had returned unexpectedly and found her passed out drunk in her bed. Oh, wouldn't that be delightful. The glass door behind her opened and she swivelled a little too fast for her head's liking. She dashed to the sink and dry-heaved into it.

"Ha! Good morning!" Anna said, her voice too damn perky for this early in the morning. What time was it, anyway? She looked up and saw the four dogs beyond the glass door, looking tired from a walk. Their morning walk.

"What time is it?"

"Quarter to ten," Anna said, walking towards her.

"Quarter to ten? Holy shit. I'm so sorry. What a horrible host I am!" She ran the water down the sink, even though there was nothing in there, or in her stomach.

"Don't worry about it. Do you want coffee?"

"Is the Pope Catholic?" Em asked then groaned. She really was a terrible host. "Oh my God, I'm sorry. That was rude. My mum uses that line all the time."

"It's fine. And it seemed like you needed sleep more than anything. So, all good. Dogs are walked and fed. Chickens are fed and out roaming the paddock. The rooster really likes to get out first, doesn't he? He's rather a dickhead about it."

Em was gobsmacked. She didn't know what to say.

"Anna. Thank you. I am … thank you," Em stammered. "God, I'm so embarrassed. I haven't drunk that much in years."

"Well, you had a pretty shocking day, to be fair," Anna said. "And, come to think of it, you may want to navigate the coffee machine on your own. I tried but failed miserably. I could never be a barista!"

Em smiled and went into auto mode to make two coffees.

"I brought over more milk from my place," Anna said. "You were out completely."

"Geezus. Sorry," Em said again, reaching into the fridge for the milk.

"It's fine. I had to go back and let out the chickens at my housesit anyway. They're not great layers, though, not like yours. I think they're pretty new to the farm."

Em nodded and handed Anna her coffee. "Well, I'll send you home with some eggs. I have about three dozen at the moment. The girls have been in overdrive."

Suddenly, Em fully realised what Anna was saying. She'd been home and returned. She didn't have to do that. She could have just stayed at her place, left the dogs outside until Em got up. But she hadn't. She'd returned to make sure Em was okay. If the tables were reversed, Em may have taken care of the farm animals, dogs included, but then she probably would have left. What kind of friend was that? But Anna was still here, now settling into the couch ... with her laptop.

The night before came flooding back in a rush. The video. The call with Asher. The multiple calls with Kennedy.

Kennedy. Didn't she call late last night? While Anna was still there? Was that real? Had Kennedy actually called at almost midnight?

She walked over to the long table and picked up her phone.

"Hey, Anna? Did Kennedy call last night? Like, really late?"

Anna nodded.

"And ... did she ask to speak to you on the phone?"

Anna nodded again.

"What did she say?" Em asked, her impatience rising. There were no new calls or messages from Kennedy, and none from Asher either.

"To stay with you until she calls," Anna said, then looked back at her laptop screen. "Which should be any minute now."

Why would Kennedy want Anna to stay with her? Had something else come through? She just wanted to know what the hell was going on. Em scrolled on her phone. She saw an email from Sue, her lawyer: they were still investigating. The source was unknown, but they were looking to see what action was needed.

"Kennedy didn't say anything about what was going on though, did she?" Em asked.

Anna shook her head. "No. But apparently Asher suggested I stay until he and Kennedy called this morning."

When her phone pinged, Em pounced on it. It was a text from Ryatt.

You available to talk?

She dialled his number immediately.

"Hey Ryatt," Em said when he picked up.

"Hi Mats. Look, sorry to be the bearer of bad news, but I wanted to let you know that there is a video circulating and... "

"I'm aware," Em said, instantly mortified that Ryatt was aware of it, too.

"Okay, well, normally I wouldn't get involved, but since you've had some other strange things happening lately, I thought I'd look into it," Ryatt said slowly, cautiously.

"Oh God! You didn't watch it, did you?" Em asked, suddenly panicked by the idea, but she knew the answer when he didn't respond immediately. "Oof. Okay."

"Sorry," he said, before continuing. "Last night, there was a message posted online, connected to the video."

"Who posted it? What did the message say?" Em asked impatiently.

Ryatt took a deep breath then plunged in. "Kat. The message was posted under a social media account in her name anyway. But it looks legitimate."

Em's world seemed to stop spinning.

"*What?* Why? I mean, why would she post it? What did the message say?" Em asked, her voice shaking uncontrollably. She couldn't believe it. None of it. Bile formed again in her throat and this time it was not alcohol-related.

"The message said: 'Everyone has secrets'," Ryatt said; but then suddenly, something clicked in Em's mind. Her mother wasn't *on* social media.

Em's phone dinged again in her hand. She looked down and this time saw Kennedy's name. She'd have to wait now.

"Wait, wait. Mum's not on social media. Any of the platforms. She thinks it's the government's way of controlling people. Why do you think it was Mum?"

Her mind was racing. She got up and got some water. The coffee was not sitting well. She drank the glass of water in five big gulps.

"It's been tracked back to her laptop, Mats," Ryatt said.

"She told me just yesterday that she had misplaced it. That she hid it somewhere in her van, but she hadn't bothered looking for it. She lost the phone last week too, and just bought a new one. Maybe someone stole it?"

"It's possible," Ryatt said. "We'll look into that. I was calling to ask if you and Kat have had one of your legendary fights lately? I remember—"

"No. We haven't fought like that in a long time. Not since …" She realised she couldn't remember when. Probably when her mum took off to Western Australia. That had scared the crap out of Em. "But it's strange. That message, I mean. I was talking to my friend Kennedy a few days ago and she said that exact line. It's been on my mind a lot. And I just talked to Anna about it last night, too."

"Hmm. Okay," Ryatt said. He fell silent.

The idea that someone had got to her mum …

"Mats? You there? Are you okay?" Ryatt asked.

But she couldn't answer. Fear ran through her. Then her mind started spinning in a direction she didn't like.

"*Mats!*" Ryatt asked, his voice now yelling through the phone.

"I'm here. Sorry," Em finally said.

"Are you alright?" Ryatt asked, his voice soft and concerned.

"I'm okay. Just … my mum," Em muttered.

She was worried, but it kind of made sense that her mum might have posted it. Her mother didn't like Callum and she was angry at the stunts he'd pulled. Would she lie? Tell her she wasn't on social media? Would her mother be angry enough to do this? Could she have thrown her own daughter under the bus without forethought? But why? What had she done to put Kat off? And that message? Would her mother really write something like that? She knew her secrets, or most of them, anyway. And she knew her mother had secrets too – probably some not even Em was privy to.

"I just don't get it," she said, finally.

"Me neither," Ryatt said. "Is that something your mum has ever said before? 'Everyone has secrets'?"

"Not that I recall. Geezus, I thought that video had been destroyed," Em said.

"When was the last time you saw the video?"

"Um, I don't know. Maybe the week after it happened?"

"Did anyone else see it? Besides you and Callum?"

"No, I don't think so," Em said. But now she wondered if Callum had shown it to … no, surely he wouldn't have been that stupid.

"That would be the question, really. Who else has seen it, and does anyone else have a copy? Because I don't believe it was your mum behind this. They could say it was her, but from what I know of your mum, this doesn't seem like something she'd do."

"Yeah. Yeah, you're right. God, this is getting weirder by the minute," Em said.

"The problem, from a forensic standpoint, is that there isn't much to go by. I sent them the other notes you got, but there's not much they can do there either. And with this one, it's three words. So there's nothing to look at from the type-token ratio perspective. If it was hand-written, we could compare it with your mum's handwriting."

"What's a type-token ratio?" Em asked.

"Forensic linguistics. Whenever there's a threat, there's usually a note or message, so it goes to the forensic linguistic team to dig into. Do you remember that case in the US about the guy who murdered his pregnant wife and two daughters to, um, cover up the fact that he was having an affair? He put his girls into forty-gallon drums, then went on telly to say they'd just disappeared? Watts, I think his name was."

"Yes, I remember it. I was living in California by then. It was all over the news."

"Well, he was caught out because of the appeal he made for his family's return. Forensic linguists watched the video after it happened, and they found some telling inconsistencies. Things that showed he was guilty. That's the kind of thing they do. They look at notes, speech, all those kinds of things, looking at subtle signs."

"Well, that's kind of cool, I guess," Em said, confused as to how this related to the sex tape. Were there people looking at the tape, over and over, trying to find clues?

"The only thing that I can think of is that your mum's been hacked somehow," Ryatt said. "It's the only thing that makes sense to me. So I have to ask: Can you share Kat's number with me? You said she had a new phone? I need to get in touch with her."

"WHAT IS KILLING me about all of this is that I have no control over the situation. Any of it," Em said to Anna as they walked down the driveway towards the dirt road. Anna had insisted Em needed some fresh air, and Em had left her phone behind, needing to be free of the constant intrusion. Ruby stuck to Em's side, while Charlie and Billy galloped back and forth. Sachin ambled on behind them.

She'd tried calling her mum since Ryatt had called, but now she wasn't picking up. That was strange, too.

"I can't think of any reason Mum would be this angry at me. To do something like this, I mean," Em said. "I know I forgot to call her on her birthday last year, but I was away, teaching at a cooking school. I was in the middle of nowhere without a signal!"

"I'm sure she understood that," Anna said.

"That's the only thing I can think of. She sounded normal when I spoke with her. But it doesn't make sense. When we talked about my coming home to Australia, when I decided it was over with Callum, she told me she was proud of me. For realising my worth, and being courageous," Em said, her voice breaking; and suddenly, she couldn't hold back the tears she'd been fighting off all morning.

Anna wrapped her arms around her. The comfort helped, but Em had never felt so lost in her life. She felt like her very solid foundation was cracking open, like an earthquake, swallowing her up. She'd thought she was strong. But this was breaking her.

"You'll get through this, Em," Anna said over Em's shoulder. When Anna pulled back, she took hold of Em's hands and stood for a moment, looking her in the eye.

At the sound of a car approaching, they moved off to the side. Bryan's blue Holden Jackaroo drove very slowly towards them along the straight dirt road. He'd gone past her gate, then past his, and now he was approaching them.

"What's he doing?" Anna asked, but Em knew the question was rhetorical.

"Let's move to the side of the road, shall we?"

"Hello ladies," Bryan said sleazily, leaning out of his window. "After watching that video of you Mathilda, my imagination is ripe with images of the two of you together!"

"Geezus ..." Anna said under her breath.

"What?" Bryan said, snickering.

"Go away, Bryan," Anna said.

"Go home, Bryan. I'm sure your dad needs you," Em added, trying to channel Shirley's bravado in dealing with this man. But when Bryan's face turned red, it seemed Bryan didn't like to be told what to do. He sat taller in the driver's seat, in order to lean further out the window.

"What the fuck would you know? You come down here, trying to be all stealth, and you think you can hide from the world, housesitting in the wilderness. It's not like you can't afford to stay in Hobart at the Crowne-fucking-Plaza. But here's a newsflash for you, Miss High-and-Almighty. We aren't as fucking stupid as you think!"

"I never said you were stupid," Em said, her voice flat.

He pointed a finger at her. "Ah, but you think that, don't you? You think you can get away with fooling the world, hiding some secret that you like women. But nah, you're just like Margo and Shirley. At least they're open about it."

"Oh, for fuck's sake, Bryan," Anna said, stepping forward. "Go home. You're spewing bullshit that you have no idea about. And leave Shirley and Margo out of this. They've done nothing to you!"

"You … you think you know everything, don't you? Well, we'll see about that!" Bryan said, full of bluster and self-confidence, then reversed slowly back to his own house.

When he pulled into his driveway, Em released her breath. He was so much like Callum.

"I may have to leave the housesit," Em said.

"Why? Because of Bryan? You know as well as I do that he's all bullshit. He may have been behind the chicken thing, but I doubt he's smart enough to work out the sex tape thing. But, hey, it wouldn't be the worst thing to sleep at the Crowne-fucking-Plaza," Anna joked.

"Yeah," Em said, tapping her side for the dogs to follow her home.

"But who'd feed the dogs, chickens and goats? As much as I would like to offer to help, I'm not sure I could handle two housesits at the same time."

Em looked over at her and smiled, grateful for her kindness.

Once they were back at Em's driveway, Anna waved her goodbye, reminding her to contact Kennedy. Resigned to her fate, Em fed the animals, then went inside, boosted the fire and pulled out her laptop. Ignoring the list of three hundred unread emails, she first opened a new email to the homeowner, John.

Hello John,

I'm not sure where you may be at the moment, but I feel I need to apprise you of a situation.

Earlier this week we had an incident at the farm, where three chickens were attacked, killed and beheaded. I've already told you about this, but there's more you need to be aware of.

Initially I thought wildlife had killed them, and therefore did not call the police. I interpreted the incident as a neighbourly prank. But the following day, I found a chicken head accompanied by a note, propped up on the front mat. That was when I got the police involved.

Since then, more information has come to light.

You may not be aware, but I am someone with a public profile, due to my husband's career. I have returned home to Australia to find solace and privacy, but events have pulled me back into the spotlight. I now have concerns that the media will discover my whereabouts. I am concerned this may cause discomfort with your neighbours, given the quiet nature of the area, and I am also concerned about further damage to your property and/or animals.

If you would prefer for me to leave, I understand, and will assist you in any way I can to find you a replacement housesitter. Until I hear from you, I will do due diligence to keep your property and animals safe from harm to the best of my ability.

I await your decision.
Em McKinney

That done, she poked the fire again, then picked up her phone. Seeing that she'd missed two FaceTime calls – one from Asher and one from Kennedy – she sent a quick message.

Hey Asher. Sorry. Got a call from Ryatt – Detective Ryatt. They think they know who leaked the video. Call me when you can. xx

As she headed to the kitchen, her phone buzzed. A FaceTime call came through almost immediately. When she picked up, she could hear music playing softly in the background. John Denver.

"Hey Asher. So sorry not to get back to you earlier. Ryatt called, then I went for a walk with the dogs," Em explained as she peered into the fridge, trying to find comfort food.

"It's okay. But you've missed Kennedy. She's heading to the airport. She's flying to Melbourne tonight. She'll be there … I don't know. Sometime tomorrow? The next day?"

Em slammed the fridge door. "She's not coming all this way because of the video, is she?"

"No, she's going for another work thing. But she's going to do some digging while she's there. Because, come on, Kat leaking the video?"

"So you know then? That they're saying it was Mum?" Em asked.

"*Alleged* to be your mom. That's what we were trying to call you about," Asher said, yawning. Em looked at the phone and saw it was close to bedtime for him.

"I don't get it," Em said, walking over and dropping on to the couch.

"It's bullshit. Just like the embezzlement thing is bullshit. Your mom couldn't even work out how to take photos on her phone until you showed her. Or work Apple Music. It just doesn't make sense. No, Kennedy's going to find out what the fuck is going on. She said she'll contact you when she arrives. But she's going to start in Melbourne, see what Callum is up to. Then she said she'll pop down to Hobart when she's done with the other work thing."

Em wondered if Kennedy knew Em wasn't actually in Hobart itself. But that didn't matter. She'd tackle that later.

"I was telling Kennedy that Kat is more scattered than anyone I know," Asher continued. "Maybe she left her laptop somewhere and someone found a way to access it, figuring it was easy money to blackmail you and Callum? Or maybe she left the campervan unlocked, and someone stole the laptop?"

Both of those scenarios made sense to Em. Except there had been no blackmail demand, and it had been almost twenty-four hours since the post went up. But why – and how – had her mother come into possession of the video? It had been baffling her all damn day.

"I've been trying to piece it together too," Em said. "I mean, if she left her phone somewhere, that makes sense. She's always doing that. I think I've bought her five phones in as many years. If she had her laptop stolen, which Ryatt seems to think …"

Em paused, realisation hitting her like a Mack truck.

"Her laptop," Em repeated. She stared at Asher on the screen of her new MacBook Pro. "She has my old laptop. That's the one that the video was on. I remember deleting it, but maybe it was still in the … what do they call it? Not the cloud, but when everything doesn't quite delete from the hard drive. Maybe it was buried in there and someone was savvy enough to pull it out?"

"And now someone else has your old laptop." Asher paused. "Em, what else was on it?"

21

I see you're finally paying attention, Mathilda.

That's good. You are finally experiencing what I did.

Your world, pulled apart, because of your very existence.

You seem to think you can control the situation.

But you can't. Only I can.

22

Just after nine o'clock, Em was curled up on the lounge, trying to focus on an episode of *Grey's Anatomy*, when the dogs leapt up, making her jump. She walked to the window to see what the commotion was about, her heart pounding in her chest. She couldn't see anything or anyone. No cars coming up the driveway. No light at all. She hoped it was just some wildlife. But when the chickens began squawking, Em ran to grab her jacket, gumboots and a torch from the mudroom, then called for the dogs. Their barking would scare anything away. She hoped.

Em stepped outside and shone the torch around but saw nothing. Creeping her way around the verandah towards the chicken coop at the side of the house, she illuminated the paddocks, but nothing looked out of the ordinary. Charlie bolted past her, jumped down from the verandah in one leap, and barked loudly towards the coop. Startled, Em dropped the torch, and watched as light bounced along the verandah, eventually coming to a stop and shining back into the house. She bent and reached for it, hoping whoever was out there didn't have an accomplice who would take advantage of her clumsiness and hack her to death.

Regaining her composure, she shone the torch outwards again.

None of the chickens were out from what she could see, and the gate latch was still firmly in place. Em walked slowly down the steps, went to the gate and let the dogs through. She peered into the chicken coop and tried to count the chickens, but they were so tightly packed into the back it was a futile effort. Something had clearly scared them.

Charlie was barking now, well beyond the coop, out towards the open field where the goats were. Em shone the light in that direction. She counted the goats, relieved to find they were all there, staring in her direction. Ruby barked quickly beside Charlie, but more like she was joining in with him than protecting anything. Billy stood plastered to her side, shivering in the cold.

When Charlie finally returned to them, Ruby in tow, Em breathed a little more easily and her tight shoulders dropped a little. She bent and patted Charlie to let him know she appreciated his efforts, but from what she could see, nothing was amiss.

"Wildlife?" she asked Charlie, and hoped this wouldn't be a nightly occurrence. The dogs had scared the crap out of her, especially with the events of the last few days weighing her down.

With the dogs inside and the house locked up, Em gave up on watching television and took herself to bed. But just as she began to doze off, Kennedy's words haunted her. *Everyone has secrets.* She grabbed her phone and re-read one of the messages Kennedy had sent the night before.

The man is a dirtbag. The more I dig, the worse he gets. Please let me release something on him.

Em contemplated the idea again. It would be nice to put Callum in his place. His text messages had not let up since the tape had been released. In the latest, he'd threatened to find her and make sure she knew who was in control. Em knew he wasn't in control. Not anymore. But allowing Kennedy to release something from the media was a risk she couldn't take. Despite Callum's threats, Em wasn't the type of person to do something like that. She cared about how circumstances affected other people, and the other people involved would be impacted far more than she would.

Besides, she had an agreement with Callum: he'd leave her business alone, as long as she didn't reveal what went on behind the scenes. But he was really testing her right now. The embezzlement piece was a major pivot, and she was tempted to give in to Kennedy. She just wasn't wholly convinced yet that Kennedy wasn't finding another way to do her job and using Asher to get it. Asher's point that Kennedy focused on reporting stories like her situation – of domestic abuse and misogynistic power plays – didn't really convince her either.

She turned over, snuggled down under the blankets and hoped sleep would come quickly. When Charlie came in and did his nightly three turns at the base of her bed, she finally felt comforted and secure.

A LOUD BANGING on the bi-fold door startled her and had the dogs bolting to the door. Charlie, who had slept in her room overnight, was now flying out of the room and to the other side of the house. Em poked her head around the corner of the bedroom to see the glass door at the end of the hallway. As she struggled to put her cardigan on against the cold, she saw Anna with Sachin by her side. Anna saw her and waved madly, with a desperate look on her face. Em followed the dogs and rushed to the door.

"I'm so sorry. I know it's early. But there's a dead goat down by the bottom gate. I was walking past and saw it. And, with everything else going on …"

"Come in, come in," Em said, ushering her and the old black Lab inside out of the cold. As Anna pulled off her gumboots, the dogs came to sniff their friend.

"God, what time is it?" Em asked, seeing it was barely light outside.

"Yeah, sorry. It's not quite seven. I'm heading to Mount Field today. There's snow up there so I thought I'd go for a hike. But I can't take Sachin, since it's a national park. Hence, the early hour for a walk." Anna closed the door behind her.

"Gotcha. So, a goat. It's dead? Are you sure?" Em said, wrapping her cardigan around her body.

"Looks dead to me. I mean, it looks to be an old one," Anna said, bending down to pat Charlie who was sniffing her leg, scoping her out. "But I wasn't sure. I'm not familiar with them."

"Neither am I. But you're right. With everything else going on, it's a worry. We heard something outside last night. The dogs went nuts, but when I went out, all the goats were accounted for. I didn't see anything." Em wondered now if someone had been out there after all. "Let me throw on some clothes and I'll go down and look. If you want, you can leave Sachin here today. I'm sure the doggies wouldn't mind his company. I don't want to hold you up."

"Oh, no. It's okay. I can go tomorrow. I'd rather stick around and help you with this," Anna said, but Em didn't want her to change her plans just because of a dead goat.

"No, you go. I can manage," she repeated, although she wasn't sure how she was going to haul a dead goat to the pit on her own. "I'll just get dressed. I'll be right back."

As she pulled on her old blue jeans and black turtleneck jumper, she considered calling Ryatt. Something else was dead in the paddock. First chickens and now a goat. Would this housesit ever go smoothly?

"Okay, point me in the direction where the goat is and I'll go and check it out," Em said as she opened the door to the verandah.

All four dogs plunged through the door, almost knocking Anna over. Em picked up her boots from just inside the door and took a seat on a chair outside to put them on.

"Seriously, I'll be okay dealing with this, if you want to go. And Sachin is okay with me today too. At least I hope he will be. God knows I haven't had the best of luck, but with the dogs, things seem to be normal," Em tried to joke, hoping Anna didn't see through the veil of insecurity about her ability to keep anything alive. She was relieved when Anna laughed.

"I'll stay. Mount Field can be tomorrow, and you're welcome to join me, if you like. It's only about two hours from here. We'd be back in time to walk the dogs before it gets too late."

Em considered it as she pulled her boots on. It would be nice to get away and enjoy nature for a while, especially with the sex tape out there.

"Maybe. Let's see what this is about first," she said, and tromped down the verandah stairs to the paddock gate, Anna following. The dogs joined them as they walked through wet grass towards the second gate, where the goats were enclosed. Em unlocked the gate and she and Anna slipped through, leaving the dogs looking rejected.

"Sorry, guys. You can follow us down the fence line, but you can't come in here," Anna said, then turned to Em. "Last thing we need is the dogs getting in the way."

"Good thinking," Em said.

At the bottom of the paddock, a goat lay on its side. Its eyes were open and its stomach was distended. Clearly dead. It was emanating a weird smell, too, like almonds, which explained why all the other goats were giving it a wide berth. Em looked around and saw three bright green leaves on the ground. One was half chewed and looked to have been spat out. She walked over and picked the other two up. She looked around. They weren't from any bush nearby.

"Look at these," she said, the leaves in her palm. "Where'd they come from?"

"Could be from someone walking the track who thought they'd throw something over the fence for the goats. Aren't goats known to eat anything?" Anna replied.

It was likely, Em mused. But now they had a more immediate worry. The pit was on the other side of the property. Somehow she had to drag the goat all the way up the hill and around the other side of the house. She felt defeated just thinking of it. She could use the wheelbarrow, of course, but getting the beast into it was going to take major muscle.

"Thanks for staying," Em said, resigned. "Looking at it and seeing where the pit is, I'm definitely going to need some help."

A voice came from down the track. "Killed something else, did ya?" It was Bryan, walking towards them from the road.

Great. That was all they needed.

"It's early," Em whispered. "How did he know we were here?"

"Creepster," Anna whispered back, staring at Bryan sauntering up the track. He wore the same stained grey track pants with a green hoodie, his dark hair greasy. When he reached the fence line, he peered over.

"Looks fucking dead to me. What did you do to it?" Bryan asked, then stood back, spreading his feet apart and digging his hands into his track pant pockets. His black gumboots were covered in mud.

"I didn't do anything to it," Em said, defiantly. "Anna said she found it this morning when she was out walking."

"So what did *you* do to it, then?" Bryan said to Anna, his tone both accusing and amused.

"Nothing. Probably died of old age," Anna said.

Em slipped the two leaves she was holding into the back pocket of her jeans and walked over to stand on the spat-out third one.

"Yeah, right. Knowing Mathilda's luck with animals around here, I doubt it. But I guess that means you're going to call your buddy, the detective. And I bet he's going to be paying me another visit. Fuck. Why don't you cu—"

"Bryan!" Shirley's voice rang out from the track. Em hadn't even seen her coming. She stormed up towards them. Em didn't think she'd ever seen her move so fast, or out and about so early.

"Go home, Bryan," said Shirley. "There's nothing for you to see here. Not unless you're going to help, but God knows you're about as useful as tits on a bull!"

"Well, fuck. The gang's all here. What? Do you all have a secret coven or something?" Bryan said, pushing away from the fence. "I'll be out today, in case your cop friend wants to have a chat. Just know, I had nothing to do with this either." He nodded towards the dead goat, then stalked back up the track, flipping Shirley off as he walked past her.

"Hi Shirley," Anna said.

"Morning, Shirley. Thanks for that," Em said, but Shirley waved her off.

"Saw him coming this way and heard the dogs last night. Figured something was up. So, what's happened here?" She looked down at the dead goat over the fence, her hands on her hips. But before Em could answer, she continued, "Ah, this one. He's an old one. John's had it for a while. Useless bloody thing. I'd just throw it in the pit and forget about it. No tears over this one."

"Well, I found something," Em said quietly, quickly looking up the track to see Bryan's retreating back. She pulled the leaves out of her pocket and picked up the chewed one.

"What are they?" Shirley asked.

Both Em and Anna shrugged.

"Not sure," said Em, "but I think I might call Ryatt, just to be sure. The dogs did go off at something last night. And I found these right before Bryan showed up."

"Well, if you think that's best," Shirley said, then looked up towards the house. "Might not be a bad idea, actually. We're going to need more help to get this thing up there and into the pit, and I wouldn't be calling Bryan back for *his* help. In the meantime, I'd move the other goats to another paddock, just to keep them away."

Em nodded, appreciative of her sage advice.

"You know, Tyler mentioned something interesting to me, late yesterday," Anna said. "He said he saw Bryan standing at his fence, watching you feed the goats the day before yesterday."

The thought made Em's skin crawl.

"Margo was talking to Tyler yesterday too," added Shirley. "He told her that he's seen a campervan at the park again. He reckons it's the same one he's seen before." Shirley grunted. "I have my doubts. There's always a van parked down there, although not many at this time of year. Too bloody cold for the mainlanders."

"So if it's not Bryan, could it be someone in a campervan?" Anna asked, as they stood around the dead goat. "I mean, it's not likely the campervan would be involved with the other stuff, but it's possible that they were the ones that threw the leaves over the fence."

"It could also be Tyler making shit up," Shirley scoffed.

But Em doubted that. The kid seemed to be genuine.

LESS THAN AN HOUR LATER, the remaining goats having been lured to the other paddock with Weet-Bix and grain, Em sat at the kitchen table with Anna, drinking coffee and eating sourdough and eggs, while they waited for Ryatt. Shirley had gone home, since she and Margo were heading to the Judbury markets.

When tyres hit the gravel outside, the dogs barked to let her know of the arriving visitor. This time Em was relieved it wasn't aggressive barking like the night before. She got up from the table and stepped onto the verandah as Ryatt made his way up the stairs.

"Morning, Ryatt," Em said. The dogs' tails wagged at him this time, knowing he was a friend rather than a foe. This morning, Ryatt's hair was still wet, and he was dressed in blue jeans, a thin blue jumper, and a parka thrown over the top. His boots, brown leather R.M. Williams, were so beaten up they looked like the ones he wore in high school.

"Hey guys," he said, patting each dog as he made his way towards Em. "Morning Mats. So, a dead goat, hey?"

"Yeah. I'll show you where it is, but come in. Anna is here. She was the one who alerted me to it earlier. We can fill you in before we go down there. I have coffee going if you're interested?" She opened the door as he kicked his boots off.

"Wouldn't say no," he said, walking through the door behind her.

"I think you already know Anna?" Em said, as she moved into the kitchen.

Ryatt nodded and took a seat at the table like he'd been there a thousand times before.

"So, you found the goat earlier this morning?" Ryatt asked, diving right in. From the kitchen, Em looked over to Ryatt and Anna talking at the table and felt weirdly comforted. It was nice to know people were on her side, even if it was over a dead goat.

Anna showed Ryatt the leaves while Em made the coffee. "We found these near the goat. They don't grow in the paddock. We think someone put them there."

He looked at them intently. "To be honest, I don't know what they are, but I can get them checked out. I think we should do a necropsy on the goat."

"That's a bit of an overkill, isn't it?" Em said, placing his coffee on the table.

Ryatt looked at her, then Anna, as if determining how much to say in front of her.

"It's not Anna, if that's what you're thinking," Em said. "She's a friend. She's helped me out already, first with the chickens, then when Bryan—"

"When Bryan what?" he asked, sharply.

"Bryan got a bit aggressive when we were all talking out on the road the other day, with Margo and Shirley. He reminded me of …"

"Callum? Doing his usual alpha male bullshit?" Ryatt asked.

Em saw Anna look at her, clearly surprised that Ryatt knew about Callum's antics.

"Yes," Em said. "So, it's not Anna behind it. Whatever you need to say, just say it."

Ryatt took a sip of his coffee, as if needing a moment to gather his thoughts.

"We've had a couple of calls about the, ah, video," Ryatt said, blushing. Em wanted to crawl into a hole and never come out. It was one thing hearing him talk about it over the phone. It was another hearing him talk about it in person.

"Okay," Em said quietly, looking away, then pulling the sleeves of her jumper down over her hands.

"We've learned that Callum is in Melbourne. Is it possible that he could have flown down here without us knowing, to do something like this? To kill the goat, I mean?" Ryatt asked.

Em shook her head. "I doubt he'd even know how. Getting his hands dirty is not something he'd do. But I did get some texts from him." She got up to get her phone from the kitchen counter. "Apparently he's not happy about the video getting out either."

She unlocked the phone, opened Callum's messages and handed the phone to Ryatt. He scrolled through, page after page, while he drank more coffee.

"There's, like, a hundred texts here," he said, exasperated. "That's harassment, Mats. And I see you haven't responded to any of them." He looked up at her.

She shook her head. "I haven't responded, no. On my lawyer's advice."

"Smart," Ryatt said. "Okay, let me make a call about getting the goat picked up and a necropsy scheduled. We'll get the leaves checked out too, just in case. I think we should just cover all bases. Between the headless chickens, the chicken head on the front mat, the notes, and now the goat, I think someone seriously has it in for you. And, while we wait, tell me what Bryan said to you."

Em replayed the scene for him. Within an hour, the Huonville police were picking up the goat and hauling it to the local vet. Ryatt asked to speak to her in private when he got up to leave. Em followed him out to the car.

"Look, I think Callum is behind the majority of what's been going on. Problem is, I can't prove it. But the, um, tape is a concern. There is the assumption it came from Kat since it looks to be her account. And as I said, that looks legitimate. But it doesn't add up for me, given what I know, and what you've said, about Kat."

"I can't work it out either. My partner's girlfriend is looking into it as well. She's a member of the media. Normally I wouldn't trust her, or someone like her, but I trust my business partner and his instincts. So, Kennedy is digging, but she's saying the same thing. Plus, no one has made any demands either."

"What does your gut say?" Ryatt asked.

"What do you mean?" Em was confused. Why would that matter? She wasn't the detective here.

"Because you've always had good instincts. Or you did," said Ryatt. Em felt the sharp barb in those words.

"Until I got together with Callum, you mean," Em said, but Ryatt shook his head.

"No. That's not what I meant. When I knew you back then, you were always very intuitive. You could read people really well. Your bullshit gauge was always on point. This is about who is harassing you, and I want to work out who's behind it. From what you know, who do you think is behind it?"

"Callum. My gut tells me it's Callum. I don't know how. Maybe he's hired someone, maybe Bryan, to harass me? But how would he know him? It's the video that doesn't make sense," she said, then paused.

How could she explain this about Callum, without exposing everything? This was one hell of a secret she'd held for a long time. But this part was Callum's secret, not hers. And if he was behind the harassment, then why would he expose this tape?

"Mats. What aren't you saying?" Ryatt prodded.

Em walked away from Ryatt, who was leaning against his car, and walked towards the gate heading to the chicken coop. As she wrapped her fingers around the cold metal, she considered her options.

She had trusted Ryatt before. The instincts he talked about included how she viewed him. But she wondered, if this got out, just how messy things would get with Callum, and she really didn't need to open that can of worms. Not when they were so close to finalising the divorce negotiations. Would this information weigh in her favour? Was she willing to throw dirt? Callum had started the slinging, though, hadn't he? When he released the embezzlement piece to the media.

Taking a huge breath, Em turned back to face Ryatt. He was standing straight now, facing her. He looked at her intently. His body language looked like he was in fight or flight mode. She exhaled, realising she had to trust him with this.

"There was another woman with me on that tape. You know that. But we weren't exactly willing participants. I mean, I knew about the woman, but ..." She shook her head. She wasn't explaining this well. "We had just moved to California, and I was completely reliant on Callum at that point. For everything. I didn't even have a visa at that point. But when we moved to America, the real Callum surfaced. I hadn't experienced it before then. Before we moved, he treated me like a queen. But once we got to California, he was ..."

"Did he ... force himself on you?" Ryatt asked slowly. She could see his fists opening and closing as he said it.

She shook her head. "No. But I was trying to keep my marriage together, so I agreed to his idea. I just didn't realise that meant being drugged, or that he would be taping us," Em said, her face feeling like it was on fire.

She took another deep breath, and when she exhaled, she felt like she was free-falling into an abyss. But she needed to tell him all of it if he was going to help her. Or most of it, anyway.

"The other woman, Kelli, was a young Hollywood actress. She was barely eighteen. Kelli was infatuated with Callum."

"And Callum ate that up, no doubt," Ryatt said.

"Yes," she replied. "He seduced her, and she fell for all his charms."

She paused again. Here it was. "If Callum is behind this, then I don't understand why. He's the one with the most to lose in this, because ..." Em heard footsteps on the verandah.

"Sorry to interrupt but ... your phone is going nuts in here, Em. I haven't looked at it, but it's pinging all over the place," Anna said, then walked down the steps from the verandah and handed Em her phone. "Look, I'm going to leave you to it, but I'll stop by later, okay?" She called for Sachin. "Call me if you need me."

"You sure she's not in on it?" Ryatt whispered, after Anna had turned the corner at the end of the driveway.

But Em wasn't hearing him. Staring at her phone, she saw multiple missed calls and one text from Kennedy that made her knees weak. With shaking hands, she held the phone up so Ryatt could see the message.

In Melbourne. Callum is MIA.

"So it could be Callum," Ryatt said.

Em shrugged.

"Look, I'm going to see what I can do to get this goat assessed quickly, then see if I can find out where Callum is. In the meantime, watch your back, okay?"

"I will," she said, gazing towards the cluster of trees and feeling as if eyes were on her.

"Just a thought, but if Callum isn't behind it, he may think you are. If he has the most to lose, as you said, then he may not be a happy boy about it."

Em nodded, knowing that was the understatement of the century.

23

Her phone dinged on the wooden table. She'd been ignoring it for the last twenty-four hours, but she knew she needed to talk to Kennedy at some point. She had been in Melbourne for close to two days now. Walking over to the phone, she picked it up, and saw text after text from Callum. Would he ever let up? She began scrolling.

Answer me for fuck's sake!

Em scrolled to the next message.

What game are you fucking playing, Mathilda? The media are on me like shit on a pig!

The name grated. Callum had refused to call her Em once they moved to America, insisting her full name sounded more sophisticated for their life in LA. Hearing Callum's voice in her head, saying her full name, made her feel dirty. She scrolled again.

You're a fucking cow, you know that? Fucking answer me!

Delightful. She slammed her phone back down on the table and burst into tears. His words were cutting, but she had had enough of it. She'd left him. She was done with his drama.

"Why did I put up with it for so long?" she asked the empty room, but she knew the answer. He was Callum Walsh, and he had charmed her, just as he'd charmed everyone else in his life.

At a noise, Em pivoted and looked behind her through the door. A small silver car was pulling up in the driveway, dust trailing behind it. Charlie began barking aggressively at the visitor. Em opened the door and saw a slim woman get out of the car. She was dressed in what Em would consider New York black, from head to toe, her spiral salon-blonde curls bouncing at every movement. The woman looked around as she slammed the door behind her. She turned towards Em.

Kennedy. What was she doing here?

"Hey there," Kennedy said.

She stayed near the car, looking cautiously at Charlie. When he stopped barking, he looked to Em.

"I'm not a fan of dogs," Kennedy said.

Em called Charlie to her. "Okay," Em said. "Let me put the dogs in the other yard. They're friendly, but …"

"Even so. Not a fan," Kennedy said, staying put.

When Em had secured them, Kennedy walked towards her.

"Thanks."

"What are you doing here?" Em asked, her hands on her hips.

"Did Asher not tell you I was coming?" Em tried to cast her mind back. "Well, he was supposed to. Doesn't matter. I'm here now. So, this is Nay-meen-ar River?" Kennedy looked around.

Em winced at the butchered pronunciation. It was an Aboriginal word, Anna had told her. Before she could correct her, Kennedy continued.

"How the hell would anyone think to find you here? Seriously! It's—"

"Peaceful," said Em.

Kennedy snorted. "Except when someone is out for revenge, or whatever it is that's going on," Kennedy said. "And holy shit. It's freezing cold!"

"Welcome to winter in Tasmania."

When Em looked at Kennedy, she saw a journalist taking in the surroundings through judgemental eyes. Did she want to let Kennedy inside? Into her world? Not really. The woman represented a profession Em hadn't trusted in years. But, looking at Kennedy shivering on the driveway, she reminded herself that Kennedy was also Asher's girlfriend.

Em smiled, but it was the smile she'd practised many times over, for when she'd had to stand in front of a million cameras at Callum's movie premieres.

"Follow me," she said. She headed up the steps to the verandah. "The fire is going inside." She kicked off her boots and opened the door, reflecting that she never would have expected to be allowing this woman into her private space.

"Thanks," Kennedy said. She followed Em's lead and began unzipping her black boots.

"Bring those inside with you," Em suggested, noticing the red soles and realising Kennedy's boots probably cost her a small fortune. Who the hell would wear Louboutin boots in rural Tasmania?

"Good idea," Kennedy said, carrying them inside in her stockinged feet. She left them by the door.

"Would you like a coffee? Tea?" Em asked. She went to the kitchen and switched the coffee maker on.

"If it's not too much trouble. I grabbed a coffee in Melbourne before I left, but that feels like a week ago, not hours." Kennedy stood at the kitchen counter, admiring Em's latest baking creations. "I see you're still baking. That's great. Asher said you were working on your cookbook while you're here. How's that going?"

"Okay. Slowly. I seem to be losing stuff. This morning it was the paddle for the Mixmaster. I used it yesterday and could have sworn I put it back on the machine after washing it. I suppose with all this other stuff going on I just seem to be losing it. Or it feels that way, anyway. Bah. It's fine."

Em knew she was rambling. Having Kennedy standing there watching her every move was unnerving. It was one thing to chat with her online or over FaceTime, but it was another thing altogether to be face to face with the woman.

"What kind of coffee do you want?" Em asked.

"Oh! Ah ..." Kennedy hesitated, which made Em think that she was probably the type to order something really complicated, like a half decaf, lite milk mocha with a caramel shot, extra hot, and extra whipped cream in LA.

"How about a hot chocolate or a cappuccino?" Em asked.

Kennedy blushed. "Cappuccino would be great. Thanks."

"So this is a work visit?" Em asked, turning to froth the milk.

Kennedy was quick to respond. "God, no! No, I'm here as your friend. I found out more of what's going on in Melbourne. I haven't reported it yet. I wanted to see you first."

"Did you find Callum? You said he was MIA." Em finished Kennedy's coffee with a dash of chocolate powder and placed it in front of her.

"Thanks, and no I didn't find him. And no one knows where he is either. The producers were tight-lipped, as expected. I talked to one of the makeup artists. They usually have an ear to the ground. He said Callum was last seen heading off to a nightclub called Revs, with one of the young female extras, a couple of nights ago."

Em rolled her eyes. Typical Callum behaviour.

"The extra was back at work the next day. She said she'd left Callum at the nightclub around two before heading home. He never showed the following morning. And, as you can imagine, the director and producers are pissed." Kennedy picked up her coffee and took a sip. "Oh, thanks for this. That hits the spot."

"He's probably shacked up with some woman he met at the club, got high and lost track of time," Em said, looking down at a broken fingernail.

"That's what they're assuming, but the director and producer are not happy campers."

"Well, he's had no trouble texting me." Em leaned against the kitchen counter, wrapping her fingers around her own latte.

"Then we know he's alive, at least," Kennedy said.

That much was true, Em thought, but something wasn't sitting right.

"Callum has pulled all-nighters at LA clubs before and still managed to get to the set the following day, said Em. "He's all about his career and his reputation, so this isn't like him at all."

Where *was* he?

"There's more," Kennedy said cautiously, her eyes focused on Em, watching her reactions. "More I wanted to talk with you about. I was planning on coming to talk to you before this Callum-missing thing happened. It's about the video ..."

Em stepped back from Kennedy until she was in the opposite corner of the kitchen. While she knew Kennedy was the one who told her about the video initially, she still didn't trust her or her intentions. Kennedy was still the media, after all. Em had trusted and been burned by the media before. And look where she was now. Hiding on the other side of the world because of the carnage they created. But Kennedy was also Asher's girlfriend, and that was the only reason Em was willing to hear the woman out.

"Look, I know it's a sensitive situation. One I don't envy. But we both know what Callum is. And ... I know there's more to the story, too." Kennedy paused, looked intensely at Em before she continued. "I am friends with the other woman in the video. Kelli. We've been friends now for a couple of years."

Em felt her legs buckle under her like she'd been whacked behind her knees. Fuck! Could it get any worse?

"I talked to Kelli when the video was leaked, and she's just as freaked out as you. She doesn't want ..." Kennedy looked down at her mug, appearing to be struggling with something.

"Oh, just spit it out, Kennedy."

"Kelli told me about the conversation you had with her after she—"

"Found out she was pregnant?"

Kennedy looked up, relief in her eyes. "Yes. And with the tape out, she doesn't want Leo ..." Kennedy stopped, looking like she'd put her foot in it.

"I'm aware of Leo," Em said. "I know he exists. So does Callum. So do his lawyers, who had Kelli sign an NDA and slapped a suppression order on her to stop her disclosing who the father is."

"Except Leo is the spitting image of Callum. Anyone who sees that tape and knows Kelli will take one look at Leo and work it out. Kelli is freaking out. She's even stopped working because of it."

"Well, she should have enough money to cover her expenses until this all blows over," Em said, her tone cold, knowing Kelli was paid a couple of million dollars for her silence. "I know that sounds horrible, and believe me, I wish I could be empathetic to her, but—"

"But what?" Kennedy asked. "She was tricked, Em. Just like you were."

"What? No she wasn't. She was fully aware of who Callum was and what she was doing!"

"And who told you that?"

"What?"

"Who told you she was aware of what was happening?"

"Callum. Who else? Plus, I was there, remember?"

"And were *you* fully aware of what was going on?" Kennedy asked. Em was silent.

"Exactly. You were told one lie. Kelli was told another. Kelli was expecting an intimate dinner with Callum. Alone. And it started out that way. He was supposed to have met her at seven-thirty but told her he was running late. So instead, he gave her directions to a hotel and told her to meet him in the hotel bar at eight-thirty. What were you told?"

Em didn't reply for a moment. Should she tell Kennedy? Callum had brought Kelli up to the hotel room at nine, and by that time, she seemed to have no inhibitions, despite finding Em in the hotel room as well.

"I was meeting him there at eight. He wanted a ..."

"A threesome?" Kennedy asked. "He told you something different than what he told her," she stated. Her delivery was matter-of-fact, and she didn't look surprised.

"He wanted a threesome," said Em, "but I didn't expect Kelli to be so young. And I didn't expect there to be drugs involved."

"And I bet you didn't expect him to film it, either. Did he drug you, or were you complicit?"

Em's head snapped back in Kennedy's direction. "*What?*"

"He drugged Kelli," Kennedy said. "Gave her something in the bar without her knowing. She said they'd already been on a few dates, and this was the night they were supposed to have sex for the first time. She went to the bathroom in the bar to throw up, she was so nervous. When she got back, she finished her drink, and they went up to the hotel room together. But by then, she said she was floating. Feeling really happy. She said she doesn't remember seeing you in the room until you were naked on the bed and going at it."

That was how Em remembered it too.

"So? Did he drug you, or were you complicit?"

Kennedy was pushing her, and Em could feel the journalist talons coming out. She shook her head. She couldn't do this.

"I'm sorry, Em. I'm really just trying to understand. Kelli is my friend. You're my friend. At least, I hope so. Asher trusts me, and I wish you did as well, because what this guy, your soon-to-be ex-husband, has done to both of you is criminal. The fact that Kelli has a child with him makes her ill, but she's also Catholic. She couldn't bring herself to get an abortion. Can you imagine how that feels?"

Em's eyes welled. She knew why Kelli had gone through with the pregnancy.

"Look. I know what it feels like to be in Kelli's shoes," Kennedy said. "I was once in a similar situation."

"What?" Em gasped.

"I was raped by my brother's best friend when I was seventeen. He roofied me."

"Oh my God ..." Em whispered.

"Yes. Miller had convinced everyone that he was the all-round American good-guy, best friends with everyone. Girls loved him. Parents loved him, including my own. He was the star quarterback. Miller's shit didn't stink. And we dated for about three months the summer after my high school graduation, before that night. My parents were over the moon at the pairing. My brother thought it was the best thing ever. Then Miller raped me. And no one believed me.

Not my mother. Not my father. Not even my brother. And when I found out I was pregnant, before I could say what I wanted, there was a wedding planned, because – surprise – Miller was Catholic. It didn't matter that I wasn't eighteen. To everyone else, I was the slut who had lost her virginity to the golden boy and had trapped him by getting pregnant. How could I dare do that to him!" Kennedy tried to smile but it was half-hearted at best. "It was a nightmare."

"What happened?" Em asked, so shocked by this information that she had forgotten what Kennedy represented – her enemy. Now she was her sister. Someone who understood.

"I ran. I'd just received a partial scholarship at Washington State University to do a journalism degree, so I packed a bag and left for Seattle. Once I got there, I terminated the pregnancy. I couldn't keep it..." Kennedy paused. Em knew the full force of that decision. "After that, I worked my ass off to get through four years of college, juggling three jobs to pay the bills. I haven't returned home since."

"Wow," Em said.

Kennedy nodded, then squared her shoulders and lifted her chin up in defiance. "I've been fighting the fight for women like me ever since. You and Kelli are no different."

"I guess we aren't," Em finally admitted. "What happened with Miller?"

"He went on to the University of Texas, on a full football scholarship. He was accused of date rape by three girls in the first year. Last I heard, he's still locked up."

"Good," Em said. "That's good."

"My only regret is that I didn't report him too. But by the time I'd had the abortion and got my life together, I didn't want to think about him anymore. I just wanted to move on. It wasn't until my roommate was date raped that I decided to do something about it." She took a drink of her now-cold coffee, then screwed her nose up at it.

Em reached over and took her cup. She dumped the contents in the sink and held the cup up, asking if Kennedy wanted another. She nodded.

"So ... you were drugged too?" Kennedy asked softly, as Em turned to the coffee machine.

Em nodded, ever so slightly.

"Do you think it was ecstasy?"

Em nodded again. Having her back to Kennedy made the admission easier. But she was no wimp. She turned back to Kennedy. Taking a deep breath, she told her the truth.

"I had a headache that night and wanted to bail on the whole idea. Callum gave me what I thought was ibuprofen, then asked me to just give it a chance to work."

"But it wasn't ibuprofen, was it?"

"No. I felt strange fairly quickly after that. I felt like Kelli did, I suppose. Uninhibited. Floaty. A few months later, when news of Kelli's pregnancy came, it was a shock."

"That was a surprise to her, too. Kelli was on the pill, against her upbringing, but she'd been sick the month before and had taken some antibiotics. She was young; she didn't know until later that antibiotics can alter the effectiveness of the pill. She didn't think to ask, and if the pharmacist did tell her that, she didn't hear it. She also said Callum said he used condoms."

"Not that night," Em said, remembering that detail vividly.

Em knew she'd said enough. She gritted her teeth, her rage simmering beneath the surface. She refused to give Kennedy any more details of that fateful night. Knowing how it had gone for Kelli was one thing, but what had happened to Em had to stay hidden.

"Well, it seems that Callum is not the golden boy he wants everyone to believe either. He's no different from Miller," said Kennedy.

Em nodded, giving her a long look. "So, what are we going to do about that?"

There was a silent understanding in the air as they contemplated their next move.

24

anic barking from the dogs, still in the outer paddock, and the sound of screeching tyres on the road outside broke the silence. Em bolted outside and looked down the hill to see a blue Ford Mustang speeding in reverse, smoke billowing around the tyres, then turning fast into her driveway.

Callum.

"Is that ..." Kennedy stopped mid-sentence, watching from the doorway as the blue Mustang drove aggressively towards them. Em couldn't think above the sound of the dogs, so she called over to hush them, but a car driving fast up the driveway, spitting gravel as it went, was good reason for them to be going off.

"Stay inside," Em threw back at Kennedy. The last thing she needed was for Callum to see Kennedy Wright with her. She didn't know if she and Kennedy were friends at this point, but she found herself wanting to protect whatever the relationship was, especially from Callum.

Em slowly walked down the steps as her ex-husband climbed out of the muscle car. He slammed the door behind him, looked around, then zeroed in on Em.

"What the fuck do you think you're doing?" he screamed, striding towards her.

His dark blond hair was styled perfectly, the result of no less than an hour in front of the mirror, getting the kinks to sit just right. His eyelashes, permanently dyed a darker brown than his hair, outlined blue eyes that raged at her. He looked like the action heroes he liked to play. But Em knew her ex-husband – the wrinkled chambray shirt he wore and the equally rumpled grey t-shirt he had on underneath were tell-tale signs of just how livid he was. Normally the chambray shirt, his signature style, would be pressed perfectly, thanks to whatever assistant had been assigned to him. But not today.

She walked through the gate, but stayed close to it in case she needed something between her and Callum.

"I asked you a fucking question, Mathilda! What the fuck are you doing?" His voice was booming, and he was now standing so close she could see the red lines in his eyes, and his mouth quivering.

Em had no doubt that Margo and Shirley could hear every syllable all the way from their house. The dogs were relentless, making their anxiety known. When Callum reached out and wrapped his hand around her upper arm, his fingers digging in so hard she knew they would leave a mark, Charlie growled behind her. She yanked her arm away and stepped to the side.

"You need to stop this bullshit now! Pull that fucking video." His voice was pure venom.

"It wasn't me. The media are saying it was Mum, but it wasn't her either." Em asked. "Think about it, Callum. What would Mum gain by releasing it?"

His face went white. Then, in true Callum form, he laughed sarcastically. "We both know what her motives would be. To get back at me. She's always hated me." God, he was a narcissist. It was always about how the world felt about Callum Walsh. He had to be adored by everyone.

"It doesn't matter who released it," he yelled. "You know what it can do, if the wrong person decides to speak!" His eyes were cold. Spittle flew from his mouth.

Em stepped back further. "You mean Kelli?" she asked quietly.

"You know perfectly well who I mean. Just kill it. Kill the video.

And don't fuck with me or my life! You know better than to do that! I will fucking kill you if people find out!"

Em stayed silent, letting Callum's words fly past her. *Don't be rattled by him. Don't be rattled by him.*

"Are you threatening your wife, Callum Walsh?" Behind her, Kennedy's voice rang out, loud and clear. "Because I just heard you threatening her. And what is it that you're hiding, Callum? What interesting facts would your fans like to know?"

Em spun around and saw Kennedy with her phone raised and pointed at her and Callum. She quickly shook her head at Kennedy.

"Mathilda. What the fuck did you do?" Callum's voice was quiet and his words slow, full of steel.

She turned back to Callum. His face had turned to full on rage.

"I didn't ..." But she knew she had to step up and stand up for herself. "Actually. Yes, I did. I told Kennedy Wright everything. And you know why? Because I trust her, more than I trust you." She saw Callum move towards her once again, but she didn't move. Couldn't move.

"Keep going, Callum. Let the whole world know who you really are," Kennedy prodded from behind.

Em heard a siren in the distance. It seemed so foreign among the quiet surroundings. Behind Callum's rented Mustang, Em saw Margo and Shirley approaching. Callum wasn't aware of their presence, only that Kennedy was filming him without his permission.

"Tell her to back the fuck off, Mathilda," he growled.

"No," Em squeaked.

He stepped up to her, his face now so close she smelled sour milk mixed with coffee on his breath. "Tell her to stop videoing, or I'll make your life a living hell," he growled, spit hitting Em's cheek. His breath reeked.

Em stepped back. Callum's nostrils flared. She squared her shoulders and took a deep breath before she said the next words.

"How is that different than the last five years, Callum? You've always done what you wanted. Treated me like I was a mere convenience. I've turned a blind eye to everything, but I'm done with that. I can't keep doing that. I left you, and our marriage. I'm not the one responsible for your behaviour. You are. You need to take ownership of your mistakes. Kelli is a good person. She deserves better."

"You don't think that whore is living the high life already?" Callum raged. "She's got a better house – and a better income – than we had straight out of high school. I made sure of that. I had to, to make sure that stupid little bitch would not run off her fucking mouth!"

"Yes, but she didn't know she'd be drugged or that you'd have unprotected sex with her. I'm sure it's not the life she dreamed of having, the night you raped her," Em said quietly. She was so quiet, she doubted Kennedy got any of her words on camera from where she was standing.

"Well, it was her choice not to get an abortion when I told her too."

"The girl was Catholic. And a virgin. And, for some reason, she thought you walked on water. Guess she got to see the real Callum Walsh, huh? Like some of us are so lucky to have experienced," Em said, sarcasm dripping from her tongue.

"Step back, Callum," a voice boomed behind them.

Ryatt. How was Ryatt there? Em whipped her head around and saw him standing next to his unmarked car, his hand resting on his holster. Oh geezus!

"It's fine, Ryatt," Em said, stepping back, trying to put some distance between her and Callum while she could.

Ryatt stepped forward.

"I will kill you, Mathilda, if you don't put an end to that video circulating," Callum whispered to Em. "And I'll bury you if this leaks." Then he turned around to face Ryatt, his hands raised like he was about to be arrested, and turned on the movie-star charm.

"All good, officer. We're just having a lovers' spat. Just ironing out some details of our divorce, which I'm sure you've read about." Callum's smile was megawatt. "Sounds like you already know who I am. What's your name, officer? Just so I can let your superiors know what an outstanding job you're doing, keeping the neighbourhood safe." Callum's eyes flicked towards Kennedy, making sure she was getting this on camera too.

"Oh, for fuck's sake," Shirley said from the sidelines. "What do you think this is? A bloody movie?"

"Shirl. Let the detective do his job," Margo said. Had they heard all that had been said?

"I know who you are, Callum Walsh," Ryatt said, his hand not moving from his holster. "I've known you since high school. Seems like not much has changed since then, either. Seems you're still a bully."

Em saw anger flash cross Callum's face again.

"What the fuck are you talking about?" Callum said, lowering his hands.

"I'm Detective Josh Ryatt. I went to high school with you and Mathilda. At Pennant Hills High. You're one of the reasons I became a police officer. To eradicate bullies like you."

"You've got to be kidding me. Joshy? Joshy from Penno High?" Callum's voice sounded just like the voice he had back at Pennant Hills. Not the voice-coached one he used now.

"One and the same. Now, I'll ask you again, Callum. Step back from Mathilda."

Callum laughed, then took a very exaggerated step away from Em, a move that was supposed to be comical, but fell flat. No one, it seemed, was buying the charms of Callum Walsh here.

Em stood dead still, but could feel herself begin to shake. No, no, no. She couldn't have a panic attack now. She had to keep strong. Face up to Callum, once and for all.

"How did you know where Em was?" Kennedy asked, suddenly at Em's side.

"Great question," Ryatt said, stepping forward. "Mathilda advised me that she had not told you where she was, Callum."

Em felt Kennedy's cold hand reach for hers and wrap around it. Holding Kennedy's hand felt odd yet reassuring. It immediately calmed her.

"Well, it was kind of easy, actually," said Callum. "I knew she was in southern Tasmania. Seems as if everyone knows that little tidbit. So I asked around. Wasn't until I was having a beer in the local pub last night that some guy told me exactly where to find her. In fact, he was more than obliging once he realised who I was."

The guy was incredible, Em thought. He truly believed everyone was a fan of Callum Walsh.

"Where?" Ryatt asked, but Callum looked confused and stayed silent. Ryatt spoke again. "Where were you having the beer last night?"

"I told you. At the local pub," Callum said.

"There's more than one pub in southern Tasmania, you moron. In case you haven't noticed," Shirley added.

Ryatt shot Shirley a look, but then Callum displayed his true self: "Oh, shut up, bitch."

"Don't speak to me that way, you little upstart! You don't want to cross me," Shirley said, stepping forward, but Margo pulled her back. Em could see the anger simmering in Margo's face too.

"We'll just be going home, Ryatt. Let you do your job. Em, love, call later if you need us. Okay?" Margo called to her, then took Shirley's elbow and turned her around, but not before Shirley shot Callum the middle finger.

Kennedy giggled and Em's lips curled into a side smile. But Callum's face wiped it away just as quickly.

"Oh, I see how it is now," Callum said, chortling. "You have the old bats looking out for you!" he laughed, then turned to her. "That's cute. Real cute."

Em looked down. She wanted to slap him. He was so incredibly rude and arrogant, it was embarrassing.

"Mats?" Ryatt's voice brought her back. "Did Callum threaten you at all?"

Em stared at him. The question floated in the air like a dark, threatening thunderstorm. She could feel Callum's threat in her heart, while his eyes bored into hers. He, too, was waiting for her answer. What was she supposed to say? Yes, Ryatt, Callum had threatened her ... but to say so would bring hell and damnation upon her, in court, in private, in texts. All she wanted was for everything to be peaceful. For Callum to be out of her life, forever.

But this confrontation, in front of people, changed things. She knew she needed to step up and admit that he had done exactly what Ryatt was asking, but where would it get her? She wasn't divorced from him yet. It wasn't over. He still had control over her. And he knew it.

"No," she whispered. "But it's not a lovers' spat, either. He's pissed off about the video." That was as close to the truth as she could get.

"Are you sure? Are you okay?" Ryatt asked.

Em hesitated, then nodded.

"Okay then," Ryatt said then turned to Callum. "Then Callum, I'm going to ask you to leave the premises."

"Why?" Callum spat out, his voice whiny like a five-year-old. "I have every right to be here. She's my wife." He lifted his arm to point at Kennedy. "And I've more of a right than that cu—"

"You'll leave," cut in Ryatt, "because there have been disturbance complaints from the neighbours, and you are the reason for the complaints."

Callum stood dumbfounded. Em wondered if he'd ever been told to leave anywhere before. Callum Walsh was always the reason people wanted to *be* somewhere. He was always the centre of attention. But not this time.

"Then I'm going to request that Kennedy Wright leave as well," Callum said eventually, thrusting his hands in his pockets in defiance. "And she needs to hand over her phone, so I can delete the video she took of me."

"There was no complaint against Ms Wright. And if I'm not mistaken, she's welcome to be here." Ryatt looked at Em, who glanced quickly at Callum, then nodded.

"Are you fucking kidding me? What the hell did you say to her? She's the *media*, Mathilda. The enemy, remember?" He stepped towards her once more.

"Mr Walsh? I will ask you once more, and once more only. Otherwise, I will arrest you for trespassing. Please. Leave the premises." Ryatt stood and waited. Callum faced Em, then looked over at Kennedy and back to Ryatt.

"Whatever is going on here, it's not good. Fine. I'll go. But you haven't heard the end of this, Mathilda! And if there's anything in the media about this, or me, then you'll be hearing from my lawyers. And you *know* what they can do."

Kennedy squeezed her hand. Ryatt looked at Em as Callum strutted to the Mustang, yanked the door handle open and got in. Em felt her cheeks burn. Callum revved the car, then spitting rocks behind him, turned the car and sped back down the driveway.

"You okay?" Ryatt asked.

Em nodded. She took a few breaths, then said, "Yeah. I'm fine."

"He did threaten you, though, didn't he? Off the record?" Ryatt said.

"Yeah, but it's not unusual. It's how he reacts when he's feeling under pressure. Because he knows that if I decide to speak up, his career is over. And that's what's making him nervous. He knows that I could destroy his life if I wanted to," Em said, then turned and walked heavily up the steps, opened the door with shaking hands, and went back inside.

25

You think you are so clever, Mathilda.

You keep thinking it's that idiot husband of yours.

Still, it's nice to have such a convenient scapegoat.

This will be fun.

26

Em was surprised when both Kennedy and Ryatt followed her inside. She wanted to be alone, to collect her thoughts, to calm her pounding heart. Callum was so pissed off about Kennedy being here and then Ryatt telling him to leave. She knew he'd make her pay. She knew that for a fact. It was how he operated. The question now was how? Maybe it had already started. Maybe he was the one behind all the things happening at the housesit.

"Mats?" said Ryatt. "I need to ask you some follow-up questions. Since this was a formal complaint."

"Can you give me a minute? I just need to use the bathroom," Em answered quickly, hoping to escape for a minute or two.

"Yeah, of course," he replied, and stood in the doorway.

"I'll make you a coffee while you wait," said Kennedy.

"Do you know how?" Em asked, half seriously.

"I exist on coffee and yoga. I know how to do both quite well, thanks very much. Now go. I've got this covered," Kennedy responded, switching on the coffee machine with attitude.

"I won't be a minute," Em said and escaped into the bedroom's ensuite.

She closed the door and took a few deep breaths, her hand on her chest, trying to calm herself. Callum showing up was not what she'd expected, but at least it answered the question of where he was. His anger at her was not a surprise, given what the video release meant, but the intensity of his anger always took her by surprise. It was quite a feat to keep that part of his personality under wraps. She really didn't know how his PR team did it. They were worth every penny he paid them.

But now others had seen how he treated her. That was new. Usually he gushed about her, about how proud he was of his wife, when he was in a public forum. In private, he called her a fat, lazy failure, and taunted her that she would never find the level of success he had.

Except his version of success was different to hers.

She had to find out who released the video. Clearly it had come from her laptop, which is probably why Callum believed she had released it. She knew her mother hadn't. So who had – and what did they have to gain from it? And how did they know how to find her mother and gain access to her laptop? That was the million-dollar question.

Em flushed the toilet, splashed her face with some cold water and ran her hand through her hair, trying to tame the mess. She grabbed a hair tie and wrangled her hair into a topknot, then headed back in to face Ryatt's questions.

When she walked out into the living room, she found Kennedy and Ryatt sitting like two old friends at the long wooden table. Coffees sat in front of them, as well as a plate of cookies Em had made the day before. Crumbs lay scattered on the table in front of Ryatt.

"Are these more of your creations, Mats? Because I'm serious, you really should open a bakery or something," Ryatt joked.

He was back to being Ryatt the friend, not Ryatt the cop. She liked this version better.

"You're a hoot, Detective Ryatt. Now, what are these questions you have for me?" Em said, and moved to the coffee machine.

"I didn't make you one, sorry. I didn't know what you wanted," Kennedy said. "Sorry about that."

"It's okay. I've got it. Like you, I exist on coffee. Just not on yoga.

Although that explains why Asher is so into it lately." Em watched Kennedy blush.

"I've been doing some more digging," Ryatt said, returning the conversation to the matter at hand. "Shirley and Margo's call came in when I was heading out this way anyway."

"So they called the police?" Em asked.

"Yes. Said they heard Callum clear across to their place and he was threatening you. Sounded like he was about to take a cricket bat to you or something. They were clearly worried."

"Nice to know the neighbours are looking out for you, and that they aren't starstruck by the Great Callum Walsh," Kennedy said.

"Yeah," Em said, although she was embarrassed by the unwanted attention.

"So about Callum's threat … are you willing to put that on the record?" Ryatt asked.

"No," Em said, quickly.

"Why the hell not?" Kennedy exclaimed. "After what we were just talking about before his highness turned up?"

Em shook her head.

"What were you talking about?" Ryatt asked, intrigued.

"Nothing. It doesn't matter," Em said, drowning out any further conversation as she began to froth milk. She could feel Kennedy's eyes burning a hole in her back.

When she was done, she turned around and leaned against the kitchen counter. "Someone released that video. It wasn't me and it wasn't my mother. She wouldn't know how. So the question is, who did? And how did they get access to her laptop? That's what you need to look into."

"Is there any chance that the video was posted somewhere online just after it happened?" asked Ryatt. "Maybe you weren't aware? Would Callum have done that for kicks, so he could access it whenever he wanted to?"

Em thought. She hadn't considered that. It would be like him to do something that sick.

"It's possible, I suppose. But he wouldn't. It would be too risky,"

Em said, then immediately swore under her breath. She had not meant to divulge that.

"Why risky?" Ryatt asked quickly. "Em. If you want me to help you, you need to be open with me. Is this something you want to talk about without Kennedy present?"

"No. Kennedy knows," Em said.

"Then why won't you share it with me, too? I'm on your side, remember?" Ryatt said.

Em picked up her coffee and joined them at the table. A FaceTime call came in on Kennedy's phone just as she sat down.

"It's Asher. Want me to bring him in?"

Em hesitated, then nodded. She still wasn't clear on where things stood between them, but he knew everything already. It would be easier to have this conversation with all three of them.

"Hey love. I'm here with Em and the Hobart detective, Ryatt," Kennedy said, her face softening significantly when she saw Asher's broad face on the screen.

He looked exhausted. Em stared into her coffee, calculating the time. It would be late afternoon for him. He would have put in a full day already, covering her part of the business as well. Guilt flooded her.

"Hey guys. Hey Em. You doing okay? You look …" Asher was like that. Always concerned about others before considering himself.

"Callum just showed up," Kennedy interjected.

"Yeah, I was about to ask if it was something along those lines. Like, you look like you've been Callummed," Asher said, nodding.

"Callummed?" Ryatt asked.

Asher grimaced and stayed quiet.

"What he means is I look like I do when Callum has been confrontational with me," Em replied. "Like he was today. When he's gone on a rant or thrown abusive comments my way."

"So today was not unusual?" Ryatt asked. "It's not just in texts that he abuses you like that?"

"What the fuck did he do?" Asher asked, his protector instincts clearly kicking in.

"Down boy. We've got it covered," Kennedy replied.

"He came to tell me to take the video down," Em said, taking a sip of her coffee.

"Demanding to know, you mean," Kennedy said.

"Asher, can I ask you a question? If that's okay with you, Mats?" Ryatt asked.

She nodded, ignoring the surprised look on Asher's face when he heard Ryatt's nickname for her.

"It sounds like you've experienced Callum this way before," said Ryatt. "Can you describe how he reacts?"

Asher seemed to look right at Em through the video screen and she nodded, giving him permission.

"It's okay," she said. "I talked to Kennedy about it earlier. Ryatt just witnessed the end of one of Callum's tantrums today."

"Okay," Asher said, and went on to describe an almost identical scene, including the threat, which had happened only two months before in the back of their café. It was the day she'd served Callum with divorce papers.

"Clearly he didn't see the divorce notification coming?" Ryatt asked.

"Oh, I told him. I told him I was done. That our marriage was over. He thought I was joking," Em answered.

Ryatt began, "I hate to ask this question, but it's one I have to ask ..."

"Ask away," Em said.

"Why do you think he wanted to hold on to the marriage? Wouldn't he be better off a free man? To live the life he wants?"

Kennedy smirked.

"Why are you smiling at that?" Em asked, but Kennedy shook her head.

"Fine," said Em. "Well, I guess that's a question I've asked myself repeatedly since I left him. He's been fighting the divorce, and I thought that was because he likes to be in control. But sometimes I wonder if it's because he knows I can destroy his career. So maybe he wants to keep me close? You know that saying, 'Keep your friends close and your enemies closer'? But then I remember that he wasn't always such a dick, and maybe he really just doesn't want to let go."

Ryatt coughed.

"Okay, so maybe he always was that way," Em admitted. "But I didn't experience it myself, not for a long time."

"Because he didn't let you see that side. Or more likely, you were probably too busy supporting him to see it," Asher said. "You've admitted that yourself. You worked, while he played. I mean, the way you describe the early days, it's all romantic and stuff, but he was using you then, too. Let's face it, with his lack of talent, he got lucky with the roles he's been given. Maybe he's bullied his way into the roles? Maybe he charms his way in? Who knows."

"Maybe. I was just happy with the stability. It wasn't until we moved to America that things started going downhill. Then something happened and he felt, I don't know, like he was stuck with me. Because I knew his truth."

"And what truth was that?" Ryatt asked.

But Em shook her head. She could reveal the secret about Kelli, but if the truth got out about what Callum did to further his career, he would destroy her, well and truly. Or kill her. That had become a real possibility, especially with the other things happening around the farm. She was starting to believe Callum was behind it all. Somehow. Some way.

"He gaslighted you. But is this thing different from the Kelli thing?" Kennedy asked.

"Who's Kelli?" Ryatt asked.

Kennedy looked at Em with an apologetic look, mouthing the word 'sorry'.

"Kelli is the mother of Callum's child. His secret child," Em said in a tone intended to shut down further questions.

"Okay. That was not the answer I was expecting," Ryatt said.

"And yes, it's a different thing," Em said, using the same tone and looking at Kennedy.

"So, why not expose him with it all?" Kennedy prodded, clearly ignoring Em. 'Hashtag sorrynotsorry' flashed through Em's mind. That was clearly Kennedy's attitude as she kept prodding. Sorry for revealing the Kelli thing. Not sorry to keep the can of worms open.

"Because I can't do that. There's too much at stake," Em said.

"For whom? You? Or for Callum? Because the way I see it," said Kennedy, pushing harder, "it's Callum with something to lose. And if you're divorcing him anyway, you aren't invested in him – or his career – anymore."

"So, this brings me back to whether Callum is actually behind the antics here," Ryatt said. "That's why I was coming out this way. I have more information, but it's connecting what I know to Callum that's the bit I can't work out. But Callum mentioned the guy in the pub—"

"Yoo-hoo, anyone home?" Shirley called from the verandah, obviously disregarding Kennedy and Ryatt's cars in the driveway.

Em got up and opened the door, finding both Shirley and Margo on the verandah.

"Just wanted to see how you were doing, pet. Especially after the interaction last week with Bryan," Margo said.

"You had the same look on your face today that you had when Bryan got in your face. But today, with that little upstart of a husband of yours, you were a deathly shade of white," Shirley said.

"I'm okay. We're just talking with Ryatt," Em said, gesturing for Shirley and Margo to come inside.

"Well, we don't want to interrupt," said Margo. "We just wanted make sure you were okay."

"Anna was walking this way, too," Shirley said. "I just saw her chatting with Tyler. But since you're here, officer, I wanted to share something I've noticed that may be of interest to you. That Bryan, across the road, he's been watching Em. I've noticed him a few times now. One time he had binoculars out, watching her come down the road."

"What?" Em said. "When?"

"Oh, two days ago? I don't know. Just not right," Shirley said, leaning over and taking a cookie off the plate on the table. There were more footsteps and voices coming from the verandah outside. Em looked out and saw both Anna and Tyler walking up. Tyler looked uncomfortable, trailing behind.

"Hey Em. Sorry to bother you, but Tyler just shared something with me that I thought you should know about. About Bryan."

Suddenly Ryatt was at the door with her, taking over. "Come in. Sounds like there's more unfolding here," he said.

Em stepped back.

"Tell him what you just told me," Anna said, turning to Tyler. "It's okay."

"Um. I saw Bryan at the fence yesterday morning, watching Em while she was feeding the goats. He was also on his front verandah earlier this morning, looking around like he was trying to see if she was about." Tyler looked down and shuffled his foot along the ground. "Or maybe looking for someone else?"

"You don't think Bryan was the guy that Callum met at the pub, do you?" Kennedy asked.

"Sounding like it, isn't it? I'm going to go over and pay Bryan a visit," Ryatt said.

"He's not going to be happy about that," Shirley said.

"I've already done some background on him, based on my first interview with him. Stay clear of him," Ryatt said, looking at Em. "I'll be back later. We're not done here." And before she could say anything, he was out the door, striding down the steps, a man on a mission.

Tyler and Anna left, then fifteen minutes later, Em finally managed to get Shirley and Margo out the door. She sat down at the table with Kennedy, with Asher still on FaceTime.

Asher, finally able to get a word in, said, "Are you okay, Em?"

"Yeah. I guess so. I just don't get it. Why is Callum always pulling my strings and why the fuck can't I just move on? I'm so tired of his bullshit! Kennedy suggested releasing something stealthily to the media about Callum and the drugs and prostitutes – but I just can't."

"But why not? Seriously, what do you have to lose?" Kennedy asked.

"It's too hard. Too messy. Too damaging. And we're not divorced yet." Em slumped down in her chair. "I just want to know why all these things keep happening to me! Don't I deserve a normal life? A sane life? Maybe it's karma."

"Karma? What do you mean? What have *you* done to piss off the universe?" Kennedy asked.

Em looked sheepish.

"Off the record," added Kennedy. "Obviously. As your friend, Em. I'm wanting to help you."

"I have something on Callum. On something he's done," Em said. Asher give a low whistle. "He threatened to kill me if I ever exposed him."

"For real?" Asher said.

Kennedy sat forward in her chair. "Did you tell Ryatt that?" she asked.

"No. Because I don't know if Callum meant it or not. But maybe he is serious."

"What did he do?" Kennedy asked like a salivating dog.

Em looked at her, wondering if she could trust her or not.

"Pinky swear, I won't say or write a word about it. Not unless you give me the green light," Kennedy said, and thrust out her little finger.

Em was quiet. Was she mad to trust her? She took a deep breath and decided to take the leap.

"Do you promise?" Em asked, then tried to think of what she could tell Kennedy that wouldn't be too damaging for her if Kennedy did decide to leak it. She thought the early story would be best. It would only damage Callum's career – and maybe resurrect someone else's.

Kennedy nodded.

"Okay. Callum was up for a huge role against an adversary, early in his career. The producers and casting director were dragging their feet on the decision. Callum knew it would be a career changer, so he called in an anonymous tip to the police, accusing his rival of domestic violence. Then he called the paparazzi. The other actor lost the role and, while the domestic violence charge was proven false, the guy was convicted by public opinion. His career was over, so Callum got the role."

"When was this?" Kennedy asked, while Asher's hands went to his head in disbelief. He'd been around Hollywood long enough to know how things like this worked.

"About five years ago," Em said, and watched as Kennedy's face reflected her mental rewind.

"Kevin Chamberlain-Holt?" Kennedy asked.

Em hesitated, then nodded.

"Holy shit! And he was good! And God, such a lovely guy. I interviewed him about that. He insisted it wasn't true. Talked about how in love he was with his wife, and I believed him. But it's as you said … public opinion."

"Do you have evidence of him doing this?" Asher asked.

Em nodded again. "I recorded Callum without him knowing. I knew it wasn't right. He found the recording about a year ago. He was livid. He erased it, of course, but I have a backup copy. Somehow I knew this would be something to hold on to."

"And he thinks you only have the Kelli thing over him now?" Kennedy asked.

"Yes. And I feel stupid. I knew what he did to Kevin was wrong. But until he found the recording, I guess I never realised his blinding ambition."

"If it's ever exposed, if this secret gets out, his career is over," Asher said.

"And you could have a normal life, Em," Kennedy said. "Isn't that what you want?"

"Yes, but I'm worried about retribution."

"But there wouldn't be any. Because as we know, once Hollywood makes up their mind, and the Great Callum Walsh tumbles, people will not be kind. All of his secrets will be out, and people will not hold back. My guess is he'd end up in jail."

"And just think of what a pretty prison bitch he'd make," Asher said, chuckling.

27

W hen Em heard a car on the driveway later that afternoon, her blood ran cold. He was back. Back to torment her again. But she quickly realised that the engine sounded different from the Mustang. She looked out the window – and gasped. Her mother's campervan was pulling up next to Kennedy's smaller rental.

What was her mother doing here? She had claimed repeatedly that she never wanted to come to Tasmania. It was why Em, not her mother, had taken the housesit.

Em glanced over at Kennedy, told her that her mum had turned up, then stepped out of the door to greet her.

Kat emerged from her VW campervan looking exhausted and worn down. Upon closer inspection, Em noticed that her mother seemed to have aged significantly in the month since she last saw her. She was wearing a long, tie-dyed dress with an old, tattered black cardigan over her slender frame. Her grey hair, usually long and straight, was pulled haphazardly into a ponytail, like it was an afterthought. To make matters stranger, she had applied a bold pink lipstick, which didn't quite fit with the rest of her dishevelled appearance. It was as if she had attempted to look put together but given up after the effort of putting on lipstick.

"Mum! What are you doing here?" Em said, stepping down the stairs and walking through the gate. Ruby was at her heels, but the other two were standing silent at the top of the stairs, as if they could tell Kat was a friend.

Kat's gaze shifted upwards, and then her whole body froze in shock. It was a familiar reaction whenever her mother laid eyes on her. Talking on the phone was one thing but being in each other's presence seemed to be an insult to her mother. Maybe it was a constant reminder of all she had lost since Em's father passed away. Kat moved her hand to her heart, took a deep breath, and nodded.

"Well. That's a fine greeting, my darling girl," Kat said, plastering on a fake smile, as she walked towards Em. When Em hugged her mother, she realised how relieved she was to see her, especially given the sporadic communication of late. But when she felt her mother's tired body wilt against hers, she pulled back.

"Are you alright?" she said. She studied her mother's expression for any hint of deception. Kat had never been able to lie to Em, at least not successfully.

"Just tired. It was a long trip and I hate that damn ferry. Got to Tasmania last night but I was too buggered to drive down. Slept somewhere up north and then took a wrong turn, so I ended up nearly on the west coast before I realised I was going in the wrong direction."

"Geezus, Mum. Come in, come in. I'll make you a coffee and find you something to eat."

Ruby nudged Kat's leg, looking for attention.

"And who is this sweet thing?" Kat asked as she bent down to give some love to Ruby.

"That's Ruby. Charlie and Billy are up there on the verandah. They're all lovely. But you can get to know them later. Come on. I have a friend inside from America. Well, not a friend, per se – a friend of Asher's. His girlfriend." Em led the way up the stairs.

"His girlfriend? I thought Asher was gay!" Kat said, following Em.

Em laughed. "Why would you think that?"

"Oh, I don't know. A vibe I got. He's more emotional, more in touch with his feelings than most men I know. I just assumed, I suppose," Kat said, as they stepped through the door.

"Interesting. Well, come in," Em said, and walked towards the coffee maker straightaway. Her mother looked like she needed a boost, and quickly.

"Kennedy, this is my mum, Kat," Em said, and watched as the women approached each other. While Kennedy had a beaming smile, Kat's face reflected caution.

Kat's eyes narrowed as she studied the stranger before her. "I know you," she said, her voice laced with curiosity. "Don't I? I've seen you somewhere."

"Probably on the telly, Mum. Kennedy is an entertainment reporter," Em explained as she scooped coffee into the portafilter.

"And you're friends with her? I thought you avoided people in the media!" Kat said, as if Kennedy wasn't standing a metre away from her.

"Normally I do, but Kennedy is different. If Asher trusts her, then so do I. And I've told her all about Callum – the good, the bad and the ugly."

"Pfft. Callum. Now there's a fuckwit if I ever met one," Kat said, dropping into a dining room chair.

"And there we agree," Kennedy said, joining her at the table. "I've always had a buzz about him but could never put my finger on it. Until I got Em's side; and this morning, he proved my instincts were right."

"This morning?" Kat screeched and swivelled in her chair to face Em in the kitchen. "Why? What happened?"

"He was here this morning. To ask about the video that was released," Em said.

"It wasn't me, love. I swear. But the computer is gone from my campervan. Last week. When I was down in Apollo Bay. Someone broke into Lorelei. That's my van," she explained to Kennedy.

"I figured that's what happened. Are you okay? Did they take anything else?" Em asked as she moved around the kitchen, making coffee and grabbing food for her mum. She looked like she hadn't eaten in a month.

"I'm fine. And no, they took nothing else. Well, nothing I noticed anyway. I called the police, but they're about as useful as a basket full of smelly underwear. Wrote up a report. That was about it."

"You didn't come all the way down here to tell me that, though, did you? I thought you never came to Tasmania." Em put a cup of espresso in front of her mother with two scones she'd made that afternoon. After Callum's visit that morning, she'd baked up a storm.

"I don't hate this place. Not here, anyway." She glanced towards Kennedy, then added, "There's something I needed to tell you in person—" She was cut off by the sound of another car coming into the driveway.

"It's like Grand Central Station around here today. I'll go see who it is," Kennedy said, leaving them alone, but then she called out quickly from the verandah, "It's Ryatt."

"Who the hell is Ryatt?" Kat said, taking a small bite of the scone.

Em was relieved to see she was at least eating.

"Do you remember the guy I dated in Year Eleven?" Em asked her mother. "I went out with him just before Callum and I got together."

"Vaguely," Kat said. "Didn't he move?"

"Yes. And I have questions I want to ask you about that. Apparently he sent me a ton of letters after he left."

Em waited a beat, hoping for an explanation, but her mother's expression remained neutral. Either she'd completely forgotten about it or she deemed it insignificant. Em put it aside, deciding to take it up with her later.

"In any case," Em continued, "he's a detective in Tasmania. It's a small world." Em heard footsteps on the verandah and went to the door. "Come on in, Ryatt."

Ryatt waved, then bent over to take his boots off.

"Don't bother with your boots. It's a constant stream of people through here today."

He looked up, shrugged and came in. He stopped, surprised to see Kat. Kennedy followed close behind.

"Well, hello Mrs McKinney. You don't look a day older than the last time I saw you," Ryatt said, clearly lying.

Em noticed him clenching his fists while he plastered on a professional smile. He had to be pissed off at her mother for not passing on the letters. Em knew *she* was!

"Oh, another bloody charmer?" Kat replied, but this time with a smile. "I remember you. Didn't you go to school with Em at Pennant Hills High School?" It seemed Kat could be just as charming as Ryatt.

"I did," Ryatt answered.

Em groaned. "Coffee, Ryatt?"

"Oh, that'd be great. Been one hell of a day," he said. "But I have an update for you."

"An update on what?" Kat asked.

"The neighbour, for now," Ryatt said.

Em placed a few more scones on the table, along with plates for Ryatt and Kennedy.

He looked at Em. "I was right," he said. "You need to keep your distance. Bryan had some charges against him in Western Australia. Catfishing. I've given him a warning, but …"

"What the hell is catfishing?" Kat interrupted. "And who is Bryan and why do we care?"

"I'll fill you in later, Mum," Em said, but Ryatt answered her questions.

"Catfishing is when someone takes on a new identity to mislead someone. In this case, Bryan was using his boss's identity to begin an online relationship with a wealthy widow. He was in pretty deep, too. Allegedly."

"And who is Bryan?" Kat asked, nibbling at more of her scone.

"The neighbour, Mum. He's been acting weird. I've had some weird stuff going on here."

"Like with the chickens?" Kat asked.

"Yes. Other stuff, too. And Ryatt is trying to work out who's behind it all," Em explained.

"It's not Callum? I thought you said it was Callum?"

"I thought it was …" Em said and looked to Ryatt.

"It still could be. He and Bryan could be connected, but the question is how. Bryan was at the pub in Huonville last night, so it could have been him who told Callum where you were. But Bryan swears he didn't see Callum. Given his history, I'm not sure I'd believe him, but without knowing whether that was the pub and what time Callum was there, we just don't know."

"It's Callum," Kat said, convinced.

"But Bryan clearly has online skills," Kennedy pointed out. "So is he behind the video?"

"I don't know yet. I can't arrest him without cause. But he's looking like a good candidate," Ryatt said. "The question is, how did he get hold of the video in the first place. You said, Em, that you thought there was only one copy, and it was erased from your laptop."

"I thought so. But Mum just said her laptop was stolen from her campervan last week in Victoria."

"There's a police report," Kat added. "But you know how those things go. On to the pile, never to be seen again."

"*Mum* ..." Em blushed, then looked to Ryatt. "Sorry." She glanced at Kat, who clearly wasn't sorry at all for the insult. She knew how her mother felt about the police. They were just as corrupt as all other government entities.

"It's okay, I'll follow that up," Ryatt said, taking the details from Kat.

"I just can't see Callum being involved with the video, though," Em said. "He's not very computer savvy. I was the one who taught him how to use email. And how to open a web browser."

"Maybe he paid someone to steal it?" Kennedy suggested.

"But how would he know where Mrs McKinney was?" Ryatt added.

"Kat. Call me Kat," she interjected. "'Mrs McKinney' makes me feel a hundred years old."

Ryatt smiled, nodding.

Em was pensive about the whole Bryan thing. How was he connected? "I don't understand the Bryan angle," she said, finally.

"Well, he has a history of stalking, too. My guess is that's why he lives at home again. According to Margo and Shirley, he told people around here he came home to look after his dad. Truth was, he came home with his tail between his legs. He has been banned from the mines, and there is a court case pending. He's due in court in Perth in a couple of months."

Kennedy said, "So he's essentially unable to earn a living if he is banned from his current job, and all other opportunities are blocked. I would imagine the mining industry would be about as tight as the entertainment industry."

"You should be a detective," Em joked. She could see how Kennedy, with her quick mind, had got to be such a good investigative reporter. She asked the right type of questions.

"That's what I was thinking, too," Ryatt smiled.

Em sat back and just listened to them bounce theories for the next ten minutes. Which was all well and good, but where did that leave her with all the drama going on?

"Well, whether this Bryan fellow is connected or not, Callum is involved in some way, and karma is a bitch," Kat said. "The boy needs to pay for the carnage he's left in his wake, and the lives he's ruined along the way. He needs to be dealt with, one way or another."

"Mum …" Em said, embarrassed by her mother's outburst – especially saying something like that in front of Ryatt.

"I agree that karma is a bitch, Mrs McKinney. Sorry … Kat. But I'll do my job and make sure the right person is charged for what's happened here," Ryatt said definitively. He looked down at his watch. "And I'd better go. I have to be in Huonville before five. Thanks for the coffee and scone, Mats. Delish, as always. Seriously, you really should think of opening a bakery or something. You have a gift." With a laugh and a salute, he was out the door.

"Well, who would have thought that tall, lanky kid would fill out to be such a dishy policeman!" Kat said, finishing off her scone.

"He's a detective, Mum, and I think they're required to wear bullet-proof vests now," Em said.

"I think most of that was Ryatt," Kennedy said, winking at Kat.

"Nice," Em groaned as she cleared the plates.

"You know, he reminds me of Jake. Em's dad. He seems sensible, strong, a protector, too. Still has an eye for you, Em, it seems. And he has a sense of humour. Gotta love a man that knows how to spin a good one."

"He reminds me of the kind of guy Callum plays in his movies," Kennedy said.

"'Plays' being the key word there," Kat said to Kennedy. "Callum could never live up to being the real thing."

"Even if Ryatt was interested, I'm still married," Em reminded them both.

"Not for long," Kat said. "But you're probably right. He's probably taken. Or gay. All the good ones are. Now, do you have a bed for me in this place? I need to crash for a while. I'd nap in Lorelei, but she needs a good airing out first."

WHEN EM WOKE the following morning, the sun was already up, and she could smell coffee. Groaning, she again realised her failures as a hostess. She was never good at it. She threw back the covers when she remembered the dogs. Kennedy hated dogs and her mum probably wouldn't have thought about taking them out, although with their morning whining, they would be almost impossible to ignore.

She grabbed her jumper, stuffed her feet into her woolly socks, used the bathroom, then walked into the living room. Kennedy was dressed in a media-ready outfit, as always. Her small bag sat by the door. Her mum sat at the table reading a book.

"Morning. Sorry …" Em mumbled, looking down at her phone, seeing it was barely eight o'clock. "Didn't mean to sleep so late."

Her mother chuckled. "I remember you sleeping away until noon when you were a kid. Anything before nine was a miracle," she said, looking a little more refreshed than the day before. They'd sat up talking until almost midnight, Kat reinvigorated after her two-hour nap in the afternoon.

"Yes, but now I have responsibilities. Like the dogs," Em said.

"Already been let out to pee. Fed too. And I let the chickens out, but I wasn't sure what the routine was there," Kat said, placing her novel on the table.

"Oh, thanks. They get a scoop of wheat, but if they went out without dramas, then great."

"Well, that rooster was a bit of a dick. But aren't most men?" her mother said, taking a long sip of whatever was in her cup.

"Most. Not all," said Kennedy, "Asher is pretty sweet. Anyway, I hate to love you and leave you, but I've got to get back to Melbourne. Apparently, there's drama on the set of Alice Kingman's new show. She's being a bit of a diva and the locals aren't too happy. So I've been called to check that out. I've booked a flight at eleven and, since we're in nowhere Tasmania, I have to hit the road." She walked over and hugged Em. "I'm here whenever you need me. I'm happy I came."

Em found herself thinking the same. She'd been a rock during the confrontation with Callum the day before.

"And when you're ready to tell your story, I'm here to share it," Kennedy said, with a twinkle in her eye.

"It won't be anytime soon, but thanks for coming. I am glad you were here," Em said, then added, "Asher was right. You're a good egg."

Kennedy's eyes softened.

"I'm glad I came. Just remember, Asher is just looking out for you. So am I," Kennedy said, then she squeezed Em's hand, wished Kat a great stay, picked up her bag and handbag, and headed out the door. Em and Kat followed her out to wave from the verandah

"Well, she wasn't what I expected," Kat mused as she drove way. "So different than she is on television. Do you know, she was up before dawn this morning, head down, arse in the air, doing yoga and looking like she was still camera-ready the entire time. How do some women do that? I look like an unmade bed most of the time, even if I put in some effort."

"It's her job to be camera-ready no matter what she's doing," Em said. "She's always on call. She was going to stay a few more days, she told me yesterday, but work beckons."

"Well, now it's just us two again," Kat said when they were back inside. "So let's do something fun today to celebrate the back of that man."

"He's not dead, Mum. He's still in my life. I'm still married to him," Em said as she made a coffee for herself.

"Not for long, my girl," Kat said. "Not for long. Anyway, I'm going to have a shower, then let's find a market. Any going on around this place?"

. . .

Two hours later, after Em walked the dogs, they drove to the local farmers' market. Walking around, Em realised it was good to get out, if for nothing more than to get her mind off things.

The day was gorgeous. With an azure-blue sky dotted with white puffs of cloud, and only a slight breeze, it felt like spring was just around the corner. A new beginning. Still, she was glad she'd brought her scarf. Dressed in her faded black jeans, her favourite cable-knit jumper and her boots, she was comfortable, but she was learning quickly that there could be four seasons in one day in Tasmania, even in the middle of winter, and that the UV rays were brutal here.

Beside her, her mother shivered. She was dressed in jeans and jumper, a beanie pulled low, but she had left her jacket in her camper-van. Em offered her jacket to her, but Kat insisted she'd be fine. Didn't stop her grumbling about how she'd forgotten about the "crap weather in Tasmania".

Em kept an eye out for a rogue photographer or, God forbid, Callum, but it felt nice to be among people. As she wandered the stalls, she picked up some fresh vegetables, and was delighted with the array of baked goods on offer. She sampled here and there, noting ingredients in her head, and unconsciously made mental notes of what the locals were buying. Em was surprised at how busy the market was.

"Well, look who it is! Hello, Em darling."

Em jumped at the sound of her name, then turned to find Margo, dressed in a long flowing skirt, boots and a dark grey jumper that skimmed the lumps and bumps. Her outfit was finished off with the most spectacular necklace in an array of blacks, greys and greens.

"Hi Margo. Wow. You look great. I love that necklace!" Em smiled at her neighbour.

Margo looked gloriously happy. The silver streak, standing out in her glossy brown curls, glistened in the sunlight. "Isn't it gorgeous? I just bought it over there at Suzi's stall. She's got the best jewellery. Not sure that it's everyone's taste, but it sure fits mine! Anyway, how are you, love? Doing okay?" Concern clouded Margo's eyes.

"Oh yeah. Drama over. Sorry about yesterday," Em said, apologising, as always, for her ex-husband's behaviour. "Oh, this is my mum, Kat McKinney. Mum, this is my neighbour, Margo."

Margo greeted Kat with a warm smile, then scanned the bustling crowd. "I'm sure my wife Shirley is here somewhere. She's probably off at the weaver's stall, deep in conversation with Annie. She can talk for hours."

Margo turned back to Em and her mother. As she looked at Kat again, her expression turned inquisitive.

"You look familiar," Margo said to Kat, her eyes scanning her face for clues as to where they may have met.

Kat looked back at Margo, scowling, and shrugged. "Probably just one of those faces," she said, then walked away, embarrassing Em with her rudeness.

"Maybe so," Margo mumbled, her voice trailing after Kat, but she didn't look convinced. She turned to face Em. "Well, I need to go find Shirley. We're going into Hobart this afternoon. It was good to see you. I hope things calm down a bit for you, darling. Meanwhile, enjoy the markets!"

And with a wave, Margo was off, casting another curious glance after Kat as she went.

28

"You do know you're not allowed visitors at your housesits, right? Unless you have permission from the owner?" Kat said as they unpacked the bags from the markets.

"Like you?" Em said, teasing her mother.

"I meant Kennedy," her mother said harshly. "What were you doing inviting the media in to stay?"

"Well, she's not just the media, Mum. She's Asher's girlfriend. And I didn't exactly invite her. She came down to tell me about what was going on with Callum. Apparently he was missing from the set in Melbourne and, as Asher's girlfriend, and a friend, she came to warn me. She was going to stay at a local Airbnb, but I just told her to stay here after Callum showed up. She was only here overnight."

"Just be careful, love. She's still the media. And you never know what her motivation is," Kat said. "I mean, couldn't she just call you and tell you Callum was not on the set?"

"Well, it was more than that, but ..."

A glance from her mother stopped Em from saying any more. "My point exactly," Kat said. "Vultures. That's what you've always told me."

Just hearing the word made Em think of Callum and his immense dislike for anyone in the media.

"Well, I was glad she was here yesterday," Em said, as she finished putting the shopping away. "I need to walk the dogs. Do you want to join me?"

"No love. I think I'll stay here. I need to do some laundry, if that's okay?"

"Sure. I'll show you where everything is."

FIFTEEN MINUTES LATER, Em was enjoying the peace and quiet of the trail down by the river, as the three dogs sniffed the ground around her. They were all off-leash, enjoying the freedom as much as she was. It was chilly, but she'd left her coat behind. Maybe she was acclimatising to the cold weather after all? It had only taken her less than two weeks. Or maybe it was her blood pressure keeping her warm. God knew it had to be through the roof. With the drama surrounding Callum, Kennedy's visit, and her mother arriving out of the blue, things were stressful.

Even her baking was off. She'd intended to bake bread and cinnamon rolls, that morning, only to realise she'd forgotten to put yeast in the bread dough or roll out the pastry last night. She was going to have to go through the process all over again.

But the visit with her mum had her ruminating. Going to the markets, in the end, hadn't been as much fun as she'd hoped or the distraction they'd needed. Even when she wasn't looking over her shoulder for Callum, Bryan, or a random photographer, her mother had kept looking at her with sidelong glances. There was always a barrier between them when they were together. It didn't matter how close they were from a distance – when they were face-to-face, there was always something there. Something unsaid.

It pained her to see her mother's face whenever they were reunited. The words her mother had spat at her when she was nineteen – words said at the end of a heated argument over her mother's need for therapy – had stayed with Em: "You're just like him." The words returned to her whenever she saw that look on her mother's face.

Em thought it should have been a compliment to be told she was just like her father. Her mother had adored him. Still spoke of him like he was a god. But the look her mother had given her when she said the words had not conveyed the same love. More like hatred. She had wanted to ask her mother what she meant – she still did – but it was so long ago. Seemed like it was just how things were, now.

When Charlie stopped at the end of the track, Em looked up. She was surprised to find they'd made it to the park so quickly. A campervan was parked near the toilets, but it looked different from the other one she'd seen here recently. This one was a Britz.

Em could see an older couple heading towards the river. Ruby barked and they turned. Em scrambled to clip on the dogs' leads, but Ruby dashed ahead, tail wagging, eager to say hello.

"Sorry!" Em called out, grabbing Charlie's lead before he could follow Ruby. Thankfully, Billy, the compliant one of the three, stood waiting for her.

Ruby bounded towards the couple, but they seemed relaxed. Finally, Em caught up. "I'm so sorry. I usually have them on a lead by now, but I got distracted," she said.

"Don't worry about it. We have four of our own dogs at home in England. We know how it goes," said the woman with a chuckle, giving Ruby a good pat.

"Do you live around here? It's a delightful spot," the man with her asked. He, too, sounded English. He bent down and patted Billy, who as usual was happy to take all the love he could receive.

"Oh no. I'm just housesitting," Em said. "But it is lovely."

"What a coincidence! We were talking to another camper this morning about housesitting. He was saying he has a housesitter looking after his farm. Isn't that right, Gerald?"

Her partner nodded.

She turned back to Em. "We have a housesitter looking after our place in Surrey. Such a great opportunity for travellers, but some do take advantage. The man was a good sport about it, but he was joking about how he should start charging his housesitter rent. Apparently she's had visitors coming and going since she arrived!"

"I only hope our housesitter is not like his!" Gerald said, straightening back up after giving Billy and Charlie a pat. "I'd have thought it's against the rules to have visitors when housesitting?"

"Oh, it is. Unless you have permission from the homeowner first," Em said.

"Yes, that's what I thought," the Englishwoman said. "Like I said, some take advantage, that's for sure."

"Well, we must get on, poppet," Gerald said, nudging his wife. "We're heading to Port Arthur this afternoon but wanted to check out this lovely little walk before we jump back in the van. Lovely to meet you." They waved goodbye.

As she watched them walk away down the track, Em felt guilty. She certainly hadn't asked John's permission for Kennedy, or for her mother, to stay. She made a mental note to email him when she returned to the house.

"THERE YOU ARE," Kat said. "I thought you'd got lost."

Em found her mother reclining on the couch, looking very settled in. She had a cup of tea next to her, her book in her lap, and what looked to be Em's fuzzy socks on her feet.

"I took the longer track. The dogs needed a good walk," Em said, hanging up her coat.

"I've been sitting here thinking about that husband of yours," Kat said, sitting up. "He really is a waste of human flesh. He needs to go. Permanently. I mean, you don't have to put up with that shit that he's dishing out to you. Leaving Hollywood was the right thing for you to do. Being on your own, it has its advantages. And being able to leave the past behind, to forget everything in your past, that has its advantages too."

Em knew all this. Her mother had said as much, repeatedly, since she'd decided to leave LA. So why did she need to say it again now? And in person? Her showing up all of a sudden was weird. Her mother had always told her she had no desire to go to Tasmania, yet here she was. On the couch. Drinking tea. Repeating the same thing she'd said only days before. And Callum was not a subject she wanted to have on repeat with her mother.

"Who was it that you met in Torquay, Mum? You said it was someone from your past. Is that what's prompting this little lecture? Because you've already told me all this about Callum before." Em busied herself putting the kettle on.

"You do know I had a past before your dad came along, right?" Kat replied, sassily. "There were just some people from that part of my life, a missing part of the puzzle that makes up my life." Kat got up and paced the room. "I was going to ..."

Kat had stopped in front of the dining room bookcase. She was staring at something sitting on a shelf.

Em walked over, and Kat started at her touch. "What the ..." Kat began, and when she turned to Em, she looked traumatised.

"What is it, Mum?" Em said, but Kat shook her head and ran to the back bedroom. Em trailed behind, surprised to see Kat packing the few clothes she had.

"I've got to go," Kat said.

Em stood there dumbfounded as she watched her mother grab her overstuffed handbag, throw her phone into the bag like it was a hot potato, and literally run out the door to her campervan. Seconds later, Em found herself staring at her mum's wet clothes, still hanging on the line, the only things that remained of her mother. She wondered what the hell had just happened.

EM TRIED CALLING her mother for the next three hours. The calls went straight to voicemail. She sent texts. They went unanswered. She couldn't piece it together. She'd walked to the bookcase to see what may have made her mother run. She could see old books, an old post-card in a frame with a hand drawn heart on the front of it, and some maps, but there was nothing obvious.

So, while she continued trying to reach her mother, she attempted to focus on baking. Her streak of things going wrong continued. She was too distracted to concentrate. Nothing was going right. First Callum's threats, and now her mother had run off. What was going on with the world?

On her afternoon walk later with the dogs, she ran into Anna. They continued on together, and when Em walked faster as they passed Bryan's place, looking determinedly away from the house, Anna picked up on it.

"What's going on? Finally worked out how creepy he is?" Anna joked.

Em filled her in on what Ryatt had told her and was surprised when Anna didn't react strongly.

"Had to be something like that. The guy is just weird. Tyler told me he's been keeping a close eye on you. He was a bit worried about it, honestly. I told him he needed to warn you," Anna said.

"He told me. And Ryatt, too."

"Oh good. He's a good kid. His heart is in the right place," Anna said. "I'll miss him, that's for sure."

"Why? Where's he going?" Em asked.

"Not him. Me. My housesit is up in a few days, and the next one just fell through. Not sure what I'm going to do, to be honest. It's only a couple of weeks, and I need to hang around Tasmania for my course. But there are no housesits available, and my funds are low. I need to save all I can for when my course starts, so I can pay for tuition and rent."

Em opened her mouth to offer Anna a place to stay, but her mind went to the couple by the river and their comments about housesits and visitors.

She said, carefully, "I need to talk to John about my housesit, and the unexpected visitors I've had. But I'll happily ask if you could stay with me, if you like? I mean, no promises, but I trust you, and you could help me out in return. I need to get my head back in my recipe book. I could use your help with the animals while I do that."

Anna's eyebrows shot up and her mouth dropped open. "Oh, that would be fab! You've got how long left on your housesit?"

"John said he'd be back on July fifth. So about two-and-a-half weeks," Em said.

"Yeah, that would work out great. My next housesit starts on the third of July. It's up north, near Penguin." Anna was smiling widely.

"Okay. I'll email him tonight and let you know what he says. I'm just hoping he won't be too pissed off about Kennedy and Mum's impromptu visits."

"From what Lukas told me when he was housesitting, John is pretty chilled," Anna said, with a little skip.

"Let's hope the chill continues. Can we keep walking a bit further down the road? I took the dogs down by the river this morning. I think a little variety would be good for them."

"Sounds good," Anna said.

On the way back, they saw Margo and Shirley in their front yard, raking leaves. Well, at least, Shirley was. Margo stood nearby near a large plastic bucket, waiting for Shirley to dump leaves into it.

"Hello, darlings," Margo greeted them. "I was just talking to Shirley about your mum, Em."

"Oh?"

"Yeah," Shirley said, straightening slowly. "Margo says she thinks she knows your mum, from when she stayed with her aunt and uncle up in Swansea on the east coast."

"Yes, I think your mum lived in Pontypool when I was about seventeen," added Margo. "She's not that much older than me, is she? I think she was mid-twenties around then. Maybe younger? Does that sound right to you?"

"I don't think so. Mum has never lived in Tasmania," Em said.

"Are you sure about that?" pressed Margo. "Because she looks awfully familiar, and when I tried to calculate ages, I think it fits."

"No, couldn't be Mum." Em was certain. "She travelled here for a short while as a backpacker, I think, but she hates it here. She said she'd never live here. I was surprised to see her here at all, to be honest."

"That's interesting, because there was a story about a woman living up in Pontypool who left suddenly with her young daughter. The woman had some kind of mental breakdown. Not that your mother seems mentally unstable, mind you, but from what I know of the story, the woman was escaping a horror house. And I *think* my uncle helped them escape."

Em stayed silent. It didn't make much sense, not with what she knew about her mum. She had lived on the mainland all her life. But after what her mother had started to say about her past earlier – not to mention her hasty departure – Em had to wonder if there was something about her past that she hadn't shared.

29

You look lost Mathilda.

It's not a good feeling is it?

Time for you to get what you deserve.

30

E m slept hard. It probably hadn't been wise to take a sleeping pill while being responsible for someone else's home. She had only taken them once before, but she desperately needed to turn her brain off. She had strange dreams of dogs whining while someone broke into her house in California. This was one of her usual stress dreams: either being robbed at The Bakehouse or being burgled in her home. It didn't surprise her, given the amount of stress she was feeling over her mother's disappearance. She still hadn't heard from her.

The first thing she did when she woke up was check her phone. There were no new messages. Nothing from her mother to explain her sudden disappearance. Resigned to the fact – and knowing that this was not the first time her mother had bolted – Em climbed out of bed and went to the bathroom, which was usually the place Ruby met her in the morning.

But there was no Ruby this morning. Odd. She walked out to the cold lounge room, kicking herself for not stoking the fire the night before, and looked around. Where were the dogs? She turned to the back door and saw Billy peering in, his face forlorn, his entire body shivering in the cold.

Oh shit! She'd forgotten to bring the dogs in the night before.

She ran to the back door and Billy dashed inside, so cold that his legs wobbled. Em grabbed the red throw blanket from the back of the couch and wrapped it around him, trying to warm him. He pranced around, clearly agitated.

"Oh Billy, baby. I'm so sorry! I'm so, so sorry!" She looked around but the other two dogs hadn't followed him in.

"Where are Charlie and Rubes?"

Billy looked to the door.

"Stay here," she said, and dashed outside, closing the door behind her to keep Billy in. He whined, wanting to follow, but she knew he'd be better inside, where it was somewhat warmer. She'd forgotten to grab her coat, and ice covered the edges of the patio. "Geezus. It's fucking freezing!"

She scoured the yard, but still didn't see the other two dogs. She ran back inside, pulled on gumboots over her flannel pyjama pants, and put her red anorak over her long-sleeved merino sleep shirt. She went outside again through the mudroom door. Still no dogs.

"Ruby? Charlie? Where are you?" Nothing. Then she stopped in her tracks when she heard whining coming from the other side of the garden. She descended the stairs, careful not to slip on the ice that covered them completely on this side of the verandah, and walked around the side of the house.

There lay Ruby, with Charlie's head on her abdomen. He raised his head, whined again, placed his head back down and continued whimpering. In an instant, Billy was beside her, the red blanket dragging behind him. She realised she'd left the mudroom door open.

Em looked back to Charlie and Ruby and went to see what was wrong. Charlie looked up again pleadingly, as if waiting for Em to help Ruby, but Em knew instantly there was nothing she could do. White foam covered the cocker spaniel's mouth. Charlie began lapping at it, but Em said, "No!" so firmly that he recoiled. He sat up, the look in his eyes reflecting his heartbreak.

Soft sobs escaped from Em's lips, the only sound in the otherwise still and heavy air – apart from the sound of her heart beating faster and louder in her ears, the blood rushing through her veins like a rapid river.

Em scanned her surroundings desperately. Sunlight peeked through the trees, casting dappled shadows on the ground where dewdrops glittered like tears. What was she supposed to do now? She didn't even know where to begin. What had Ruby eaten? Em searched the ground frantically, but there were no obvious clues. Had Charlie consumed it too? Maybe. If Billy had eaten it, he would surely be dead by now; he was already skin and bones and shivering from the cold temperature. Despite feeling distraught over losing Ruby, Em couldn't help but feel relieved that it was only her – so far.

She tried to think straight. Whatever Ruby had ingested, there was a chance that Charlie had eaten it too. She needed to call the vet immediately … but then something about Ruby caught her attention again. Although her body lay on its side, her head was twisted in an unnatural position. Did she collapse suddenly and fall like this? Em leapt up, causing Charlie to jump at the sudden movement, and grabbed the blanket from Billy, gently draping it over Ruby's lifeless body.

"Charlie. Billy. Come on," she said and ran back towards the house. Billy followed, but Charlie remained. "Charlie. Come on. We're getting help." This time the German shepherd followed slowly, turning back repeatedly to look at his dead friend.

Em ran into the kitchen and pulled John's housesitting binder from the bookshelf. She riffled through the pages and found the vet's number. Looking at the clock on the kitchen wall, she saw it was barely eight o'clock. The phone rang and rang and rang. She got voicemail. She dialled again, and this time, someone picked it up on the fourth ring.

"Huon Valley Veterinary Hospital. May I help you?" said a gruff male voice.

"Hi. Hello. My name is Em and I'm housesitting for …" She blanked on John's last name. "I have three dogs that I'm looking after. I think one has been poisoned, possibly two. I …"

She hesitated. Should she admit that she left them out overnight? He'd find out anyway.

"I left the dogs out accidentally overnight," she went on. "It was a mistake, but I woke this morning to find one at the back door, while the other two were out in the garden. One of them is dead and I don't know if the other one has been poisoned too. But I … I don't know what to do." She knew she was talking fast, but she just wanted to get all of the information out there.

"Okay. First, what kind of dogs are they?" the voice said.

"Um, the dead one is a cocker spaniel. The other one I'm concerned about is a German shepherd, and the third one is a greyhound."

"Ah, yes. Are you at Neeminah River?"

"Yes," she said, surprised.

"Got it. Charlie's the German shepherd, Ruby's the cocker spaniel, and … Billy's the greyhound. So, the cocker spaniel is the one who passed away, correct?"

"Yes," she said, putting her hand over the phone when her voice cracked. "But I'm also worried about Charlie. Billy doesn't seem to have any signs, but Charlie seems lethargic. But that may be sadness, too. I don't know." She let out a sob.

"Okay. We'll get to the bottom of it. Can you tell me more about Ruby's condition?" he asked. Em began to speak, but the words stuck in her throat.

"Take a breath," the vet said. Em did as instructed, then began again.

"She's lying on the ground, on her right side. She's got white foam around her mouth, and her eyes are bulging. And her head is … it's at a weird angle." Tears crept down her cheeks, as she thought about Ruby's body.

"Hm. Okay. Definitely sounds like a poisoning of some kind. I don't think the owner puts bait traps down, but do you see anything around? Any meat or food around?"

"No, nothing. I feed them inside, in the mudroom. And I haven't seen any baiting either, although I'm not really sure what that would look like."

"Okay. The head thing is odd, so let me just grab some things here and I'll be out in about ten to fifteen minutes, okay?"

"Oh, thank you. I don't know what to do," she said, her voice catching again.

"You're on the left on Willow Road, right? The house with the wrap-around verandah?" There was no point talking about house numbers, since no one numbered their properties out this way.

"Yes, that's right. Thank you. I'll be waiting," she said.

She hung up, wiped her eyes and went into action. She needed to move fast. She threw some clothes on quickly, then realised she needed to re-start the fire. She needed to get Billy warm. Both dogs looked at her like she was crazy in her manic state. Charlie whined, as if asking why she wasn't doing more for their dead friend lying out in the yard.

"I've called for help," she said, stopping to give them both long soothing pats, trying to calm them as well as herself.

Ruby was dead. How could she have forgotten to bring the dogs in last night? But her mother taking off like that had thrown her for a loop. And Margo's comments about her mother possibly having lived in Tasmania had her distracted, too. It was all too much, but she vowed never to take a sleeping tablet again. Especially with alcohol!

Tears came again, but she wiped them away quickly as she placed kindling and a firestarter into the wood heater. She reached up to grab the matches. Billy wandered over, nuzzling his head into her shoulder. He licked her tears and the gesture made Em stop what she was doing. She turned and sobbed into Billy's fur, while Charlie wandered over and sat patiently at the back door.

Em heard the sound of a vehicle coming up the driveway. Pulling back from Billy, she opened the matchbox she'd been clutching and lit the fire. She closed the door of the wood heater, leaving the flue open, and walked to the mudroom to grab her jacket and boots again. She got to the front door just as the elderly vet was getting out of his Toyota Hilux.

"Morning. Are you Em?"

She nodded.

"Doctor Woods. I'm the main vet at the clinic. Want to show me where Ruby is?"

Em nodded again. "Thanks for coming. I really—"

"It's no problem," he said. His words were clipped but his eyes were empathetic. As Em led the vet around the house and out behind the garden enclosure, he slipped on latex gloves. The red blanket was wet around the edges now from the dew on the grass. Dr Woods removed it and took a close look. He checked Ruby's breathing first, then her eyes, and finally inside her mouth.

"Definitely poison," he said, looking around. His tone was suddenly icy and when she looked at him, his face looked angry.

"Oh God. I … I found three decapitated chickens last week, behind the shed. I thought it was a natural predator. But then one of the heads was sitting on the front verandah the next morning, with a note." Em stumbled over her words. "I … I called the police when it happened."

As her words poured out, the vet's face remained hard, but his eyes softened just a little. He lifted Ruby's head and found it limp in his hand.

"This is odd. Her neck has been broken, and my guess is it wasn't a natural break. Someone has killed this dog intentionally. Wait, what's this?"

Under Ruby's head lay a piece of paper. Dr Woods lifted it with his gloved hands. "What did the other note say?" he said, inspecting the note. "The note with the chicken head?"

Em hesitated, then said "Welcome to the neighbourhood."

He looked back down at Ruby. "Hmm," he muttered.

"I thought it was just a neighbourhood prank. Someone who doesn't like housesitters?"

The vet nodded. "Well, this one is a lot more threatening," he said and held out the note in his gloved hand so she could read it.

The bitch is disposable. Just like you.

"This … this …" She couldn't finish the sentence because of the lump in her throat.

"Did you call the police about this incident yet?"

Em shook her head. "No, but I've been in contact with Detective Ryatt about the other incidents. I think he works in Hobart."

The vet's eyebrows shot up.

"My name is Mathilda Walsh," she said. But when he looked confused, she added. "I'm married to Callum Walsh, the actor."

"Ah, yes." The way he said it made her want to cringe. He seemed to pick up on her discomfort. "The, ah, information about you and your ex-husband has been in the news a lot lately," he added.

She nodded, then nodded uncomfortably.

"Last night, I left the dogs outside by mistake. Because of—"

"I think you should call the detective again," interrupted Dr Woods. "As soon as you can. Because this was no accident. And this note confirms it."

WITHIN TWO HOURS, Ryatt was there with three other policemen. They secured the area as a crime scene and began scouring the property.

She stayed inside on their instruction. Billy was curled up on the blanket next to the fire, but Charlie hadn't left her side. He was looking for comfort as much as she was.

"There's someone here who says they know you," a policeman said, poking his head in the door. "Anna, from down the road?"

"Yes, please let her in," Em said, and felt immense relief. She'd called Asher and Kennedy to let them know what was going on, but she'd forgotten to call Anna.

"Can I bring Sachin in?" Anna asked, looking worried. Em nodded. "The policeman said to keep a tight hold on him," Anna added.

"Yes," said Em. "We don't know what else may be out there." She called for Sachin while Anna closed the door behind her.

"What do you mean? What's going on?" Anna asked, taking off her jacket and hanging it up on the peg just inside the door.

"Ruby is dead. I ..." She hated to admit it, but there was no getting around it. "I accidentally left the dogs out last night. Fuck, it's been bad, Anna. So bad. Mum left suddenly yesterday, and I have no idea why. I tried calling her but ..." She couldn't even begin to tell her about the note.

And just like that, Em lost it. Tears flowed. Anna came to her, but Charlie was between them, and the dog was not moving. Anna reached out to Em to try and console her.

"Look, leaving the dogs out happens. I've done it before. Everyone has at one point, I'm sure. But your mum? What's that about?"

"I don't know." Em sank on to the couch. "We didn't fight. She just kept on looking at something on the bookcase, like, staring at it, then got up quickly and announced she had to go. I tried calling her, texting her. I ended up giving up and went to bed." Em looked over at Anna, stricken.

"I'm sure she's okay," said Anna. "She's got to be, right? She's *your* mother. You told Ryatt about your mum leaving yesterday, right?"

Em nodded. At a knock on the glass door, she looked up.

"We're going to take the dog to the vet hospital and do a necropsy," Dr Woods said. "The police have cleared that, but they're still looking around."

"Okay, thanks. Will you call me and let me know what the necropsy finds? That way I can let John know too."

"I will, but we have his information. We'll reach out to him direct-ly," he said, looking at Anna with suspicion.

"Yes, okay. Thank y—" The door closed.

"Wow," Anna said. "But why do they need to do a necropsy?"

Billy got up and nudged Anna's leg, looking for his own comfort now Sachin had pushed him off the dog bed in front of the fire.

"Because Ruby was poisoned. And it looks like her neck was also broken on purpose," Em said, the tears starting again.

"Oh shit," Anna said, taking a seat on the couch. "Who the fuck would do that? And why?"

THE POLICE PACKED up their gear an hour later. The neighbours who'd gathered at the fence all scattered and disappeared back into their houses, the grapevine no doubt blooming with the juicy news.

Anna stayed to help Em with Charlie and Billy, along with the chickens and goats. The police had found no further evidence of bait-ing, so she was free to let the animals out. But they hadn't found what Ruby had eaten, either.

Em spent the next hour on FaceTime with Kennedy and Asher, trying to piece together what had happened. Em couldn't imagine Callum being responsible, but Kennedy was still convinced he was involved, somehow. Nevertheless, the escalating threats were serious business. Ryatt now had Bryan at the top of the list, while also trying to find a link between him and Callum.

"I'd suggest putting together a list of all of your friends and acquaintances. Anyone you may have argued with, disgruntled employees," Ryatt had said. The problem was, that list was small. There weren't that many people she'd remained close to.

"Whoever did this is seriously pissed off," Ryatt had added.

When Em got off the phone, she found Anna, now back from walking the three dogs, staring at the coffee maker, willing it to create a flat white all on its own. "I had every intention of making you a coffee, but, um …"

Em hadn't had coffee at all that morning, with all the commotion with Ruby. Looking at the clock, she saw it was close to one in the afternoon. She hadn't eaten all day. No wonder the headache was setting in.

"I'll make it," Em said. "It will give me something to do. I just feel so guilty about Ruby. I mean, she was the most beautiful dog, and she didn't deserve this."

"No, she didn't, but it's also not your fault," Anna said, pulling the milk from the fridge.

"Oh, I got an email from John last night," remembered Em. "I need to call him and tell him about Ruby. The vet was going to call him, but I need to let him know too." She knew she was rambling. She flicked off the coffee maker, not realising it was already turned on, then turned it on again. "Anyway, I'd asked him if he'd be okay if you stayed here with me, once your housesit is over. I explained that your next gig had fallen through. He said it was fine and that he may extend his trip. He even offered you the housesit, if I didn't want to extend my time. I mean, I'm happy to share it with you, if you want to do that?"

"Wow, seriously? I mean, you said you'd do that, but I didn't want to get my hopes up, you know? Are you sure?" Anna put the milk down on the kitchen island.

"Yeah, I mean, why not?" Em said, twisting the portafilter onto the machine. "It would give me time to keep baking. And with all this other shit going on, it would provide another pair of hands, so I don't do something stupid again, like leaving the dogs out. But …" Em looked down. "*Yesterday* he was okay with it. After today, it may just be you staying. He'd be an idiot to keep me on."

She hoped she could stay, but of all the incidents that could happen during a housesit, losing chickens and then a beloved dog was unforgivable. Who'd want her to housesit for them after this?

"Well, the Smiths return tomorrow, so if you and John are still good with it, it would help me out a lot," Anna said.

"I think it would be great," Em said, but she knew her tone was flat.

"I'm just relieved that I can be here to help you," Anna said. "I can't imagine what this is like."

THE GOSSIP VINE WAS, indeed, ripe. When Em and Anna walked the dogs later in the afternoon, Shirley stepped out of her house and practically ran down to the gate.

"What happened? Where's Ruby?" she said, skipping all polite salutations. Em was quickly learning it was Shirley's style, not intentional rudeness.

"She died. Someone poisoned her," Anna said, taking the lead. They'd agreed not to mention the broken neck. At least not yet.

Shirley looked directly at Em.

"Don't blame her for it," said Anna. "She found Ruby this morning, already dead."

"Who would have done that? I know John doesn't have that kind of thing on his property. Bait, I mean," Shirley said.

Em wanted to keep walking, but before she could nudge Anna to do so, Pete came out of his house with Tyler.

"Is everything okay?" Pete asked. He wore a pair of denim jeans and a flannel shirt which, after seeing him for the last two weeks in his chef's uniform, was a bit of a shock. Em had been starting to wonder if his work gear was the only clothing he owned.

"Ruby, the cocker spaniel, is dead. Poisoned," Anna said, taking the lead again. Tyler looked shocked, while Pete's worry lines ran deep, like he was trying to make sense of the words.

"And the cops came all the way out here for *that*?" said a voice behind them. Em turned and found Bryan standing ten metres away. "That shit happens all the time. What with bunny bait readily available."

"What's bunny bait?" asked Tyler, and Bryan's face flashed with exasperation, as though it was a stupid question to ask.

"What's bunny bait, Bryan?" Pete repeated, his tone cold as he put his arm around his son's shoulders.

"Just what it sounds like," Bryan said. "Bait to kill bunnies."

"A lot of people use it to get rid of rabbits and the like. It's used extensively to keep the rabbit population down around here," Shirley said. "We don't use it. It's inhumane."

"Doesn't it kill the wallabies and other native animals, too?" Tyler asked.

"Yes. Although they don't go advertising that," Shirley replied.

"And the cops came out, just because the dog was poisoned? Seems a little far-fetched, but maybe it's because, you know … you're famous and all."

Everyone stared at Bryan. Em cleared her throat, and heads turned to her.

"Ruby wasn't just poisoned, Bryan. Someone broke her neck." Em's voice trembled with rage. "So, add in the chickens being decapitated, the note that was left on the front verandah with one of the chickens' heads, the poisoned goat, and now this, yes, they're looking for who is responsible. Because they believe someone is doing it on purpose. Someone who takes pleasure in causing pain and suffering to innocent creatures." She locked eyes with Bryan.

The group's jaws collectively dropped. Yeah, she knew that would shut them up. They were all aware of the chickens and goat that had been found dead, but they had no idea about the threatening notes, or the chicken head left on the welcome mat. In this moment, Em just wanted to finish her walk and leave Neeminah River behind. She'd had enough.

"Wait on," Bryan said. "What do you mean, someone broke her neck?"

"Em," Shirley said, causing Em to stop in her tracks. "We don't understand. Someone is doing all this intentionally?"

Em turned. The dogs looked at her like they wanted to walk on, too. Their energy had waned like hers had. They wanted to get this over with as much as she did.

"I can't make sense of it either," she replied. "All I know is that three chickens were killed last week. The next day, a chicken head and a note appeared on my doorstep with the words 'Welcome to the neighbourhood'. At first, I thought it could be someone from around here. But then, a goat was poisoned shortly after. Then when a sex tape was posted online, a video I believed to be destroyed years ago, my mother was accused of posting it. But it turns out her laptop, which used to be mine, was stolen from her campervan last week. Now she's gone missing. And this morning, Ruby was found dead." She scanned the faces in the crowd, trying to gauge their reactions. "So excuse me if I seem rude or preoccupied, but my mind is racing with all of this. And if I find out any of you are connected to these events, I promise you will face the full force of the law." She directed a stern look at Bryan once again.

"Hold on! You don't think one of us did any of this?" Bryan exclaimed, folding his arms in front of him, defensively.

"I don't know who did it. But the more things that happen, the more pissed off I am."

With that, she turned on her heel and walked away, leaving Anna to deal with everyone's spluttering. She almost felt guilty about that, but anger boiled in her chest, fuelling her determination to uncover the culprit and put an end to their cruel games. Her guilt and despair had morphed into a fierce rage. She was ready to find whoever it was who was playing mindfuck games with her.

31

"We've been asked by John to return Ruby's body to you, with the direction for you to dispose of it in the pit," Dr Woods said when she went to the vet's office later that afternoon.

Em was taken aback. She had assumed the vet practice would cremate the remains. The thought of dropping poor Ruby's body into the pit seemed like a cruel and unfeeling way to get rid of a beloved pet. Maybe John didn't want Ruby's body to be dug up by devils, Em thought. The metal sheeting that covered the pit would keep them out.

"Sadly, her death was caused by the broken neck," Dr Woods said. "It could be that someone came across her and broke her neck to put her out of her misery, given the poisoning, but I'll leave the investigation to the police. I've sent my report on to them."

Em hadn't considered that. Maybe someone had done that, but why in the middle of the night – and why would they not have knocked on the door to alert her? Why leave her body in the backyard? It was deeply suspicious, and she was more than ever convinced it was connected to everything else going on.

They handed Ruby's body to her in the same red blanket she'd grabbed from the couch. The one she'd wrapped around Billy to keep him warm, then used to cover Ruby's body until Dr Woods had arrived. Now, she hoped the red blanket wasn't something John wanted to keep, because she was going to drop Ruby's body into the pit still wrapped in the blanket. At least she could offer that small comfort to the sweet dog.

Lifting the body from the back of her 4WD when she arrived back at the house, Em couldn't look at it. Charlie and Billy came sniffing around, but Anna called them back. They looked to Em then to Anna, and when Anna called them again, they obeyed.

"John wants me to put Ruby in the pit. I'm just going to put her body near it for now. I need a moment before I toss her in," Em called.

Anna nodded.

She wove her way around to the side of the house, past where the poor dog had died, and laid her beside the metal sheeting over the pit. She wanted to find her favourite chew toy and bury that with her. Maybe the old dog bed, too. But was that pushing it too far? Would John be pissed off that she did that? She should probably only put organic matter in there. That's what the instructions in the housesitting binder had said. Organic matter only. Fine. The blanket would have to suffice.

Em walked inside, feeling like a heavy weight was on her shoulders. She couldn't shake off the feeling of doom.

"You okay?" Anna asked when she walked inside.

Em nodded.

Then Anna asked, "Can I share something weird with you?"

Em looked at Anna, who looked really uncomfortable standing at the edge of the hallway. She hesitated, then nodded.

"I was putting some things in the bathroom, you know, unpacking, while you were gone, and I found something strange in the medicine cabinet," Anna said, her tone unsure.

"What did you find?" Em said, distracted by the thought of how she would get Ruby's body into the pit gently.

Anna replied, "I'll show you. I didn't want to touch anything in there, but this spot seemed odd for something like this."

Em looked up and had a sinking feeling. What was about to happen *now*?

They made their way to the back of the house where John's

bedroom and ensuite bathroom were located. Anna opened the medicine cabinet above the sink. Em hadn't entered John's room except to change the sheets, and had only been in the bathroom once, just to confirm that it was clean before Anna arrived. Inside the cabinet, on the middle shelf and hidden behind some shaving cream, was an old iPhone.

"Weird, right? Who would put a phone in the medicine cabinet?" Anna asked, then looked back at Em. "Hey Em. Are you okay?"

Em felt like the blood was draining from her body.

The phone had a clear plastic case with red strawberries all over it. It looked just like the one her mother had on her phone. The phone she'd lost recently. Em struggled to take it in. Surely it couldn't be …

Anna reached out, but Em grabbed her hand.

"Don't touch it!" she screamed. Anna stopped, her hand in mid-air. "Would you go and get my phone from the kitchen? I'm going to call Ryatt," Em said.

Anna dashed past her and ran to the front of the house. Meanwhile, Em looked around. Nothing was out of the ordinary, with the exception of a few things of Anna's lying around the room.

"How much did you touch in here?" said Em, when Anna came back.

"Oh, um, the toilet. The taps, of course. The cabinet when I opened it. I didn't move anything, though. I saw the phone and thought it was creepy. Especially since the camera part is facing out. Some homeowners have cameras in their houses, which they're supposed to disclose to housesitters. I didn't think to ask you if John had any."

"No, he doesn't," Em said, leaning in to look closely at the phone.

"But it doesn't make sense to have a camera in the medicine cabinet either, which is why I thought I'd tell you about it."

Em nodded, her phone to her ear. Ryatt's phone rang once, twice, then a third time, before he picked up.

"Ryatt," he said gruffly.

"It's Em. Remember how I told you that my mum lost her phone?"

"Yeah. Last week, right? It was why she wasn't calling you?"

"Yes. Except. Well, I think we've just found it," she said, not taking her eyes off the strawberry cover.

"What? Where?" Ryatt said.

"Anna just found it sitting behind some shaving cream in the medicine cabinet in the master ensuite. The case is the same as Mum's, and the phone looks like the older model like Mum's."

"It's at your housesit? What the ..."

"I know!" Em shrieked. The whole idea that it was her mum's phone was unnerving.

"Don't touch it. Look, I'll call you back," Ryatt said, and the line went dead.

Em stared at the phone for a moment, then raised her own phone and took photos from as many angles as she could think of, including showing the case up close and from further back to show the phone's position in the cabinet. When she'd finished, she sent them all to Ryatt.

The longer she looked, the more she was convinced it was her mother's phone. The question was, why was it in the medicine cabinet, here with her?

"I NEED to go and put Ruby in the pit," Em said, once she'd told Anna what Ryatt had said. "Not that I want to do that to the sweet girl. But I can't leave the body just sitting out there."

Em had gone from bewilderment to anger to rage and back again over the course of the last two hours. Now she was back to being confused about what was going on. With the note beneath Ruby's dead body, and the phone in the cabinet, things weren't adding up. She couldn't see Callum doing this, no matter how desperate he was.

"I'm going to go out to the pit, say some words, then put her in the pit as carefully as I can," Em said, grabbing her jacket.

"I'll come with you. That cover is heavy, remember?" Anna said.

"Do you want to let Billy and Charlie follow? I'm sure they'll want to say goodbye too?" Anna suggested as she grabbed her coat.

Em hesitated, then nodded. The yard had been cleared by the police, so there was no danger to them. Billy hadn't stopped looking sad all day, and looking at Charlie broke Em's heart. He looked lost.

"Yes. That's a nice idea," Em said and called to the dogs.

"Ruby was such a beautiful spirit," Anna said, as they rounded the corner of the house and walked towards the large, enclosed garden. Em couldn't say anything, she was so lost in her own grief.

The pit lay just behind the garden, hidden from sight from the house. When they arrived at the metal lid, Charlie and Billy seemed to hold back. Charlie growled but Em shushed him gently. Taking a deep breath, she lifted the blanket that was wrapped around Ruby. She looked to be at peace, at least, Em thought. She ran her fingers through the softness of Ruby's velvety ears one last time. When Anna walked closer to the pit, Charlie growled again. Em covered Ruby with the blanket again.

"Charlie. It's fine," Em said, then turned to Anna. After the chickens, Em knew the lid was heavy and best moved by two people. "If you can help me lift the lid aside, we can say a few words and then lower Ruby in together. Is that okay?"

Anna nodded.

Together, they stood on either side of the pit and lifted the lid cautiously. Charlie let out a low growl, while Billy barked, which was unusual for the greyhound. What was going on with them today?

Suddenly, an overwhelming stench filled their nostrils. Em glanced at Anna, who looked like she might be sick. They quickly dropped the lid back down with a loud clang. Charlie and Billy both retreated in fear. But then, Charlie turned around and barked fiercely at the pit.

"What the hell is that smell?" Anna asked, covering her nose and mouth. "God, it's toxic!"

"Surely it's not from the chickens," Em said.

Anna half shrugged.

"It's probably from the goat we put in there. If you can lift the lid, I'll look down into the pit," Em said.

Anna hesitated, then nodded reluctantly. She pulled her jumper up over her mouth and nose in an attempt to mask the smell, then bent down again to lift the lid.

"Wait," said Em. "The pit is deep. Let me just turn on the torch on my phone so I can see down in there. Okay. Ready?"

Anna nodded and, her voice muffled through the jumper, said, "Ready as I'll ever be, but I can't promise I won't hurl afterwards. That smell is rank!"

"Just vomit away from me, okay?" Em said, wryly. "Okay, go."

Anna huffed and Charlie growled again. When the lid was lifted enough for her to see further down, Em held her nose and covered her mouth before turning the light into the abyss.

"Holy fuck! Close it! Close it!" Em shrieked, and fell back onto the grass, her fingers clawing into the dirt.

Anna let the lid drop. "What? What is it?" she screamed, reacting to Em clawing herself as far away as she could get.

"Em. What's in it?" Anna asked, her eyes so wide she looked almost cartoonish.

"I … I don't know," Em stammered. "But it's not the goat. It looks like … like a body." Her body was stiff from shock and her eyes stung with tears.

"What the *fuck*?" Anna said and reached out to open the pit again.

"*Don't!* Don't open it. I think … I only saw part of the body but …" Em began sobbing. The image in her mind of the body at the bottom of the pit was shocking. It was curled up as if in a foetal position, the head not visible due to the shadows of the pit, but she could see the shoulders and the back. "We need … we need to call the police."

"Fuck. Fuck. *Fuck*," Anna said, pulling her phone from her pocket. "Who the fuck would do that?"

Em's blood ran cold. "Wait," she barked. "Wait. I … Oh …" She scrambled to the nearby bushes and vomited over the waxy shrubs. Vomit dripped down the leaves. "It couldn't be, could it?" she whispered as she fell to the ground, her hand landing in a trail of her own sick.

"Oh my God, Em. Are you okay?" Anna asked, but Em couldn't answer.

The image was firmly in her mind. She shook her head and shuffled further backwards on the grass. She kept shaking her head. She couldn't speak. It wasn't real. It couldn't be real. Who would do this?

"Oh God …" Em said, shaking from the shock.

"Em, what's going on?" Anna asked, the phone in her hand, ready to dial.

"I think … I think it's Callum," Em whispered.

"*What?* What do you mean?" Anna asked, her own voice echoing Em's shock.

"The shoulder. He has a tattoo on his left shoulder. A Southern Cross. And the body. In the pit. It has a tattoo … like Callum's. Just like Callum's. Oh my God, this can't be real."

"I'm calling the police," Anna said, dialling 000 and hitting the green call button.

Em brought her knees up and wrapped her arms around them. She rocked back and forth as tears rolled down her cheeks, then sobs took over. Images of Callum's body swam in her mind, over and over.

"Who'd do this?" she mumbled, over and over. She was so cold. When her entire body began shaking, she felt Charlie nuzzle her armpit. She reached over to stroke his soft grey fur. He lay down next to her and she let the dog's presence calm her.

"Where's your phone, Em?" she heard Anna say, but it sounded like Anna was in a long tunnel. She looked over and saw Anna suddenly at her side, as if she'd snapped her fingers and Anna had disappeared from in front of her only to rematerialise beside her.

Em next became aware she had a blanket around her. Billy was pacing back and forth, agitated. Em called to him, and he came slinking over and lay down so that Charlie and Billy were either side of her. Billy's nose nuzzled under her leg as he looked to provide comfort, too. How did dogs always know when someone needed them? Billy, Charlie and, oh God, Ruby! She'd forgotten about Ruby. She looked over and saw the dog's body still wrapped in the frayed red blanket. They'd have to … No. She couldn't think of the … She continued to stroke Charlie's head in long, smooth strokes. He reminded her of the dog she'd had when she was little. When her dad was still alive. What was her name? She'd come to them abused, hadn't she? Wasn't that what Daddy had told her? Sasha? Was that her name? That sounded right. She was sweet, too.

"Em!" Anna yelled. "Where's your phone? We need to call …"

But all Em could hear were sirens coming from somewhere.

"Never mind," Anna said, and a minute later, she thrust the phone in front of Em's face.

Em recoiled, thinking Anna was going to hit her with it, but then

Anna started doing something with the phone. Dialling someone. The sirens got louder.

"Ryatt? It's Anna," she said, her face taut with concern and … was that anger?

Em was confused. Why was Anna angry? It was Em's husband …

"Oh, God …" Em leaned over, pushing Billy out of the way to dry heave into the grass. When nothing came up, she sank onto her back, her body splayed out on the grass. This time Charlie and Billy both came to her at once, sniffing her. Charlie lay down and put his head on her stomach, much like he'd done with Ruby. Oh, poor Ruby. She was such a sweet dog.

"No, not good," she heard Anna say next to her. "We've found a body. On the property. Em thinks it may be Callum."

Em heard the words Anna was saying but she couldn't comprehend what was going on. She looked over at the pit again as someone opened the gate behind her. She saw Anna wave them over from the corner of her eye.

"Over here," Anna shouted to whoever it was.

But all Em could do was lie on her back and think of the image in her head of what lay at the bottom of the pit, patting Charlie's head in long, broad strokes as she wondered who the hell would kill Callum.

32

"**M**ats?"

She heard Ryatt's voice, but her tears blurred his face. She sat outside on the back verandah while ambulance people poked at her, a silver blanket now wrapped around her. The shivering continued. From beyond the fence, in the outer paddock, Charlie and Billy watched the commotion around the house. Sachin sat staring at Em with his big brown eyes.

"Mats. I need to ask you some questions," Ryatt continued.

He'd grilled Anna already. There had been lots of nodding from Anna in response to Ryatt's barrage of questions. Em wasn't sure whether she could speak, let alone answer any questions. She still wasn't sure what she'd seen, although she remembered people pulling a body out of the pit. A body. A naked body. The tattoo.

"Callum," she whispered. It couldn't have been him, could it? She looked up, blinked rapidly, then stared at Ryatt, who looked at her with barely concealed worry under his detective gaze.

"Yes, Mats. It was Callum," Ryatt said, so quietly against the thrum of noise around them that she could barely hear him.

"How? Why?" she asked, but she was afraid to know the answers. Callum. Callum was dead. Her husband was dead. Callum, her husband, was dead. It was like a never-ending reel playing over and over.

"We're trying to determine the answers to those questions," Ryatt said, taking a seat next to her. "But right now, are you okay? Can I get you anything? Margo and Shirley are going to take you back to their place. Okay?"

"Why?"

It was all she could ask. Why? Why had this happened? And why Callum? He was a shit to everyone who knew him, but why would anyone want to kill him?

"Why what?" *Why everything,* she thought. "Why can't we let you inside?" he asked.

She nodded.

"Because we need to rule you out as a suspect," Ryatt said, cringing.

"*Me?*" she screamed.

Heads turned her way. One detective, someone she'd seen Ryatt talking to only moments before, looked at her with cold, steel grey eyes.

"We need to rule you out. It's part of the process," he said, guiltily.

His face showed concern, but after looking over at the other, presumably more senior, detective, Ryatt turned back to her, his eyes back to what she'd come to recognise as his 'official' expression. His eyes, too, were cold.

"Did you see Callum last night or this morning?" Ryatt asked.

She shook her head.

"Did he call you, text you?"

Again, she shook her head.

"When was the last time you saw him?" Ryatt asked.

"The other day, when you were here," she said quietly.

Ryatt wrote something down in his notebook. "And you've not seen or heard from him since?"

She shook her head again.

"Will you let me check your phone to confirm that?"

She nodded again.

"I need you to verbally give me permission to do that, Mathilda."

Hearing Ryatt use her full name was like having a bucket of ice water dumped on her head. She didn't remember the last time he'd called her Mathilda. It had always been Mats.

"Yes," she squeaked. "Check my phone."

"Did you know where Callum was staying?" Ryatt asked. "When he came down to see you?"

She shook her head again.

"And has anyone mentioned anything to you as to his whereabouts?"

The question threw her. It seemed loaded. Had Kennedy said that he was back in Melbourne when she spoke to her yesterday? She didn't think so, but she wasn't sure.

"I don't think so. I assumed he went back to work on the movie. In Melbourne," she said, but the days and hours were a blur. She couldn't remember what anyone had said or done.

"We'll check that," Ryatt said, then looked up. "Okay, I'm going to give you over to Margo and Shirley. They're going to take you home to their place. I'll be in touch. Okay?"

"How?" Em asked.

Ryatt looked at her quizzically.

"How'd he die?"

"We don't know. That's what we are here to figure out." He glanced over at the senior detective, who was now walking away towards a cluster of people near the pit, then looked back at her. "There appear to be no fatal injuries to his body," he said, very quietly. "He had a broken leg and arm and a lot of bruising, most likely from being thrown into the pit. There'll be an emergency autopsy today, given who he is. Was. We'll know more later."

"Okay," Em said, then found herself being guided by Margo's hand and soft words to Shirley's car.

Anna already sat in the back seat, while Shirley was in the driver's seat.

"Come on, darling. Let's get you warm," Margo cooed.

. . .

SHE HEARD voices from another room, but, looking around, couldn't place where she was. Surrounding her were massive bookcases lining the walls, filled with romance and mystery novels and an assortment of gardening, cooking and knitting books. Em was snuggled down under a wool comforter with a beautiful patchwork quilt over it. She suspected an electric blanket was also under her. She wanted to stay here forever. But something was pinning her down at the end of the bed. She looked up and saw Gracie curled up at her feet.

At Em's movement, the dog raised her head, then tilted it like she was asking if Em was okay. That's when reality hit her like a ten-tonne truck.

Callum. Callum was dead. Her husband was dead. The reel in her head returned. But now added to it was the thought that she was a suspect.

The voices outside the room got louder, but Em couldn't make out all of what was being said.

"... but what if they think she ..." Shirley bellowed, before being hushed by Margo.

"... did do it, it would have been an act of self-defence," Anna whispered loudly. "You saw ..."

"... so focused on Em? She didn't ..." Shirley said.

Margo shushed her again.

Em threw back the covers. Gracie jumped down and nuzzled the door open. Em looked down and noticed she was wearing the same clothes that she'd had on earlier, and her body ached like she was a hundred years old. She felt heavy and weak. She stood, but dizziness overwhelmed her. There was a faint smell of urine lingering in the air, from the cat, Kumquat. Em fell back down onto the bed, and when she looked up, Margo stood in the doorway.

"Hello, love," Margo said simply. "How are you doing?" It was a question that Em had no words for.

Shirley appeared over Margo's shoulder. "I'll make you some tea. Or would you prefer coffee?"

"Tea is fine. Thanks." She stood again, wobbled, but kept her balance. "Toilet?"

"Next door over," Margo said. "We'll be in the lounge room when you're ready."

When she walked out into the living room a few minutes later, she was surprised to find Kennedy sitting in the living room with Anna and Margo. Shirley was banging around in the kitchen.

"Kennedy?" Em didn't know why she was here. How she'd got here. Wasn't she supposed to be in Melbourne by now? Or LA?

"Hey, girl." Kennedy stood, looking camera-ready as always, and stepped forward to hug her.

"What are you doing here?" Em asked.

"I came to help," Kennedy said. "I was still in Melbourne when I heard. Anna called me. Asher is on his way, too. He'll be here sometime tomorrow. We're still trying to reach Kat."

"Mum. I should call her," Em said. "Where's my—"

"Ryatt has your phone," Anna said. "He said he'd try and reach your mum, too."

Em nodded, then sat on the couch. "How long was I out for?"

"A while. It's okay. You've had a shock," Margo said.

Shirley thrust a mug of tea in her face. "Don't know how you have it, but I put sugar in it for the energy," she said, smiling awkwardly.

"Thanks," Em said, and took a sip of the steaming brew, then recoiled at the sweetness. It was enough to rot teeth.

"How much sugar did you put in that tea, darl'?" Margo said, turning to Shirley.

"Same as I put in my tea. Figured she needed the boost."

"It's fine," Em said, placing the cup on the coffee table in front of her. "So, what's going on? Have they figured out what happened with … ?" She couldn't finish the sentence. Saying it out loud made it real.

"Not yet," Margo said.

"But the media are blaming you," Shirley butted in.

"Shirley!" Margo snapped, then turned to Em. "We know it wasn't you, love, don't worry."

"And don't worry about the media, I'm on it," Kennedy said, "but I need to know if you're okay if I release a statement on your behalf?"

Em nodded.

"We'll draft it together, okay?" Kennedy said. "Make sure it's clear you aren't involved."

"Why would they even think that?" Em croaked, confused. "He was my ..." Her voice caught. "My husband."

"The video," Shirley said. "People think it's a revenge killing." That got her a laser blast look from Margo.

"The video?" Em asked. "The *sex* video?"

Shirley nodded.

"I wrote up what we talked about, Em, just in case," Kennedy said.

"In case of what? I didn't do it!"

"We know that, love. And so does Ryatt," Margo said, soothingly.

"People are twisting the truth and trying to put pieces together without knowing what's real and what's bullshit," Shirley added.

Margo sighed, but Em appreciated Shirley's no-nonsense manner at this point. At least Shirley knew what was going on and didn't treat her like she was a delicate flower. Even though, right now, she felt like one.

"Yeah, without knowing what Callum was really like," Kennedy added. "Their beloved 'son' is dead. That's all they see."

"Right," Em said.

"We're all behind you, Em," Anna said. "Whatever you need. Tyler has the dogs. Pete said they'll take care of the animals for as long as you need."

Em looked at Anna, who stood at the kitchen door, and remembered that she'd been in the process of moving in with her for the rest of the housesit. Em felt a mixture of horror and guilt. Would Anna even want to stay with her, now? First she'd had to help deal with Ruby. And then Callum. She'd been there with her when she'd found him.

"I'm so sorry," said Em.

Anna shook her head. "Not your fault."

"But you were about to stay with me. Help with the housesit," Em said.

Anna shook her head slowly again. "That's not important. We'll work something out."

"You can't go back to the house, anyway," Margo interrupted. "Not until we hear from Ryatt."

"It's still an active crime scene," said Shirley. "They're trying to locate John to let him know, too."

John. The homeowner. Her stomach plummeted.

"God, that poor man," Em said. "He thought he was just getting a housesitter. Instead, because of me, he's got dead bodies."

33

Hours later, sitting silent in her hotel room in Hobart, Em felt lost and alone, despite having had people buzzing around her all day. People kept asking her if she was okay, if she had everything she needed. But all she needed was her mother. God, even to know where she was. No one could get hold of her.

It would be just like Kat to turn off her phone and disappear for a while. What had freaked her out so much that she'd disappear like that? But with this, with Callum dead, surely she'd come back?

Sitting there, staring at the stark white walls, the reality of the situation hit her again, hard.

She had no one anymore.

Callum was dead. Her mother had bolted. She had … no one.

She thought of Asher, currently flying to Melbourne, and wondered if their friendship had changed. He'd told her when she'd left LA that he wanted out of the business; but he'd been there for her, supporting her, as her friend over the past few weeks. Would things be weird when he arrived?

Her mind went to Ryatt. She thought she had a connection with Ryatt, too, but he'd kept his distance all day, staying in official mode.

No one to comfort her, to hug her, to tell her it was going to be okay. Right now, she felt like she was in a chasm of loneliness. She wanted to cry.

The media were everywhere. At the end of the driveway. At the end of the road. In Huonville. Two television vans had even followed them to Hobart. It was just like LA, only ten times worse. Once in her hotel room, Em had cried until her sinuses were overwhelmed and her head screamed from the congestion.

She stood and made her way to the window, her heart heavy. The lights from the marina pushed back the darkness. In any other circumstance, she would have found it breathtaking, but all she felt was a deep sense of loneliness. The room felt suffocating, yet she couldn't bring herself to face the outside world. She craved comfort, yet feared what awaited her once she stepped through the door.

Resigning herself to what was to come, she washed her face in the bathroom and opened the door to the suite's living space. She was surprised to find Kennedy and Anna sitting on the couch, talking quietly and sipping on glasses of red wine. Em couldn't believe it; they had stayed with her. She'd figured they'd just dump her at the hotel and leave. But here they were, settled in. She guessed Kennedy had her own hotel room somewhere, although she hadn't asked where. Anna could have stayed with Margo and Shirley. But then, thinking of the underlying smell of Kumquat's urine, Em thought maybe not.

Kennedy smiled at Em, got up and poured a glass of wine for her from the bar, where six bottles of red wine stood waiting.

"Figured you'd need this. It was either red wine or crap whiskey from the bar, so I opted for the wine."

Kennedy topped up Anna's glass then her own, and returned to the leather couch. Em sat heavily in a blue velvet chair opposite them.

"I was just sharing stories with Anna, telling her about my family," Kennedy said casually, as if they were a couple of girlfriends hanging out for the night.

Em nodded, and Kennedy carried on with her story.

"My dad would have had a one-way express ticket to hell, if there is such a place," Kennedy continued.

Em listened to her talk, thankful that she wasn't being bombarded with questions about how she was doing or feeling. Kennedy continued speaking as if there wasn't a storm brewing beyond the door. Em opened her mouth to ask if they'd heard from Ryatt yet, but Kennedy stopped her with a shake of her head, like she could read her mind, before continuing with her tale.

She chuckled darkly. "Actually, hell would have been too kind for my dad." Anna's eyebrows lifted in curiosity. "Have you guys seen the show *Supernatural*?" said Kennedy.

"Yes, loved it," said Anna.

"There was a character on it. Crowley. The King of Hell. That was my father personified. He was always the one who schmoozed everyone, full of charm, but my dad was without the hint of a heart. Come to think of it, Crowley *had* a heart – he'd just buried it under the King of Hell persona. But my father lacked that. He had a way of charming people and then taking advantage of them, whether it was material or otherwise. Whatever it was that made him look good. He was all about appearances. My mom was dependent on plastic surgery and later Valium, while my sister battled addiction for years until she ultimately overdosed in a dirty alley in Los Angeles, about fifteen years ago. And when I became pregnant as a teenager after being raped by the golden boy quarterback, Dad couldn't even look at me. As if it were my fault and I had brought shame upon the family."

"Geezus. Is he ..." Anna hesitated, unsure of whether she was allowed to ask questions. She took the plunge anyway. "Is he still alive?"

Kennedy shrugged. "Don't know. Don't care. I was told he was dead, but I didn't ask how, where or why." She took a long sip from her wine glass.

Em wondered how deep Kennedy's emotional scars ran. Having a dad like that would scar anyone.

Kennedy shifted in her chair, looking uncomfortable. "I have a question for you. I was talking with Asher about this, and, um...."

Em took a deep breath. "What's the question?" Kennedy looked toward her and grimaced.

"What are you going to do about a funeral, once the autopsy is completed?"

Em shook her head. She hadn't thought about that, but she suddenly hoped that his PR team and agent could handle it.

"I can't think about all that yet. I keep wondering where Mum is. Given what's happened, I'm really worried about her now. She hasn't called, has she?"

Kennedy shook her head. Em sighed, then turned to stare out the large glass windows. Where was she? Where was her mother?

"I had a dream about my parents," Em began, her voice soft. "Mum was vibrant all the time when Dad was alive. I just remember them being happy. There was always music playing in the house, whether Dad was home or not. But when he was home, my parents used to put on a record and slow dance together. They'd include me sometimes, but most of the time, it was just the two of them. Mum has spent her whole life missing him. I thought she was going to die of a broken heart. Since then, she's been dealing with depression on and off for years. It's why she moves around a lot now. Best to keep moving, she tells me. The ghosts can't find you then."

Anna and Kennedy were quiet, taking sips of wine here and there while Em spoke. Her own wine glass, clenched in her hand, had remained untouched.

"We stayed in Coonawarra for a little while, after Dad died, but it was too hard for Mum. Memories were everywhere, and she had to eventually accept that Dad wasn't coming home to us. When I was about five, we moved to Ballarat, I think. Then we lived with a guy and his son, but I'm not sure where that was. After that, it was Brisbane, I think. We just kept moving after that. After Dad, Mum seemed lost. She was lost for a long time."

"And you have no brothers or sisters?" Anna asked.

"No. Mum told me she had a hard time with my birth. Something to do with some stuff that happened before she met Dad. She always called me her miracle baby."

Em's smile was sad, but the memory of her words was a lovely one. Her mind jumped to one night, when they lived in the house in Ballarat, and she had a flash of a boy's face. She remembered how longingly he used to look at her mother, like he was desperate to have a mother of his own.

Kennedy's phone pinged beside her. She reached over for it. "Well, shit. AP has just blown up," she said, her fingers scrolling over her phone.

"Who's AP?" Anna asked.

"Not who, what. Associated Press," Kennedy said, her eyes skimming the news bulletin.

"What are they saying?" Em asked.

She'd been expecting this, but Kennedy's face went hard, her fingers to her mouth as she read the media bulletin.

"Kennedy? What's the story?" Em asked, but she was also afraid to know the answer.

"Hmm...," Kennedy mumbled, focused on her screen.

"Just tell me," she said, resigning herself to facing whatever had been released. Em knew how these things worked, but being on this side of the story was like being trapped in a small, suffocating room with no escape. The grief had finally caught up with her, and she could feel the walls closing in around her.

"Better to know than not," Kennedy said.

Em nodded. "Go on then," she said, mentally putting her armour on.

"The media is blaming you for Callum's death," Kennedy said. "They're saying that it was a crime of passion."

Kennedy turned the phone around for her to see. There, at the top of the web page for the *Sydney Morning Herald* bore the words she would never, in a million years, believe she'd ever see.

AUSTRALIA'S FAVOURITE SON, CALLUM WALSH, MURDERED BY WIFE

"Oh my God!" Em said. Kennedy turned it back around, scouring the page.

"Read it to me. I want to know what they're saying."

Kennedy looked at her and paused, and when Em nodded, she started reading out loud.

"Mathilda Walsh, award-winning ... blah blah blah ... left her respected position after ... blah blah blah ... to spend a year travelling.

While she was housesitting a property in southern Tasmania, Callum Walsh's body was found buried in the backyard," she read.

"Well, nice to know they got some parts of that correct. Keep reading," Em said. Anna got up to get more wine.

"A source for the *Sydney Morning Herald* has shared that the tape released to the public only weeks ago, showing blah blah blah … was released by Mathilda's mother, who has a history of mental instability. As previously reported, Mathilda's mother, Kathryn McKinney, spent time in Adelaide's psychiatric hospital in the early eighties for undisclosed reasons. The source claims that Callum Walsh was outraged by the tape's release, but it was his wife, Mathilda, who made threats against anyone responsible for leaking it. Amidst all the accusations and chaos surrounding their ongoing divorce case, it seems that Mathilda Walsh reached her breaking point. More allegations have been made against her, and her impending arrest is reported to be only days away."

"Fuck me!" Anna exclaimed, outraged.

Em found comfort in her friend's words, but she also knew the media's tendency to twist the truth. As did Kennedy, who sat gnawing on her thumb nail.

"I need to tell you the full story," Em said, suddenly.

Kennedy's head shot up like a gun had just gone off.

"There's more," Em said.

She sat back in the blue chair and took a long, deep breath.

34

Ah Mathilda.

Your world is crumbling.

It's such a pleasure to watch.

Now you will face the ultimate humiliation.

Being accused of something you didn't do.

35

"You told me, Kennedy, when we talked about Kelli, that everyone has secrets. Well, there's another part to Callum's secret that still isn't public. And I have a secret as well. One that no one knows about. Not even Asher."

Anna opened her mouth to ask a question, then closed it again.

"Do you want me to … take notes, or just listen?" Kennedy asked, awkwardly.

Em understood her struggle between being a friend or a reporter. "Hit record on your phone," she said, and saw disbelief in Kennedy's face.

"You sure?" Kennedy asked.

Em nodded. "The media need to know the truth, and if they're going to persecute me, they at least need all the facts."

"I already have enough to set the story straight, Em. You don't need to tell me anything else," Kennedy said, but Em knew she had to let the truth out.

"There's more to the story of why I left Callum," she said.

Kennedy nodded, stood, and rummaged through her handbag for a small recorder. She pressed record on both her phone and the recorder, then nodded to Em.

"Kelli wasn't the only woman Callum got pregnant," Em said.

Kennedy did not look surprised, but Anna looked confused.

"Let me give you some background, Anna, so you know what's going on," Em said. "Callum has a secret child with a woman named Kelli, born after he drugged us both and essentially raped us."

"Not essentially," said Kennedy. "He *did* rape you."

Em nodded. "That was the sex tape that was released. That's why he was so pissed off and showed up in Tasmania. Callum gave Kelli and me ecstasy, so it looked like we were having a great time, but the truth was a lot more sinister than that. Kelli was an actress. She had been working with Callum on a movie, and thought Callum was God's gift. When he invited her to his hotel room, she thought it would be just him."

"What hotel was this?" Kennedy asked. "Never mind. I don't need to know."

"No, I get it. You need the facts to confirm what I tell you. It's the same as what Kelli told you. It happened in, let's just say, a famous hotel that's known for risqué things happening. In Hollywood. I don't think we need to name and shame the hotel. They had no idea what was happening.

"Anyway. Kelli was a virgin, which we didn't know until later on. She was barely of age, which Callum did know, but I didn't. I thought she was over twenty-one. She looked it, anyway. And she was Catholic, which wasn't something we knew until later either. But when she turned up at The Bakehouse one morning, wanting to speak with me, it all came out. She was pregnant. She couldn't reach Callum, which was no surprise. He was a 'one night only' show with the girls. He had a saying about that, I learned later, but it's not a nice one, nor one I'd repeat."

Em took a sip of wine. The others did the same.

"Anyway, Kelli refused to get an abortion, and so Callum's PR team went into action and put Kelli on full lockdown. They set her up in a condo, gave her a stipend, had her sign an ironclad non-disclosure and support contract, and locked Kelli and her baby away. They wanted her to move overseas, but she refused. Good for her, I say. She had her family's support, but she wasn't allowed to tell them who the father was. All was fine for him for a while. But now others know about what happened. Or have figured it out," Em said, looking at Kennedy.

"It's not hard, when Kelli's little boy is the spitting image of Callum when he was little," Kennedy said, turning to Anna. "There are photos of Callum as a kid online. When I went digging, I figured out the boy's paternity pretty quickly. It wasn't hard. I eventually had a conversation with Kelli, who reluctantly told me the truth, but it was on condition of anonymity."

"She spoke to you? After signing a contract?" Anna asked.

"Not at first. But I told her there were others," Kennedy said. "I initially lied to her to get the truth. I didn't know then what I know now. And, I know. It was wrong. There are days I truly I hate my job."

"Except you weren't lying," Em said. "There *are* others."

Kennedy nodded. "Yeah, I've been discovering that. I just found a girl in the UK named Monica last week."

"Yep, Monica is in England. She was seventeen at the time. That was about three years ago. There was Ines in Sweden, last year. She was barely eighteen. She had an abortion. There's Fiona in New Zealand. She was eighteen, almost nineteen. She wavered over keeping the baby or having an abortion. She was also Catholic but was smart enough to see the writing on the wall. That was four years ago. Then there's Celia. She's Canadian. That's when things started getting very messy. Celia is fifteen. When Celia came forward, that's when I left. I didn't want to hide Ca—" She found she couldn't even say his name. "His secrets anymore."

"Holy shit," Kennedy said. "I had only discovered Monica."

"You would have discovered the others, soon enough. Although Callum's PR team are very good at their job."

"Apparently! I've heard none of this on the gossip pages I follow," Anna said, then blushed. "Followed. I stopped following them after I met you and saw what happened on the other side."

"I need to change careers," Kennedy declared. "I've been thinking about it for a while. I'm sick of the bullshit."

"The bullshit is one of the reasons I escaped LA," Em said, but Kennedy knew that part.

"Everyone has secrets," Kennedy said.

"Including me," Em said. She took another deep breath, knowing she had to get it all out. "I got pregnant at the same time as Kelli, but I decided immediately to have an abortion. No one knew. I told Callum that I was heading to Canada to check out a cooking school in Toronto. Instead, I checked into a Seattle hotel after visiting a clinic."

"I'd do the same," Kennedy said.

"The problem is, I've always wanted to be a mother. But when I realised I was pregnant with Callum's child, it felt wrong. I didn't want anything more to do with him. It just took me a while to work out how to get out of the marriage. The abortion was easy. But when Celia turned up pregnant, claiming he raped her, I really had to wonder how many other women he'd done this to. I knew about Kelli, but Celia's story made me feel sick, knowing what I already knew."

"You weren't an accomplice, Em. You were a victim as much as they were," Kennedy said.

"I hate that word, victim," Em said.

"Survivor, then."

"Did you know what he was doing?" Anna asked.

Em hesitated. "I knew about Kelli, of course, but not about the others. Not until Celia. After she showed up on our front doorstep, he got blind drunk. That's when I confronted him about it. He spilled it all then. He told me I needed to keep my mouth shut, or else."

"He threatened you?" Anna said.

"Yes, and it wasn't the first time. But this is all why he showed up in Tasmania," Em said. "Why he was so livid. Because he suspected that if the Kelli story got out, the rest would too, and he'd be ruined."

"This is why I need to write the story," Kennedy said. "His career is one thing. How he got there, I mean. But we're talking about the man, and the lengths he went to. Thinking he's God Almighty and could treat women like trash. Drug them. Rape them. We need to put out a statement. You need to be cleared by the police first, of course – and you will be – but the bigger story about Callum needs to go out shortly after."

"I don't know," Em said. "I don't want all those other women to get hurt. And really, it's more a 'he said, she said' scenario at this point. I only know what Callum told me."

"Would the women be willing to talk? If I talked to them?" Kennedy asked.

Em shrugged.

Kennedy went on, "I could tell them Kelli's story, if she was okay with that. Without naming her, of course."

"I don't know. Honestly, they're likely under contracts too."

"Well, I already found Monica, and I already have Kelli's story. Did you sign a contract with his PR team?"

Em shook her head.

"Then we dig around and find these women. Then I write the story on the real Callum Walsh. Because as shocking as it is that he's dead, the fuckwit is where he deserves to be," Kennedy said. "And where he deserves to be is in hell, and without the 'Australia's Favourite Son' title."

"That makes me sick now," Anna said.

"Me too. And this, ladies, is the part of my job I *do* enjoy," Kennedy said. "Bringing the fuckwits down."

EM'S MOUTH felt like a dried-out sponge when she woke the following morning, but finding some water would have to take a back seat, because right now she needed to know where her mother was. She rolled over and grabbed for her phone on the bedside table, but found the space empty. Opening one eye, she scanned the room and remembered where she was. Then the realisation that Ryatt still had her phone sank in. *Shit.*

The thump of the hotel door in the living area startled her out of bed. She grabbed her jumper from the chair and pulled her pants on. Every part of her body felt heavy, like she was being pulled down by wet cement. Not only was she dealing with an overwhelming situation that would make anyone feel heavy, but she'd also, unsurprisingly, overindulged in wine the night before.

She opened the bedroom door, and the smell of strong coffee and something greasy filled the room. Her stomach rumbled, although she wasn't sure if it was from too much alcohol swimming in there or from hunger. Probably both.

When she walked into the living room, she was shocked to find Asher standing there. He was dressed in worn jeans and a black peacoat, a wool skull cap pulled down over his ears. He looked as if he hadn't slept all night. He probably hadn't, Em thought, if he'd just folded his immense body into an economy seat all the way from LA to Melbourne.

"How's it shakin', bacon?" Asher said, throwing his backpack down and striding over to her.

His arms wrapped around her, and she slumped into them, sobbing against his jacket. His hands rubbed her back methodically. He didn't try to quieten her. Didn't try to soothe and stop her. He just stood there, holding her, letting her get it out. It was everything she needed. When she was spent, she pulled back. Snot covered his coat.

"God, sorry," she said, wiping it away.

"Don't worry about it. Needs a wash anyway. I had a toddler sitting next to me on the flight who unfortunately vomited right as we were taxiing to the gate in Melbourne," he said with a smile, looking down at her.

She craned her neck up to see him, having forgotten just how tall he was.

Kennedy held a coffee out to Em. "I wondered what that smell was." She smiled at Asher and pinched her nose.

How was the woman looking so bright-eyed and perky this early in the damn morning?

"Bless you," Em said, taking the cup. "What time is it?"

"Almost noon," Kennedy said.

"What?"

"Here. I got you this, too. It's a bacon and egg roll with barbecue sauce. Anna said it's a sure-fire cure for a hangover," Kennedy said, handing her a greasy paper bag. "Besides, you didn't eat dinner last night, so you need to eat."

"How are you not feeling the same?" Em asked, opening the bag. The smell hit her afresh and her mouth, oddly, salivated.

"Wait. Where is Anna?" Em asked, looking toward the other bedroom.

"She drove back to Neeminah River. We heard from Ryatt this

morning. The farm is clear. He said we could go back today, but suggested we spend another night here. The media are everywhere down there. Anna went back to check on the animals."

Em opened her mouth, but Kennedy hastily added, "They're all fine. Tyler? Is that the kid's name?"

Em nodded.

"He's got it covered, but Anna wanted to do something to help, so she's going to go and check the chickens, and take the dogs for a long walk, since Tyler has school and his dad had to get to work."

Em felt oddly uneasy about receiving so much help. Not that she didn't appreciate it.

"Now, eat that thing, and drink your coffee," Kennedy demanded.

"Babe, do you need a shower? You can use the shower in my room."

Asher looked at Em with questioning eyes. She smiled back, although she knew it was half-hearted. It still felt a bit weird with Asher, but he was here.

"Thanks for coming," she said.

"It wasn't even a question, Buttercup. Just instinct," Asher replied, returning her smile as he grabbed his backpack and headed out to Kennedy's hotel room.

36

"It's been days. What do you mean you can't get hold of him?" Ryatt was on the phone, his tone impatient. "Keep trying. Contact the Western Australian police again. Get them to track him down."

It had been three days since Callum's body was found. Ryatt was back at the housesit, still trying to piece everything together. Em wasn't sure what he was looking for. Every possible photo had been taken of the scene. The neighbours had all been interviewed for the umpteenth time. No one had seen a thing. At least, nothing unusual. Nothing was out of place either. But Ryatt was convinced he'd missed something.

Em watched him pace the verandah outside the bi-fold doors. The fire was on, thanks to Anna (using Shirley's fire-building technique), but Em still felt cold down to her bones.

"When are they releasing the body? Have they said?" Anna asked, folding a grey woollen blanket and placing it over the back of the couch. Em had been wrapped in that blanket all morning.

"No, not yet. I need to contact ..." She couldn't bring herself to finish the sentence.

"Kennedy said she was going to help you with that," Anna said, but Em knew Kennedy was already doing enough by trying to keep the media at bay. Between Asher and Kennedy, they'd kept them far away from Em, for which she was grateful. She couldn't believe that the media continued to imply that she had murdered Callum. The police had denied Em's involvement – although by the way the local police kept looking at her, she had her doubts. She'd already told Ryatt the full story of Callum's background. Somehow Ryatt wasn't surprised to hear the details, which made Em wonder if he already knew what Callum had been doing.

"Was there a woman in Australia?" Ryatt had asked the day before, but she said she didn't think so. "If there was, it might explain all the crap that's been happening to you. Maybe it's a scorned woman, out for revenge? Or maybe they were setting you up to take the fall?" Ryatt suggested.

Em was initially shocked at that idea. She'd paused to think. Surely no one would be that manipulative? But then, she wasn't naive. They'd been blackmailed before.

"Maybe, but I haven't heard of anyone here," Em had said, eventually.

"I'll check with his PR team. Maybe he thought a girl in Australia was too close to home?"

Callum had loved his fans in Australia. They'd been the ones to boost his ego whenever he felt he wasn't getting ahead in the US. When he wasn't getting the exposure he wanted, he'd pop home for a week, show up in Byron Bay where the paparazzi would go nuts for him, and return to LA with an ego the size of a monster stadium. She'd hated those trips.

But it wasn't just Ryatt digging. Kennedy was champing at the bit to release the story on the real Callum Walsh. After getting the all-clear from Ryatt, Kennedy had contacted Monica and talked to Fiona in New Zealand. Neither woman was hard to find, once the news of Callum's death was public, despite the fact that Ryatt hadn't been able to release their contact information to Kennedy. Not that he hadn't wanted to, he had admitted. He was clearly on Team Em.

But Kennedy had also interviewed Celia. She was reluctant at first, but with her parent's support and encouragement, had decided to get involved. Her parents had wanted to make it clear from the start that Celia had nothing to do with Callum's murder, and neither did they.

"I can't do anything until they release the body, so it doesn't really matter what …" She opened the cupboard and took out fresh coffee cups, then stopped. She'd forgotten what she was doing. She'd been all over the place, all morning. "I was thinking …" Em began again.

She had been rehashing everything over and over, talking out her theories to Anna for three days. Now, Anna smiled at her, ready to hear today's theory. She was a better friend than Em could ever imagine herself to be.

But before she could speak again, Ryatt came through the door.

"Ryatt …" He looked up, his cheeks red from the cold. His eyes were hard, but when they locked with Em's, they softened immediately.

"We still can't get hold of John. Which is strange, given it's all over the media," Ryatt said. "You really don't know where he was headed?"

Em shook her head. "No, sorry. All he said was he'd be out of reach. I assumed he was in the middle of the outback."

"He'd still be reachable though, right?" Anna interrupted. "When I was travelling across the Nullarbor, there was cell coverage most of the way. And most travellers have satellite phones if they're heading up the west coast or going inland. It's just common sense and encouraged everywhere," she added.

Em chimed in, "You're right. Mum carried a satellite phone for a while, since not every place has a reliable signal from Telstra." She had temporarily forgotten that detail, as Kat had lost the sat-phone a few years ago and hadn't replaced it.

"Yeah," Ryatt said, looking like he was mulling an idea over. "We've contacted the main police stations all over WA and the Territory. They're all keeping an eye out for him."

"I've been thinking—"

Ryatt's phone rang again before Em could finish the sentence. He held up a finger to ask her to wait, then walked back outside. Ryatt had heard all her theories too, just as Anna had.

"Tell me your theory, Em," Anna said, walking over to the kitchen.

"Okay. So, it started with the chickens, right? The chickens were slaughtered. Three of them. Does that mean three victims? Does that mean Callum and me, but who else? Mum? But then there was only one chicken head. But the note kind of pointed to it being a neighbour. Maybe a decoy, since all of the neighbours were cleared there. I mean, they may have past wrongdoings ..."

Em paused, thinking of Bryan.

"But with the chicken head," she continued, "there was only one head. And so maybe that means there is only one killing?"

She knew she was talking in circles. She wasn't making much sense even to herself, so she probably wasn't making sense to Anna either. Still, she continued with her theory.

"Then there was the sex tape. It doesn't seem related, but it had that social media post, about everyone having secrets. But it made me wonder ... What if Lukas, the previous housesitter, is behind all of this? Maybe someone hired him? Maybe he's a psychopath and we were all wooed by his charms?"

She knew she was grasping at straws. She was thinking through everyone who would, or could, have been involved. At this point, all of Callum's victims were cleared, just as she was, although the police were still looking into their families and partners. Retaliation was, after all, the strongest motive.

"Doesn't explain how Lukas could be in Melbourne the night of the chicken head," Anna said, taking a seat opposite Em at the table.

Em was on her fourth cup of coffee that morning, but it sat in front of her, ice cold. Her head was buzzing. Anna looked at the door and watched Ryatt pace as he made yet another call.

"How long is he going to be here today? Do you know?" Anna asked.

Em shrugged. "He said he was going over the crime scene again, to work out some theories."

"Hmm. Well, it can't be Lukas. I told him about Callum. He was just as shocked as we all were. And the police spoke to him. He said there was nothing in the pit but some old goat bones the morning he left, and he's been in Adelaide for the last week. So it's not him either."

"Yeah, didn't think so. Just playing it out," Em said, as Ryatt came back into the room.

"Mats, I have a couple of questions for you," he said, without any preamble and certainly not caring that he was interrupting a conversation.

"Sure, ask away," she said, her tone flat. She was tired of the questions, but she knew he had to ask them. They didn't seem to be getting them any closer to finding out who killed Callum. "Do you want a coffee? I'm making another." She got up.

"Ah, no. Thanks. I've had my fill for today," he said, then looked at her uncomfortably, as if hesitating to ask his question.

"Just ask, Ryatt," she prompted.

"Do you want some privacy?" Anna asked, standing quickly.

"No, it's fine. You know it all anyway," Em said.

"Well, I'm going to have a shower. Give you some privacy anyway," Anna said and walked quickly out of the room.

Ryatt took Anna's seat. "When was the last time you spoke to John? Do you remember?" he asked.

"It was when I asked him if Anna could stay. Um ... I can't remember when it was. Days ago. Maybe three or four? I have the email," Em said, reaching for her phone, relieved to finally have it back from Ryatt.

"But you didn't actually speak with him?"

Em shook her head as she scrolled through her emails.

"No. I've never spoken to him. All our communication has been through email," she said, her brow furrowed as she scrolled. She'd already told him this. "Here it is. The last email from John."

She thrust her phone at Ryatt so he could read the email himself. He leaned forward and read it quickly.

"So," he said, looking down at his watch, "that email was sent five days ago. But he didn't say where he was?"

Em shook her head.

"Okay. But he said he was planning to return on the fifth of July. It's now the, ah, twenty-third of June," Ryatt said, looking at his watch again.

"Sure," Em said, unsure of what day of the week it was, let alone the date. She had no clue, either, of where this was all going, but something nagged at her.

"He said he was thinking of extending it, which is why it worked out with Anna. She needed a place to live until her next housesit. She's starting her course in January, in Hobart."

Ryatt sat back in his chair. "Well, it's his whereabouts now we're concerned with. No one seems to know where he is. We tracked his phone number, but the phone seems to be turned off. Last ping we got from the phone was Melbourne."

"That's weird, because Lukas, the previous housesitter, said that John was in 'woop-woop' and that he checks in 'here and there'. I just assumed it was the outback somewhere," Em said. "And, considering I emailed and got a prompt response five days ago, he's bound to respond soon. I mean, I sent him a quick email about Ruby but haven't heard back yet. I assume that's because the vet was able to get hold of him directly."

"And don't you think that's odd?" Ryatt asked. "The vet called, and the call went right through. As in, he spoke to him, and everything was sorted quickly. But when you and I try, nothing."

"Maybe the vet has a different phone number for him? But I'd assume the number he's left is either his mobile or the sat-phone. Maybe the number we have is his mobile and the number the vet has is his sat-phone?" It was the logical explanation in Em's mind.

"Yeah, we've tried both," Ryatt said, rubbing the stubble on his chin.

"One is bound to reach him, in case of emergency. Maybe it has to do with timing and availability?" Em proposed. She knew she probably wasn't helping the case, but she had no other explanation.

"When I interviewed the neighbours, they all said John was a lovely man. They all seem to like him. Works in Hobart four days a week as a vehicle inspector. Walks his dogs. Helps his neighbours when they need help. Quiet but charming. That kind of thing," Ryatt said.

She nodded. "That sounds like the man I communicated with, too," she said.

"And you said that he's a friend of Kat's? Would she know how to contact him?" Ryatt asked.

"No, he's a friend of a friend, I think. Mum was a bit unclear about all that. I just know that there was a housesit in Tasmania, and Mum didn't want to do it. So she suggested me for it."

"Okay. We'll put that aside for now. Although with the way this thing has escalated, you'd think he'd be reachable."

Em shrugged.

Ryatt said, "With every other piece of this puzzle, there's been a note attached, or you've received something else within the first few days. But it's been three days now and you've not received anything this time. I'm starting to wonder if Callum's murder is even connected with the other things."

Em was surprised. How could they not be connected? But she'd been thinking about the notes herself that morning.

"Maybe it wasn't Bryan who notified the media as we suspected," she said. "What if whoever murdered Callum did that? What if his goal is to frame me? To frame me for Callum's murder? What if *that's* the message?"

There was a flash of something across Ryatt's face, but he quickly shut it down. He was in official mode, and whatever it was, she couldn't read it.

"The thing that has me worried is Mum. I still don't know where she is," Em said, as she got up to put another log on the fire. "She would've heard about this by now. What if she's in trouble?" The thought made her heart race with panic. As much as she tried to push the thoughts away, they continued to gnaw at her mind, leaving her feeling helpless and conflicted.

"You haven't heard from her at all?"

Em shook her head, closing the wood heater door.

Ryatt said, "I called her and left her a message when Callum was found. She never got back to me. I assumed she would have called you."

"No," Em said. "And for something like this, she'd show up. Or at least call me. And if someone is out to frame me, wouldn't they want to frame me for her murder too?" She put her hand over her mouth. Where had *that* thought come from?

She went on, "I mean, I am seriously worried. I just want to know if she's okay. Three chickens were killed. Does that mean three killings?

Maybe Callum was just the first? And Mum left here so fast. But why was her old phone here?" She was back to spinning. "I remember Mum picking her new phone up, from right here on the kitchen counter, and tossing it in her bag like it was the enemy. Then she left. But right before she ran out, she was staring at something on the bookcase ..."

37

I am getting dizzy watching you all go around in circles.

You really have no idea. About any of it.

I'll have what I want soon, Mathilda.

And you'll be left with nothing.

38

"I don't know what to do, Em," Asher said with a hint of discomfort.

Em turned to face him while putting away a cup and noticed his unease. She had no idea what he was talking about. But seeing him anxious and unsure was unusual; Asher was never this way. He radiated confidence in every situation. Maybe he was talking about washing the dishes? She had offered to do them earlier, but he insisted on taking care of it himself. Did he even know how? He had employees at The Bakehouse for tasks like these. Whenever he baked, there would be a trail of dirty utensils and pans left in his wake. His co-workers called him Pigpen behind his back.

"I'm just as weirded out as you are that you're doing the dishes. I should take a photo as evidence," Em joked and looked into the sink to find Asher scrubbing a pan vigorously, causing the non-stick coating to flake off. She considered handing him the tea towel and taking over before any more damage was done. "Have you ever washed a dish before?"

"What?" he said, looking up. "Oh, no. Not that. I was talking about the business." He looked down, rinsed the pan then put it on the drainer. Reaching out for the tea towel, he leaned back against the water-soaked counter.

"Forget the dishes. I'm talking about The Bakehouse. What should we do with it?"

"Oh." Em looked down.

"Asher, baby. I don't think now is the best time to talk about that," Kennedy said gently from the couch. She and Anna were seated at each end like bookends, both with laptops on top of their blanketed laps.

"No, it's okay. We should. You want out. You said that when I left," Em said, her tone colder than she meant it to be.

"I really don't," Asher said, exasperated. "I love that place. So do you." He looked at her with ... Em couldn't interpret the look on his face. Was it pity? Guilt?

"But you *told* me you wanted out," Em said, crossing her arms over her chest.

"Maybe it's better that we sell. I mean, you have no ties to LA anymore," Asher said, grimacing at having to speak of her situation.

Em realised he was right. With Callum gone, there was nothing holding her there. Not that Callum would have tied her there once they were divorced, but she had thought it would be years before she could leave.

"Do you want to sell?" Em asked.

She watched his face zoom through a million emotions. After a few long moments, with Kennedy now watching from the couch, Asher slowly shook his head.

"Then why did you say you wanted to? Why did you say that when I said I wanted to come home for a while?" she screeched.

Asher flinched. "Because, Buttercup, you needed to get away from him. From his bullshit. And you needed a way to go, guilt free. I was trying to give you an out."

"Are you freaking kidding me? I've been thinking this whole time that you were pissed off with me! That this friendship, this bond we have, was all bullshit!"

"What? No, Em. That wasn't it at all," Asher said, his face solemn. "I've been worried about you. I have been for ages."

"I thought it was because you were worried about the paparazzi always hanging around, and how some of our customers were put off by that. And then there was the embezzlement thing."

Asher gasped. "I knew that was bullshit as much as you did. I never believed that stupid fucking rumour, because you know as well as I do that we do the books together. And we check each other, every time. Even the accountant called and asked me what was going on. He knows it's bullshit too."

"Then why?" Em yelled. "Why would you say that you wanted to sell?"

She knew she was raging about more than their miscommunication. But it felt good to yell and scream, and she knew Asher could take her wrath.

"Because I wanted you to be able to walk away and not look back. To give you a clean break," he said calmly. "LA was not the place for you anymore. It's still not the place for you."

"Just tell me what you really think, Asher," she shrieked.

"What I really think is I love you. You know that. And I want the best for you. Do I want to sell? No. I want to keep our bakery going. I freaking love that place. But it's not right for you. I just want to give you an out."

"I can give myself my own out, thanks very much. And I don't want to sell it either. Maybe you're right. Maybe I don't want to be in LA anymore, especially after this. God knows I'll be hounded like a rabid dog. Labelled as Callum Walsh's killer. Not his wife. Not his ex-wife. But his killer. Whether I killed him or not."

"And we all know you didn't," Kennedy said, now standing on the opposite side of the counter from them.

"No, I didn't," Em said, the reality of the situation deflating her. She slumped against the counter.

Asher walked over to her and opened his arms. She stepped in and his arms engulfed her. She sighed, and after a moment, pulled back. She wanted to cry, but she was all cried out. She didn't want to give up The Bakehouse. It was their baby. She'd poured all of her dreams and heart into that place. But Asher was right. She didn't want to be in LA anymore either.

"I'll think about it," Em said, resigning herself to the truth. "But right now I think I'll be a bad hostess and go to bed."

"Sounds good. We're going to head back to our Airbnb. We'll be back in the morning," Kennedy said. "Come on, Ash."

THE FOLLOWING MORNING, with Charlie, Billy and Sachin sniffing the ground around them, Em and Anna walked silently down the trail. Anna walked in front, while Em lagged some distance behind, her head trying to make sense of the last few days.

On one hand, she'd still not heard from Kat; but Em had discovered her mother's phone charger behind the bedside table in the spare room earlier that morning. Could that explain her mother's silence? A dead phone? But surely Kat would have learned by now where to pick up another one?

Next on Em's plate was dealing with Callum's funeral. Ryatt had said they'd receive the autopsy results later that day, and she could begin moving forward with the arrangements afterwards. Callum's PR team was eager to get everything arranged. Em had no clue where to even start with all of that. Callum's parents were no longer alive, and his brother Zeke was struggling with alcoholism somewhere in Queensland. Even Callum's sister Didi wasn't doing well; she had four children from four different men and had recently moved in with a fifth man whom she'd claimed was 'the one' three years ago at their last family gathering. Since then, they hadn't heard from her. But Em suspected that Callum had been secretly sending money to his siblings through his lawyer. She couldn't help but wonder how they would manage now without that source of income. Just thinking about it made her shudder. She knew she would have to discuss this with her own lawyer soon enough, especially since Callum had no will. Em had been unsurprised by that news from his lawyer. The man thought he was invincible, after all.

As she walked the path, she thought about what Asher had said the night before. How he was only trying to help her break away. Be free of the mess her life had become. His swooping in and helping after they'd discovered Callum in the pit spoke of who she knew him to be.

Her rock. The one who was always there for her. His declaration that he would be willing to sell the bakery was the most unselfish thing he could have suggested. He'd forgo his own dream to make her life better. She didn't know what to do with that.

They'd stepped off the track and back onto the road when Margo pulled into her driveway. Two days before, she and Shirley had driven up the coast to visit Margo's aunt. The dust-covered RAV4 made Em question where this mysterious aunt lived. When Anna had mentioned their trip to Swansea, Em had imagined them travelling to a charming cottage by the sea.

As Em and Anna approached the driveway, Shirley was already out of the car and pulling Kumquat in his carrier from the back seat. Margo was around the back of the car, lifting bags out of the boot.

"Hey Margo. Hi Shirley. How was your trip?" Anna called.

Margo turned around at Anna's voice. Shirley just waved as she headed to the front door, struggling with the howling cat in the carrier.

"Hello, darlings. Em, I need to chat with you," Margo said, looking flustered for the first time since Em had met her.

"Is everything alright?" Em asked. Margo's hair was a mess, and she looked like she hadn't slept for days.

"Oh, yes. I suppose," Margo said, but she didn't look convinced of that. "My Aunty shared some information with me. Information I think you'd want to know."

Shirley came back outside and walked over to the car. "Ugh. There's that bogan again," Shirley said, looking over Em's shoulder.

Em turned to see Bryan on his verandah, smoking a cigarette. He was dressed in his usual stained track pants, but today he had a red hoodie on, emblazoned with the letters "LA" in white. Em cringed.

"I wouldn't pee on him if he was on fire," Shirley said. "I thought the menace was the kid. But mark my words, that one is behind it all." She nodded in Bryan's direction. "Although I'm not sure how he could be such a mastermind. The man clearly has a roo loose in the top paddock."

They all turned and looked to Bryan, who stood upright, flicked his cigarette onto the lawn, then turned and went inside.

"He's the least of it," Margo said, turning back to Em. "Do you have a moment Em? I really need to tell you …"

"Stop jabbering on out here, Margo. Come inside. All of you. I'll make tea," Shirley said in her no-nonsense way. "You'll want to hear this, Em."

They each took a bag from the car and followed Margo and Shirley inside, leaving the dogs to roam outside. Shirley took two cold bags into the kitchen, while Margo went off to the bedroom. Em followed Shirley. Anna walked over to pat Kumquat, who was already perched at the top of the cat scratcher, watching over his kingdom.

"You know that time-out contraption will never work for this cat, right, Shirley?" Anna said, stroking the cat. "He needs his freedom."

"Yeah, I've been wondering about that. Every time I put him in it, he pisses on something else as soon as he's out. But Barb in town swears by the thing for her two dogs," Shirley said, placing milk and orange juice in the fridge.

"Dogs and cats are a world apart, Shirley. Just put the thing away and notice how Kumquat reacts. I promise you, he'll be a much happier cat," Anna said.

Em could hear the cat's purring all the way from the kitchen.

"I'll try it and see," Shirley said. "Barb is as mad as a cut snake, so who knows what she's thinking half the time."

When Shirley opened the second cold bag, Em saw some beautiful, homemade-looking lamingtons. She started salivating. "Yummo!" she said. "They look divine!"

"Margo's aunty made these yesterday. We're still not sure if the old girl is going senile – she's ninety-eight after all – but she sure can whip up a lammo."

"They look amazing," Em said, wanting to push on one to see how well it bounced back, checking the freshness of the chocolate and coconut-covered cake.

"Taste bloody good, too," Shirley said. "Now, Margo's about to burst like a bloody dam with the info she found out from Aunty Nell."

Just as her name was mentioned, Margo came out of the bedroom and walked to the kitchen. She helped Shirley grab the teacups and milk and, not wanting to waste any more time, began sharing what her aunty had said.

"I wasn't quite sure if it was true when she first started, mind you, but then Aunty Nell pulled out an old photo album."

Em and Anna perched on some battered old bar stools in the kitchen as the two older women shared the telling of the story like well-rehearsed ballet dancers.

"I told you that I thought I recognised your mother. She's a bit older than me. But when I saw her at the markets, I could have sworn I had met her before. Then I pieced it together. It was when she lived up the road from Aunty Nell and Uncle Ray."

"When was this?" Em asked, confused.

"Well, it was a couple of times. When I was young, maybe sixteen or seventeen? Then I saw her later. I must have been in my mid-twenties that time."

"Twice?" Em asked. "That doesn't make sense. She said she backpacked in Tasmania when she was eighteen, nineteen, but then she left. She told me she's never been back. Not until a week ago, that is."

"Well, I'd say she doesn't want to remember, or she doesn't want to tell you about it. Not a surprise, though, given the circumstances," Margo said, putting lamingtons on a plate while Shirley bobbed tea bags in the teapot.

"What circumstances?" Em asked.

Margo reached down into the pocket of her long cardigan and pulled out two photos. She passed them to Em.

There, plain as day, was Kat. The first photo was Kat with an infant that wasn't Em. Her mother had to be no more than twenty. Maybe a bit older. Her mother wasn't smiling into the camera. Em flipped to the next photo. This one showed a young boy scowling while Kat held another infant. She wasn't smiling in this photo either. And this time, the baby was her. She'd seen photos of herself as a baby with her mum and dad, so there was no doubt in her mind that the baby in the photo was her.

"I don't understand. Who's this boy?" Em asked, although he looked familiar.

"That, my girl, is your mother's son. He lived with his father in Pontypool."

"My mother's son?" Em asked. "She doesn't have a son."

"Well, according to Aunty Nell, there was a Katherine with a Mathilda living in Pontypool. Katherine was married to Rusty, who turned out to be an abusive husband. After about nine years, she met a drover in Swansea, where she worked. When she ran off with the drover, she was pregnant. She left the son behind with the husband."

"What?" Em could hardly breathe, let alone form words.

"Yeah, Katherine's husband was very bad news, according to Aunty Nell."

"Why would she leave her son behind?" Anna asked.

"That's what people in town were wondering," Shirley chimed in.

"This second photo ... is this the same boy as the baby in the first photo?" Em asked.

"Yep, that's Russell. The son. And that's you, Em," Margo said, pointing at the baby. "When Kat came back, and you lived in Pontypool. That's why, when I saw your mum the second time, I thought she looked familiar. You didn't live there for long. Kat knew what Rusty was like. Apparently the son was becoming like his dad, and Rusty wasn't doing anything to help matters. It was my Uncle Ray who helped Kat escape the second time."

Em stared at the photo. She remembered the boy standing in the middle of the road. She'd watched him as they drove away, out the back window. Em remembered being in the back seat of a white ute, staring out, seeing the boy in the road, looking lost. Broken. Then his face changing to white-hot rage.

"When Rusty found out Uncle Ray helped Katherine get away, he was ropable. Manic, apparently. He killed a couple of Uncle Ray's sheep, including their prize-winning ram. He killed their dog too, just after that." Margo looked at Em for a long time, then took a sip of her tea.

Em wrapped her frozen fingers around the cup in front of her and stared down into the milky brown liquid. She didn't know what to do with this information. Her mother had a son. A son she'd abandoned. Why? And why had her mother lied to her? Had she done it on purpose? Or was this just a part of her past she wanted to leave behind?

"There was no stopping Rusty," Margo continued. "The police were called, but they didn't do anything. There was no proof he did any of it."

"Oh my God," Anna said.

Margo nodded, and with tears in her eyes, told them the final piece. "Uncle Ray died not long after Kat left the second time. Rusty was a suspect in Uncle Ray's death."

Em looked up from the cup, shocked.

"Unfortunately, charges were never laid," said Margo. "Rusty was in tight with the Swansea police back then."

"Oh geezus, Margo, I'm so sorry," Anna said, reaching over to squeeze Margo's hand. Em nodded, speechless. But there was one more thing Em needed to know.

"Is he still alive? Rusty?" Em asked.

"No. Rusty died about twenty years ago," Margo said.

"How …" Em began. Her hands were shaking. "What happened to Uncle Ray?"

Somehow she knew what Margo was about to say before she even said it.

"Car accident. Driving home to Pontypool. His brakes failed."

Em nodded slowly, swallowing the lump in her throat, and felt the wind go out of her.

Margo's uncle had died exactly the same way her father, the drover, had died. Failed brakes.

39

"Where is she?" her mum demanded as she came barrelling in the door a few hours later, her hair flying, her jacket hanging off one shoulder. She tossed her bag across at the wooden dining room table, where it skidded across the surface and thudded heavily to the floor.

When her mother wrapped her arms around her, Em stood dead still.

"What happened?" said Kat, then leaving no time for an answer, she poured out her explanation. "Sorry, sorry. I was up near Launceston, and I thought I turned left on the highway, but somehow turned right. I was almost at Stanley, on the north-west coast, when I realised my mistake. So, I turned around and missed the turn again, and ended up in bloody St Helens on the north-east coast! I turned around again and ended up in some place on the other side of Cradle Mountain. Zee-something. Zeehan?" She shook her head. "Anyway, doesn't matter. I got directions, headed south, and then I was told after Queenstown that I had to turn around again, because there was snow on the road and my van wasn't equipped for it. So, I backtracked again ... but, oh it doesn't matter. Here I am. Finally."

This was typical of her mother. She couldn't find her way out of a supermarket.

"You have GPS on your phone, Mum," Em said, flatly.

"Oh, I lost my phone again," Kat said, flippantly. "Somewhere up in Launceston. I don't know. I didn't find out what happened until two days ago, when I popped into a café for a coffee. It's all over the news!"

Kennedy and Asher had been hovering by the door with Anna, but Asher now ushered them all outside. They knew she was angry at Kat. It had been all she could talk about since she'd arrived back from Margo and Shirley's to find Kennedy and Asher sitting on the verandah.

"Callum's dead," Em said, repeating the reel in her head. "My husband is dead."

"Well, I know that much!" her mother said. "Who did it? Was it you?"

Em gasped. How could her mother even think she could do something like that?

"No!" Em said, stepping back, away from her mother.

"Well, I wouldn't blame you. The man was a prick. A dickhead. The worst kind of man there is," Kat said.

While Em agreed that Callum had his faults, she couldn't agree that he was the worst kind there was. She'd heard worse. Like the kind of man her mother had been married to, apparently.

"He didn't deserve this, Mum. I was moving on with my life. He was going to be out of it. I don't know who killed him, but he didn't deserve it."

"Oh, he deserved everything that was coming to him," Kat said, but Em began to worry about the look in her mother's eyes. It was if she wasn't quite there, and she wondered if her mother was high.

"Are you ..." Em began.

"*What?*" Kat demanded.

"*On* something?" Em asked. She knew her mother dabbled with pot, but she'd never known her to drive while high.

"No. I'm just livid!"

Em was nearly dumbfounded. "Livid? Why?" she yelled.

Her mother looked at her. "Because the prick got the easy way out instead of facing the music," she said, looking around the house as if seeing it for the first time. Her eyes zeroed in on something on the bookshelf.

"Like your husband, you mean?" Em asked.

Kat's head whipped around.

Em was so angry at her mother for not telling her about living in Tasmania before, being married to another man before – yet she was devastated at the same time. Why would her mother not tell her about this part of her past?

"What do you mean?" said Kat. "Your father was—"

"I'm not talking about my father," Em said, and watched her mother's face go pale.

"What are you talking about?" Kat's voice was barely a whisper.

"You heard me. Your first husband. The one you were married to in Tasmania. The one you lived with and had a son with, up near Swansea. Where I lived too, apparently."

Her mother rocked on her feet, then stumbled to a chair at the table.

"How do you know?" Kat asked.

"So it's true? I know because Margo thought you looked familiar, remember? When she went to visit her Aunty Nell in Pontypool, the same Nell who was married to Ray, the same Ray who helped you escape Rusty, Margo asked questions. Turns out, Aunty Nell has quite the memory."

Em walked to the kitchen counter and grabbed the two photos Margo had given her. She thrust them in Kat's direction.

"Where did you get these?" Kat asked, her voice cracked.

"Aunty Nell had them. Why didn't you tell me? Is it true that I have a half-brother? Do you even know who my real father was?"

"How dare you!" her mother spat.

"How dare I? You've kept this from me, all this time, and now you're mad at me for asking questions?" Em strode to the table and looked into her mother's face. Her whole body was trembling.

"I ... I was coming to tell you. When I came last time. I just ... I just ... couldn't," Kat said.

"Couldn't or wouldn't?" Em spat at her. "God, this is so typical of you, Mum! Things get hard, so you leave. Just as you always do. Last time, without explanation, you just left. So now I want to know about Rusty. That was your husband's name, wasn't it? Rusty? And why didn't you take this boy with you? Is he yours? Why would you abandon him to this man? How, Mum? How could you do that?"

Em realised she was screaming at her mother. She'd had enough lies. Heard enough stories of why they were always running. Why they never had friends. Now it made sense that she'd shut Ryatt out of Em's life. He was getting too close to them.

Tears ran down Kat's cheeks. Her body shook uncontrollably. She said softly, "I didn't take him because he was just like Rusty. Just like his father. I wasn't sure we were safe with him."

"He was a little boy, Mum!" Em yelled.

Kat shook her head. "He was twelve and he was already vicious. He had the evil gene in him."

"So it's true, then. You were married to the boy's father?" Em stepped back and crossed her arms over her chest. She was not letting her mother get off that easily.

"Yes. I married Rusty when I was nineteen," Kat said. Taking a deep breath, she reached into her pocket and plucked out a wad of tissues. She spread them out, found a clean one and blew her nose.

"Go on," said Em.

Kat pointed at a chair. "You need to sit down."

"No. I'm fine to stand, thanks," Em said, not moving.

Kat took a deep breath, then looked up at Em with pain written all over her face. "I was married to Rusty. Then I ran away with Jake. It was not a good situation with Rusty." Kat took another breath and started tearing the tissue to pieces. "When Jake died, I was devastated, but I didn't have a breakdown. Rusty called the cops. Anonymously. He told them I had tried to kill myself. Somehow he'd found out about you. They put me on a seventy-two-hour psych hold. That's when you went to stay with Mrs Boyle, across the road. You stayed there for two weeks. She was your temporary foster carer," Kat said, her tears returning.

Em stood stock still.

"I was deemed an unfit mother. But Rusty swooped in, just as the seventy-two-hour hold was up, and 'saved the day'," Kat said in a mock-jovial tone. "That's the impression he gave the cops, anyway. He told them I'd run off with a drover and he'd finally found me. Just in time, he told them. Rusty was not one to mess with."

She blew her nose again. Em stayed silent.

"I heard from Nell and Ray occasionally," Kat continued. "And when Ray died, I knew Rusty was capable of doing something like that. He used to joke about how easy it was to mess with someone's brakes. I used to check them every time I went anywhere, just in case. Do you remember that? I still check them."

"So, you weren't married to Dad, then?" Em asked, pushing on.

"No," Kat said, looking up at Em. "I was never married to Jake."

Em gasped. She had been led to believe her parents were married all this time. "So, what about the boy?"

"Russell," Kat said quietly, as if she'd not spoken the boy's name in years.

"Rusty wanted him named after him ..." she trailed off, staring out the window. "It was bad with him, Em. I watched Callum. I could see the same traits coming out in him. Rusty was charming. Everyone loved him. It was just behind closed doors that things were bad. He locked me up in the shed in the middle of summer when I was four months pregnant with Russell. He thought I'd been flirting with someone in the café where I worked. I wasn't, of course. I'd only asked the guy and his wife how their holidays were going. But Rusty could turn anything around. He wasn't averse to tying me up, drugging me, when he thought I wasn't complying with him. At first, he'd beat me in places people couldn't see. When I got brave and wore short sleeves, showing the bruises, Nell and Ray noticed. Rusty wasn't happy about that, either."

"Callum didn't do that to me, Mum. Beat me, I mean. But that's not the point. Why did you go back to Rusty? When Dad died. Why the hell would you go back to a man who abused you?" Em asked, just as her phone rang. She looked down, saw it was Ryatt calling and chose to ignore it. She needed to finish this conversation with her mother first. "If he was so horrible and you had got away from him, why didn't you just stay away?" Em had a million questions swirling through her head.

"I didn't want to go back, but I had no choice. The police in South Australia wouldn't release me on my own. I had to be in someone's care, and Rusty was still my husband. My next of kin. So he dragged me back to Tasmania. Dragged us."

"And you just went with him? You didn't fight for us? For the life we'd made with Dad?" Em asked, although she knew it was a cruel question to ask. She didn't mean it, but she was angry over her mother's lies.

"No. I've never forgotten Jake. But I have long suspected Rusty was behind his death."

Em gasped.

"He died in a car accident, remember. Failed brakes. Just like Ray. I still don't know how Rusty found us."

"Is that why you've always been running? Is that why you don't like Tasmania?" Em asked.

"Part of it," Kat said cryptically. But she didn't explain any further, and there was another question Em needed the answer to.

"So, who is my father? Jake or Rusty?" Em asked, dreading the answer but needing to know it all the same.

Kat didn't answer. Silence filled the room.

Em waited for as long as she could.

"Mum? Why can't you just answer the question?"

Kat shook her head.

"You've kept me at arm's length ever since that fight we had ten years ago," said Em. "Is this why? Or some other reason?"

It seemed that question was easier for Kat answer, as she snapped back quickly, "Because you threatened to lock me up! In a psych ward! Just like Rusty did. And who do you think was still my next of kin? If Rusty knew where I was, what do you think would happen to me? Or you!"

"He's dead, Mum. Rusty died years ago, according to Margo," Em said, but Kat shook her head, as if she didn't believe it. "Surely you already know that much."

"Russell ..." Kat said, her voice cracking.

"He died too, apparently. Margo said he moved to Melbourne after

Rusty died. Someone in Swansea heard he died in some kind of hunting accident, in Queensland."

"No," Kat said, glancing towards the bookcase again. Then, abruptly, Kat stood. Em looked over to the bookcase, trying to see what had caught her mother's attention.

"I've got to go," Kat announced, grabbing her coat from the back of the chair.

"What?" Em said, stunned. "You're leaving again? *Why?*"

Her mother turned and wrapped her bony hands around the back of the chair, as if trying to hang on. "I've just got to, Em. I've got to sort something out."

"This is so fucking typical. You always leave. When Dad died, you left me to deal with my grief with Mrs Boyle. Then you ran away to Western Australia when all I was trying to do was help you deal with your grief! And now, when I tell you that I know about your past – my past – you're running again? You can't even face me. You can't even tell me the truth!"

"There's something I've got to do," her mother repeated, crying. "It's complicated."

"Fuck that, Mum. You never face responsibility," Em screamed. "You're so fucking selfish! Dad died on his way back to us. He loved us. He wanted nothing more than to be with us. And now I find out that your husband killed him and that I may not even be his child? And that you have a son? What am I supposed to do with all of that information?"

"You don't know what it was like," Kat said, her face racked with pain. "What it's still like."

"What? To try and get away from someone who has control over your life? To hold someone's secret? To live with someone who is arrogant and self-absorbed? You don't think I know what that's like? Then you haven't really noticed my life that much, have you? Now, I find out I have a brother? A life I knew nothing about, let alone remember? And you can't even talk to me about that!"

Her mother shook her head, now weeping loudly.

Em had had enough of the self-pity. "Before you ran to Western Australia, you said I was just like him. I thought you were talking about Dad. But you weren't, were you? It's why you hate being around me. So, who am I like? Just tell me. Am I not Jake's daughter? Am I Rusty's?" Em screamed at her mother, letting everything out. Her anger at her mother for abandoning her, then and now. Her anger at Callum. Her anger at whoever had been doing these evil things.

Kat looked long and hard at Em, then pulled her jacket tightly around herself and walked out the door. Just as she always did.

40

E m sat on the verandah steps, waiting for her mother to return. She had serious doubts that she would.

Em was still enraged, but at the same time felt horrible for unleashing on her mother. All she could think about was that her mother's actions had consequences. They'd affected Em's life, too, in ways she couldn't even see. Didn't her mother understand that?

There was more to it. More her mother was not saying. She didn't know why she felt that, but her instincts screamed at her.

"What's the deal, banana peel?" Asher said, approaching the steps with Anna, with Kennedy trailing behind. They'd all gone out to walk the dogs while Em talked to her mum, but Em was pretty sure half the neighbourhood could've heard their argument.

Asher had Billy on a lead. Anna had Charlie. Both dogs looked worn out but happy. Em couldn't say the same for Kennedy. She was typing on her phone like a woman in a rage. More guilt flooded Em. Asher and Kennedy were still managing the media for her, a full-time job if ever there was one.

"How was the walk?" she asked.

Anna unleashed Charlie who trotted towards her. Asher looked back at Kennedy and undid Billy's lead. But, as wary of dogs as

Kennedy seemed to be, they seemed to be the least of her worries at the moment.

"Good. We walked along the river to the park and back. Well, not quite to the park. It was filled with vans. Probably some of the media are camped down there," Asher said.

"More vans than usual, for sure," Anna said and wandered off towards the chicken coop.

"Wonder when they're going to give up and move on?" Em said to Asher as he sat in the fading sunshine beside her. They watched Kennedy walk the last few metres, her head down, her feet in auto along the gravel driveway.

"She's had her head in that thing for days," Asher mumbled.

"Hmm…," Kennedy said, then looked up at them when she finally got to the verandah. She looked conflicted. "I've been asked for an exclusive."

"Will that make it all go away?" Em asked, knowing the answer was unlikely to be yes.

"Maybe. Depends," Kennedy said.

"On what?" Asher asked, leaning to the side to let Billy pass by. A moment later they heard the thump as Billy collapsed behind them on his dog bed.

"On what we tell them," Kennedy said.

Charlie sat down beside Em, looking for pats. She appreciated, once again, his need to comfort her.

"Yeah," Em said, mulling that over.

Kennedy's head was back in her phone.

"How was the chat with Kat?" Asher asked Em, bumping her with his shoulder.

"Not great. I'm surprised you didn't hear the whole thing from the track," Em said. "I unleashed on her. So now she's gone again."

"Gone?" Kennedy asked, looking up in surprise.

"Yup. Typical Kat move. When things get hard, she runs. The story of my life. Always moving, running from something. I guess I know from what now."

She didn't blame Kat for always looking over her shoulder, but once Rusty was dead, she wasn't sure why they kept moving. Was it because of the boy? Kat's son? Em couldn't quite bring herself to call him her brother. She didn't know him. And she never would, now she knew he was dead.

"Do you know where Kat went?" Asher asked, but Em shook her head.

"She'll pop up again at some point," Em said, resigned. "It's her MO." But this time, Em wasn't so sure. She'd said some harsh things to her mother.

"What do you want to do about the media?" Kennedy asked, bringing them back to the emergency lighting up her phone. "There's speculation all over the place. That you've been having affairs. That you killed Callum because you were jealous of his success."

Asher laughed at that one.

Em just smiled.

"We need to get them off Em's back," Asher said. "Enough is enough."

"Agreed," Kennedy said. "But the only way to do that is release something. How do you feel, Em, about releasing what you've already told me?"

Em wrinkled her nose. "Maybe. I just don't know about the timing. It would be great for the world to know what Callum was really like, but he was still my husband. You know?"

"But was he a good husband?" Kennedy asked. The question was clearly rhetorical.

"Let me think about it. With this crap with Mum, I'm not really in the right frame of mind for another media onslaught. Besides, I should talk to Ryatt about it first. I don't want to get in the way of their investigation. Nor do I want it to look like I'm the bitter wife looking for revenge."

Charlie laid his paw on her leg. She looked down at him and caught his eyes. It was if he was telling her he was her protector.

"I need to call Ryatt back anyway," she went on. "He called while I was talking with Mum." She continued to stroke Charlie's head.

Anna returned, her jumper stretched out with round lumps protruding from underneath.

"Eggs. Lots of them," Anna said. "I may ask Tyler to come over tomorrow and help me clean out the coop. It's ripe. I feel like I stink of chicken shit. But the girls are locked up for the night. They don't seem to care. And I gave the goats some feed while I was at it."

"Thanks Anna. Seriously. For everything," Em said.

Anna smiled and shrugged, then walked past her and into the house to put the eggs away.

Beyond them, the sun set, and with that the cold began seeping in. Kennedy shivered and Em felt the cold coming up through the wooden planks.

"I need food. Should I make us some dinner?" Em asked, her stomach taking that very moment to rumble loudly. She got up from the step slowly, making Charlie jump up. "Sorry, I know I've been a shocking hostess." She turned to go inside.

Kennedy chuckled behind her.

"I think you're excused," Asher said, watching as Billy rose slowly, stretched and then craned his neck when Asher bent down to pat him.

"Can we get pizza delivery here?" Kennedy asked.

This time, it was Em's turn to laugh.

"Hm. I'll take that as a no. Damn," Kennedy said, bending over to unlace her sneakers. Billy knocked her off balance as he bullied his way to the door to get inside to the warm fire. Charlie stayed on Em's heels as she kicked her shoes off and walked to the kitchen.

"You know, I can whip up some pizzas," Asher said, taking his muddy boots off at the door.

"I'm not sure what we could put on them," Em said over her shoulder as she opened the fridge. "I haven't bought groceries in a while, and we've eaten all the stuff the neighbours brought over."

"Do you have any wine?" Kennedy asked.

Anna, having put the eggs away, went to the pantry and pulled out the last two bottles. She held them up like they were champion's cups.

"Lovely," Kennedy said, sighing.

"We'll head into Hobart tomorrow. Now, I think there's some pizza dough here … I made it the other day. Do you want to see if it's usable, Asher?" Em said, finally finding it buried behind a bag of shredded cheese.

When Asher nodded, she tossed the dough to him on the counter, followed by the cheese.

"I'll see what else we can use for toppings," Em said. She found potatoes in the pantry, then remembered the rosemary bushes lining the courtyard. She thought she had some pesto in the fridge, too, and suggested the combo for their pizzas.

Kennedy laughed. "I think you are the only person I know who can whip up a gourmet pizza at the last minute, scraping together random things you find. If it were my house, you'd be lucky to find a tub of expired Chobani and some mouldy cheese."

She poured wine into four glasses that Anna had placed in front of her, and it was then that Em realised Anna's sobriety had ended right after they'd discovered Callum's body in the pit. Not that she could blame her.

"Well, most of us don't eat out six nights a week, trying to win over celebrities," Em teased, as she watched Asher work the pizza dough in front of him.

"This dough looks fine, Em. And it looks like there's lots of it. Guess you've been baking while you've been here?"

Em smiled. "I was, until ..." Em felt the cloud of doom return.

"You'll get back to it," Asher assured her.

Charlie sniffed towards the counter, curious to know what was happening.

"We need to build that fire up, so we can get this dough to rise again," Asher said.

Anna raised her hand and went to work on the fire, before announcing she was heading off to have a shower before dinner.

"I'll go cut some rosemary," Em said, and Charlie followed her, wedging his nose into the crack of the door to open it for their escape. Seeing the door open, Billy lumbered up and joined them outside.

The cold air hit Em in the face and she felt the chill down the back of her neck. Charlie barked into the air, to let all predators know who was king, while Billy pranced over the dew already forming on the ground to a nearby tree. He lifted his leg and Em swore she heard him sigh.

With the clipped rosemary in hand, she ascended the stairs and looked out from the verandah while she waited for the dogs. The sky was clear, and the stars were starting to appear. Before coming here to Neeminah River, Em had never seen so many stars. They looked so close that she felt like she could reach up and touch them. Tonight, the horizon looked to have a green glow, but she was tired and probably imagining things. It had been a long day.

She called the dogs back in, and found Kennedy peeling potatoes as Asher rolled out the dough.

"I never imagined you even being in a kitchen, much less peeling a potato," Em teased, walking to the sink to wash the rosemary.

"Well, I was raised to know how to cook the basics. I just don't. I'm too busy for the domestic life," Kennedy said. "But I am surprised that Asher knows how to make pizza."

"He knows how to make the pizza dough. Let's not get carried away," Em said.

"Well, I thought I'd start trying to make it, but I couldn't find the pesto. It's not in the fridge, and I couldn't see it in the pantry," Asher said.

"Typical guy. It's probably right in front of you," Em said, moving to the pantry.

She moved the coffee and the container of sugar aside and stopped dead. Another phone sat on the shelf. It had a different cover from the last – this one had apples all over it. But Em knew immediately that it was Kat's phone – the phone she'd just replaced. The one she had apparently lost in Launceston. So how did it get here and into this pantry?

Em picked it up and, coming out into the light of the kitchen, turned it over when she felt something taped to the bottom. It was a piece of paper with a message written on it.

If I can't have her, neither can you.

"Oh fuck," Em said and dropped the phone on the kitchen bench. She ran to the dining table and grabbed her own phone.

"What's going on?" Kennedy asked, but Em shook her head.

She found Ryatt's number and stood tapping her finger against the phone, willing him to pick it quickly.

"Mats? Glad you called. I ..."

"Mum's phone is here," she began, but she knew that didn't explain it well enough. "Her new phone. Her replacement. The one she just lost in Launceston. And this one has a message taped to the back of it."

"What does it say?"

"If I can't have her, neither can you," Em said, quickly.

"It says *what*?" asked Ryatt.

Em repeated the message to him again.

"I'm in Hobart right now, but I'm on my way. Did anyone else touch it?" Ryatt said impatiently. She could hear running, then the dinging in his car as he started the engine.

"No. Just me," Em answered.

"Bag the phone. Don't let anyone near it," Ryatt said. "I'll be there in about thirty minutes."

Em hung up when she heard his siren going. She wasn't sure why the situation warranted a siren, but at least he'd be here sooner with it on. She grabbed a sandwich bag from the pantry, picked up the phone with it and turned it inside out to enclose the phone.

"Ryatt's on his way. He said not to touch the phone," Em said to Kennedy and Asher, who hovered nearby, their mouths open.

While she paced, waiting for Ryatt, Em walked to the bookcase, eager to try again to find what her mother had been staring at. She wondered again about the framed picture, but then something else caught her eye. A photo lay face-down on the floor near the front of the bookcase.

She picked it up and turned it over. It was a photo of Em when she was about five, with a dog that looked a lot like Ruby. But she had never had a dog like Ruby growing up, and she wasn't familiar with the background, either. She thought of the other photos that Margo had given her. She shook her head in denial. This couldn't be real. How did this photo even get here?

"Did anyone put this photo here?" she asked, turning around to face Asher, Kennedy and Anna.

"Oh, sorry," Anna said. "I saw a book that looked interesting but when I opened it, the photo fell out. I meant to pick it up, but Charlie started barking manically outside. Sorry. What's the photo of?"

Em held it up.

Kennedy walked over to look. "Geezus. Who is that?" she asked.

"Me. And I think it was taken in Pontypool."

Em looked down at the photo again. The dog had a big black cross over its face. And Em's face in the photo had a target drawn over the top.

41

"So you think this is you?" Ryatt asked half an hour later, as they sat at the dining room table. Beside him was the phone Em had found in the pantry. He had looked at the note, photographed it, then forwarded it to someone in his division. Now he was staring at the photo between then.

"Yes, I think so," Em replied, shocked that she was looking at a photo of herself with a bullseye drawn over the top.

"And where did you find it?" Ryatt asked Em, but Em looked over to Anna.

"Um, I was looking at the books on the bookshelf," Anna said. "When I grabbed one out, the photo just fell out and fell to the floor. Charlie started barking outside, and I forgot to pick it up when I came back inside."

"And you didn't see the photo until just now?" Ryatt asked Em.

"No," she replied. She couldn't stop looking at the photo, wondering what it was all about.

"How old do you think you were in this photo? My son is seven, but you look to be a bit younger here than he is. I'm going to say you were about five? Would that be right?"

Em looked at Ryatt, shocked. "You have a son?"

"Yeah – didn't I tell you?" Ryatt looked confused.

Em shook her head. "Ah, no. Are you married?"

Suddenly she felt like a fool, thinking there was still chemistry between them. That he cared about her. But no, he was just doing his job.

"No. Single as a bird. Ethan's mum ran off with a French backpacker when he was just a baby. Just been him and me ever since," Ryatt said. "Sorry, I thought you knew."

"No," Em said, slightly relieved to hear he was single, but still shocked to hear that Ryatt was a single dad.

"I'll bring him over another time to meet you. In the meantime ..." He pointed at the photo.

"Yes. I was probably around five," Em said. "When Mum was here, I confronted her about the photos Margo gave me. Turns out, she does have a son. And, if this is in Pontypool, like Margo says, then it must have been just before we left. I remember a kid standing in the road when Mum and I left. He looked ... I don't know. Lost? Heartbroken? That had to have been him. Russell. Mum's son."

"Geezus," Kennedy said.

"But why wouldn't she have taken him with you both then?" Anna asked.

"She said he was evil when I asked. I don't know why the first time, though."

"Could have been a custody arrangement," Ryatt said. "Back in those days, they usually sided with the mother, but if Russell's father had something on her, then that would have tipped the scales."

"The mental instability," Kennedy said. "Remember what was leaked to the press? You said that her time at the psychiatric hospital was not public record ... Maybe he had something on her before that, along those same lines?"

"Okay, but if both Rusty and Russell are dead, what's with the photo from the bookcase?" Em said.

"That's what I was calling you about earlier," Ryatt said. "I can't find any record of Russell's death, in Queensland or anywhere."

"But Margo said—"

Ryatt cut her off. "I know, but I dug deep. There's no record of a Russell Duggan after his booking on the ferry to the mainland. Which, by the way, coincided with right after his dad died. I think Russell is alive, and he's changed his name."

"But why would he do that?" Anna asked. "What did he have to gain?"

"New life?" Asher asked. "With a childhood like that, wouldn't you?"

"I think it's more sinister than that," Ryatt said, looking back at the photo, then over at the phone encased in the plastic bag beside him.

"What do you mean?" Em asked.

Ryatt looked at her. "This is just a theory, okay?"

Em nodded, waiting.

"I think Russell may be behind all this."

"But why? And why is the photo here? In this house?" asked Em. She couldn't piece it together.

"Holy shit," Asher said.

Em looked over and found his face a weird shade of grey. He shook his head.

"What?" Em said.

"Why? Why do you think that?" Kennedy asked impatiently, the investigative reporter on high alert.

"We need to find something written by Russell," Ryatt asked. "We may be able to link it back to the notes. Maybe there's a pattern to them?"

The others nodded.

"I don't understand. What am I missing that all you seem to have figured out?" Em demanded.

"Look at the photo again, Em. That looks to have been done by someone who wants revenge. Think about it. If you are Rusty's daughter, then you got to be with the mother Russell lost. He was left behind."

Em felt like the blood was running out of her body.

"Exactly," said Ryatt, "Em. I think Russell is your homeowner. John."

"What?" Em whispered, her voice barely audible.

"Problem is, we still can't find him. We tracked his campervan down to Western Australia, but it was a dead end. The couple who were driving it stated they rented it through a service in Victoria and that they picked up the keys at a locked box. They never met the owner, but they had his email address. When we checked, it was the same email address he gave you. And that's also proving to be a dead end."

"You can't find the IP address from the sent emails? That's how we find people." Kennedy blushed. "I know, it's unethical as hell."

"I have someone looking at that. But at first glance, the IP is buried deep," Ryatt said.

"What about that campervan Tyler mentioned? The one that's been down at the park so often?" Anna asked. "I know it sounds weird, but what if that campervan is John ... Russell ... just staking Em out?"

"What campervan?" Ryatt asked.

"Tyler said that he thinks there's a campervan down at the park, parked by the river, that he's seen before," Anna said. "It's not uncommon, but there was something about it that he thought weird."

"I've seen campervans there myself, and when I mentioned them to Shirley and Margo when I arrived in Neeminah River, they said tourists park there all the time. It's a good spot for free camping, given the toilet block has a shower," Em added.

"But Tyler has seen the same one on multiple occasions?" Ryatt asked.

"He thinks so," Anna said. "I can go ask, if you like. He should be home today."

"I'll go get him. He's the kid across the road, yeah? About sixteen?" Asher said.

Anna nodded. Asher grabbed his jacket and ran out the door. Charlie followed, and Em let him go. Tyler would recognise Charlie and know it was okay to talk to Asher.

"He said this morning that there's a van that's been parked down there for a couple of nights. I just assumed it was the media," Em added.

Ryatt pulled his phone from his pocket, hit a button then put the phone to his ear. "Smith please. It's Detective Ryatt from Hobart," he said, staring down at the photo on the table. "Smith, it's Ryatt. We have a lead, but I'm going to need you to check out a campervan parked at the Neeminah River. No details yet, but I'll call you back as soon as we have more information. Tyler, the kid across the street, has noticed it's been there for a few days."

"The track down at the bottom paddock," Anna said. "It leads to the park."

Ryatt nodded, acknowledging her comment.

"Apparently there's a track from the property that leads to the park," Ryatt repeated. "Yep, that one. Okay. Call you with details soon. Thanks."

"Have you ever seen a photo of John?" Ryatt asked, putting his phone back in his pocket.

Em shook her head.

"Without a name, we can't find what he looks like either. I've done a search on John Young, just in case they are connected, but you can imagine that doesn't lead to many places. I even checked vehicle inspectors in Tasmania, since Shirley said that's what he does. But there aren't any vehicle inspectors that go by the name of John Young. Plus, the only two inspectors taking holidays at the moment are a woman in her thirties and an Asian bloke who's just about to retire."

"I wonder if Shirley or Margo might have a photo," said Anna. "I'll go and ask them." She dashed towards the door.

"I'll call them," Ryatt said, and, standing up, scrolled through his phone. "Faster this way." He walked to the glass door.

"Hello. It's Detective Ryatt. Sorry to bother you, but I'm with Em at the property and we wondered if you or Shirley might have a photo of John? Yes, that's right. Of John Young ..." He seemed to listen for a long time. "Oh really?" he said as he glanced back at Em. "Yes, that would be great. Yes, we'll be here. Thank you."

Ryatt returned to the table. "Seems we're in luck. Margo and Shirley had a Christmas party last year. They have a photo with John. Seems he was a bit of a reluctant participant at first, but after a few drinks, he lightened up, according to Margo. They are going to find the photo and bring it over."

Em nodded as she continued to stare at the photo. She couldn't seem to take her eyes off it. The resemblance between Ruby and the dog in the photo was uncanny. It made her skin crawl.

"Em," said Anna suddenly. "What about the room?"

"What room?" Ryatt asked.

"The locked room. There's always some place that the homeowner locks up in a housesit. A cupboard, a room, a shed. It's where they keep their valuables while they're away," Anna explained.

"Show me," Ryatt said.

"Didn't you check it when you checked the house before? When Callum died?" Kennedy demanded.

"No, we just checked outside," Ryatt said. "There wasn't any reason to come into the house."

Asher returned with Tyler, and Pete trailing behind, just as Ryatt was inspecting the lock on the door.

"Where is everyone?" Asher called from the lounge room.

"We're in here," Kennedy called, poking her head out from the hallway.

"You guys don't happen to have any bolt cutters, do you?" Anna asked.

"I think there's some in the shed," Tyler said.

"I'll go with you," Pete said.

"Crowbar would work too," said Anna.

"Wait!" Ryatt shouted and everyone froze. "Just to be clear and make sure we're all above board. Mats. Do you have any proof stating you are the occupier of the property? Like an agreement with Russell?"

"Yes. It's all through the agency," Em said.

"And it's documented?" Ryatt asked.

Em nodded.

"Good, because I can only search the premises when the owner or occupier consents to the search. Without that, whatever we find will not hold up, even if we find incriminating evidence. Do you have a copy of the agreement?"

Em nodded, ran back to the table and picked up her phone. Scrolling through, she found the app with her housesitting agreement, then handed the phone to Ryatt. Quickly, he scrolled through the document. He looked down at his watch, then back at the phone.

"Good. Just confirming it's within dates," Ryatt said, and handed Em back her phone. "Okay Tyler, we'll take a crowbar or something similar if you can find one."

The lock rattling behind them caused Ryatt to look back. Kennedy was doing everything she could to open it with her bare hands. Ryatt walked over and placed his large hand over the lock.

"Maybe you should wait in the lounge room. You all should," Ryatt said.

"No way!" Kennedy said, but when she saw Ryatt's intense look, she backed down. "Fine," she said, and squeezed past him.

Em remained beside him. She wasn't going anywhere. This was her life. Her family. Suddenly the idea of that made her feel ill. Was she actually related to this man?

"Tyler," Ryatt said, when the kid returned, "can you tell me anything about the campervan you saw at the park?"

Tyler handed Ryatt the bolt cutters, then stood nervously at the edge of the hallway and the living space. His dad stood behind him. He looked back, saw Pete nod, then turned back to Ryatt.

"Um. It's a white one, a GoCheap or Tassie Explorers, something like that. But it was fairly new, not one of those beaten-up or painted ones. I never saw anyone around it, just the van. There's often a campervan down there so you never know if it's the same van or not. But it stuck out, because the number plates changed, but there was always the same red mark on the back right hubcap."

Ryatt pulled out his phone again and dialled.

"Smith please. Detective Ryatt. Yep, I'll wait." He cradled the phone in the crook of his shoulder and looked closely at the lock. He nodded over to Pete to turn on the light switch he was standing next to, to make a better inspection.

"Smith? Ryatt. Yep. White van. Either GoCheap or Tassie Explorers. Those are usually the Toyota HiAce model... Yep. And there's red mark on the right hubcap." There was a long pause. "Okay, I'm at the house. Yes, I'll be here. Thanks." He hit the end call button and slipped the phone back into his pocket.

"I suggest you all join Kennedy in the living area," Ryatt said firmly, but while everyone else retreated, Em stood her ground.

"If you're sure," said Ryatt.

Em nodded.

With a quick snap to the lock, he looked back at Em again. She clenched her hands together to stop them from shaking. She wasn't sure if she was ready to see what was behind the door. If there was anything there at all. But something told her the answers would all be there.

With a deep breath, Ryatt turned the handle, then reached around to turn the light on with his still-gloved fingers. When the room was illuminated, Ryatt exhaled a stream of explicit language. Em felt like she wanted to vomit.

Covering every inch of one wall were photos of Em's and her mother's life. Photos of when they were working one of the Sydney markets, when Em was a teenager. A photo of Em with her mother beaming into the camera at her high school graduation. Another photo of them laughing at Em's twenty-first birthday party. Her mother, blowing out candles on her fiftieth birthday cake. It looked like they were photos taken from one of Em's personal social media accounts.

Another wall was dedicated to the design plans for the house renovation, with interiors taken directly from Em's Pinterest boards. Her dream boards. Information about housesitting, including her profile, was pinned next to them. Beside that was information about campervan sites, including how to rent out his own campervan and the cost of renting one in Tasmania.

Ferry schedules, newspaper articles about Em's life in LA, and more photographs of her and Callum lined the last wall. There even looked to be journals stacked on the desk.

Ryatt moved closer to the campervan information.

"Son of a—"

His phone rang. He grabbed it from his pocket and punched it.

"Ryatt," his pissed-off tone evident to whoever was at the other end. "Fuck. Find the van. He's been here the whole fucking time. I have enough here to arrest him. Yep. Okay."

He turned to Em, who felt like she was in an alternate reality. She'd seen this kind of thing on television, but never in real life.

"The van isn't there, but Smith is putting a call out on it," Ryatt said.

Em nodded and turned; and when she saw a photo of her father, dead on the side of the road, everything went black.

42

"I don't think she's slept well in days," Em heard Anna say through the dark fog that surrounded her.

"Mats?" She thought she could hear Ryatt calling her name, with anguish in his voice. She tried to open her eyes, but pain shot through her skull.

"Close those blinds, would you?"

Yes. That was definitely Ryatt. He was right next to her now. She could hear his rapid breathing.

"I think the other detective is coming up the driveway," Asher said.

Em tried again to open her eyes.

"Come on, Mats. That's it. Open your eyes," said Ryatt.

"God, my head," was all she could get out.

Then it all came flooding back. The room. The photo. Her father.

"The room," Em croaked.

A knock on the front door made her try and sit up. A detective walked in. The one who'd been here when Callum died. Ryatt's boss.

"What happened?" he demanded.

"Fainted," Ryatt said, standing and leaving Kennedy to look after Em. "We opened the padlocked room based on other evidence found this morning. The owner of this house is definitely our guy." With that,

Ryatt nodded towards the hallway to show the other detective the way.

"Babe? Can you get Em some water, please?" Kennedy asked Asher over her shoulder, then looked back at Em.

Em looked towards the padlocked room. She flashed to the walls, plastered with images and plans.

"Em?" Kennedy asked, handing her water. She took it with a shaking hand.

"I'm fine," Em finally said, although she felt far from it. Ryatt's phone rang from the locked room, the sound reverberating down the hallway. All eyes turned that way.

"Ryatt speaking," he said. There was a long pause. "What?" He went quickly to the front door and opened the door a little way to peer at something outside.

Em heard the slow crunch of gravel on the driveway. Her eyes zeroed in on Ryatt's movements. She tried to stand up, but Kennedy pushed her down.

"I'm fine! Let me go!" she snapped, but Ryatt turned in a rush.

"Stay here. Do not come outside," he barked, urgency giving his voice a harsh edge as he frantically pulled on his boots near the door. He ran out, then stuck his head back inside the room and shouted instructions for everyone to stay away from the locked room, emphasising the word "evidence" as he slammed the door shut again. Charlie barked from inside, the sound echoing off the walls, sensing something major was happening outside. Even Billy was on his feet, but he looked confused by all the commotion.

"What's going on?" Kennedy demanded from Em's side.

Asher shrugged helplessly but moved towards the front door to investigate. He bent down to peer out the peep hole and recoiled in shock.

"Holy shit," Asher said.

"What?" Kennedy demanded.

Asher turned to face Em, his expression grim. "There's a white campervan in the driveway. I think it's Russell, or John, or whatever his fucking name is, sitting in the front seat. Ryatt has his gun drawn on the passenger side and there's another cop at the front with his weapon out too."

"What?" Kennedy exclaimed. She was on her feet now, rushing to the door.

Em saw an opening. She darted towards the door, burst out onto the verandah barefoot and made a beeline for the gate. The dogs chased after her, barking loudly and adding to her already heightened sense of panic. She had one goal in mind: get to Russell. She had to find out what had happened with her mother. Where was she? What had he done with her? And why? Why would he do this?

When she reached the fence, the dogs came to a sudden stop, as if sensing too much danger beyond this point, but she continued on.

"Mats! No! Stay back!" Ryatt's voice echoed through the air, but Em was too blinded by her fury to listen. All her rage was directed at the man sitting in the driver's seat. She faced him through the windscreen.

He had the same green eyes as she did and, as he smirked at her through the glass, she saw a similar dimple in his right check – but that's where the similarities between the siblings ended. His frame seemed tall and lean, and there was a rough edge to him, making him appear much older than early forties.

"Are you Russell?" she screamed.

The smirk turned into an evil smile. When her question went unanswered, she ran around to the driver's side window to confront him. The policeman ordered Em to step back, but she paid no attention. She pounded on the glass, desperate for answers. The man on the other side of the glass smirked at her, taunting her with his wriggling nicotine-stained fingers.

"Where's my mother?" Em demanded, her voice shaking with fear and anger. But instead of answering, the man sneered and flipped her off.

"Hands on the wheel!" the policeman shouted.

"Where's Mum!" Em repeated, then watched in horror as Russell took a swig from a water bottle that Em immediately recognised as Kat's, the same one she had been using for years.

"Where is she? What did you do? Why would you do this?" Em shrieked, her voice quivering with rage.

Russell's eyes narrowed into slits. "Because of you, you stupid bitch!" he spat, his voice hoarse and filled with venom. His voice was scratchy, like he smoked five packs of cigarettes a day.

Through the passenger side window, beyond Russell looking at her, she saw Ryatt's head turn towards the back of the van. Instinct told her to keep Russell's attention focused on herself.

"Why? Just tell me why," Em pleaded, her voice shaking with emotion. "The chickens, Ruby ... and Callum? How could you kill my husband?"

"Do you ever think about anyone else but yourself, princess?" Russell's voice was muffled by the glass separating them, but she heard his words. "It's always been about you. But she was my mother, too. And she left me there with Dad. He was your father, too! But no, she took you and never looked back." Russell's face contorted with hatred.

Her mother was right. He had an evil streak. But hearing the truth about who her father really was left her speechless.

Suddenly, the back door of the van swung open, jolting Russell's attention away from Em. Someone grabbed her from behind, and Em spun around to find Bryan with a finger pressed to his lips, silencing her screams. He quickly pulled her down into the shadows behind the bushes.

"Just shut up and listen. The fucker fooled us all," Bryan hissed, fear and anger radiating from every word. "And they called me the catfisher! Listen to me, you're in danger with this bastard. Just trust me, okay?" Em barely had time to process his words before Bryan yanked her away, heart pounding as she struggled to piece together what was happening around her.

"What the hell?" Russell roared as he burst out of the driver's side door. But before he could react, Ryatt appeared from behind the van.

"On the ground, now!" Ryatt yelled, his gun aimed at Russell's chest. Instead of complying, Russell stood there with a twisted smile on his face.

"Now, Russell!" Ryatt bellowed.

"It doesn't matter anymore. She's dead," Russell sneered, and pulled the water bottle from inside his jacket.

Instantly, a gunshot echoed through the air. Em screamed, the first shot still ringing in her ears as another shot rang out. Everything unfolded in front of her in what felt like slow motion. Russell crumpled to the ground. Ryatt stood facing Russell, his handgun by his side.

Bryan's words snapped her back to reality. "She's not dead," he said, crouching beside her. "Your mum. She's barely alive, but she's here, in the back of the van. I looked in before."

Em shot up off the ground and rushed past Ryatt to the open door at the back of the van. "Mum!"

Kat lay motionless on the bed inside, looking almost lifeless. Em's heart threatened to stop beating until she noticed a faint rise and fall in her mother's chest.

"Two ambulances on the way!" the senior detective shouted, kneeling down beside Russell and shaking his head at Ryatt.

It was all happening too fast, but Em knew one thing for sure – they had to get her mother help, and fast.

43

Em's head throbbed as she walked into the house later that night. She'd had one hell of a day.

"Hey. How's Kat? Is she okay?" Asher asked impatiently from the kitchen.

Em put her bag down and nodded slowly. She had insisted that Asher and the others leave her at the hospital hours ago; someone needed to take care of the animals, especially since they had all piled into one car to follow the ambulance without considering the logistics of returning later. Ryatt had come back for her afterwards, after completing his report with his team, and driven her back to the Huon Valley.

"Yeah. Russell tried to poison her. They were able to pump her stomach and they're confident she'll make a full recovery. She's been sedated for now. She was pretty agitated. She kept screaming Russell's name, then mine. She'll most likely be released tomorrow, maybe the day after. She asked if you were with me, Asher. When I told her you were, that seemed to calm her down." She smiled at her friend, who currently had his hands in dough.

"And Russell?" Kennedy asked, holding a glass of wine out to Em.

She indicated the wine to Ryatt, but he shook his head, then his car keys. Kennedy smiled and nodded.

"In the morgue," Em said. She had no sympathy for the man, although she knew that between her and her mother, they'd have to decide what to do with the body. Right now, it was almost too much to process. Not only was 'John' her brother, but he was responsible for all that had happened. But the reason he did it, and why he killed Callum, remained a puzzle that Em couldn't work out.

"Are you hungry? Margo and Shirley were here for a while. Tyler's dad sent over food from his restaurant, so they stayed for dinner. Shirley's a riot and her Margo is just a sweetheart, isn't she?" Kennedy said.

Em appreciated her trying to lighten the mood, but there were still so many questions she wanted answers to. She was glad Ryatt was here.

"No, I'm okay," Em said. "Maybe later. My head is just spinning for now. The wine may calm it, so thanks for that."

She walked over and took a seat in the lounge room, being careful not to spill any wine from the full glass. Ryatt sat in the chair opposite her.

"Tell me why," Em asked. One big question had been spinning in her head all night.

"Why what?" Ryatt asked.

"Why did Russell do all this?" She took a large drink from the glass.

"He was trying to frame you, Mats. He had journals in his van. Pages and pages of notes and ideas. There were even notes to you in there. Threatening ones. Callum turned out to be a convenient way to frame you. He wanted you out of the way so he could have your mother all to himself. I don't think he planned to kill Callum, but when Callum came down here to confront you about the video, it made him an easy target. From what I can piece together, Russell was the guy Callum met in the pub. The guy who told Callum where you were. And let's face it, if the guy got Callum talking, it would have been easy for him to see what an idiot Callum was."

"Wow, okay," she said, astonished that Russell had been that calculating.

"And, if he stroked his ego enough, Callum would have gone along with whatever Russell said," Kennedy said.

"I agree," Ryatt continued. "Callum probably came back at a time you weren't here, which meant Russell could kill him, dump the body, and be out by the time you were back. And since you were going through a messy divorce, and with Callum's body found where you were housesitting, well, it all played into Russell's hands."

"*Damn*," Asher said from where he stood leaning against the kitchen counter, picking dough from his fingers.

"Not to freak you out, Mats, but we believe you were Russell's original target. Callum was just easier. Russell probably figured out he could just set you up and get you out of the way, and tarnish the relationship you had with Kat, in one fell swoop, and he'd have his mother back to himself."

"The piece I can't work out," Kennedy added as she walked over and sat next to Em, "is if Russell wanted to be with his mother, why would he have Em housesit? Why not just bring his mother here?"

"He probably tried. But she's always hated Tasmania," Em said plainly. "She's been very vocal about that to me."

"Russell tried to get her here, according to his journals," Ryatt explained. "He wanted to reconcile with his mother in Tasmania, but she refused. So he met up with her in Victoria. But when she came down to see Em shortly after that, he was not happy. That's when things escalated quickly. We still need to talk to Kat, but we think she was coming down to tell Em about Russell."

"Oh my God!" Em yelped. "She said she wanted to tell me something, but she left before she could."

Ryatt nodded.

"She left because of something on the bookshelf." Em got up and scanned the bookcase again.

"What book did you find that photo in, Anna?" Em asked from the other end of the room.

"Ah, the one on auto-mechanics," Anna said, standing to join Em at the bookcase. "That one," she said, pointing to the well-used book on the shelf. "I was looking at it because my car has a rattle."

Em considered whether her mother would have been interested in the book. Rusty had been an auto-mechanic, so it could have been that – but then her eye went back to the framed postcard. Em slid it out of the frame and turned it over to look at the back. It was empty of writing,

"Maybe this freaked her out," Em said. "This postcard. Maybe she sent it to him?"

Ryatt stood and came over to take a look for himself.

"There's no writing on it, though," Em noted.

"Could've sent it in an envelope? Less obvious that way?" Ryatt suggested, as he looked at it closer. "It looks like Ballarat. In Victoria."

"We lived there for a while when I was about six or seven," Em said.

"Maybe she worked out that Russell was the man who lived here when she saw the postcard? I'll ask her about that when she's out of the woods, Mats. We'll get to the bottom of it. Things are still being pieced together."

Ryatt looked at her like he wanted to hug her, but he was still here in an official capacity. They had already sealed off the locked room. Em was just waiting for him to tell her she needed to pack her things and leave. And she would. Soon.

"What I can't get over is that the guy has been in Tasmania the entire time," Asher said. "That's just creepy."

"Not the whole time," Ryatt said. "He was with Kat in Victoria. We think that's when he got her computer and took her original phone."

"Probably when he dumped his campervan, too," suggested Anna.

Ryatt nodded.

"And the notes he left for Em?" asked Kennedy. "He must have thought of those ahead of time."

Em walked back to the couch and curled up on it, her arms wrapped around a pillow.

"I think once Em was on the hook for the housesit, he planned it out. Explains the notes in the van. The ones written to Em." He looked pensive for a few moments.

"How much time was there, between you agreeing to housesit and you being here?" Ryatt asked.

"A couple of months," Em said. "I had to talk to Asher about The Bakehouse and get that sorted, and then finalise some things with my lawyers. I was originally supposed to arrive a few weeks before."

"Which is why Lukas was here," Anna interjected.

"Yeah, I wondered about that," Ryatt said, returning to the lounge room to stand in front of the wood fire. "I wondered why he would bring in another housesitter first."

"To make it look legitimate. Or to test the surveillance?" Kennedy suggested.

"Probably both," Ryatt agreed.

"But the chickens, and the chicken head, and the goat? He had to be here for that. And for Ruby," Em said, her voice breaking. All that loss. And for what? So he could screw with her?

"All those times Tyler saw his campervan down at the park ... God, I feel sick now for ignoring him," Anna said.

"I know. Me too," Em said, her voice cracking again. Tears formed.

Kennedy stroked her back.

Em turned to Ryatt. "When you talked to Mum, did she know about Russell? That he died?"

"Yes, I told her," Ryatt said. "She didn't seem too upset, but she was pretty doped up."

Charlie stood and walked towards Em. He nudged her leg, just like Ruby used to do.

"Oh God, what will happen to the dogs? To the animals?" Em asked Ryatt and was surprised when he just shrugged.

"Leave it for tonight," he said softly. "You need some rest, just as much as Kat does. She knows you're okay. She knows where you are. Go in and see her tomorrow."

Tears trickled down her face.

"I've got to go," Ryatt said. "Need to get home to Ethan."

The reminder that Ryatt had a son made Em feel guilty. Ryatt had been with her all day. How did he handle being a single dad with such a time-consuming job?

"God, I'm so sorry. You should have been home hours ago!" Em said.

"Nah. I've got great parents who spoil him rotten. They're constantly on call and luckily live just down the road from us," Ryatt said.

Em was surprised to hear that.

"Guess that's another thing I forgot to tell you. I'll fill you in later. For now, rest up. I'll call in the morning." His eyes flitted towards the hallway. "We'll have the room finished up tomorrow, but don't go in there, okay?" He put his boots back on in the doorway. "I think they've put a lock on it anyway." With a wave, he was gone.

"You know what I don't understand? Why would he try and kill your mom?" Kennedy asked as she settled into the chair Ryatt had vacated. "He seemed pretty obsessed with her, so why kill her?"

Em's phone rang. She looked down and was surprised to see Ryatt's name on the screen. She doubted he'd even made it to the end of the driveway. She hit the green button.

"Hey, Mats. Look, I just got a message from my Senior Sergeant. The team have just discovered something interesting in the campervan. Have you seen anything in the house that could be something that he'd be listening in with? Like a baby monitor or some kind of small device on a shelf?"

Em looked around but didn't see anything in the living room.

"I don't think so. I can't see anything here," Em said.

Kennedy mouthed to her, "What are you looking for?"

Em moved the phone away from her face and said, "Listening device. Do you know what to look for?"

Kennedy's face registered the same shock Em felt at the notion. Then she nodded and went on the hunt like a bloodhound.

"We're looking. Kennedy says she knows what to look for," Em said.

"If you find anything, don't touch it. There'll be someone out in the morning to take a look, okay?"

"Okay." Em watched as Kennedy, Anna and Asher all scoured the room.

"Here!" Kennedy called, pointing to something Em had assumed was an air freshener on the bookshelf. "That could be something. Maybe a camera?"

"Kennedy thinks there may be a camera here," Em said to Ryatt.

"Like a nanny cam?"

Em didn't know what that was, so she repeated the question to Kennedy, and Kennedy nodded.

"Kennedy says yes," Em said.

"Okay, don't touch it," said Ryatt. "Hold on a minute." She could hear him typing something. She waited. "Okay, the Senior Sergeant is requesting you vacate the premises for the time being. Sorry. I know it's late."

"It's okay," said Em. Being there was making her uncomfortable anyway, especially with the locked room looming in her mind.

"Maybe go to where you went after Callum's death," Ryatt suggested.

"Okay."

"I'll talk to you tomorrow." Ryatt hung up before she could say anything more.

"We've been told to leave," Em said. "Ryatt suggested we go back to the hotel in Hobart. I'll be closer to Mum there, too."

"We'll come with you," Kennedy said, looking to Asher, who was already cleaning up the kitchen.

"But you've got the Airbnb!" Em said. "Wait. The dogs and other animals. I've got to get someone to look after them."

"Anna? Could you stay at the Airbnb and keep the dogs there? I think they said they were dog friendly when I booked," Kennedy asked, picking up her phone.

"Ah, sure. And if they don't allow dogs, I'm sure Tyler will help out," Anna said. "He's helped before. He's still feeling bad after—"

"Oh God! He shouldn't!" Em said, cutting her off. "He's still a kid. I don't blame him!"

"I'll contact the hotel, then the Airbnb. Babe, you okay with that?" Kennedy looked up at Asher as her fingers flew over her phone.

"Yep," Asher said, staring at the dough he'd just formed into the perfect loaf. "Just trying to work out what to do with this ..."

"I'll take it and share it with Margo and Shirley in the morning," Anna suggested.

"Good. I'd hate for it to go to waste," Asher said, and went on the hunt for something to wrap it in.

"Okay. Airbnb sorted. Anna, I'll give you the address. It's just down the road in Glen Huon. And I couldn't get into the Macq 01, but I got a suite at the Henry Jones nearby. So, lots of room."

Em was stunned. How did Kennedy do all of that so quickly? She felt like she was in a time warp and unsure of what to do next. Right now, the walls of her life seemed to be closing in again. She had yet to unpack the truth of who her real father was. But she wasn't quite ready to face that yet.

44

It had been two long days since the confrontation with Russell, but it felt like an entire week had passed. Despite the numerous questions she had asked, some still remained unanswered. Sitting in the hotel suite with her mother, Em knew that Kat held the key to unlocking the last of those unanswered questions.

Ryatt had already interviewed Kat, but refused to share any information with Em, insisting that she speak directly with Kat instead. They had plenty of time to fill as they looked through photos and letters from Russell's campervan, most of which were in piles on the table between them. Everything had been photocopied and the originals placed into evidence. They'd get the originals back eventually. If they wanted them. Em wasn't so sure. Ryatt had promised the police would finish at the house by early afternoon, but Em couldn't decide if she wanted to return there. The house was filled with death, and memories that she desperately wished she could erase.

Part of her felt tied to the house. Perhaps it was because of the dogs, or maybe it was the kindness of the neighbours who had reached out and helped her. Whatever it was, Em was grateful for their support. Shirley and Margo had driven to Hobart that morning to offer their support and assistance. They'd brought more food from Pete and comforting words from all, expressing how sorry they were about what had happened. Shirley was unusually verbose. She talked about her disillusionment about John – or Russell – non-stop, saying how wrong she'd been about him.

"I'm usually good at sussing people out, but he pulled a fast one, even on me! I thought he was a nice fellow. But holy shit! I feel like I need a bloody good shower every time I think of him!"

Margo simply hugged her tightly, letting her know that they were there for her whenever she needed them.

Even Bryan had surprised her. He'd surprised all of them, really. She still had no idea where he had come from that day, or why he'd stepped in to get her out of the way. She needed to ask Ryatt. Or Bryan – but she hadn't seen him since the day it happened.

Now, with Asher and Kennedy out buying lunch for them all, Kat seemed dazed as she looked through the old photos Russell had kept. Some of them had singed edges, like they'd been tossed on a fire then rescued.

Kat stared down at a letter she'd written to Russell.

"You asked me why I didn't take Russell with me," Kat said, running her hand across the words. "Rusty was good friends with the local cops. They all went to school together. Played rugby together. Went fishing together. After Jake died and we were back in Pontypool, I asked Rusty for a divorce."

Em looked up from the photos in her own hand.

"So Dad – Jake – wasn't my real father," Em said flatly. Russell had all but said so, but Em wanted her mother to confirm it. Her mother shook her head.

"No. He wasn't. At least, not biologically. But Jake was your dad in all the ways it mattered."

Em struggled with this reality, but after seeing the pictures of Rusty in front of her, she knew without a doubt that she was his daughter. She shared the same broad, muscular build as her father, and the same fiery red hair. Despite her childhood memories of Jake being larger than life, he had actually been lean like her mother.

"It makes sense now. Em said, staring at one particular image of Rusty.

"Why you always reacted the way you did whenever you first saw me. Especially if it had been a while."

Her mother looked up with a confused look, then saw the photo Em held in her hand. She looked up at Em and nodded solemnly.

"Sorry about that. Some days, seeing you…it catches me off guard."

The tension was thick between them as the truth continued to sink in for Em.

"Why aren't there photos of dad? Did you not keep any of them?"

"Rusty burned them all," her mother said sadly.

Em opened her mouth to ask something more, but Kat started speaking.

"When I found out I was pregnant again, I knew I had to get out. I was still married to Rusty when I left with Jake. Jake and I didn't, ah, consummate anything until we were well out of reach. I was too scared that Rusty would find out and kill Jake. Turns out, I was right to be scared. Anyway, after we were away, I couldn't tell Russell where I was, because I was so afraid Rusty would come after us and drag us back to Tasmania. But that happened, too."

Kat shook her head rapidly, like she was trying to refocus her thoughts into a narrative that made sense. She got up and walked to the window.

"When we were back in Tasmania, after Jake died, I asked Rusty for a divorce. He almost killed me that night. Tied me up, then beat me. He was worried I'd run again, I suppose. He left me in the shed for three days. No one knew where I was."

Kat turned around to face Em, and Em could feel her heart breaking at her mother's anguish.

"Well, actually, Russell did," Kat continued. "Rusty made him check on me. To make sure I was still breathing, I suppose. I made sure Russell looked after you since Rusty wanted nothing to do with you. Rusty didn't know that you were his. I don't know why. I guess he just assumed you were Jake's daughter. But I was so afraid that he'd find out somehow. That's why we kept moving. I'm not sure when he worked it out.

"But while he had me tied up in the shed, Rusty got papers drawn up. He used the mental hospital against me, to prove to the judge that I was mentally unstable. He was the one who had me committed. His plan was to get full custody of Russell. I didn't know about all this at the time. Not until Ray told me and helped us escape. He'd heard about it all while he was in the pub. Rusty's mates were all laughing about it. Ray and Nell saw the writing on the wall, so they gave me money and helped us get away. Told me to leave Russell, because Rusty would find a way to track me down to get Russell back. They told me to leave and never come back. They promised they'd keep an eye on Russell for me, let me know how he was doing, but I didn't hear anything from them after a year. That's when I found out that Rusty had killed Ray. Had cut his brake lines. Just as Rusty killed your dad. By then, Nell was too scared to say anything or keep in contact with me." Kat's tears traced a path down her cheeks.

"So, did Rusty kill Dad?" Em asked, remembering the photo of her father in the locked room.

Kat nodded. "They couldn't prove it, but after Ray died, I knew. It was exactly the same way."

"But didn't Rusty die that way, too? Car accident? Brake failure?" Em asked. Kat looked surprised. "That's what Margo told me. That he died when Russell was about seventeen. Failed brakes coming home from Swansea. Just like Ray."

"Then Russell must have killed Rusty," Kat said matter-of-factly, as if she wasn't surprised by the information. She picked up another pile of photos and began sifting through them.

"Maybe," Em said, not wanting to add any more stress to her mother's already fragile state. She'd just found out her son was a killer. And now, multiple times over.

"I remember Russell," Em said.

Kat's head shot up.

"That day we left Pontypool. He was standing in the middle of the road. At least, I think it was that day. I was only about five or six, I think."

Kat nodded.

"I was looking out the back window as we drove away. I didn't know who Russell was, when I remembered this at first. He was older.

Thought it was just some random kid. The son of some guy we stayed with once."

"I never told you Russell was your brother," Kat said. "I didn't know if we could all get away together. If we had, I would have told you. But I wanted to keep you away from him initially. When we first got there, when you were little, he was very angry. He was a teenager, full of rage, and something told me never to leave you alone around him. He was jealous of you. But he came around for a little while. By the time Rusty put me in the shed that time, he was a good kid, happy to have his mum home and all that. But not long after that, I saw pieces of Rusty arise in him. I'm sure Rusty was feeding him with bullshit. By the time we left, he was back to being angry and jealous."

"I don't remember Pontypool at all," said Em. "I just remember that day. I remember him running out from around the back of the house when we were driving away. He was filthy dirty. I remember that. But I also remember the look on his face. He looked betrayed and devastated at the same time. Then *really* angry."

"I imagine he was all of that," Kat said. "I was leaving him. Again. And with Rusty. But I had no choice. I could never have taken him with me. Once I knew what Rusty had done with the custody agreement ..." Kat's voice trailed off.

"How did he find you?" Em asked. "Russell, I mean. Was it recently?"

"About a year ago, I suppose. I have no idea how he found me. I guess he'd had his eyes open and his ear to the ground."

"Hm ... I guess."

Em continued looking through the photos. She stopped at one of Russell and studied it, noticing their resemblances and their differences. While Em's hair was red and curly, Russell's was grey and wiry. While Em was curvy, soft and attractive, Russell was sinewy, hard looking, cunning. She wondered how her mother went from being scared of this man to accepting of him. Probably just blind mother's love, she mused. But something niggled at her. Something Callum had said in an interview a few years before.

"Wait. I think I know how he found you," she said, sitting up straighter. "Remember that interview Callum did about two years ago with *People* magazine?"

"No," Kat said, still looking through the photos. She held one out to Em. It was a picture of Russell as a boy, with the dog that looked a lot like Ruby. In the photo, Rusty stood next to Russell and the dog, a shotgun slung over his shoulder.

"Rusty killed this dog. Ruby, her name was. She was Russell's greatest joy. But Rusty declared all females were useless one night, tied her up, and ran over her with his car."

"Oh my God!" Em said, shocked. It explained Ruby's death, and the note that had been left. As they went through photo after photo, pieces of the puzzle fell into place.

"What were you saying about an interview?" asked Kat.

"Callum mentioned you in it. Said he found his success because of family, and how amazing their support was. He was on the outs with his own family at the time. I think he was trying to throw up the middle finger at them. So he said he had the best mother-in-law. He mentioned you by name. Said you were a freelance jewellery designer, currently working the market scenes around Sydney. Maybe that's how he found you."

"He always was one to embellish the truth," Kat said, shaking her head.

"I remember that interview specifically because I had asked him repeatedly never to mention you in interviews," Em said. "I wanted to protect you. We had a huge fight about it. Callum was enraged because he felt he'd finally made it, being featured in *People*. Truth was, it was a couple of paragraphs, promoting some movie he was currently in."

"I told him many times to keep me out of his Hollywood crap," Kat said.

"Now I understand why," Em said.

Kat nodded. "Now you know why," she repeated.

"What I don't understand is if he was as evil as you thought, back when he lived with Rusty, then why did you reconnect with him?" Em asked.

"Because he was my son. I abandoned him. I felt I owed it to him to at least see him. And I made sure we were in a public place at first. But he was charming. He didn't seem to be like Rusty at all – except with hindsight and all that, turns out he was *just* like Rusty. I'd forgotten Rusty was charming like that, once upon a time. But we reconciled, or so I thought, over what happened. I told him about the custody thing, and I told him why I couldn't take him. He seemed to understand that. After a while, when it seemed that we were closer, he invited me to his house. I said no. I thought it was just too soon. That was about six months ago, but I didn't realise this was the house he was talking about. I did tell him about you, and what was happening with you and Callum. I didn't mean to, but he was curious about you. The next time I talked to him, he said he had a friend who needed a housesitter. He asked me if I wanted to do it, since I'd told him I had done that during my travels here and there, but I said I wasn't interested in doing a housesit in Tasmania. That's when I suggested you. He said he'd ask his friend, and … well, you know the rest."

"You kept looking at something on the bookshelf when you were there. Was it the postcard in the frame?" Her mother looked up at her again, this time with one eyebrow raised. "Ryatt said it looked like Ballarat.," Em said.

Kat nodded.

"After Shirley suggested that John might be off travelling with a secret lover, I thought that was who the postcard was from. I had no idea that was what you kept looking at."

"I couldn't write anything on any of the postcards, so I put them in an envelope and sent them to Ray and Nell. There was never a return address. The only thing that was ever on the postcard was a heart. I guess I wasn't really thinking with that one. I just wanted to let him know I was still thinking of him when I first left. After that, a bunch of market friends around Australia would send them randomly to Russell for me. A lot of them were in similar situations, so we'd help each other out here and there. I needed to keep my tracks covered. But it was always a simple postcard with a heart on it. Nothing else."

It made sense now. So did all the moving around.

"When you saw the postcard, did you know then that it was Russell's house?" Em asked.

"No, but I knew something wasn't adding up. I didn't understand why his friend had that postcard. So I left, and I went to ask Russell directly," Kat said, then sighed. "Stupid me. I should have just called him."

Em had to admit, she wouldn't have confronted Russell with it face to face, and was surprised her mother had, especially since her mum knew the rest of the story of what had gone on with Em's housesit. But then, her mother had always been impulsive.

"I have a question," Em began, staring at the stack of letters and postcards on the table. Some were from her mother to Russell, but most were unsent letters from Russell to their mother. Her mother's face was tense as she turned to look at her. It was as if she had aged a decade overnight.

"Ryatt said he sent me letters, years ago, when he left Pennant Hills. He said he gave you a letter to give to me, and then wrote me a bunch more. Do you remember that?" She looked over to her mother, expecting her to deny it, or at least tell her she couldn't remember, like she had before. She was shocked when her mother nodded quickly.

"What happened to them?" Em asked.

"I threw them out," Kat said. She sighed. "I couldn't risk you going to Tasmania."

"But you knew how much Ryatt meant to me," Em said.

"I did. But I was scared. What if Rusty had found you? Tasmania is not that big of a place." Em understood her mother's reasoning, but she couldn't help feeling like things could have been different if she had known the truth about her past. But now, she saw the depth of her mother's fear and realized that she had been right to protect her from Russell and his father. His father. Em couldn't bring herself to claim Rusty as her own.

Silence filled the room, as both dealt with their own memories and emotions.

"Did you want to read the journals?" Em asked Kat after a while, but her mother shook her head. "Ryatt found a letter, written to you only a few days ago. Did you want to read that?"

Kat shook her head again.

"Should I read it?" Em asked.

Kat shrugged.

"Ryatt said it explains a lot," Em said, turning it over.

"Then read it. I don't want to. I already know what happened."

Em sifted through the photos and the letters and found the confession letter at the bottom of the pile.

She sat back, took a deep breath and unfolded the photocopied letter.

Dear Mum,

I didn't think it would come to this. All I wanted was for you to love me. To be with me. I bought a house in the Huon Valley, renovating it just for you. But I should have known you wouldn't come. Dad always said you wanted to live with all the hoity-toities in the Huon. I get it now. You wanted to be anywhere but in Tasmania. It wasn't just Pontypool.

But what I don't understand is why you loved her enough to keep her with you, but not me? When you left the first time, with that fucking drover, you should have taken me with you. Instead, you left me with Dad. You knew what he was like! Why didn't you come back and get me? You could have easily taken me from school or when Dad was up at the pub in Swansea. It would have taken him days to realise I wasn't home. Fuck, he wasn't even home for days on end. It would have been easy.

When you came back, I thought you'd be here forever. Dad said you were an ungrateful bitch. That you'd come back with your tail between your legs. He wasn't happy that you had HER with you! Neither of us were. But I was just glad you were back.

But you didn't stay long, did you? Six months. Not even a fucking year. Then you left. Again. And you took her. You still didn't take me with you.

Why??? What did I do? Why couldn't you have taken me with you, too? I would have ... fuck, I don't know. I would have put up with her if it meant I was with you. But no, it was her. Always her. She was the chosen one.

Well, I showed her, didn't I?

To be honest, she was fun to fuck with. The chickens first, then the goat. Ruby wasn't planned, but when that stupid dog showed more loyalty to HER than she ever showed me, it was an easy decision. Would've offed the shepherd too, if I'd had more time. Fucking dogs.

And why? She's just another whore. I mean, look at what the news said about her! She had sex with women while she was married. Filmed it too. Yeah, found that on your computer. That was a lucky break. And then there was her stupid husband. Fuck. He was pissed off about the video. But he was so easy to kill. Got him drunk then put poison in his drink when he got up to fuck some slut in the bathroom.

Women do that, you know. Use poison more than any other method to kill. Read about that online. So, I figured if SHE was going to kill him, for revenge or some shit, she'd use poison. Worked, too. After I dumped him in the pit, I waited. I knew they'd look at her for it. All just part of the plan.

I love you, Mum.

Your loving son,

Russell

45

A few hours later, in a café with downtown Hobart buzzing around them, Em shared a coffee with Ryatt, Asher and Kennedy. They'd left Kat at the hotel to rest.

"It's a lot to take in," Ryatt said, watching her closely.

"He killed his own father. How'd he know how to do it? He was still a teenager, wasn't he?" Kennedy asked Ryatt.

He nodded. "He got the idea from Rusty, from when he killed Ray."

"Just like with Dad?" Em asked.

Ryatt nodded. He paused, looking like he had more to say.

"Go on, just tell me," she said.

"Rusty was responsible for killing your dad. Russell had the details in his journal. Rusty died the same way Ray did, and ironically on the same stretch of road, too. It was deemed an accident, but people questioned it."

"Why?" Kennedy asked.

"Rusty was a mechanic. People couldn't understand how he could have ignored the maintenance on his own truck."

"So why didn't Kat want to come to Tasmania?" Asher asked.

"Mum didn't know Rusty had died. She thought he was still in

Tasmania, so she was afraid to come down because, as she said, everyone knows everyone here. Especially those who grew up here."

"That's a pretty true statement," Ryatt said, chuckling. "It's like two degrees of separation here."

"And Russell didn't tell her Rusty had died?" Kennedy asked.

Em shook her head. "I guess not," Em said. "But I suspect, even if she did, she wouldn't have come unless she really had to."

"And telling you about Russell was one of those 'really had to go to Tasmania' moments," Asher said. "Except she didn't tell you."

Em nodded.

"And she didn't know it was Russell's house?" Kennedy asked Em.

"No. Russell told Kat the property belonged to his friend, John Young," Ryatt filled in.

"She told me earlier that she once loved Tasmania, but Rusty put a dark stain on it," Em said, spinning her now empty mug around, staring at it.

"It would have been hard for her, living in a remote place like Pontypool. Especially with no way to get around," Ryatt said.

"Yeah, she said there was no one around there back then, except Nell and Ray. And after Rusty killed their dog ..."

Asher and Kennedy gasped. "He killed their dog?" Asher said.

Em realised she'd forgotten to share that nugget with them. "Yeah, Margo said Ray and Rusty had some disagreement. Next thing, their dog is gone. He killed Russell's dog, too. Her name was Ruby," Em said, remembering what her mother had told her. "The same as the dog he adopted last year. She was a replacement, apparently."

"Ruby was the one he killed at the house?" Kennedy asked. "Isn't that a sign of a psychopath? Killing animals, I mean."

"Usually a sign to watch for in kids, for sure," Ryatt said.

Kennedy nodded.

"Is that why Ray helped Kat escape? Because of the dog?" Asher asked.

"One of the reasons. They saw what was going on. Mum and I talked to Nell on the phone yesterday. She was quite distraught about the whole thing after seeing it in the news. But she was happy to talk to Mum again, and glad to finally have closure about Ray's death."

Em felt so bad for the elderly woman. None of this was her fault.

"So, after Russell killed his father, what happened? Where did he go?" Em asked. She'd asked her mother, but she'd shrugged. She didn't know.

"That's the interesting part. It's why we couldn't find him," Ryatt said. "He changed his name to John Smith when he moved to Melbourne. It was right after he killed his father. He moved to Queensland for a while, changed his name again to John Jones, then he moved to the Northern Territory. When he got to Western Australia, he became John Young. He lived in WA for over a decade. Worked in the mines for a while as a mechanic."

"Did he know Bryan?" Em asked, wondering if there was a connection.

"Yeah, turns out they were friends for a bit," Ryatt answered.

"So why didn't Bryan mention that? When you interviewed him?" Em asked.

Ryatt smiled. "He did. But Bryan was friends with John Young, not Russell Duggan. Russell never told Bryan that he grew up in Tasmania. Bryan was the one who told him about the property across the road when it went on the market. So Russell bought it and renovated it. Russell was the mastermind behind getting Bryan back to Neeminah River to spy on you, it turns out. He used Bryan's dad as an excuse, knowing his dad was the one thing Bryan would go home for."

"He played on his emotions," Kennedy said.

Ryatt nodded, then continued on. "Once Bryan was back, Russell asked Bryan to keep an eye on the housesitters for him while he was away. But it got tricky, because Bryan became obsessed with you, once he knew who you were. I guess that made things a bit harder for Russell to come and go as he pleased, with Bryan's binoculars trained on you the whole time. According to his journals, he had to send Bryan on a wild goose chase once in a while, just to get him out of the way."

"Bryan is the guy across the road?" Asher asked. When Ryatt nodded, he turned to Em. "The same guy who helped you the other day. Wasn't he the same guy who scared the crap out of you?"

Em nodded.

"Right! Then I'm confused," Kennedy said, sitting back in her chair.

"Me too!" Em admitted.

"Yeah, well it turns out Bryan isn't as sleazy as we all originally thought. He has his moments. Racist, yes. Homophobe, yes. But the catfishing was all part of Russell's scheme. In the end, Bryan was just as much a victim as the woman involved." Ryatt continued, "I don't want to defend Bryan's actions – he's still a sexist bogan – but he's innocent when it comes to Russell's lies, and he ended up losing his job because of them."

"Damn," Asher said, sitting back in his chair.

"And how was it that he was right there on the spot the other day?" Kennedy asked.

"He'd been watching Em, which kind of came in handy. He'd seen Russell drive past earlier with Kat in the passenger seat. She was agitated, pointing towards the house, but Russell was shaking his head and pointing further down the road. Then Bryan saw Asher run over to Pete and Tyler's and take Tyler back to the house, so he could tell something was up. When he saw Russell return without Kat in the front, he was suspicious. So he crept over and hid behind the bushes. While Russell was busy yelling at you, Em, Bryan was the one who looked in the back of the van and alerted me that she was there and only just breathing. I still don't know how Russell didn't see him, but I'm damn glad he was there."

"Yeah, we were too," Asher said.

"He's an angry guy," Ryatt said, "but once the truth comes out – and it will come out, as we've shared those parts of Russell's journals with the Western Australian police – Bryan will be cleared. He'll at least be able to get his job back. I think that's what was pissing him off. He was stuck. He couldn't find work, doing what he knew how to do well. He's said it's time to put his dad in a home, so I think they'll probably sell up, and he'll move his dad over to Western Australia with him."

"Good. He may be a good guy underneath, but there was no reason for him to be such a dick," Em said.

"Yeah. I know. Some guys still need to be reminded that women should be respected. I think the mines cultivate a misogynistic environment, and Bryan's been in it for a long time. Not that that's any excuse."

"Why the hell did you run out of the house in the first place, Em? That was crazy!" Asher burst out.

"Yeah, it was," said Kennedy.

"I needed answers. And I needed to know where Mum was," Em explained. "And if Russell had already killed her, which I thought was the case, I wasn't going to let him just get away with it and never know the truth."

"Even so, don't do it again. Like, ever," Ryatt said.

"He was drinking from Mum's water bottle," Em said. "That's when I really knew he knew something."

"He was poisoning himself," Ryatt said. "The same stuff he gave Kat. She would have died if it had been much longer."

"That's when you shot him," Em said. "When he grabbed the water bottle."

Ryatt nodded. "Except I didn't know that's what he was pulling out from his jacket. Or what it contained. I just reacted."

"Mum said he was just like his father. That she was scared of him," Em said after a while. "But he'd charmed her into reconciling, and she fell for it. Completely fell for it. I think that's what's haunting her the most."

"That's the bit that's haunting me, too. Why did he try and kill her?" Kennedy asked.

"Because she probably figured him out," Ryatt said. "The confession letter was the clincher. He was a lost little boy, rejected by his mother. And she was rejecting him all over again. Kat wanted Russell to meet his sister, but he wanted nothing to do with Em. He wanted Kat to himself. When he realised that wasn't going to happen, he wanted to make sure that Em couldn't have Kat either."

"The note we found on the phone in the pantry," said Em. "'If I can't have her, neither can you'."

Ryatt nodded. "The journals go way back. He talks about life in Pontypool as a kid. What his father used to do to him. The day his mother left with the drover. It's all there. Russell was one fucked up man."

"I don't know whether to feel relieved or angry," Em said quietly.

"I'd be fucking angry," Kennedy said.

"And I am," Em said. "But I'm also relieved. Selfishly, it means I have an answer to all that happened. As in, I know now who killed Callum. But I also have the answers to all the strange things that kept happening. I was piecing it all together earlier."

"What do you mean?" Ryatt asked.

"Early on, I thought I kept losing things. Or forgetting things, anyway. Like, the matches. One night I had them next to the wood stove, and the next morning, after the dog walk, they were gone. I could have sworn they were there the night before. And my coffee scoop. I always kept it in with the ground coffee, ready to go. But it disappeared. Same with my slippers."

"Well, we all lose things," Asher said, nudging her with a smile. "You've been losing your marbles for a while now. Admit it."

She had to smile. It had certainly felt that way.

"Nah. Em's right," said Ryatt. "They found those things in his van. And there were notes in his journal about Mats forgetting stuff."

"So, what now?" Asher asked. "I mean, not to be crass, but … it begs the question. The property? The animals."

"The house, the property, all of it, will go to Kat," Ryatt said. "Russell had no will, and she's his next of kin."

"She won't want it," Em said, knowing her mother. "She's already told me she's leaving as soon as she can. She wants to go back to the mainland."

"What about you?" Ryatt asked. "Would you stay?"

Em wasn't sure if he was asking as a friend, as a detective or as something else – but there seemed to be hope in his eyes.

"I don't know," Em said. "It'd be kind of weird. Russell used my Pinterest boards when he renovated the house. They were my dream-house boards. Especially the kitchen. But I don't think he knew they were mine, because I'd created them under Mum's name for privacy reasons. He must have thought it was *her* dream kitchen, *her* dream bathroom … But also, the house has kind of got the stench of what's happened there. Mum should sell it."

"Nothing that a good sage burning won't cure!" Kennedy joked.

"I'm sure those neighbours of yours can fix you up there. Margo, for sure!"

Em thought about the house. She had fallen in love with it the minute she drove her 4WD up the driveway. Despite the circumstances, in some ways she'd found comfort there. Even the neighbours had surprised her over the three weeks since she'd pulled up to the house. They'd come to her aid, rather than turning away from her, especially when she needed their support. She'd found friendships where she didn't expect them.

"Could you stay, knowing what you know? Maybe not in that house, but in Tasmania?" Ryatt asked.

It seemed an odd question to ask. There was a lot she did know, but looking at his earnest face, it seemed there were a lot of questions still unanswered.

So Em just shrugged, because, right now, she didn't know the answer to his question. Not yet, anyway.

EPILOGUE

S ix months later

EM LOOKED out from the verandah to see Charlie sniffing around the bushes. Billy was lying beside her rocking chair, sound asleep.

"I don't think this is ever coming off," Kennedy bellyached, scrubbing vigorously at her grape-stained feet. "And I have an event in New York in two weeks. I was planning on wearing my new Louboutins!"

"It's a good thing it's winter in the US, then, isn't it?" Em chuckled.

Kennedy huffed, then kept scrubbing. They'd spent the day stomping grapes at a local vineyard. It had been Asher's twisted idea of a fun vacation activity.

"Do you two want a glass of wine? Or one of my famous dirty Mexican martinis?" Ryatt shouted from the kitchen.

"That man continues to surprise me. He knows how to find crazy-ass killers. He knows how to make wine which, I have to admit, I was surprised to learn today. He knows how to make an American cocktail. And now I learn he cooks? What is he cooking in there anyway?"

"Fettuccini carbonara. His speciality, he says," Em responded, then yelled back to Ryatt through the open bi-fold doors, "We'll always go for your speciality!"

"Great," Kennedy groaned. "Stained feet and carbs. I guess you've made a cheesecake or something for dessert?"

"Actually, I made my lemon cheesecake squares," Em said, knowing they were Kennedy's weakness. Em had made them for the bakery for years now, and they were one of the most popular recipes in her new cookbook.

"Are you trying to kill me? I have to fit into my damn dress, remember?"

Em did remember. Her best friends were getting married in six months, at the beach, with a reception at The Bakehouse, which Asher had agreed to keep running. Em was staying on as partner – just a distant one.

"You know you're fabulous, whether you're a size four or a size twenty-four, right?" Em said, smiling over at a still-scrubbing Kennedy.

"Hey, do you guys want homemade garlic bread with Ryatt's pasta?" Asher asked from beyond the gate. Nearby were Asher's two favourite playmates: Ethan, Ryatt's son, and Bert, Em's newly rescued beagle, who was currently at Ethan's heels as they ran crazily together through the paddock.

"I could whip some up with those baguettes I made yesterday. Might be a good way to use them up, actually," Asher suggested.

Kennedy groaned again.

"Here you go. Two very cold, dirty martinis," Ryatt said, a red striped apron over the top of his jeans and button-down shirt.

"Asher, mate? How about you? Beer, wine or martini?" Ryatt asked as his eyes, shining with love, followed his son having a grand time with the dog.

"Who the hell *are* you?" Kennedy asked, throwing the scrubbing brush back into the bucket and taking her drink from Em.

Ryatt beamed. "Josh Ryatt. Chef extraordinaire. Dad to the best kid on the planet. Boyfriend to one fine Mats McKinney, who happens to be everyone's dream pastry chef. Friends with the uber-talented Asher Fowler and his fiancée, the famous Kennedy Wright, who published the exposé of the century. Oh, and a measly old police detective in my spare time." His smile was wicked.

"Good answer," Kennedy replied, and raised her glass to him.

"I'm really glad Kat sold you this property," Kennedy said, watching Asher with Ethan. Kennedy and Asher had no plans to have kids of their own, but Asher was turning out to be Ethan's favourite uncle. Whether it was official or not, it didn't matter. They were bonded for life.

"She didn't want it. She couldn't get past how the property was a means to an end for Russell," Em said.

"And you're still building her a studio?" Kennedy asked.

"You know that's more for you guys, right? For when you come and visit. And Anna, for when she's on a break from university. She'll need a place to hang out too."

Em looked up to the old barn that sat at the top of a nearby hill. She hadn't even realised it was part of the property when she'd arrived here to housesit six months ago. "It'll be here for Mum when she needs a home base, but that won't be for a while," Em said.

"Where is Kat now?" Kennedy asked, her eyes closed, relishing the martini.

"She's heading back to Coonawarra, determined to recapture the time when she'd been truly happy, she said. Coonawarra is the best place to start that journey, she told me, now she's not worried someone's going to drag her back unwillingly to Tasmania." Em sipped her own drink.

"Asher said Margo and Shirley are meeting up with her next month? In some place called Broken Hill?" Kennedy said.

"Yeah," Em said. "They've all become fast friends. She's got to know everyone around here in the last few months. Mum was saying she was thinking of doing that long walk Aubrey and Tom talked about. The one in Spain. Maybe sometime next year."

"The Camino? Really? I can't imagine Kat hiking," Kennedy said.

"Mum is surprising me with all kinds of things lately. Walking across a country seems the least of it," Em said.

She looked over Kennedy's shoulder, beyond the paddock, down towards the river. She could hear the cold water hitting the rapids. The late afternoon breeze flittered through the tall gums that lined the river. The sun, already making its way behind the nearby mountains, gave the property a soft glow.

Despite everything that had happened here, Em was home. With her friends' help, she'd cleaned out the house of all of Russell's belongings. They'd donated most of it, but Em had kept the long wooden table. It had been perfect for laying out everything for her cookbook, including gorgeous new photos.

Now the table was covered with plans for her next project: her new bakery in Huonville. She planned to call it *Just a Bite*. Shirley and Margo had introduced her to some real estate agents who were on the hunt to find the perfect place for her, and Pete had volunteered to help her source kitchen equipment when she was ready.

She thought about the spot where the pit had once been, feeling grateful to Pete, Tyler and Ryatt for their efforts in filling it with dirt. Em had carefully planted yellow roses – her favourite – in the place where Ruby's body had been discovered. Near where the pit had been, she had placed a stone plaque for Callum, with more roses around it. Kennedy's article had exposed who he truly was, and because of that truth, Em would let the weeds do their thing. But he was still a human being, and she felt she'd honoured that fact. She was satisfied knowing the women he'd sexually assaulted had all shared their stories, and that with her lawyers' help, she had set up a trust in each of their names so they could go on living their lives freely and with purpose.

Shirley had asked her, only last week, if she was happy being here. Em had told her she wasn't quite sure yet; but when she thought of the question again now – with her friends around her and the sound of Ethan laughing with the dogs; with the bleating of sheep on the nearby hills and the cool breeze meandering through the nearby gum trees; and with the feeling of love and support from her friends and neighbours – Neeminah River was home. The place she had always dreamed of.

Russell could never have realised what a gift he was giving her.

THANK YOU!

Hello from Southern Tasmania,

I hope you enjoyed THE HOUSESITTER! Seriously, thank you so much for picking up a copy—it means the world to me.

Since this book was published, I have been blown away by the messages I have received from readers. Some of you had opinions on the characters, others commented on the setting —it's always fascinating to hear what sticks with you. As an author, I *love* hearing your thoughts. The good, the bad, the in-between—I want it all!

So if you've something to share, please send me an email at Tara@ taramarlowauthor.com or visit me at https://www.taramarlowauthor. com/contact

If you're wondering what's next, I have a few other books published. BENEATH THE SURFACE is my first domestic thriller, set in Sydney, Australia. It's the story of Grace, a seventeen year old who has been on the run with her father since she was five, but she doesn't know why. BENEATH THE SURFACE is the story of Grace discovering her truth.

You can find a sample of this novel below, but I will warn you, I have trigger warnings at the start of this book.

https://www.taramarlowauthor.com/books/beneath-the-surface/

Before I go, can I ask you a small favour? If you enjoyed THE HOUSESITTER (or even if you didn't), would you mind leaving a quick review? Honest reviews mean everything to authors these days —they help books find new readers like you.

Here's the Amazon link: https://amzn.to/3VZpbWs

Here's the Goodreads link: https://www.goodreads.com/book/show/214644421-the-housesitter

Thank you so much for spending your time with THE HOUSESITTER. It's a gift to have readers like you.

Gratefully,
    Tara

ACKNOWLEDGEMENTS

I wish to acknowledge the Tasmanian Aboriginal Community and their elders past, present and emerging. The palawa people are the first storytellers, song-singers and knowledge keepers of lutruwita and their connection to the land, sea and stars remains strong.

I named the fictional setting for THE HOUSESITTER, Neeminah River as Neeminah means mother in the local Indigenous dialect. It was important to me to recognise the local Aboriginal community but also to use a word that tied in with the story. Thank you to Jonathan Berry and Jamie Bantick, two members of the melukerdee people, traditional owners of the land in Tasmania's south-east, for your help in finding the right word, and for your permission to use the language.

The idea for THE HOUSESITTER came from personal experience as a housesitter. In 2017, my husband and I began travelling the world full time. We did this for almost three years, using housesitting to keep costs down. It was a priceless experience.

While our housesitting experience was unlike Em's (thank goodness for that), we had some unique experiences. Some, in particular, left a beautiful, lasting impression, like the housesit that inspired this story. Thank you to Kaye and Lindsay, Deb and Bill, and Emma and Clive. We are grateful for your ongoing friendship.

Thanks to the Facebook group 'Chat 10, Looks 3 Community'. I loved the amusing suggestions for one-liners. I hope the ones I chose added more depth to Shirley's character.

My thanks to Reece and Sabrina, who are a part of my Camino Family, for their assistance in finding the perfect place for Em and Asher's bakery in California.

My Tasmanian writing community are amazing. Thanks to Simone,

Pauline, Kew, Annie, Lisa, and Linda. There are many words to express my gratitude, but it comes down to this: I'm honoured to be in such brilliant company.

My editor, Lisa Neale, turned my pocket of coins into a gold nugget. As an indie, we like to feel like we have control, but it turns out the professional knew a lot more than I did! Thank you Lisa. I am grateful for your guidance and look forward to working on the next book with you!

The Lovelies - my incredible 'street team' - are GOLD. This is book four for me and through every draft, every brain freeze, every Facebook post, and every moment in between, I am lucky enough to have a great team around me. When they read the early versions of the manuscript, they gave me the feedback I needed to hear. When they read beta versions, they answered questions that identified holes, patterns, mistakes, and more! Even with the proofread, they picked up things I never saw! I will say it again, as I do in every book - I LOVE my beta readers. I truly could not do this without them. To Laura, Angela, Kim, Toni, Linda, Grant, Annie, and Meredith (who told me she walked headfirst into a parked truck, while reading a beta version on her phone, because she was that engrossed in the story) - Thank you!

I love the wisdom and laughter my hydrotherapy ladies bring to the pool each week. Some weeks it's the highlight of my week. When I need to let everything go, it miraculously happens whenever I step into the pool. These women have made me feel like I'm a New York Times bestseller when there were days I've wanted to quit. Thank you all for your words, for your support, the laughter, and the encouragement. And thanks to Ali for keeping us all moving!

While writing this book, I went through two major medical events. One was with my health, the other happened with my husband. While we could have avoided the experiences with closer attention from our doctors, we were fortunate to receive the medical care we needed without going bankrupt and without having to wait too long. We are definitely grateful for that. When faced with serious medical situations, you gain a clear understanding of who your people are. I feel incredibly fortunate to have such a powerful circle around us. Thank you to

Ang, Sue, Shane, Melissa, Nicole, Meredith, Laura, Kim, Amanda, Sharon, and Jerry for being there for us - and for checking in.

There are two people I'd like to call out in particular: Sharon Boggon and Jerry Everard. Thank you for believing in me, for helping me process what I wanted from life, and ultimately, for helping me figure out who I wanted to be. Your advice always seems to be the words I need to hear. And oddly, I'm grateful to that weird couple we met on day three who brought us together.

I can't go without acknowledging the two most important people in my life. My daughter Nat brings a fresh perspective to my days, allows me to rant at odd times, and shares crazy memes with me that keep me laughing, especially on the days I need it. She reminds me that life is an adventure, and we're all just along for the ride. I'm so freakin' proud to be your mother, Nat.

And, then there is my gorgeous husband, Richard. After over twenty years together, I can't imagine life without him. He makes me laugh. He keeps our life rolling along in order for me to write. (Granted, some days, his twenty questions drive me nuts, especially when I don't know the answers.) When I compare the person I was when we met, to the person I am today, I am stronger, more confident, and a better person - and it's because Rich was by my side throughout that journey, nudging me when I needed it most. I look forward to seeing what the next twenty years will bring, especially now we're settled into our lovely cottage by the river.

Last of all, thank you to the librarians, the booksellers, and the readers. Without you all, I would not still be publishing books! I love being on a first name basis with my local librarians and booksellers. I love getting emails and messages from readers, letting me know how much they've enjoyed my books.

It truly is a joy to sit in this chair, knowing my words resonate. Thank you.

AUTHOR'S NOTE

The inspiration for THE HOUSESITTER came from a specific housesit my husband and I did in Victoria. While being given the tour of the property, we were told that if anything were to die while the home-owners were away to 'just put the carcass in the pit'.

Initially, I was horrified, but my country upbringing helped me understand the reasoning behind it... then my creative mind kicked in. I looked over at my husband on the other side of the metal plate, the one covering the dark cavernous hole, tapped my finger to my lips, and smiled deliciously. I knew there was a story to be told there.

Housesitting was an amazing way to travel. But I could not write a book about housesitting without featuring some of the beautiful animals we met along the way.

Billy was a rescued greyhound. Ah, Billy. Billy and I bonded deeply. It still hurts my heart, knowing he won't be around the next time I visit. But he lived his best life in the end, and I hope he's zooming around heaven's paddocks, just for the fun of it.

Gracie was also a rescue, after spending her early life as the mumma in a puppy-mill situation. Thankfully, Deb and Bill adopted the gorgeous Australian Shepherd, and they treated her (justifiably!)

like the queen she was. When I began writing THE HOUSESITTER, I knew I had to include Gracie somewhere in this story. I only hope I did this sweet girl justice.

Ruby in THE HOUSESITTER was an amalgamation of a couple of dogs we looked after. One 'Ruby' was a greyhound who had the other two dogs chasing her orbit. It was this Ruby that inspired the line, Boys, am I right? There was another Ruby, a cocker spaniel, who possessed the velvety ears. Ears that soothed my anxiety amid a tense time. I can still remember how they felt in my fingers.

Sachin was a black Labrador that we looked after in Oxfordshire, England. I knew Sachin, with his ambling ways and tender heart, was perfect to be Anna's sidekick. I will always remember the moment Sachin and I locked eyes right before we left the housesit. It was like he knew he'd have someone who would always remember him with love.

But it wasn't just those we looked after while housesitting that were included in this book.

Charlie was my German shepherd growing up. We adopted Charlie when I was five, and he almost made it to my twenty-first birthday. He was my companion and my protector. I never felt scared or worried when he was around. It's been a long time since Charlie has been around, but he still owns a piece of my heart.

In the epilogue, I mentioned Bert as Em's new rescue. Bert was technically my sister's dog, but she left home not long after we adopted him. Bert was a beagle/cattle dog mix - you can imagine how stubborn he was with that mix! But he was also much loved, and I know he'll live on, living his best life in Em's world, just as Charlie, Billy, and Gracie will.

There were many more animals I could have included, but I guess I'll just have to save them for another book. Oh! And goats do love Weetbix, by the way.

If you haven't already figured it out, I am a huge advocate for dog adoptions, especially when you hear the stories of what happened to (real life) Gracie. She's just one story I could share, amongst many.

So, to all the animal rescuers out there: you have my respect and gratitude! I look forward to adopting our own dog(s) soon.

The book is also a nod to our housesitting days. If you would like to know more about housesitting, check out my non-fiction book, HOUSESITTING: A BEGINNERS GUIDE.

ABOUT THE AUTHOR

Tara Marlow is a bestselling Australian author renowned for her work in suspense and women's fiction. After a two-decade corporate career in the United States and a subsequent stint as a travel writer, she now dedicates herself to crafting compelling narratives about women overcoming insurmountable challenges and discovering their true selves.

Visit Tara online at
thecrackpotwriter.com
to sign up for her monthly newsletter.

You can also find Tara online here:

ALSO BY TARA MARLOW

BENEATH THE SURFACE

"Heartbreaking...heartwarming...sad...joyful...overwhelming! I can't say enough about this book. I would give it six stars if I could."

- Vickie Waters, Goodreads Review

CAMINO WANDERING

"This is a book every Camino traveller will want to have not just read, but as [a] woman and a Camino walker, one we want to own and proudly have in our personal book collection, taking pride of place."

- Agnes Allen, Amazon Review

THE DECISIONS WE MAKE

"What Tara does masterfully is build characters who she lets tell their own stories. And in places that sound breathtaking and untamed and fully brought to life."

- Kim McDaniel, Amazon Review

Available where books are sold.